Broken Through

Adam and Grace
Book Two
By J.C. Paulson

Copyright August 2018
ISBN 978-0-995975620
All rights reserved

No part of this publication may be reproduced
in any way
without express permission
of the publisher and author.

One

She still had that fucking dog. He told her to get rid of it months ago, but no. The dog was undeniably there, panting and standing guard, as he let himself in the back door. He knew the dog wouldn't bark. Never did, when he came by, after the first couple of times.

Fury filled his head with thudding blood. If she had listened, maybe this wouldn't be happening. Maybe. But it wasn't just about the damn dog. She had betrayed him.

He went for the dog's throat with a chain, but the beast was too fast for him. It sprung, snarling, teeth bared, and crunched into his forearm. *Fucking hell.*

He clenched his teeth and with his left arm drew a handgun from the inside pocket of his jacket. Aimed. Fired.

The dog fell to the kitchen floor, twitching. Dead in seconds.

His face twisted into a mirthless grin. One job down. One to go.

*****

Grace Rampling drew a hand across the back of her neck, under her heavy tangle of auburn curls. It came away dripping with sweat.

Hell, she swore under her breath at her desk in the newsroom of the StarPhoenix. Why, she wondered, did the damned air conditioning always break down on the steamiest days of the year? It was invariably repaired just in time to freeze everyone in place by August. Today, when the mercury showed thirty-five degrees Celsius outside, it was only marginally cooler inside, and without the benefit of breeze.

Saskatoon, a rapidly-growing city of just over two hundred thousand in the middle of the Canadian Prairies, was noted for its lovely summers. Occasionally, lovely tipped over into ridiculously hot. Its citizens usually embraced the heat, or at least coped with little complaint, because it beat the heck out of the long, frigid winters.

Thirty-some degrees indoors, though, was a different matter.

"Bloody hell," Grace repeated out loud to Lacey McPhail, her friend and colleague. "I'm going to stick my head in the sink. I'm melting."

"Me too," said Lacey, her smooth face dotted with pearls of perspiration. "Does this have to happen every time it's approaching two hundred degrees outside?"

Grace grinned at Lacey's exaggeration, as the two reporters grabbed their purses, makeup within, and headed to the washroom. They drenched paper towels with cold water and applied them to their necks, faces and arms.

"What a hot summer," complained Lacey, who wasn't good with heat. "I guess it's our reward for surviving an extra-cold winter. Stupid continental climate."

Grace agreed a temperate climate would be more comfortable, but she had once endured the blast furnace of Australian summer for two months, along with the contiguous collapse of a relationship with her former boyfriend of two years, Mick Shaw. This was better, apart from the lack of air conditioning, especially considering the turn her life had taken recently. A mere three weeks ago, she finally connected body and soul to Adam Davis.

At the moment, though, she was not just physically but sexually overheated, and bereft.

Grace peered at herself in the mirror, attempted some facial touchups and tried not to think of the nights they had spent together. Lacey cocked her head and smiled sympathetically at Grace's huge, liquid brown eyes and furrowed brow.

"Missing him?" she asked.

Grace sighed. "It's that obvious?"

"Oh yes. Yes, it is. When's he coming back?

"Another week or so."

"Let me try to distract you. Want to go out for dinner one night this week? We can call Suzanne, see if she wants to come. Haven't seen her in ages."

"Yes. Sure," Grace said vaguely.

"Hey, Rampling. Hello? Are you okay?

"I'm fine," she lied.

Lacey gave Grace another sympathetic look.

"Do you need help on that crash story, by the way?" she asked, as they returned to their desks.

"No, I can handle it. There aren't many details yet; no sign of the speeding car, no arrests. Thanks, though. And dinner would be great."

*****

Detective Sergeant Adam Davis of the Saskatoon police force was in Los Angeles at a North American police conference, to be followed immediately by a second conference on psychological profiling. Police Chief Dan

McIvor liked to send his detective sergeants and inspectors to the annual events as often as possible, budget allowing. They were, he said to Adam, helpful forums from which to gather new ideas, connect with officers facing similar policing issues, and hone skills such as profiling and researching.

"I know you went a couple of years ago," McIvor said to Adam. "But you're the right guy to go this year."

"What about Pearson?" Adam asked hopefully. But he knew the answer. McIvor hated Inspector Terry Pearson almost as much as Adam did.

"No way," said McIvor.

Adam still looked unconvinced, which McIvor apparently took as modesty.

"Look, Adam, your work on the bishop's murder was brilliant. That was some kind of crime solving. Go share it."

Due to his chief's enthusiasm, Adam had been obliged to hastily pull together a presentation on the bishop's murder, complete with photos, overhead slides and handout. God damn it, thought Adam, I don't have time for this. Worse yet, I'll be away for two weeks, aching for Grace. He wasn't sure he could stand it. He was having trouble getting his butt into work as it was; how was he going to manage two weeks away from her, when twelve hours was a problem?

Adam met Grace in March, over the body of that bashed-up bishop. She was covering a story about a gay choir booted from holding a concert in the sanctuary, and got more than she bargained for. She literally stumbled over the corpse.

Adam was captivated, as he had never been before, the second he saw her rising from her hiding spot between two pews. The next three months were torture, as he tried to stay away from her. Grace was his witness in the murder case, and later became a victim to violence herself. Legally and ethically, they couldn't go near each other. Three months later, they finally fell, explosively, into each other's arms.

Now he was in L.A. Three days into the first conference, he already pined for Grace. He called her in the evenings, before the obligatory social events started, and tried not to talk about making love to her.

It never worked. The conversations would start with his heart rate soaring at the sound of her rich, low voice, and end with him sitting disconsolately on the edge of the bed, head bowed.

After he had finally made love with Grace for the first time, Adam had fallen asleep — unintentionally, fearing one of his nightmares would awaken him and terrify Grace. And so it had awakened him; but she was undaunted. After pulling him back into bed, she crawled up his body, touching and licking every inch of him, to both comfort and arouse him. He could hardly stand remembering it. He missed her, and her bed.

"Grace. How was your day?"

"Hot," she said, giving the word a whisper of innuendo. "It's thirty-five degrees here today. How is it there?"

"Also hot. It's bloody L.A. in the summer, and if we were right on the coast, we'd be fine. But it's brutal downtown."

Talking about the heat had Adam envisioning Grace in a cool, light dress outlining her slim figure, with a deep décolletage, and wishing he wasn't. Her breasts made him crazy. How long would it be before just the thought of her didn't arouse him?

"Have you given your presentation yet?" she asked, breaking into his reverie.

"No — tomorrow. I'm dreading going over the whole case again, but I suppose it'll be good practice for when the bishop's killer goes to court."

The trial for the man who had murdered Bishop Howard Halkitt was still pending. Crown prosecutor Sanjeev Kumar had told Adam it might go to court in the winter; he was still preparing what he hoped was an iron-clad case, with Adam's help.

"Any interesting stories today?" Adam asked, ready to temporarily forget the bishop's case.

"A few. There was a bad car accident — some idiot flying down a Nutana street in an SUV and smashing into a Smart Car. The speeder drove away; the Smart Car was crushed. Amazingly, the driver lived, but he's in bad shape. He'd be dead if the SUV had hit the driver's side.

"I can't understand how people can even get up to such high speeds on those narrow streets," Grace added. "We're still waiting to find out more from your shop — whether they've caught him yet, if he was DUI, et cetera."

"How fast was he going?"

"Police say he could have been going ninety kilometres an hour, based on witness observations and the state of the Smart Car."

"Wow. That's insane."

"But I think I'm going to get to talk to James. I gather he's on communications duty today, still being stuck in the office. I'm looking forward to it. He's so lovely."

Adam knew it was ridiculous, particularly since James was gay, but he felt a tiny pang of jealousy. Grow up, he said to himself.

"You're lovely," he said, huskily.

Grace felt her body heat rise even further to the compliment.

"Hush, Adam. Don't unlock the zoo. I'd like to keep my animals safely inside until . . . later."

"I'll try to behave," Adam said. Then he didn't. "I want to kiss your neck right now. Then your lips. Then the rest of you. Hell."

"God, oh . . . Adam, stop it. I'll never make the next week."

"Neither will I."

After they hung up, and Adam was hanging by a thread in his lonely hotel room desperately considering having phone sex with Grace, an idea came to him.

First thing the next morning, he called his boss; feeling very guilty about it, he also called Grace's.

And then he called his travel agent.

Two

The next day dawned just as hot and even muggier, in both countries.

Grace dug out the skimpiest dress in her closet and added the lightest little bolero sweater, in a large weave, over top — in case someone from the public showed up at the office. She slipped her feet into sandals, and slicked on a trace of lipstick and mascara. Makeup would end up sliding down her face anyway, so why bother with more than that?

Driving to the office from her little bungalow in the Buena Vista neighbourhood, in her air conditioned vehicle, she wondered if the same amenity would be available today at the office.

It was not. It was so hot the day before, the managing editor had come out into the newsroom and told the staff they could wear pretty much whatever they wanted, as long as it was barely decent.

"No cutoffs, no tank tops, no muscle shirts," warned Mark Williams, sweat streaming down from his temples and coursing down both cheeks. "Everything else is pretty much fair game."

Melting brains on journalists wouldn't do. But it was just as hot today, if not worse.

Grace put down her bag, started her computer, and greeted Lacey, who had beaten her in by a few minutes.

Seconds later, Grace's phone rang. She sighed. The phone rang all the time. No peace. She saw it was Alison, the receptionist, and sighed again: there was probably someone in the reception area asking to pitch a story to a reporter. Couldn't it wait until after nine in the morning?

She picked up the phone.

"Hi, Allie. How are you? Melting?"

"You bet. God, it's hot. Grace, there are flowers for you here. Do you want to come and get them, or should I send them up next time Dorothy does deliveries?"

"Depends. Is it cooler than thirty-five degrees where you are?"

Alison checked the little thermometer on her desk. "Yep. Only thirty-two."

"I'm on my way."

Grace grabbed her security card, stuck it in the pocket of her dress, and feeling rather free without her purse and reporter's gear, skipped down the winding staircase.

"Wow," she said, upon seeing the massive bouquet of white and red flowers, partly visible through semi-opaque cellophane wrap. "Wow. It's not even my birthday."

Alison's eyes were wide with excitement. "It's a big one. Open it, Grace!"

Grace lifted the bouquet off the high counter in front of Alison's desk and took it to the coffee table on the other side of the lobby. Bending slightly at the waist, she untied the ribbon at the top and undressed the gorgeous, fragrant bunch. Red roses. White, frondy chrysanthemums. Beautiful.

Snagging the unusually large card off the top — it was not the usual florist's mini-offering — she opened the envelope and read:

Grace.

I've had time to think, alone in this cold hotel, in this steaming city.

And what I think is, I miss you. I crave you, day and night.

You've tapped the shell. You've broken through.
I can hold on, if I know you're on the way.
Come to California, Grace. — Adam

Grace turned bright pink, breathed "Oh, Adam," and sank onto the blue leather couch, shaking.

"Grace!" said Alison, extricating herself from her boxed-in desk and dashing over. "What's wrong?"

"Nothing. It's just such a surprise."

Alison put her arm around Grace's shoulders. "Are you sure?"

"I'm fine, Allie."

But she had to take the elevator back upstairs; she couldn't trust her legs to get her up the long winding staircase, and she had a massive bouquet of flowers to carry besides. What was she going to say when she got back to the newsroom?

She understood immediately what Adam was telling her: her efforts to soothe and support him, after years of struggling with the post-traumatic after-effects of being shot and nearly killed, were helping him. Healing him. She was breaking through his pain. He was shaking off the awful nightmares. He felt less of a victim, counterintuitively less of a superhero — and more of a man.

When the dreams did come, she would hold him until he calmed, then make love to him in the deep night. She was amazed and thrilled that she could help this beautiful man, this fierce police officer. Besides, she loved the soothing, and the sex.

There was more in the envelope.

As Grace returned to her desk with the enormous bouquet, Lacey looked up and raised her eyebrows.

"Adam?"

Grace nodded, and handed her the second piece of paper in the envelope. The note she kept to herself, slipping it into her dress pocket. The larger paper was a printout of an airline itinerary, detailing a flight from Saskatoon to Calgary to San Francisco, eight days away. Her name was on it.

"Oh, my God," breathed Lacey. "Holy shit. Is this a surprise?"

"Completely. I hope I can make it happen. It's so soon."

"He didn't, like, you know, ask or anything?"

"No. It's the first I've heard of it."

"That's so romantic I can't stand it," said Lacey, to a shushing noise from Grace.

Grace's phone rang again. This time, it was Mark.

"Hey boss, what's up?" answered Grace.

"Hey Grace, can you come into my office for a minute?"

"On my way."

"Hi, Grace. Take a seat," said Mark when she arrived two seconds later.

Grace thought the expression on his face was odd. His lips were twitching, as if he was trying hard not to break into an ear-to-ear grin, but he looked guilty, too.

"What's up?" she asked, baffled.

"I see you got some flowers."

"Yes. Why?"

"I kind of knew they were coming. Adam Davis called me. He wanted to know whether you could get away if he booked an impromptu trip. He felt terrible, for what it's worth, about giving me the head's up first, but it was the only way he could figure out how to surprise you, and still make it work."

Grace was silent for a moment.

"He's a pretty nice guy, Grace," said Mark, who seemed to interpret her silence as being upset about Adam going over her head.

Mark had been impressed by Adam's handling of the bishop's case, and how hard he had tried to protect the StarPhoenix reporters from potential harm. He had said so to Grace, several times.

"I know," said Grace, who was actually having trouble absorbing the fact her boss and her lover were conspiring to put her on a plane. Whatever worked, as long as she could see Adam as soon as possible. "So what do you think? Can I get away?"

"Of course. You deserve it. You haven't been away since you got back from Australia. How long ago was that? This time, though, don't get any ideas about staying away, damn it."

Grace laughed. "I can't see it happening. Thank you, so much."

"No problem. I hope it's relaxing and fun."

She doubted it would be relaxing, which was more than fine with her, and wondered how soon after work Adam would call. Her spine tingled at the thought. It was going to be a long day of anticipation.

"So?" asked Lacey.

"He gave me the time off. Please don't tell anyone, Lace. I don't know if I can stand the knowing looks of all my colleagues."

"Promise."

Grace tried to focus on the boring report on her desk, but found it impossible. Instead, she mentally multiplied eight days by twenty-four hours, and started the countdown.

Until her phone rang. Again. But she knew the number and happily picked up the phone.

"Suzanne!" Grace answered. "How are you? I haven't seen you for so long — too long. Lacey and I were just talking yesterday about calling you, to see if you're free for dinner this week. How are you, and when can we get together?"

"How about now?"

"What's wrong, Suzé?" asked Grace, hearing the sombre tone in her friend's voice.

"This might be a story, *belle amie* — a sad story. My neighbour's dog went missing yesterday. We found him this morning, dead in the alley. He'd been shot."

"Shot. Seriously? Are you sure?"

"*Oui.* The SPCA came out and confirmed it, although it was obvious. They took Argo — that's the dog's name — and said they would also call the police."

"Oh no, Suzanne, I'm so sorry. Do you want to have lunch right away? I can do it. Meet me at the restaurant on Temperance and Fourteenth? What's it called now?"

"I forget too. Ridiculous. I'm only four blocks away. Used to be the Sweet Carrot, then something else . . . say half an hour?"

"Sure, I can make it by then. See you there, Suzé."

*****

Who would shoot, actually shoot, a dog in the middle of Nutana? An asshole, Grace thought. A nut case? Dog hater? She headed over to the desk and told the city editor, Claire Davidson, what Suzanne had said.

"Claire, someone has found a dead dog in a Nutana alley — shot in the chest, if you can believe it. A friend of mine just called; the dog was her neighbour's. I'm meeting her for lunch. Sounds like a story. What do you think?"

"Absolutely. God, that's awful. Where's the dog now?"

"At the SPCA. They're going to call the police. I don't know if or when a press release will come out. But we know the dog owner, or at least the owner's neighbour, so we can do better than a brief, one way or the other."

"Great . . . uh, sorry. If you know what I mean. We'll talk when you get back and see where you're at. I'll keep an eye out for a news release."

Ten minutes later, Grace pulled up near the restaurant inhabiting a former pharmacy building. It was a local favourite, situated right in the middle of the lovely area of Nutana. Grace always admired the tree canopy overhanging the well-kept older homes, separated by long, grassy boulevards.

Suzanne Genereux was waiting for her and had snagged a table in the bustling little diner now known as D'lish. Grace often thought her friend looked remarkably like the actress Sandra Bullock, although considerably shorter and somewhat younger. She had the same fresh, glowing complexion; enormous, slightly almond-shaped brown eyes; wide mouth with perfect white teeth; high cheekbones and a long, thick drape of chestnut hair. Suzanne came from a French farming community, and to this day often mixed her first language with English. Men found it entrancing, along with the rest of her.

"Suzé," said Grace, to get her attention. Her friend jumped up with a smile; they embraced and got in line to order Tuscan black bean soup and mixed green salads.

Suzanne added an espresso to her order. Grace settled for water, squeeze of lemon. Too damn hot for coffee, thought Grace; but Suzanne could drink coffee any time of day, any time of year, keep her cool and still sleep like the just and righteous.

Grace envied that. She loved coffee.

"So," began Suzanne, "tell me everything. Last I heard you had, ah, connected with the handsome police officer. Is all well?"

"Yes, thank you," said Grace, a little primly. While she didn't mind talking about Adam with Suzanne, she was completely floored and intensely aroused by the thought of the man arranging for a rendezvous in California. She was quite sure she wouldn't get through a conversation about the situation — at least, not in public.

"Suzé, there is so much to say. I can't talk about him right now, at least not here. He's away. I miss him — a lot. And it's only been a few weeks since . . . well, we got together."

"*C'est bien. Je comprends.* We will drink wine together soon, and you can tell me what you can tell me. But you are well? Healed? Not unhappy?"

"I am. Well, I mean. Healed," said Grace, who had overcome the wounds of two violent attacks in the spring. At least, the physical ones. "And disgustingly happy. Makes one wonder if it will continue."

"It will. I can feel it."

"Thank you," said Grace, putting her other hand on top of Suzanne's. "How are you, Honey?"

"I'm okay, *merci*. But perhaps we won't talk about that here, either."

"Of course. So. Tell me what happened."

"I told you about Argo, *oui*? Well, it was horrible. My poor neighbour. Sherry is her name. She came to my door this morning and told me Argo was missing. She asked what I thought she should do, so I suggested we go look for him.

"We walked around the neighbourhood for an hour, and finally went into the alley. Bruno was straining on his leash and barking and sniffing, and I had no choice but to follow him; he's so big, he pulled me along. And there was Argo, with a hole in his chest, under a pile of branches." Suzanne sniffled, and looked down.

"God, that's terrible," said Grace, reaching for her friend's hand again.

"I couldn't help thinking of how shredded I'd be if that was Bruno."

Grace knew Suzanne was very attached to her enormous, affectionate black Newfoundland. At the hip, really.

"I know, Honey. Then you called the SPCA?"

"Yes. They came and picked Argo up, and took him away. They said they would call the police. But something also happened the day before. It bothered me at the time, although it didn't seem like a big deal — but now, I wonder."

"What?" asked Grace, taking a spoonful of her rich, spicy soup, which had been delivered as Suzanne spoke.

"I was working on a graphic for Hedonism, that new bar, and admiring the sunshine and thinking how quiet and lovely my neighbourhood is, and suddenly there was a big noise. A slam, I would say. A few minutes later, there was a bang. I thought it was a car backfiring. A minute later, a car squealed down the alley, spitting gravel against the garage doors. I went to the back door and looked out, in time to see the car turning the corner onto the street."

"And now you think these noises, and the speeding car, might be connected to Argo?"

Suzanne nodded, her mouth full of arugula and shredded beets. "What if the person in the car killed him?" she asked, between bites.

"Suzé, there was a very bad car accident yesterday. An SUV smashed into a Smart Car. According to witnesses, the SUV was going very, very fast; police say he could have been going ninety kilometres an hour. There was a short story in the paper today."

"I haven't had time to read the paper yet," said Suzanne, who had been busy with Sherry and Argo. "Where was the crash?"

"Lansdowne and Tenth Street. Just a few blocks from here."

"That's a bad corner, for some reason. I see. It might have been the same SUV."

"Could it be? What time did you hear all the noises?"

"Early afternoon, about one-thirty or two."

"We got the press release from the police about three, three-thirty, so the timing works. Do you remember anything about the SUV? Colour, age, dirty, clean? Anything?"

"I only saw it for two seconds, as it turned onto the street. It was a dark colour, maybe black or navy. And I don't know why I'm saying this, but I have the sense it was a newer model. It seemed shiny, clean, new. But again, two seconds. Only an impression."

"You have to call the police and tell them about this. I'd bet the farm on this being the same guy."

"Should I come back downtown with you?"

"Good idea. I'll call James Weatherall and tell him we're coming. Do you think I could talk to your neighbour? This is starting to look like a pretty big story, what with Argo being shot and what could be the shooter crashing into a car at ninety-K."

"I'll ask her. She's very upset. I don't know if she could handle an interview yet."

"She may not have a choice. We'll talk to the police first, and see how Sherry is feeling later."

As they left the restaurant, Grace called the police station on her cellphone and asked for James.

"One moment please, Ms. Rampling," said the officer answering the phone. After the bishop's murder and discovery, pretty much every cop knew Grace Rampling, if they hadn't known her already from her court reporting.

"Hello, Grace. How are you?" said James, picking up on his extension.

"I'm fine, James. How are you? How's the leg?"

"I'm almost finished here in purgatory," said James. He couldn't wait to get back on active duty after having been shot in the spring. "I'm cleared for action."

"Glad to hear it, James. Listen, are you available by any chance in about fifteen, twenty minutes? It's a long story, but a friend of mine may have some information about the speeding SUV. And a dog."

"Do you mean the dead dog? The SPCA called a while ago. What's the connection?"

"That's what she needs to tell you about. Can I bring her down and introduce you?"

"Absolutely. I'll be waiting for you."

"Great. See you in a few minutes, James."

Twenty minutes later, after Grace parked her car in the StarPhoenix lot and she and Suzanne made the two-minute walk to the police station, James was greeting them in the reception area.

"James Weatherall, Suzanne Genereux," Grace introduced them.

"Very nice to meet you, Ms. Genereux," said James, with a small, courtly bow. "We can use Adam's office for our chat. Follow me."

"Please call me Suzanne, *Monsieur*," said Suzanne, smiling rather warmly at the handsome police officer in reaction to his bow. Grace had told her a bit about James in the spring, and Suzanne knew he was gay; but it didn't hold her back from a little flirting just the same. For her part, Grace was a little surprised. She hadn't seen this side of Suzanne for years, but she was glad to.

"*Merci bien*," he said, smiling back. "And call me James. This way."

Wishing they were not going to Adam's office, Grace followed James and Suzanne up the stairs and down the hall. As they settled into the three chairs, she tried to ignore the fact of Adam's missing presence. She ached for him.

James belatedly remembered to offer them coffee.

"No way, James. I can't drink your station coffee. Suzé, say no. I mean it," said Grace. "It's unbelievably bad."

"*Non, merci*," said Suzanne, with a laugh. "I am a *connoisseuse du café*, and perhaps I don't need to try police station coffee. And I just had one. Thank you, though."

"So what's going on? Grace said you might have some information about this crazy driver we're looking for. He could have killed the guy in the Smart Car. He's still critical. Oh, wait . . . do you know what I'm talking about, Suzanne?"

"*Oui*. Grace explained over lunch."

"Perfect. What can you add to this investigation?"

"Well, I was working — I work from home, you see?" started Suzanne. "I'm a graphic designer. And early in the afternoon there was a very loud sort of slamming noise. It could have been a car door, but it was so loud I jumped. Then seconds later, there was an even louder bang. I thought, perhaps, a car backfiring?"

She again explained how she heard the speeding vehicle scatter gravel against the garages on her block, and saw it turn the corner.

"I don't know anything about SUVs, or any other cars, but it looked fairly new."

"And the dog?"

"My neighbour's dog went missing yesterday, and this morning we found him in the alley, dead. My dog smelled him, and found Argo under some brush. He had not been run over, which is what one might expect, *oui*? He had been shot."

If the timing lined up, the driver of the SUV shot a dog, sped off at ninety, crushed a car and almost killed a man. And was missing, to boot. The police had started looking for him, first by cruiser and then by plane, within minutes of the crash; but he had disappeared.

"Had you ever seen the vehicle before?"

"No."

"We will have to talk to your friend, and soon. I'm sure she's very upset, but it is important. Here's my card. Call me — later this afternoon, if possible. We want to find this guy."

"I'll do my best. I don't know if she went to work, but I doubt it. I'll run over as soon as I get home."

"I'll drive you back," said Grace. "Later, James."

*****

Sherry Hilliard had not gone to work.

She had called in, at first, to say she would be late. After finding her dog dead in the alley, and after running home in a blur of tears, she called the dental office where she worked as a hygienist and said she was still feeling unwell.

Sherry roamed around her home. She tried making tea, and ended up boiling the water away. She did not have a drink, although that would have helped. But Sherry was trying not to drink, even when she was frightened. It had gotten her into far too much trouble.

She dragged herself into the bathroom and had a cool shower; it was so very hot. After donning a light robe, she wandered back into the living room, towelling her hair.

An envelope lay on the coffee table.

Hands shaking, she tore it open and found a single sheet of white paper folded inside. Typed words. No signature.

Sorry to hear about your dog. It's so easy, isn't it, to hide a body in the bushes? Or, really, anywhere. Best not to talk to anyone about it.

And take care, Sherry baby. I'll see you soon.

Sherry took the note to the sink and burned it to a cinder.

Three

Half an hour later, Grace and Suzanne banged on Sherry's door. They had tried the doorbell, but there was no answer.

"Sherry! It's Suzanne!"

There was a long pause before Sherry appeared, her swollen eyes and red nose testaments to a day of weeping.

"Oh, Sherry," said Suzanne, putting her arms around her neighbour. "Such a bad day. I'm so sorry. Can we come in for a minute?"

"Okay," said Sherry, turning and leading the way into the kitchen.

"Sherry, this is my friend Grace. She's a reporter at the StarPhoenix."

Sherry just nodded at Grace, who smiled back. "Nice to meet you, Sherry."

"We just got back from the police station," Suzanne said as the women sat down at the table. "I had to tell them about something that happened yesterday."

Suzanne yet again described the noises and events, and explained about the speeding SUV and the crash.

"They would like to interview you about Argo, Sherry. His death is bad enough, but the SUV driver who may have killed him could also have killed a man. They asked if you would prefer to go to the station, or have someone come and interview you. I said I would ask you, because you're having such a bad time."

The expression on Sherry's face changed from grief to something more inscrutable. Grace didn't know Sherry, but thought the switch was strange. *She's hiding something*, thought Grace.

"Do I have to?" asked Sherry.

Now Grace was really surprised. Why wouldn't Sherry want to talk to the police? But she let Suzanne do the talking.

"I don't know, Sher. I don't think so, but it might help find Argo's killer. Why wouldn't you want to talk to them?"

Grace mentally blessed Suzanne for asking the question.

"I don't think I could be any help," said Sherry. "I don't know who killed Argo, and I don't want to talk about it."

Grace didn't understand. If someone had killed Bruno, hell yeah, Suzanne would be talking to the police. Sherry's reaction was weird.

"Do you want to sleep on it? I told the constable I'd let him know what you decided. But he was hoping to talk to you today. He said it was very important to catch the speeder. Especially if he killed Argo."

Sherry didn't respond, again, for a moment.

"Can you tell him I'll come down to the station tomorrow morning? I can't face it today."

"I will. I'll tell him to expect you — when, maybe ten?"

"Sure. Whatever. Suzanne, I think I'm going to lie down now. I don't feel very well."

"Of course. Give me a shout if you need anything, okay? I'll be home the rest of the day."

"I will. Thanks, Suzanne. I appreciate it — everything you've done."

"We'll see ourselves out," said Suzanne. "Take care of yourself, *mon amie*."

Grace and Suzanne went next door to Suzanne's home.

"That was odd," said Grace. "Why do you think she's so reticent about talking to the police?"

"I don't know. I don't really know her all that well."

"She's not telling us something. Let's call James and tell him when she's coming. Then I better get back to work."

*****

Half an hour later, Grace told the city editor what she knew, which wasn't a heck of a lot more than the police had revealed in the press release.

"Maybe we'll know more tomorrow," she said to Claire. "Sherry, the dog's owner, will be at the cop shop at ten."

At five, Grace tidied her desk, tucked her cellphone into her purse, grabbed her keys and said goodbye to Lacey.

She was wildly anticipating Adam's call, particularly this night, after the flowers arrived with his note and the airline itinerary. She had no idea what he would say, nor what she would say. Her stomach was taut under the tension, the wondering.

Once home, Grace poured a glass of cold white wine and added two cubes of ice, then ran the glass over her perspiring forehead. A change in the weather would be more than welcome, she thought. Maybe a nice thunderstorm to clear the air.

Taking her phone, she went into the back yard, which was shady and slightly cooled by a light breeze whispering through the trees. Grace loved her little patio, surrounded by a low wall with flowers and vegetables growing on the other side of it — mostly tomatoes, a couple of zucchini plants, peas crawling up a trellis. So civilized, she sighed contentedly to herself.

Her mind returned to the Adam conversation, pending. She couldn't keep her mind off it, or off him. Grace had never believed in crap like love at first sight, and definitely believed in taking things slowly, her relationship with Mick Shaw notwithstanding; but she fell hard for this man the second time she saw him. Grace remembered the moment, looking up into his face, her body instantly responding; then quickly looking down to cover her confusion. She knew she would have fallen for him when they met in the cathedral — and had been profoundly impressed by his policing prowess, as it was — had she not been so rattled by stumbling over the dead body of a high-ranking cleric.

Occasionally, she asked herself if this was simple infatuation with the most beautiful man she had ever seen, not to mention intelligent, authoritative, sexy, masculine and brilliant at his work. The list of attributes was endless. And sex with Adam was like nothing else she had ever experienced, which was definitely colouring her opinion of him. He was focused, passionate and expert but also sincere and responsive. She felt alive, sexy, and strangely both vulnerable and powerful in his arms.

It was terrifying to feel like this about a man. Grace had to admit to herself she was scared — not just by her own overwhelming feelings, but by Adam's physical power. What if, one night, she couldn't manage his dreams? Assuming, of course, that he wanted her to.

They had only been alone together a few times. Where was this going?

Deep in her heart, she was both sure and very afraid it was Adam, or no one.

The phone rang. Damn. He was calling earlier than usual, and she wasn't sure she was ready. Nor could she wait another minute.

"Grace," said Adam when she picked up the phone, beating her to the greeting in the big, warm, thrumming baritone she mentally added to his attribute list. She could never mistake his voice for anyone else's.

"Adam," she said, her own voice husky.

"Are you coming to San Francisco?" he asked, without preamble.

Grace had been toying with making a flippant answer, to avoid the intensity of the conversation, to lighten things up while he was so far away. "It's an offer I can't refuse," or "depends; will you be there?" or something equally stupid. She often used such humour to defray uncomfortable or intense situations. It had gotten her into trouble more than once.

The gravity in his voice told her this was serious for him — as it was for her. She was just having trouble handling her roving emotions. Grow up, Grace, and face this beautiful thing, she told herself. It's all you've ever wanted.

"Adam. Oh . . ." suddenly Grace was fighting tears. "Thank you for your note. I don't know what to say."

"Oh, no, Grace, don't cry," said Adam, hearing the tears in her voice. "Just say you're coming. Come on, Grace. Say you're coming."

"I'm coming, Adam. Of course I'm coming."

"I want to make love to you for four days straight."

"Adam, don't. Don't say that. Eight days to go. Well, seven. Please, I can hardly stand it as it is. But I thought you were in Los Angeles? Well, I know you're in Los Angeles. Why San Francisco?"

"Because it's too damn hot here, and in Saskatoon. We'll go north up the coast, walk on the beach in the mornings and hide in the shade in the afternoons. I'll meet you at the San Francisco airport, we'll rent a car and go."

"You're brilliant. How did you come up with that?"

"Lust. I admit it. Wanting you," said Adam. "Let's get away, be together. Learn some things. Eat food. Drink wine. Talk. Make love. And not melt — at least, not because of the sun — while we're at it. What do you think?"

She was speechless. What was this incredible man saying? Was she hearing him right?

"Tell me, Grace. What do you think?" asked Adam, a tiny edge of anxiety creeping into his voice.

Grace swallowed hard.

"I love it when you say, 'tell me.' You do it a lot, do you realize that?" she said. "It's an invitation to speak, and be heard. I can't believe you've done all this, and, and, yes, I want to eat and drink and talk and . . . make love. With you. Now."

By the end of her answer, Grace's voice was trailing off. The thought of being alone with Adam somewhere in California made her tremble.

"Hold on, Grace," he said, emotion thickening the words.

Did he always know exactly what to say? Grace wondered.

"Hold on, Adam," she said, from deep in her constricted throat.

For a moment, neither spoke, overwhelmed by the emotional conversation. Grace pulled herself together and asked, "I know this might sound stupidly practical, but what should I bring to wear? What will the weather be like, where we're going?"

"The days should be warm, maybe hot, but not an oven like at home or in L.A. right now. Evenings will be cool, or cooler anyway, so bring a sweater, maybe a light jacket? A dress in case we go somewhere special for dinner?"

"I'd love that," said Grace. "But forgive me, is this not costing the Earth? Can I contribute? It's not like we're going out for dinner and a movie."

"I haven't been on a decent holiday for four years. I've been home to the farm for seeding and harvest, a few weekends away, but that's about it. This is on me. It's the least I can do. Please. Let me."

"How would this be the least you can do? You're flying me from Hades to the California coast, for God's sake."

"We can talk about it when we see each other. By the way, anything new about the car accident you mentioned yesterday?" said Adam, abruptly changing the subject away from the financial topic.

"A lot," said Grace, and told Adam about Suzanne, Sherry, Argo and the car spitting gravel in Suzé's alley. She also told him about taking Suzanne to see James, and meeting Sherry.

"Something's off here," said Adam. "Do we know if a neighbour hated the dog or something? Even so, killing it seems extreme. Shooting it is bizarre."

"I agree. Suzanne definitely thinks something weird is going on, and so do I. Sherry acted very strangely when we asked her to talk to the police. She didn't want to."

"That is weird. Do you think she's protecting someone?"

"I have no idea. That seems to make the most sense, though." Grace sighed. "I can't wait to see you, Adam."

"And I you. Hold on, Grace."

*****

The loudest crack of thunder Suzanne had ever heard shocked her out of sleep. Or was it a tree coming down in the storm? Bruno had awakened, too — he was barking his head off as Suzanne leaped out of bed and slammed the bedroom window shut. Rain was hammering through, and splattering onto the floor.

She flicked the light switch but, of course, the power was out. It always went out in powerful lightning storms, and even not-so-powerful ones. Suzanne waited a few seconds until the next flash allowed her to see well enough to get to the living room, where a candle awaited on the coffee table. Lighting it with the matches she kept nearby, she took it into the kitchen and dug a flashlight out of the junk drawer. Bruno was right on her heels. For a big dog, he was sure a wimp in bad weather.

Turning on the flashlight, she directed its beam through the kitchen window into the back yard, worried the big noise had signalled a tree or a big branch crushing her garage roof. A small mess of branches and twigs left by the howling wind littered the yard, but she saw no serious damage. She clicked off the light and stared into the dark.

In the sudden light of a massive fork of lightning, she detected movement. She caught it on the periphery of her vision, at the edge of perception. Someone was out there, in the crazy July storm. It was three in the blasted morning, and the world sounded like it was going to crack apart. But someone, or something, was out there in the rain, wind and lightning.

The presence seemed to walk through Sherry's yard, and slip in through her back door. Maybe it was Sherry? Between the deafening howls of wind and cracks of thunder, Suzanne heard something else — a cry. Or the storm was playing havoc with her senses.

Still . . .

She picked up the phone to call Sherry, but the power had been off for too long. It was dead, and so was her cellphone. Lightning must have hit a tower. There was no service. It was the middle of the night during the storm of the summer, if not the decade, and someone was out there.

And Argo had been shot.

She couldn't call the police, nor text them — there was no such thing as 911 text service.

Suzanne and her flashlight, followed closely by Bruno, returned to the bedroom, where she pulled on jeans and a T-shirt. Slipping on sandals and throwing a raincoat over her head and shoulders, she crept out the door, leaving Bruno behind.

Soaked within seconds despite the raincoat — the wild winds were driving rain under its hood — Suzanne hurried up the path to her neighbour's home and knocked loudly on the door. There was no candlelight, no flashlight. She rang the doorbell, knocked again, and called Sherry's name.

Nothing. She tried the door. Locked.

Suddenly terrified, Suzanne gave her own little cry, turned on her heel and ran the few steps back to her home. She pulled the door open and dashed inside, locking it behind her. Shaking and on her knees, she flung her arms around Bruno's enormous, warm and stalwart body.

Four

Grace awakened to pounding on her front door. Her heart lurched; it was early in the morning, still dark even in July, and raining like hell with claps of thunder following explosions of lightning. It sent her back to the horrific night in March when a deranged man broke into her house and assaulted her. Who would be knocking at this hour, during a storm?

Well, she couldn't ignore it. Slipping out of bed, Grace hit the light switch, and immediately realized the power was out. Hell, she thought. Hell, hell, hell.

By the time she made the hallway, she could hear the voice behind the door.

"Grace! It's me, Suzé! Open up, for God's sake."

Relief flooded through Grace, followed immediately by concern. What was Suzanne doing at her door at this hour, in this weather?

"I'm coming!" she shouted, over a fresh rumble of thunder. Seconds later, she threw open the door to reveal her drenched friend.

"Suzanne, what is going on? Come in . . . get in here, you're soaked."

"Do you have power?" asked Suzanne, shivering. "Doesn't look like it," she added, surveying the dark house, as Grace rummaged through the kitchen for a flashlight and towels.

"No. Do you?"

"No. No power, no phone. Grace, I'm scared. Something happened, next door. I tried texting and calling you. Did you sleep through that big clap of thunder? I thought the world had ended. *Le dernier jour.*"

"It did wake me up — it was insanely loud, wasn't it? But I must have gone back to sleep. Oho, here's the flashlight. Give me a sec and I'll find you a better towel and maybe a blanket. You're freezing, by the look of it. I can't make you tea, though."

Grace found a big, white, fluffy towel and put it on her friend's head, then wrapped the TV-watching blanket from the couch around her shoulders. She found some cold tea in the fridge, and poured them each a glass in the beam of the flashlight.

"What do you do when the power's out and your phones don't work?" asked Suzanne, through chattering teeth.

"I don't know, Honey. Try to calm down. We're okay right now. We're safe here together. Warm up for a second, then tell me what happened."

Suzanne took a big gulp of her iced tea.

"I think there was someone trying to get into Sherry's house," she said, then explained what had happened, and described the sound she thought she'd heard.

"Could it have been Sherry herself in the back yard?" asked Grace.

"It occurred to me, but I don't think so. What would she be doing back there with no flashlight? It was pitch black, except during flashes of lightning. I thought maybe she'd be out there checking her trees, too, but I could see my garage and trees through the back window during the lightning. She'd be able to as well. And there were no lights inside — no candles or anything. What should I do now?"

"We. What should we do now. Well, we could wait until the phones come back on, and call Sherry. If she doesn't answer, we could call the police. Or, we could drive down to the police station. It depends how worried you are. You were there."

Suzanne thought for a minute.

"You know, I've seldom been so terrified in my entire life, if ever," she said. "My head says I may be overreacting, in the bad weather and everything. But my stomach says something is wrong."

Grace had to admit the very last thing she wanted to do was climb into a car in the wild storm and drive downtown, then admit to the police they were frightened and worried about Suzanne's neighbour.

But Suzé's gut was pretty reliable. Grace hoped she was right about Adam, too, when she had said over lunch she had a positive feeling about their fledgling relationship.

"I'll put on some clothes," Grace said. "You warm up. We'll brave the storm and get down to the cop shop."

"You think it's the right thing to do?"

"Yes, I do. Your feeling about those noises you heard the other day appears to have been bang on. So let's go. We can't do anything from here."

As she threw on jeans and a T-shirt, it occurred to Grace that this night would be playing out much differently if Adam were in her bed. He had the communications, the weapons, the team, the investigative know-how and the power to take control over this strange and potentially terrible situation. But he wasn't there. She had been alone. So had Suzanne. But now they were together, and they would have to manage.

Then she wondered if Sherry had someone to rely on, besides Suzanne. It didn't, so far, seem that way.

*****

The drive downtown was insane. Rain hammered on and poured down the windshield, rendering the wipers useless. It was utterly black in the widespread power outage, which had also taken out the street lighting; it was impossible to see anything beyond the car's headlights — except during ear-splitting, eye-dazzling forks of lightning.

It was so noisy, Grace and Suzanne were forced to shout at each other. Grace was trying to be Suzanne's second set of eyes, because driving around broken tree branches — some of them very large — was also part of the stormy obstacle course.

"Shit! There's another one on your right," yelled Grace.

Suzanne swerved.

"Damn. That was a big one. Do you think we'll notice in time if a whole tree has fallen across the street?" Suzanne shouted back.

"God, I hope so."

It was the most violent, longest and wettest storm in years, the two friends had agreed as they climbed into the car. There had been a spectacular rainfall in the early eighties, when they were young: almost one hundred millimetres of rain in fifty minutes had flooded basements across the city and Grace hadn't forgotten the storm's aftermath, rescuing her toys and cleaning out the silt and sewage.

This was worse.

The bridge was a river, ending in an enormous puddle at its base. Suzanne blasted through the two-foot-deep pool, as Grace prayed the brakes wouldn't quit on them.

A few blocks later, they pulled up in front of the police station, and the two women stared at each other.

"What a trip," said Grace. "Was it as bad getting over to my place?"

"Pretty much," said Suzanne, earning big points for bravery from her friend. "Thank God we don't live too far apart."

Taking deep breaths, they pushed the car doors open into the pressing wind. Heads down, they dashed to the front door of the station and were instantly soaked again; the rain was so heavy, it was like running through a waterfall.

A cursory evaluation of each other in the vestibule provided the conclusion nothing could be done about their drenched, makeup-free, drowned-rat-like appearances. Resigned, they approached the desk.

The young police officer on duty, whose widening eyes registered amazement at their wild, wet and dishevelled appearance, grinned at the two women.

"Enjoying the weather?" he asked. "Sorry. Seriously. Are you two okay?"

"We have not been blown into the river, electrocuted by lightning, or smashed by trees, if that's what you mean, *Monsieur*," said Suzanne. "I wouldn't say we are okay, however."

"No. I suppose not. How can I help?" asked the officer. "I don't know if we have any towels or blankets or anything. Joan?" he called over his shoulder. "Do we have anything blanket-like?"

Sergeant Joan Karpinski, who helped determine the identity of Grace's attacker in the spring and was promoted on the strength of her efforts, emerged from behind a door.

"I don't know — hey, Grace! How are you doing? Wait. I think that was a dumb question. Why don't you come in? I'm Joan Karpinski," she added, introducing herself to Suzanne and holding out her hand. "Let's go in this room, over here on your right."

Thank the gods, thought Grace. Failing Adam, she'd take Joan any day. Joan was smart as hell and super easy to talk to.

"Hey, Lorne, look who's here," Joan shouted over her shoulder.

Lorne Fisher came into the room, barely making it through the door. He was easily the most massive man Grace had ever seen, and certainly the largest cop on the force. Grace remembered Lorne from the bishop's case in the spring; they greeted each other, she introduced him to Suzanne, and Grace dove in.

"Suzanne's worried about her neighbour," she explained as they settled into chairs with bitter java. It was definitely the first time Grace was grateful for cop shop coffee, which was, at least, hot; the station had generators to provide power during outages.

"Worried enough to drive down here during the worst summer storm in twenty years," Joan observed. "Maybe thirty. That's pretty worried. Suzanne, give me a quick version of what's going on. I assume we're going to have to get over to your neighbour's house."

"If you don't mind me butting in for a second — in the hopes of speeding this up — do you know about the dog who was shot yesterday?" asked Grace. "And the SUV crashing into the Smart Car? We came down to talk to James about it."

"Yes — I read the report. You're *that* Suzanne, the witness who saw the SUV in the alley, then. What happened to bring you down here now, in this weather?"

"The storm awakened me," Suzanne said quickly. "There was a huge clap of thunder — so loud I wondered if one of my trees had come down, crashed onto something. I looked out the kitchen window with my flashlight. Then I turned it off, but a few minutes later, in the lightning, I saw someone moving in my neighbour's — Sherry's — back yard. I thought the person went into the house, and I don't think it was Sherry. And what would she be doing outside in this weather, without a flashlight?

"I couldn't call anyone. Neither of my phones worked because of the power outage. I went over and banged on Sherry's door and I shouted, but there was no response. And no candles, no flashlight inside. The door was locked. Then I became very frightened, and ran back to my house.

"I drove to Grace's and explained to her, and now, *nous sommes là*. Here we are," she added, realizing she had switched to her mother tongue.

"I see why you're concerned," said Joan.

"Oh!" said Suzanne. "I thought I heard a sound, a cry. But I could be wrong. It's so noisy with the wind and rain and thunder."

"Okay, Suzanne. Let's go and have a look, shall we? Do you want to stay here, or go back to Grace's?"

"Fat chance, Karpinski," Grace said, her reporter's hat firmly in place.

Joan sighed. "I guess I can't prevent you from going to Suzanne's house, can I?"

She shook her head. "I don't think so."

"We'll take a police SUV," said Joan. "You can follow us. We'll meet you in the lobby in two minutes."

Joan and Lorne Fisher gathered keys and put on their jackets; they already wore their duty belts, fully equipped with mobile communications, guns and myriad other gear.

Stopping at the front desk, and with time against them, Joan asked the young constable to contact James Weatherall and Charlotte Warkentin, the detective constables on call that night.

"Tell them no sirens, and no lights as they get close. What's the address, Suzanne?" she asked.

Suzanne gave it, and they were away.

*****

Tucked into her car, with a blanket Joan had unearthed at the station, Suzanne slumped in her seat; Grace had taken the wheel. Perceiving her friend's exhaustion, Grace wondered if she might doze off on the short trip up to Nutana, across the river from the police station.

Grace was having the opposite reaction. As they neared Sherry's house, her tension rose. She was much more concerned about Sherry now that the police were obviously taking Suzanne so seriously. While Suzanne nodded off, Grace vibrated, and wished she had brought a reporter's notebook.

Hopefully, thought Grace, Sherry had been asleep, and the person Suzanne thought she saw was either a phantom or a friend.

The SUV dodged tree branches and puddles the size of ponds; Grace followed Joan's lead. They arrived within ten minutes down the street from Sherry's house. Dimly, Grace could see a second police vehicle across the street; the rain, while still pouring down, had let up enough to allow her to see a few metres. There was a scarf of light on the eastern horizon. The dawn was coming.

"Stay here," said Joan, stopping at Suzanne's vehicle. "Or, go into Suzanne's house, but I'd rather check it out first, in case it's one of those power-outage break-and-enter sprees."

"We'll stay here for now," said Grace.

"Sherry Hilliard? Is that right?" Joan asked Suzanne.

"Yes," said Suzanne, drowsily.

Joan and Lorne walked a few paces and met James and Charlotte on the sidewalk. All four advanced on the house, as Joan quietly explained what she knew. All the officers already knew about the dog being shot and the SUV crash. Was this related?

James and Charlotte went around the side, to check the yard, garage and back door. Drawing their guns, they crept silently along the narrow sidewalk beside the house. Joan and Lorne walked up to the front window, and tried to peer in; it was black inside.

Nothing for it but to try the front door, and it was, as Suzanne had said, locked.

"James," said Joan quietly into the mobile phone, "it's locked. We're going to knock. Be ready."

"Copy that," said James.

Lorne, the big man with a big fist and a voice to match, hammered on the door and rang the doorbell at the same time.

"Police," he called. "Please open the door, Ms. Hilliard."

No response. They waited a moment longer.

"Police!" yelled Lorne, banging again. "Open up please!"

He turned to Joan and shrugged.

"How do you want to get in?" he asked. "Want to check windows, or break down the door?"

"Just a sec," said Joan. "James, is the back door locked, too?"

"Yeah. No windows open along this side . . . just a minute . . ." he sloshed through muddy puddles to the other side. "No windows open here, either." He pulled on one of them. "Locked, too."

"Looks like we're breaking in. Lorne's going to try this door with his shoulder. Otherwise we'll get the ram. Standing back now."

Lorne, who in the spring had almost single-handedly carried a wounded James out of a tiny basement with a little help from a bleeding Adam, unloaded his power onto the door. It caved easily, crashing to the floor.

The police officers walked over the door and into the house, first going straight through to the back to let in the detectives.

Still no power. Still no light. All four officers turned on high-powered flashlights, and beamed them around the kitchen and living room.

"Sherry Hilliard! Can you hear me? It's the police," said Joan, heading for the woman's bedroom. The door was closed; Joan opened it, but Sherry was not there. Only a mess of sheets and a comforter thrown aside, possibly because of the heat. A dog bed. A dresser. Clothing carpeted the floor.

Lorne was in the other tiny bedroom, and James had taken the bathroom. No one there.

It took them thirty seconds to check the main floor, but as they searched, there were no signs of basement stairs. This odd, old house didn't have the usual steps off the kitchen. Finally, in the floor of the second bedroom's closet, they found a trap door covered with a mat.

"This is creepy," said Joan, shining her light on the floor. "Can we even get through the hole?"

"Maybe," said James. "No way Fisher's getting in there."

"Nope," agreed the man with the wide shoulders and massive chest. "But I can open the door for you guys."

It came up easily enough, revealing nothing but a black hole; but an odd noise emanated from the gloom. James prepared to head down as Joan flattened herself on the floor, shone her light in and peered around. There wasn't enough of an angle to see much, but there was a ladder.

James handed his flashlight to Joan and started down the flimsy rungs, as Joan lit the way so her colleague could see where he was placing his feet.

"Anybody down there? Sherry?" she called.

The sound of a splash heralded James's arrival at the bottom, explaining the strange noise. Joan dropped a flashlight down to him.

"There's a lot of water coming in here from the rain and . . . oh, my God," the three officers above heard him say. Then they heard him gag.

It was a tiny room. Covered in blood. What James Weatherall saw was Sherry Hilliard's body propped grotesquely against the wall, head flopped to one side, naked from the waist down. She was nearly exsanguinated from being stabbed, countless times.

Five

James would later tell Adam that the crime scene was the worst he had ever attended, and that included car crashes.

The little basement, not much more than a crawl space, was awash in bloody rainwater. That, combined with the victim's pale face above her slashed body, her legs sticking out like a doll's, made the scene utterly surreal.

James sloshed over to the body from the foot of the ladder and said grimly, "No need to take her pulse."

"What happened?" asked Joan. "Do you want me to come down there?"

"She's been stabbed, and slashed. Maybe a dozen, fourteen times. I'm wading in blood and water."

"Jesus. I'm on my way down. Lorne, call it in and get the crime scene people here right now." He immediately stomped out of the room, pressing a speed dial button.

"Charlotte, can you light the way for me?"

Joan crept down the rickety ladder. Splashing down at the bottom, she saw Sherry Hilliard in James's light as he crouched before her body.

"God. What kind of a freak did this? I'm guessing she's been raped, too," he said. "Look at the bruises."

"Christ," said Joan, staring at Sherry's ravaged body. "We have to get crime scene here pronto, and then get her out of here before we all go under water. Char," she called up. "Tell Lorne crime scene has to get here right now. Sirens and lights. Right now. This basement's going under water. We have to move."

"Copy that, Joan," said Charlotte, then shouted, "Lorne! Tell them to get here pronto. Basement's flooding. It's going to put her under water."

"Gotcha," said Lorne from the living room, and Charlotte could hear his big voice rising, demanding speed from the crime scene investigator.

"Shit! Grace and Suzanne are still outside," Joan called again. "We have to say something to them before they hear those sirens. Char, can you ask Lorne to check on them?"

"You got it," said Lorne to Charlotte's request, then stopped. "Hell, what am I going to say? Their friend has been brutally murdered and raped, and is bleeding out in a flooding basement? Fuck."

"You'll have to tell them she's dead. Keep the details out of it; say we don't know what happened yet. Go back to Suzanne's house with them. Who knows what's going on here? Make sure they're safe."

"Okay."

Even from the basement, Joan and James could hear Lorne's heavy sigh, his heavier footsteps heading across the floor and over the broken door.

The sky was brightening as Lorne walked over to Suzanne's car. While it was still raining, it wasn't pouring; the storm was moving off.

Suzanne was asleep when his tap came at the window. Grace's head snapped around; she must have been dozing, too. She poked Suzanne.

"Lorne," said Grace, rolling down the window. "What's going on? You've been in there quite a while."

"I'm sorry, Grace, Suzanne. I'm afraid it's bad news."

"How bad?" asked Grace.

"I'm very sorry to tell you this, but Ms. Hilliard is dead."

In that moment, Grace knew she would never doubt her friend on anything, ever — even if she mentioned aliens had landed.

Suzanne gave a little cry, and Grace could see tears welling up in her eyes.

"Oh, no," said Grace, putting her hand on Suzanne's shoulder. "What happened?" she asked Lorne.

His eyes widened and he shook his head. Don't ask that question, his body language told Grace. "I'm sorry. We just found her. We don't know yet."

"Okay," said Grace, turning to her friend. "Honey. Should we go inside, see if we can warm up, get some tea? Maybe the power's back on."

Suzanne nodded speechlessly. Tears slipped down her face as she pushed the door open, stepped out of the car and started to weave toward her house.

"Oh, no, oh, no," Grace heard her crying, as she opened her own door. Then Suzanne doubled over, in the middle of the street, and leaned to one side.

"Suzé!" shouted Grace, leaping out of the car toward her friend.

But Lorne Fisher was there first. He dove toward Suzanne as she collapsed, and scooped her up in his colossal arms before she could hit the pavement. She was out cold.

Grace lurched back toward the car, snatched the keys out of the ignition and led Lorne to Suzanne's front door, fumbling to unlock it. She flicked the light switch; the power was back on.

Bruno awaited them in the tiny entrance, barking and jumping in a frenzy, nearly tripping Lorne as he carried Suzanne to the sofa and laid her gently down. Grace saw the concerned look on Lorne's face as he crouched beside Suzanne and took her pulse, as she tried to calm Bruno.

Uh oh, she thought, something's happening here. Lorne Fisher was not, by thousands, the first man to think her friend was beautiful; but the kindness in his expression, mixed with admiration, was a moving thing to behold.

Suzanne's eyes fluttered open and her gaze landed on Lorne. It took many seconds before she spoke, as she recovered, confused, from her faint.

"*Allô?*" she said, questioningly. "*Monsieur? Que s'est-il passé?*"

Lorne looked at Grace.

"She's asking what happened," Grace explained, coming over to the sofa and kneeling by her friend. "Her first language was French. Her English will kick in again soon. Suzanne, I'm here. This is Lorne Fisher, the police officer, remember? He caught you when you fell in the street. You fainted, Honey. How's her pulse?" she asked Lorne, quietly.

"Okay," he said. "How are you, Suzanne? How do you feel?"

"Dizzy. Tired. Oh! *Mon Dieu*," she said, suddenly remembering why she had fainted. "Sherry's dead, isn't she?"

"Yes, I'm afraid so," said Lorne. "I'm very sorry."

"What happened to her? Can I see her?"

"I can't tell you, yet, what happened. We're still investigating. And I'm sorry, no, you can't see her." He flicked a warning look at Grace, which was not lost on either woman.

"It's bad, isn't it?" asked Suzanne, in a very quiet voice.

Lorne pressed his lips together, and gave one, very slight nod. Family and friends cared very much about how someone died, once they had absorbed the initial bad news. They wanted to know their loved one had not suffered. Sherry was Suzanne's neighbour, not her sister; but it was much the same thing. There was no reassurance in this case.

Sirens. The crime scene investigators were almost there. At the sound, Suzanne gave a violent shiver. Her hands flew up to her face and covered her eyes, but she couldn't stop the sobs that wracked her body. Lorne took her back into his arms and she threw her own arms around his neck, crying and shaking.

His face registered amazement, then settled into a study in misery. Grace felt so sorry for him. She remembered carrying the same expression on her own face, as she waited for and wanted Adam in the long weeks after the bishop's murder. She was pretty sure Lorne had fallen for Suzé, and hard.

Lorne held Suzanne, and Grace stroked her back, trying to soothe her. Eventually, with a shudder, Suzanne let go of Lorne and actually smiled at him — although shakily.

"*Merci*," she said. "*Merci*, Lorne. For catching me, and for your sympathy. You are very kind."

Lorne, colouring, was apparently struck dumb as he looked into Suzanne's lovely, if puffy, face. Grace wanted to save him.

"Lorne, thank you," she said quickly, to fill the silence. "I would never have been able to catch Suzé, much less get her into the house. Should I make some tea? Coffee?"

Lorne cleared his throat, and rose from the couch.

"Thanks, but I have to get back next door. First I'm going to check the basement, and take a look in the bathroom and bedrooms," he said to Grace; but he was staring at Suzanne.

"Of course," said Grace, feeling a little unsettled by his concern, "but I'm sure Bruno would have caused a fuss, if anyone was here."

Lorne nodded, but headed downstairs just the same.

"No one down there, but there is a little bit of rainwater," said Lorne, returning. He quickly checked the other rooms on the main floor. No sign of interlopers.

"Will you two be okay? I have to get back. And we're right next door."

"We'll be fine," said Grace. "And we have Bruno."

As Lorne turned to head out the door, Suzanne reached out and touched his hand.

"Thank you, again," she said.

"You're welcome, Suzanne. My pleasure. Just doing my job."

"Even so."

Grace followed Lorne to the door, and asked quietly, "How bad is it, Lorne?"

"I didn't see her. She's in the basement with James and Joan."

Grace folded her arms and raised an eyebrow at the big cop. "Give me a break."

Lorne gave a heavy sigh.

"It's really bad, Grace. About as bad as it gets. Look, I promised Joan, no details. Short form, she was stabbed."

"Let me know when we can report on it. I'll stay here with Suzanne until I have to go to work; I'll see if I can find someone to come and be with her. Do you think she's in any danger? Was it personal, or is some undiscriminating lunatic roaming around out there?"

"I'd say it was personal, but it's hard to know for sure. It's probably not a great idea for her to be alone, to be on the safe side."

"Hell. Are you sure?"

"Yeah. We don't know anything right now. I better get back."

"Yes, of course. Sorry to hold you up, Lorne. Thanks again for scooping up my friend. She's usually such a tough girl, but I think this was all too much for her."

*****

When the crime scene people arrived, Joan turned the basement over to their investigators and the detectives. She crawled back up the ladder, soaked past her knees in icy, bloody water, shivering from being partly immersed for so long.

As the ranking cop on shift that night, she had calls to make.

Once out of the trap door's hole, she slogged into the living room. With Adam away, she tried Inspector Terry Pearson first. No answer. As usual.

It would have to be the chief of police, who was either still in bed or just getting up. He was not going to be a happy man. She looked up his emergency cellphone number on her contact list and dialled him, hoping he was up.

"McIvor," he answered, sounding alert.

"Chief, it's Joan Karpinski."

"What's up, Karpinski? I assume it's bad, since you're calling me on the emergency cell before six in the bloody morning."

"It's very bad, Chief. We've found a woman stabbed to death in her basement. She was cut so many times, she lost most of her blood. What's bizarre is that this is the woman whose dog was shot the other day. And the crime scene is a mess, Chief. Her basement is at least a foot and a half under water by now, because of the storm, which is seriously messing up our investigation. I thought you should know."

"What's happening right now? Is crime scene there?"

"Yeah, they're doing their best. But the water keeps coming; it's stopped raining, but the ground is saturated and it's still seeping in. It's a leaky, crappy old basement; I don't think it's even concrete. We have to get them all out of there soon. Plus, it's bloody. We'll all have to get checked out — me, James, the crime scene guys. And the coroner. He's on his way."

"Shit, are you're kidding me, Karpinski? Get them out of there as fast as you can. Have you called Pearson?"

"Yes, sir. No answer, sir."

"Right. I'll meet you at the station as soon as you can make it."

"Thanks, Boss. See you there."

"And Karpinski. Get to the doctor first. I mean it."

"Yes, sir. Thank you, sir."

McIvor hung up and mumbled "fucking Pearson" before returning to his wife, with whom he was having breakfast.

"Why did I send Adam Davis to California, Bev? I could sure use him right now. Damn it."

"Because you're grooming him, dear, as I recall. A bad scene, I gather?"

"A very bad scene. I'm going in right away."

"You could call Adam. Would that help?"

"It would, and I will. He'll need to be up to speed on this, anyway — unless we're lucky enough to find this murderer today. I can always use his take."

*****

Grace beat the police chief to it. It was five in the morning in Los Angeles, but she had to call Adam. She needed to hear his voice, and his opinion on what to do next.

Adam's phone rang. Pick up, pick up, Grace said to him, over the miles.

"Davis," he answered, after the fourth ring.

"Adam, it's me," said Grace. "I'm so sorry to wake you. Something terrible has happened."

"Grace," said Adam, immediately alert. "Are you all right? Tell me you're all right."

"I am. I'm fine and safe. But there's been a murder, and I needed to hear your voice."

"What? A murder?" said Adam, voice rising as he swung his feet to the floor. "What the hell is going on, Grace?"

"It's this case, the one that started with the car crash and the dog being shot. Suzanne's neighbour, the dog's owner, has been murdered. Stabbed. I don't know the details, and I don't know what to think. How worried should I be about Suzanne? I'm with her now. To be exact, I'm in her kitchen and she's taking a hot shower. We had a terrible storm last night, and both of us were soaking wet and cold . . ."

"Grace," Adam interjected. "Slow down. Start at the beginning and tell me what happened. Why were you wet and cold?"

Grace realized she had been rather incoherent. She was very tired, and the night's events had been bizarre. Like she needed more bizarre, after what had happened in the spring.

"I'm sorry," she said again. "I'm not making much sense. Let me start over."

She recounted the lead-up to the murder, told him about the storm and Suzanne knocking on her door in the wee hours, how they drove down to the police station through bucketing rain, and that Sherry Hilliard was stabbed to death next door. She also told him Suzanne had fainted, and Lorne Fisher caught her before her head hit the pavement.

"Go, Lorne," said Adam. "Then what?"

"She woke up, realized what had happened, and he hugged her and she hugged him back. It was . . . well, I'll tell you what I think when I see you. Anyway, Lorne said he wasn't sure if Suzanne should be alone. Adam, should we cancel our trip, do you think? Have you heard from your department?"

"Not yet, but my phone is lighting up. I think the chief's trying to call me. I'll call him back. But Grace, please listen to me. I will do everything in my power to make this California trip happen," Adam said, his powerful voice becoming more adamant with every word. "I'm not the only goddamn detective in the Saskatoon Police Service. I want to be with you, away from work, away from home, and we are going."

"You may not be the only, but you're the best goddamn detective," said Grace, a laugh of relief burbling in her chest. The intensity of his voice hit her, and she melted in its embrace. "And the best lover," she added, softly.

"How do you know?" asked Adam, teasingly, but bursting inside.

"My body told me. She's never wrong. Very reliable as a witness."

"You must know by now I've never made love like this. It must be you."

"Oh. Oh, Adam," Grace breathed, then pulled it together. "But you have to call the chief back. Before you go, and I know this is an unfair question since you just learned about this, what should I do about Suzé?"

"I'd be led by your gut. If Fisher or James feels this murder is personal, and most homicides are, Suzanne is likely okay. But if your antennae say something else might be going on, listen. Could Suzanne leave town for a couple of days?"

"She could go visit her parents on the farm. I'll talk to her about it. It would definitely make me feel better."

Grace heard Adam grunt.

"The chief is calling again," he said. "I have to go, Grace. I'll call you back later, as soon as I can. Maybe I'll have a better take on this case by then. Bye, beautiful."

"Bye, Adam."

Adam caught the chief's second call on its last ring.

"Good morning, Chief. I hear there was a murder overnight. What's going on?"

"You're not going to believe this, Adam," said McIvor. "Brace yourself."

Six

Adam did brace himself, but it didn't help much. What Dan McIvor was telling him over the phone was, even for a police sergeant, hard to take in.

"It's one of the worst crime scenes I can recall, Adam, by Karpinski's description," said McIvor. "The woman was stabbed so many times, there was not much blood left in her body. A quick examination indicates she was raped first, too. We're waiting for forensics to confirm.

"Her blood was all over the basement, but because of a wicked storm we had last night, it was mixed with rainwater coming in from outside. Our people were wading in that, for fuck's sake."

Jesus, thought Adam, closing his eyes. "How long ago was this? Have they seen doctors yet?"

"They either have or they're on their way. I called the public health people and put the fear of God and hell into them if they don't see our officers immediately. Christ, I hope the victim comes back clean. How much pressure can I put on McDougall to speed up the autopsy, before he gets his back up? You know him pretty well."

Jack McDougall was the city's chief forensic pathologist, and after 45 years in the position, even the police chief didn't often get away with telling him what to do. McDougall was a tough old Scot, immovable as

Hadrian's Wall, but he was also the very best at what he did.

"I think you could make a damn good argument on this one, since our own people's health is at potential risk," said Adam. "Jack can be difficult to talk into anything, but if you flatter him enough, you can expedite an autopsy. I've pulled it off a couple of times. Offering Scotch helps."

"I'll give it a go. So any gut feelings on this? I know it's unfair to ask since you're not on site, but bloody hell, Adam, the public is going to flip; and women are going to ask if they're safe. They'll wonder if it was a home invasion, or what the hell. We'll have to be careful about releasing details. But it looks personal to me."

"Was there forcible entry?"

"No. No sign of it. And both doors were locked when we arrived."

"It sure as hell sounds personal. Who spends that kind of time cutting someone to pieces, not to mention the sexual assault, if it isn't? And no forcible entry. But Chief, what if we're wrong? There is at least one woman in the neighbourhood who might be at risk, if the killer knows she directed the police to the crime scene, or thinks she saw him. I'll bet my salary he wasn't expecting the victim to be found so quickly."

"Grace called you."

"Yes. As I'm sure you know by now, the neighbour is one of her closest friends. Grace is quite worried."

Adam told Chief McIvor about his relationship with Grace in its early days, which was really only three weeks ago. He wanted to clear the air about falling madly for one of his witnesses, and a victim in a former case, as quickly as possible. He also wanted to clarify any conflict rules, should he and Grace cross over on a case he was working and she was covering for the paper.

This time, there weren't a lot of options. It was a murder case Grace was involved in through her friend. They'd have to work it out when he returned to Saskatoon. Or sooner.

Adam heard his boss heave an exasperated sigh.

"If it was my friend, or my daughter, or my wife, I'd be fucking worried too," said McIvor. "I hope I wouldn't have to worry if I was the average Saskatoon woman. Can you persuade that young woman to get the hell out of Dodge? Or at least get her to move in with a friend for a few days?"

"Grace is going to suggest to Suzanne that she visit her parents out near St. Denis. It might work out okay, as long as her folks have decent Internet on their farm. She runs her graphic design business from home."

"Tell her to persuade hard. Can you also connect with James and Joan, and get on a game plan? I'd like to see something by this afternoon. Sooner, if possible."

"I'll call them next, Chief."

"Thanks, Adam. When the hell are you coming home?"

"I'll get back to you on that. Later, Chief."

It did sound personal, Adam reflected. But it was still important to cross-check the crime with other cases. Don't make assumptions.

One of the policing clinics in L.A. had hammered home that point. There had been considerable talk about cross-checking at the conference because the United States had just established its National Missing and Unidentified Persons list, or NamUS. Canada had no similar system yet, and Adam, as a Prairie cop, knew like few other how desperately it was needed.

He called James.

"You just come off the desk after being shot, and now you have to wade around in a bloody basement?"

"Hi, Sarge," said James. "Yeah, well. It's always something."

"Are you okay?" Adam asked in a different tone. "Have you seen the doctor? Has Joan?"

"Yeah, we both have. I'll be okay. So where do you want to start?"

"Let's start by going over our cold files. It may not provide any insight, but we can't assume. We know some of those perps are still out there.

"We have eight unsolved missing women cases in the Saskatoon region, and there are twenty-three missing in the province, last I checked. Let's see if any of the women murdered in the last couple of years were killed in similar ways; and if any of the missing women have anything in common with Sherry Hilliard. Have you found the SUV yet?"

"No."

"It's probably hidden in a garage somewhere. Shit. We need to find that vehicle. Let me think about what we can do, short of putting out a public plea for assistance, to find it. Have we checked the paint left by the SUV on the Smart Car?"

"Yes. I haven't seen the report, but it should come today."

"Licence number?" asked Adam, with little hope.

"No. Suzanne didn't see it and the Smart Car victim is still in a coma. No one else has come forward."

"Maybe the paint will be a clue. And it's likely the bastard has had the SUV fixed and cleaned by now. What about the dog? Any clues there? What kind of a bullet killed him?"

"The dog's autopsy hasn't been completed yet," said James. "I'm hoping for DNA but it's unlikely."

"Yeah, I doubt it. Unless he bit the attacker before he could shoot him," said Adam, ruminating. "Can you see it? Man comes for dog, planning to kill it, but before he can hit it or drug it, dog bites man. Man goes into fury and shoots dog. It is possible there's DNA in the dog's mouth. Make sure they check.

"Also, whoever is on crime scene at Sherry Hilliard's house should check for dog blood. I'm sure he cleaned it up, if he did kill the dog inside, so we'll have to use luminol and ultraviolet.

"But I bet he didn't brush the dog's teeth."

*****

Adam hung up with James, and seconds later, his cellphone rang again. Hell. He knew that number.

"Davis," he answered.

"Davis," said the voice of Inspector Terry Pearson, mimicking Adam. "It's Pearson."

"I know."

"What the fuck are you doing going over my head and calling the chief?"

"I didn't call the chief," said Adam. "He called me."

"Riiight," said Pearson.

"Look, Terry. Those were my people on the case. He called me."

"Karpinski called him."

Obviously, the inspector had finally had a chat with the chief.

"She likely couldn't reach you, Inspector," said Adam, nailing it.

"She should have called me. You should have called me."

"I haven't had time, Terry," said Adam, ignoring the second jab at Joan. "I've been on the phone since five. Which is when I learned about all of this."

"You should have called me first. I'm writing you up for this, Davis."

"Go ahead," said Adam evenly. But despite the ice in his voice, he had lost his temper. Pearson was always threatening stupid shit like "writing him up," probably to cover his own incompetence.

And Adam hung up on his direct superior, leaving him fuming at the other end.

*****

"You either have to go home to the farm, or come home with me," Grace said firmly to Suzanne. "The police — well, Adam and Lorne — don't think you should be at home. I'm sorry."

Suzanne, towelling her hair after her shower, looked wearily at Grace. There was no point in arguing. But Suzanne had work to do, and was hesitant to leave her home. And of course, there was Bruno.

"I can't come home with you," said Suzanne. "It's a huge imposition. Look at my dog, Grace. He's bigger than your couch. Besides, wouldn't I be safe with him here?"

Head tilted, Grace just looked at Suzanne. She didn't want to point out the dog next door had been killed, leaving its owner alone and unprotected. She waited for her friend to realize what she'd said. It took a few seconds.

"Oh," said Suzanne in a small voice. "Right."

"I think you should consider going home for a few days, Suzé," said Grace. "This must be an awful shock. Why don't you and Bruno hang out with me for a day or two, and then head to the farm? It won't be much fun here with police all over the place, and with crime scene tape around Sherry's house, people walking by will gawk and maybe ask you what's going on. And what will you say?"

"*Oui, belle amie.* Good point. *Merci.* I will come, for a day or two. And I will think about going to see my parents."

Grace hugged her friend.

"It'll be okay. I'm so glad you're coming. I don't know if I could sleep wondering how you're doing here."

"I might have some trouble sleeping too. I'll start getting organized, and see you after work?"

Grace paused. Well, she thought, not much could go wrong in broad daylight with half a dozen police officers next door. She hoped.

"Sure. Let's plan on meeting at five at my house?"
"I'll be there."
"You promise." Grace wasn't asking.
"Yes."

Suzanne drove Grace home, dodging yet more tree branches and other detritus from the storm; but the sun was out, the rain had stopped, and the day was glittering with summer promise. It was very hard, thought Grace, to fathom the night's events in the light of morning.

Seven

At seven-thirty, Grace left a quick voicemail message for the city editor with basic information about the murder, and managed to make it into the newsroom by nine.

"Do you have the press release from the police yet?" she asked Claire Davidson, after dropping her gear at her desk.

"I just read it. Holy shit, Grace. What in hell happened last night? You look exhausted."

Grace pulled up a chair across from Claire and told her the whole story.

"The police officer who caught Suzanne when she fainted said it was grim," said Grace. "He wouldn't give me any details. But this is going to be an awful story."

"Yeah, and you can't write it. But you can give your details to . . . well, to whoever is going to write it. You were not just on scene, your friend is involved."

"I know, I know, I'm too close to this one. You don't have to explain, Claire. Who are you going to assign?"

Claire looked around the newsroom.

"Well, Lacey did a great job on your case. I'll ask her. It'll be a rough go, so I don't want her to take it on if she doesn't feel she can."

But Lacey agreed with gusto to taking on another huge local crime story. Grace started typing out notes and questions to ask the police about what happened the night before, and Lacey got on the phone with police communications. They put her through to James.

"Hey, Lacey."

"Hey, James. How are you doing?"

"I'm okay. Tired. It was a long night. Can't wait to catch this freak." He paused. "You'll have to ask me questions and I'll see if I can answer them."

"Let's start with how she was killed."

"She was stabbed."

"In her home."

"Yes."

"At what time?"

"We don't know yet. We found her at dawn. About four-thirty."

"How did you find her? I mean, who called it in? It wasn't a crime in progress, as I understand it. Did someone hear or see anything?"

"A neighbour called us, worried about having seen something unusual next door. But you know that."

"I know I know that. But I have to ask. This woman's dog was killed less than two days before she was murdered. Do you think there is a connection?"

"We don't know yet."

"Any other details you can give me? Do you have a murder weapon, where was she stabbed — on her body, I mean — and do you have any leads on the killer?"

"No, no, and no."

"Was she stabbed twice? Three times?"

James sighed. Damn reporters, always wanting exact details.

"More than once."

"What do you mean, more than once?"

"We have to wait for the autopsy, but she was stabbed more than once."

Lacey's mental antennae stood straight up. How many times had the killer cut her?

"Where was she found, exactly?"

"In her basement."

"And where is this home?"

"In Nutana. I can't say more, honestly. And I know Grace knows where this house is, but for God's sake, don't publish the address. Please. I'm asking all the media not to publish the address. It will come out, but there are reasons why we don't want the whole damn city showing up there to gawk."

"I'll talk to Claire. For now, I'm sure she'll agree. So last question: do you know if this was a personal or a random attack? Early days, I know, but is there any indication it was personal or random?"

"No. We think it was personal because of the . . . ah, nature of the attack. Unfortunately we can't say for certain."

"Have you released her name yet? It's not on the presser. Obviously we know it, but have you reached her family?"

"No. Not yet. I don't think her family lives in the area."

Grace, who was listening to Lacey's side of the conversation, passed her a note; a thought had just crossed her mind. *Hilliard.* The name rang a bell for Grace; she had gone to high school with a girl who had the same last name, of mixed Indigenous and Scottish blood. Pretty, dark-haired Sherry looked as if she could have similar heritage.

"I understand from Grace the victim may be Indigenous. Does her background have any bearing on the case?" Lacey and Grace, and everyone else in policing and reportage, knew that Indigenous women were victims of crime at a rate well above the average.

"I don't know. Thanks for telling me. I'll look into it, but for now, no comment."

"Damn it, James. This isn't going to make for a well-rounded story."

"I know. I'm sorry. The autopsy will take a few days, at least. Likely more. Give us a few hours, will you, on the name?"

"Yeah, of course. Want to tell me off the record what the hell is going on? At least, why you guys are being this cagey about the details?"

James paused.

"We just can't say much yet. We need to know if it's personal, which is bad enough, or random, or something even worse. People are going to be worried and we have to catch this guy, so we have to be careful, and not create fear if it's unwarranted."

"Okay. But we have to run as much information as we can, because it's our job — not just yours — to serve the public interest. And that means warning women to be careful, if they need to be."

"I know, I know. It's a tough call, Lacey. I'll get you more in a few hours if I can."

"Thanks, James. I see the spot you're in. We'll do our best to walk the line."

"Appreciate it, Lacey. Later."

"Later, James."

After consulting with Grace and Claire, Lacey avoided the address, the victim's name and limited herself to saying the woman had been stabbed.

For now.

*****

It hadn't taken long for the lab to bring back a verdict on the paint left by the speeding SUV on the tiny Smart Car.

Joan Karpinski was in James Weatherall's office when a constable brought in the paperwork, and flopped it on the desk with a little flourish.

"That was fast," said James. "I told Adam it might be on my desk today, but I thought I was being overly optimistic. Thanks," he said to the constable, who gave a little salute and left.

Joan and James immediately opened the file. The paint was indeed black, not navy. High-end, super-hard finish, European; possibly a German paint made by BASF or Siemens.

"We're looking for a pretty expensive vehicle here," said Joan.

"I know who to call," said James, picking up the phone. "A friend of Bruce's sells expensive cars. He can tell me quickly which brands are available in Saskatoon, and which ones might use a high-end German paint."

James didn't say Bruce Stephens, his partner, owned one of those expensive cars. Bruce was an investment banker, and didn't mind spending his stacks of money. He had made a casual friend in the owner of Luxury Motors, where he had purchased his sleek, silver Audi.

James looked up the number and punched the buttons on his phone. When the receptionist answered, he identified himself and asked to speak with Nick Delacroix, immediately if possible.

"One moment, Constable," said the receptionist in her most mellifluous tones. "I'm fairly sure he's in the store, somewhere. I'll have to track him down."

Two minutes later, the line crackled.

"James. How the hell are you," said the voice on the other end.

"I'm fine, Nick. You?"

"Great. I hope you two are planning another pool party soon? The last one was steaming. Anyway, Lissa said you needed to talk to me right away. What's up?"

"I'd like to know how many car brands in Saskatoon would have high-end European paint, in a super-hard, high-gloss black. The lab thinks it's German."

"Hmmm. Well, we have three brands — Mercedes, Porsche, Audi, as well as Volkswagen, so it depends how high-end we're talking. We have Jags too, but they're made in England. The competition has the Italian brands, some of the English brands, and BMW."

"So all of those would qualify for high-end European auto paint?"

"Yeah. I mean, there are a few other European brands like Fiat and Aston Martin, but very few of those are sold here. We Prairie folks like our bigger cars."

James very much doubted those were the brands in question.

"Great, thanks for the information. I'll let you know if we plan another shindig. Or Bruce will. It sure as hell is hot enough for a pool party."

"Tell Bruce to get his car in for servicing," said Nick, who could be heard tapping the keys on his computer, apparently checking the Audi's record. "It's time. Let me know if I can do anything else to help."

"I will. Thanks, Nick."

"We're looking at four car makers," James said to Joan after hanging up. "At least four: BMW, Mercedes, Audi, Porsche, and maybe VW. I don't know if all of them make SUVs; we'll have to find out. I know BMW and Porsche do, and obviously VW."

"And I bet all of them make black ones," said Joan. "I'd guarantee it."

The desk constable was back at the door.

"The guy in the Smart Car," he said. "He didn't make it."

Eight

Grace and Suzanne curled up on Grace's couch that evening, with Bruno taking up most of the floor space in the living room. They tried to relax, drank some wine and ate spring rolls dipped in peanut sauce. A stir-fry was on the menu for dinner, but Grace was afraid she would doze off before she could make it, she was so exhausted.

The phone rang. Grace excused herself and answered it; she was sure it would be Adam.

"Grace. How are you and Suzanne holding up?" he asked, without preamble. As usual.

"Stupid tired," said Grace. "What an awful night. And a long day. She's here with me. How are you? What did the chief say?"

"He wanted to discuss how to move forward with the investigation," Adam said. "I think he was gearing up to asking me to come back, but he managed not to. I'd rather, instead of spending this weekend with nothing to do, except, of course, for next weekend."

"Yes. I'm with you there."

"There has been a development," he added, slowly. "I'm afraid the man in the Smart Car died from his injuries."

"Oh no, Adam. That's terrible." Grace paused. "Any further developments on the other part of the case?"

"Not much. We have an idea what kind of vehicle hit the car, but that's about it. But of course, our primary witness, apart from Suzanne, has died. We have two victims. Shit."

Adam couldn't yet tell Grace about the horrors found in the basement, nor did he want to; but holding back was stilting the conversation, as was the fact Suzanne was right there.

"Grace, I wish we could really talk. I can't wait to see you. How long will Suzanne be with you?"

"I'm not sure. She thinks she may head to the farm Sunday or Monday — before I leave, anyway, although I told her she could stay here."

"Well, make sure she takes care, all precautions, and staying away from her house for a while would be an excellent idea. Tell her so from me."

"I will."

"I miss you."

"A few more days, Adam," said Grace.

Hanging up, she returned to the couch and Suzanne, who had devoured her last spring roll.

"I'm sorry, Grace. *Désolée*. You would like to make love to Adam over the phone, I think. But I am here."

Grace smiled at her phrasing.

"I'd rather make love to Adam in person. It's fine, Honey. You will keep me from longing for him quite so much, and I appreciate it. Let's have dinner."

*****

The weekend passed uneventfully, compared to the last few days. Since Grace couldn't report on Sherry's murder and was no longer the weekend reporter, she was off the hook at work; so she and Suzanne hit the farmers' market, walked along the verdant riverbank, went out for dinner with Lacey and relaxed as much as possible.

Grace wondered, occasionally, what the police were up to; but there was little hope of finding out. They were being very careful with the information they were releasing, and Adam couldn't tell her much.

With Suzanne constantly nearby, conversations with Adam were somewhat less intense and greatly abbreviated; but Grace was nonetheless grateful for Suzanne's presence. It kept her from thinking every other minute about whether she would be going on her upcoming trip, and what would happen when she saw Adam again. Being constantly aroused was exhausting.

On Monday morning, Suzanne started packing her little car, shoving her computer, files, clothes, dog food and Bruno into it for the trip home. Her parents' farm wasn't far, but she still had to get everything in.

Grace went with Suzanne to help her pack. By the time everything was crammed inside, she was helpless with laughter. The small sedan was packed to the roof, and Bruno looked quite alarmed at being tucked into the back seat, surrounded by boxes and unable to turn around.

"It will only be forty minutes, *mon vieux*," Suzanne said to Bruno, comfortingly. "Sit now, Bruno. Sit *down*."

Grace sank to the curb, shaking with hilarity, as Suzanne drove away, waving in the rear view mirror. Grace was left to her life. She went home to get ready for work.

The morning air was fresh and clean, but the July heat was building again. Suzanne was looking forward to driving through the flowering canola fields, breathing in the sweet, heady aroma of healthy crops. But before she even made it to the edge of the city, Suzanne realized she had forgotten her printer. Damn it. Suzanne turned around and headed back.

Stopping in the driveway alongside her garage, she debated leaving Bruno in the car, but he looked so miserable, she let him out.

"All right, *mon vieux*. Come along. But be a good dog when we have to leave again."

She unlocked the door with a tiny frisson of misgiving, but Bruno was calm; he obviously didn't notice anything amiss. Suzanne relaxed, grabbed the printer, popped it in a box and made a stop in the bathroom before struggling the box and Bruno into the car.

Finally, she hit the highway. Fifteen minutes later, the car began to shudder. *Merde*, what now? She hadn't had the car maintained in a while, but it chose this time, this moment to act up? What was wrong with it?

Black smoke coming out of the exhaust — she could see it in the rearview mirror — scared her enough to pull over onto a gravel road leading off the highway. She put on the flashers and clambered out of the car. *Fuck.*

Knowing precisely nothing about vehicles, popping the hood was pointless. How would she know what had gone awry? And would the damn thing blow up in her face?

Diving back inside, she grabbed her purse with shaking hands, put Bruno on his leash, pulled him out of the back and rummaged for her cellphone. Who should she call? A tow truck? She didn't have a towing company on speed dial. Her father? Maybe — she was almost halfway home.

Suzanne thought for a couple of minutes as she watched cars fly past her on the highway. No one stopped.

Just as she decided to call her father, a truck slowed down; the man inside turned his head in her direction, and pulled over a few metres ahead. As the vehicle backed up along the shoulder of the highway, she realized it was a tow truck.

A young man hopped out of the bright red vehicle.

"Hello, miss," he said. "What's happened? Car break down?"

"Yes. Thank you so much for stopping. It started to shudder and then black smoke came out of the exhaust. It was quite scary. I pulled over and have been standing here wondering what to do."

"I'm taking this truck out to Humboldt. Brand new, this baby. We have a dealership out there. Let me see if the boss is okay with me hooking you up and taking you back to Saskatoon first . . . are you from Saskatoon? I'm Dustin, by the way."

"Thank you, Dustin. Yes, I'm from Saskatoon. It would be much appreciated."

Dustin pulled out his cellphone and punched some buttons.

"Hey, Boss," he said, when someone answered. "I have a lady here by the side of the highway. Car seems undriveable, but I haven't looked under the hood yet. Any chance of giving it a lift back to the city before I head to Humboldt?"

Garbled noises from the other end. A laugh from Dustin.

"Yes, she is," he said. "Okay, I'll get on it. Thanks." A pause. "You bet."

He turned back to Suzanne. "The boss says no problem. Let me take a look under the hood. Spectacular dog, by the way. What breed is he?"

"He is a Newfoundland," said Suzanne. "Bruno. He is indeed a wonderful dog. And very expensive to feed."

"I guess," said Dustin, with a bark of laughter. "So, about the car; if it needs to go to the shop, how will you get to wherever you are going?"

"I can call the . . . people I am visiting. They can pick me up."

"I can also take you there, or bring you back to the dealership."

"No, no. I will be fine, and I have all these things I must take with me. I'll call now, in case it has to go in."

Suzanne called her father, explained the situation in rapid French, and was assured he would be there soon. Dustin's head reappeared from around the car's hood a moment later.

"Dead on four wheels," he declared. "Black smoke was a bad sign. It'll have to go in."

"I think I have no choice?"

"Not much of one, I'm afraid. We'll take the car in, let you know what's wrong and give you a quote, if you are okay with giving us your cell number?"

"Yes. Okay."

Suzanne gave him the number as he punched it into his cellphone contacts.

"We'll get back to you by the end of the day, or first thing in the morning, latest."

"*Merci*. Thank you so much, Dustin."

With her saviour's help, Suzanne pulled suitcases, computer equipment, enormous bags of dog food and other items out of her car, and placed them carefully on the side of the ditch. Dustin hooked up the car, and waited until Suzanne spied her father's truck coming over a hill.

"There he is," she said.

"Okay, great," said Dustin. "I'll be in touch."

He was back in the tow truck before Suzanne could say goodbye.

Nine

Adam had dreaded the days between the two conferences, and they were bad enough as he thought incessantly about Grace and their upcoming getaway. At least he was busy and distracted, working long distance with his team to solve the murder of Sherry Hilliard.

The detectives started poring over the missing women files, and other potentially-related cold case files. James set up a video link so Adam could see the case room, with photos of the missing women plastered up on the walls.

"In the Saskatoon area," said James, "we have eight missing women. They're the ones to the right," he said, indicating so Adam could see which photos were which.

"There are also four non-missing cold cases we've dug out so far, to my left. Two of the women are dead. We've reached one of the women who survived her attack, and are going to see her tomorrow."

"Is anything jumping out at you?" Adam asked. "Anything that connects Sherry to any of the others?"

"Sherry has Indigenous blood. Grace thought it was worth checking on that; she had a friend with the same last name, apparently. Six of the eight missing women are Indigenous. The other two are Caucasian. Three of the eight were sex trade workers. We're sorting through murdered women over a five-year time span now."

"What else do we know about Sherry? Anything about what she did in her personal time?"

"We're working on it. The Winnipeg police have informed her family in Manitoba. The sergeant there will do a first interview today or tomorrow.

"Which reminds me," added James. "You'll remember the detective sergeant from London who helped us on the bishop's case, Jeannette Villeneuve? She's in Winnipeg now. They headhunted her for an inspector's job and she took it. Doesn't hurt to be bilingual in Winnipeg, plus I hear she speaks some Cree."

"She was fantastic when we reached out to her in March," said Adam. "Maybe we'll hook up with her again on this case, since the victim's family is in Manitoba. Either way, I'll give her a call and congratulate her."

Adam was pleased for Villeneuve. She was a hell of a cop, and welcome to follow the tendrils of his cases around the country any time. He would definitely return the favour if it ever became necessary.

"Have you contacted the dental office yet?" Adam asked.

"Charlotte's calling this morning. We'll see what we can get without a warrant. We're expecting privacy objections on getting a client list. Do you want me to get on the warrant right away?"

"Yeah. Call Sanj Kumar and get the thing rolling, even if something comes from Charlotte's conversation that points to our killer. Let's get the prosecutor's office onboard as soon as possible."

"Right. How's it going in L.A.?"

"It's going okay. I have a profiling workshop in half an hour, so I'd better hit the shower. I'll call you back this afternoon. And welcome back. Man, I missed you."

"Thanks, Adam. I missed you guys, too. Talk to you soon."

*****

If a man could have two right hands, Charlotte Warkentin and James Weatherall were Adam's.

The three detectives had been working together full-time with Adam as sergeant for two years. They were tight, effective. Adam admired James's passionate policing, and Charlotte's incredible head for detail. Coming close to losing James earlier in the year had made Adam realize how much he cared for his constable. And, he credited Charlotte with saving his life and his career. To say he was extremely fond of her was a huge understatement.

Several years ago, after Adam had been shot on the job and sidelined from work for several months, he had spiralled into a dark place. He was drinking far too much, and allowing women who threw themselves at him — and they were legion — into his bed. Desperate and confounded by the post-traumatic effect of his injuries, he sought solace in all the wrong places.

Charlotte confronted him one morning when he came into work seriously hungover and viciously angry about being reassigned to a desk job he hated. She asked him what the hell he thought he was doing. He nearly told her to go to hell, then collapsed. Charlotte dragged him through the process of healing, and he would never forget her kindness, concern and support.

Now, as James worked with the Winnipeg police on piecing together a profile of Sherry Hilliard, Charlotte was gearing up to get information out of the dental office where the dead woman had been a hygienist. She called and asked to speak to the partners, made an appointment, and drove to the clinic.

It was located in a strip mall on the east side of the city, in a fairly prosperous part of town. There were five dentists in the practice, three male and two female.

Indeed, the practice itself looked prosperous as Charlotte walked in. The décor was glass and chrome, the waiting room chairs were an elegant dark purple, and every single one of them was occupied by a waiting patient.

"Good morning," said Charlotte, presenting her identification to the receptionist. "Constable Charlotte Warkentin, Saskatoon Police. I'm here to see Dr. Dunlop and Dr. Hillier. I have an appointment."

The receptionist looked at the plainclothes officer suspiciously, and then at her warrant card.

"One moment, Constable," she said, getting up and going into the treatment area.

Seconds later, Dr. Dunlop came out to greet her. "Constable Warkentin. Please come in. I hope this won't take too long. As you can see, we have a waiting room full of patients."

"I hope not, too, doctor," said Charlotte.

As they walked down the hall toward a private office, Charlotte measured him up. He was in his thirties, perhaps early forties; close to six feet tall, ash blond hair, blue eyes, neither fat nor slim, somewhat muscular.

Dr. Leah Hillier, dark, short and slender, was in the office waiting for them. She stood and held out her hand.

"Constable Warkentin. Please, sit down," said the young dentist. "I was devastated to hear about Sherry. What a horrible, horrible thing. What can we do to help?"

"Thank you for seeing me on such short notice," Charlotte said. "It's very important we find this killer as quickly as possible, of course, and you can help. First of all, I understand there are five of you in this practice? How many other staff members do you have here?"

Leah Hillier nodded. "We have six dental assistants and eight hygienists — well, seven, I guess," she said. "And three receptionists."

"Are the other partners in today?"

"No. They work three or four days a week, as do we. Usually, there are two to four dentists in the office on any given day," said Hillier. "We also offer emergency service on weekends. It keeps us busy."

"What was Sherry like in the office?" asked Charlotte. "Was she well-liked? Outgoing or quiet?"

"I'd say she was well-liked," said Don Dunlop. "Quiet. Hard worker."

Leah Hillier nodded. "I wouldn't say she was close to anyone particularly, except maybe to Carol? As Don said, she was fairly quiet."

"I'd like to speak to Carol. Is she in today?"

Hillier shook her head. "She will be back in the office Wednesday. I can ask her to call you."

"Thank you, but I would appreciate getting her home or cell number. I need to speak to her as soon as possible."

"I'll ask Jenny to give you the numbers on your way out."

"Thank you. Are you aware of any patients who may have paid special attention to Sherry? Anyone who disliked her, or liked her particularly?"

"A number of patients would ask for her," said Dunlop. "She was thorough, but patients said she was as gentle as she could be during the cleanings."

"Any who disliked her?"

Both dentists shook their heads. "Not that we know of," said Dr. Hillier.

"Is there anything else you could tell me about Sherry? Anything at all? For example, do you know what she did in her spare time? Did a man ever pick her up at the office, or drop in to see her?"

"I don't know anything about her private life," said Dunlop. "And I don't recall a personal visit. We discourage it, anyway."

Hillier nodded in agreement. "I think she was from Manitoba," she added. "I hired her, and I seem to recall that from her application. And she had a dog she was very attached to. There was a picture of him in her pod."

"We will need your patient list," Charlotte said. "I know it might be uncomfortable, but obviously the most important thing is to catch Sherry's killer."

Dunlop frowned. "Is that necessary?"

"Yes. We will get a warrant if we have to. Well, thank you again. If you could tell your receptionist to give me Carol's numbers, I'll be off for now."

Jenny reluctantly gave up Carol's personal numbers. Charlotte thanked her and smiled warmly. Honey before vinegar was Charlotte's motto — at least until the shit sandwich had to be served. She headed for her car, and before getting in, called Carol Hall.

There was no answer on the landline, but Carol picked up when Charlotte called her cellphone.

"Hello, it's Carol," said a cheery voice. There was a lot of traffic noise in the background.

"Carol Hall? It's the police calling, Constable Charlotte Warkentin. I'm sorry to bother you, but it's about Sherry Hilliard's death."

"Hello, constable. I thought someone would be calling," said Carol, with a little sigh. "How can I help?"

"I'd like to chat with you face to face, if possible."

"Sure. How soon do you want to meet?"

"Today, if you can. It's very important I speak with you, Carol."

"How's this afternoon? I'm out running errands. Day off, lots to do."

"This afternoon would be perfect. Can we meet at your home? Or would you prefer to come to the station?"

"We can meet at my home, sure. Before the kids get home would be best. I don't want them overhearing us. Say two-thirty?"

"I'll be there. If you could give me your address?"

Carol provided an address in the Lawson Heights neighbourhood, and Charlotte thanked her. "See you this afternoon."

*****

Carol Hall lived in a tidy split level home on a quiet street, with pictures of her kids and husband adorning almost every wall. The place exuded domesticity.

"Coffee? Tea?" asked Carol, once Charlotte was settled at the dining room table.

"Don't go to any trouble," said Charlotte. "I'm fine."

"Well, I need a cup of tea. Something stronger would be better, but it's the middle of the damned afternoon. So may I make you a cup?"

"Thank you. I could use one, actually."

Once the tea had been poured, Carol sat across from Charlotte and said, "Okay, shoot. What do you want to know?"

"Dr. Hillier said Sherry was the closest to you of all the staff members. Would you say that's right?"

"Yeah, I guess so. As close as she'd let me get. She was a little — I guess private would be the word."

"What can you tell me about her?"

Carol looked at Charlotte for a moment or two.

"Sherry was a little messed up, Constable."

"In what way?"

"She had a bit of a drinking problem, a while ago," said Carol. "The booze went along with looking for love in all the wrong places. I don't know where it came from, but she was battling some kind of demon. Anyway, she quit the booze a few months ago, and was doing very well. I was proud of her."

"When you say looking for love in the wrong places, can you give me an example?"

"I can. And I will. I'm going to have to quit my job, though." Carol paused. "I knew it was going to happen, so I guess now is as good a time as any."

Charlotte waited quietly. This sounded important, at least to Carol, who took a deep breath and plunged in.

"A little over a year ago, I was at the office late, until around dinnertime. I can't remember why — probably a patient or two took longer than usual. It was getting dark when I left, and I was climbing into my car when I saw Sherry getting into another car. It wasn't her car.

"She kind of looked around, furtively I thought, and dove in on the passenger side. Then the car backed out and took off, rather quickly. Here's the thing, Constable. Dr. Dunlop was behind the wheel."

Charlotte blinked. "Why did she get into Dr. Dunlop's car?"

"It's what you'd think. I asked Sherry about it a couple of weeks later; she was acting strangely, more quiet than usual, and she jumped every time he'd walk into her pod. It was pretty obvious when you add in the night she drove off with him. I took her out for a drink and asked her, straight out, if she was sleeping with Dunlop. It took some convincing, but I got her to talk. She admitted it."

"Why did you do that? Press her on it, I mean?"

"Because having a relationship with Dunlop is a bad idea. He's married. And he's her employer, for heaven's sake. I wanted to tell her to get away from him. There was no way it was going to end well."

"And did she?"

"Amazingly, yes. She did break it off. Good for her."

"How long ago?"

"Right around the same time she gave up the booze. She was cleaning it up. So, a few months ago, I guess. Three or four?"

"Is Dr. Dunlop known for extra-marital affairs?"

"Sherry wasn't the first. I doubt she'll be the last. The man's a predator. I hate working for him, but it's still going to be weird to leave. Can you give me a few days to get my quitting hat on?"

Charlotte shook her head.

"I'm sorry, Carol. I have to talk to him as soon as possible."

Carol sighed. "I thought you'd say that."

"Do you have any reason to think Dr. Dunlop might hurt Sherry?"

"No, not really. I doubt Sherry would threaten to tell his wife, and she certainly wouldn't tell anyone in the office. I don't think he's violent; just arrogant, thinks he can fuck . . . excuse me, have sex with anyone he wants."

"Carol, you have been incredibly helpful and I'm so sorry if this will affect your professional life. We are very grateful," said Charlotte.

"I was going to leave anyway. Eventually. Not to worry, Constable. I'll get another job."

Charlotte stood up to leave, and held out her hand.

"Oh, one more question," she said. "What kind of a car does Dunlop drive?"

Carol gave a mirthless laugh.

"He has several cars. He drives two most of the time to the office, depending on the weather and his mood. In the summer, he likes to show off his silver Porsche.

"In the winter, it's his black SUV."

Ten

"No way," said James when Charlotte returned to the police station and told him about the interview with Carol Hall. "We have a boss who had an affair with our victim, and also drives a black SUV? What model is the SUV?"

"Carol wasn't sure, but she's quite sure it's an expensive one, based on how it looks."

"Adam's calling in before the end of the day. I'm for going and picking up this guy right away. Not sure if Adam would see any other plan of attack. Do you?"

"I think we have time to brief Adam. Carol Hall told me a lot of stuff Adam should know, and not just about Dunlop. For example, Sherry had a drinking problem. But yeah, we should interview him ASAP."

"I'm going to text Adam and see what time he wants to talk. I'll warn him there's some big news, and we should jump on it."

James heard back from Adam in minutes. He would call at four-thirty Saskatoon time, and would James set up the video link again?

Yes, he would. He had forty minutes to wrestle with the imperfect technology.

*****

At about the same time, Grace's phone rang in the newsroom. "H. Genereux" was on her telephone's screen, so she scooped it up immediately.

"Suzanne," said Grace. "How are you? You obviously made it to the farm."

"*Bonjour,* Grace. I am here, yes, and it's lovely. Bruno is beside himself. Chasing butterflies in the garden, if you can believe it. It's very undignified."

Grace burst into laughter at the image, particularly since Bruno's worried face earlier in the morning had put her on the ground. Maybe she should get a dog.

"But, it wasn't so easy to get here," Suzanne said.

"Why? What happened?"

"My car died."

"What? What do you mean, died? Like on the highway?"

"Yes. It started to shudder and spew black smoke. I pulled over, of course, and then it quit on me. I hadn't, I admit, done any maintenance on it for a while. Rotten timing."

"Oh, no. Are you all right?"

"Oh, yes, I was able to pull over. And it didn't explode. We're fine."

"Do you know what's wrong with it? Where is it now?"

"Not yet. It's at a place called Luxury Motors."

"Very funny," said Grace, who intimately knew the age and condition of Suzanne's car.

"No, seriously. As I was standing by the side of the highway, trying to figure out what to do, a tow truck came by. A nice and rather attractive young man hopped out and offered to help."

Hmm, thought Grace. This renewed interest in men and male company was fairly recent for Suzanne; first her playful flirting with James, despite his sexual orientation, and now this comment about the young man. Grace couldn't help but wonder if and how Lorne Fisher might fit into the picture.

Suzanne was three years into mourning her fiancé, a soldier who had died in a roadside bomb attack in Afghanistan. She had loved him fiercely, and worried constantly about his safety. Her worry had been validated. When Leo died, Suzanne had collapsed with grief, and when she could function at all, focused on work to distract herself. Once the graphics designer at the StarPhoenix, she walked away from the craziness of daily newspaper work, built an office in her home and retreated into a quieter life.

Needing some companionship, she eventually found Bruno and started to regain a little joy in life. But she had repelled every advance from every man. She wasn't sure she could ever be with anyone other than Leo.

"Well," Grace said, vaguely, "thank goodness the tow truck turned up. How long will you be at the farm, do you think?"

"I don't know yet. I might stay a week. Papa will bring me in to deal with the car when I have to on Thursday or Friday."

"Be sure to text me, Suzé. Tell me what's happening, and when you go in to pick up the car."

"Of course. When do you leave for California?"

"Thursday, early in the morning. It'd be great if you'd stay at the farm until we get back, Suzanne."

"Don't worry about me. Have a wonderful time with your Adam."

*****

Adam called James and Charlotte at four-thirty sharp, and the video conferencing equipment was actually working. James was getting the hang of dealing with its fits and hiccups.

"James. Char. What's up? Sounds like you've got something," said Adam.

"A couple of things," said Charlotte. "One could be huge. It turns out Sherry Hilliard had an affair with one of the clinic dentists, Don Dunlop. Guess what kind of a sporty car he drives."

"A Porsche. Or a Mercedes."

"Right on the first one," said Charlotte. "How do you do that? And what else?"

"Two cars? Don't tell me the other one is a black SUV."

She nodded vigorously. "Hot little sporty car in the summer, big black SUV in winter or for fun, like golf, apparently. He appears to know how to match the vehicle to the season and the reason, if nothing else."

"Who did you get this from?" Adam asked.

"A co-worker of the victim, Carol Hall, also a dental hygienist. She saw Sherry get into Dunlop's car when she was late leaving the office one night, a few months ago. She braced Sherry on it, and Sherry admitted she was having sex with Dunlop. Carol told her to cut it out, and apparently Sherry did break it off some time ago. And, she had a drinking problem. Carol Hall says she quit drinking maybe three or four months ago, and was doing pretty well."

"We had the same information out of an early interview with the family," James put in. "Winnipeg police chatted with her mother, although briefly so far. She was upset, of course, but managed to answer some usual questions about boyfriends, lifestyle and so on. She said she didn't know much about her recent romantic life; and she also thought she quit drinking a while ago."

"What do you want to do, Adam?" asked Charlotte. "Do you want us to pick him up right away?"

"Does he know you talked to Carol?"

"He knows I have her phone numbers, yes. I don't think he knows I've talked to her yet, but he might assume so."

"You met him, Char. Do you think he could be Sherry's killer?"

Charlotte thought for a moment.

"Honestly, no gut feeling. Looks bad, but it's certainly circumstantial. Saskatoon is rotten with big black vehicles. He's arrogant, but that doesn't make him the killer. We have to find out what kind of an SUV he drives, if it has the premium paint we picked off the Smart Car, or if it's domestic. I doubt it, though, considering his bank account and his other car. There's enough to ask him about, for sure."

"Do you think Carol Hall is in any kind of danger, or trouble?" Adam asked.

"She knows she would get fired for what she told me. She's going to quit first. So yes, she's in trouble. In danger, though, I don't know."

Christ, Adam thought; how many women were the police going to have to try to protect? In the spring, it was Grace and Lacey. Now it might be Suzanne and Carol Hall. But in the final analysis, they had to protect all women, and how was that done?

"The affair with the victim and the black vehicle give us more than enough to talk to him. Did he tell you anything at all this afternoon, Char?"

"He did say her patients liked her and often asked for her. She was gentle with the cleanings. But he didn't seem overly pleased I was there, and encouraged me to keep it short."

"I love him already. Pick him up. Let's see what he says about the affair, and let's get a look at his car. Anything else I should know?"

"Not much else," said James. "We're piecing together the bio on the victim. We've set up an interview with one of the cold case women who survived her attack. And Suzanne Genereux is at her parents' farm."

"Great progress. Text me later with an update and we can decide if we need another conference or phone call."

"You bet, Adam. Later."

James pulled the plug on the conferencing equipment. Then he and Charlotte prepared to go find Dunlop. And his car.

*****

James and Charlotte hopped into a cruiser and drove south, to an elegant, expensive neighbourhood not too far outside the city, where huge homes spread their square footage over multi-acre lots.

At their knock, an equally elegant and expensively-dressed woman answered the door.

"Can I help you?" she asked.

"Police. Are you Mrs. Dunlop?" asked Charlotte, producing her badge. The woman nodded.

"Is Dr. Dunlop at home, please?"

"No, he is not. What is this regarding?"

"We have a few questions for him about his former employee, who was killed four days ago. When do you expect him?"

"I'm not sure," she answered. "Perhaps if you leave your card?"

Charlotte produced it. "Does he have a cellphone with him?"

"Yes. He doesn't like me to share the number, however."

"He'll have to make an exception in this case," said James.

The woman hesitated. Was there a tiny snap of fear in her eyes? Or just annoyance?

"All right. I'll give you the number," she said, and did so. "But he often doesn't answer if he's busy."

"Do you know where he is, Mrs. Dunlop?"

"I believe he is golfing. I'm not sure which course he's on today. He often golfs the Willows and Riverside, but he also has friends at the Saskatoon East course. He didn't say."

"Does your husband drive a black SUV, Mrs. Dunlop?" asked Charlotte.

"Yes. Along with other vehicles."

"What make and model?"

"Why is that relevant?"

"Please answer the question, Mrs. Dunlop."

"It's a Porsche Cayenne, if you must know. Don has a particular liking for Porsches."

"A newer model?"

"Yes. About two years old. Anything else I can do for you?"

"Is the vehicle here?"

"No. He takes it when he goes golfing."

"Please give Dr. Dunlop my card when he returns," said Charlotte. James also handed his over. "He can call either of us. As soon as possible. Thank you, Mrs. Dunlop."

The dentist's icy, beautiful wife said nothing. She slammed the door and went inside.

As they returned to the police car, James texted Adam while Charlotte tried Dunlop's phone, getting no answer.

They got on their phones and called every golf course in town, starting with the three most exclusive ones. Don Dunlop was not on course at any of them, nor was there an upcoming tee time with his name on it.

"Where is he, do you think?" asked Charlotte.

"In bed with another woman," said James. "Guaranteed."

"He's going to be a little hard to find, then."

"Yup."

*****

"I'm thinking of getting a dog," Grace told Adam in the evening, during their daily phone call.

"What kind of a dog?"

"A big dog. Extremely big. The kind that looks silly galumphing after butterflies in farm gardens."

"What made you think of that?"

"Bruno. He stole my heart today. He looked so alarmed, so miserable and so funny crammed into Suzanne's car. Then, when he got to the farm, he lost his mind with joy, being outside and free, chasing bugs in the garden. Suzanne described it to me. I'm so grateful she has him."

Adam's voice changed.

"Grace. Having a dog, especially when you're a woman living alone, is a great idea. But as the Sherry Hilliard case shows, it's not foolproof, either."

"I wasn't thinking safety," said Grace. "I was thinking companionship, hilarity and possibly adoration. Adam, what's bothering you?"

He made a restless noise.

"Did you know there are eight missing, possibly murdered, women in Saskatoon, and a bundle of cold files? You'd hope having a dog helps, or an alarm system. And I suppose they do help, but it's not the whole answer, as the death of the victim's dog shows."

Oh no, thought Grace. He sounds so frustrated, so angry about this case. And he's so far away.

"There's a lot more going on than I know about, than you can tell me, isn't there?" she asked.

"I'm afraid so."

"I hope I can distract you from this case for a few days."

"I know it."

"I hope you're taking care of yourself. I . . . I worry about your dreams. I want to be there if it happens. Please do something relaxing, or fun or . . . or something."

"I'll be fine. Grace, I want you. Two more days."

*****

Adam was not fine.

The heat was so oppressive, Adam decided to go for a swim in the hotel pool instead of his usual run, trying to exhaust himself. He felt a demon rising, and he wanted to kill it, or at least subdue it, before it attacked.

He dove in, stroking to the end. Turn. Stroke. Turn. Stroke. Long arms and legs smoothly dividing the cool water. Adam tried to concentrate on his movements, instead of the fear in his brain.

But Adam awakened at the usual time in the dark hours, sweating and crying out. The victim in his dream was not Sherry Hilliard, bled white in her rain-soaked basement. And, unlike so many dreams in his past, it wasn't himself, either. It was, of course, Grace.

Heart pounding, Adam got out of bed and went to the hotel room window. He stared at the churning, simmering city below, then suddenly slammed his open hand against the window.

He was not just angry about the fucking nightmares but craving Grace, wanting hard, dying to feel her body in his arms and to reassure himself she was fine. What the hell was going on back home?

He wasn't going to let her out of his sight, or possibly out of bed, for four days.

He pressed his aching, naked body against the air-chilled window and closed his eyes against the city.

Eleven

Saskatoon sweltered, day after day, in thirty degrees Celsius and north of that. The heat wasn't doing Don Dunlop any favours. He appeared at the police station before seven in the morning with dark bags under his eyes, slightly rumpled shirt under his expensive suit and hair badly needing a wash. Sweat slipped stickily from his temples and down his cheeks.

"I'm here to see Charlotte Warkentin and James Weatherall," said Dunlop to the front desk sergeant, reading the names from the officers' cards.

"One moment, sir. I'll call Constable Warkentin. Have a seat."

Charlotte peered through a one-way window at Dunlop, curious about the state he appeared to be in. He looked pretty awful. But he must have made it home, at some point: he had the cards they had given his wife in his hand.

She allowed herself a grin. Things were likely not harmonious in elegant south Saskatoon last night. Make that early this morning. Charlotte went out to meet him.

"Good morning, Dr. Dunlop," she said, offering her hand. "Thank you for coming down."

"Good morning, Constable."

"Follow me, please, sir. We'll go down to the interview room. Coffee?"

"Yes. Black. Thanks."

If anyone had ever looked like he needed coffee, it was Dunlop. Had he been up all night? Charlotte asked another officer to get the coffee, then ushered Dunlop into the little room. The phone rang immediately; it was Adam, who was conferencing in on the interview.

Charlotte turned on the recorder. "This is an interview with Dr. Donald Dunlop, dentist. In attendance are Adam Davis, detective sergeant, Charlotte Warkentin and James Weatherall, detective constables. Detective Sergeant Davis is joining by telephone. Dr. Dunlop, thank you for coming in."

"You're welcome," he said, a bit faintly.

"We have some further questions regarding the death of Sherry Hilliard, Dr. Dunlop," Adam began. "I'd like to start with your relationship to the victim. Did you have a relationship outside the office with Ms. Hilliard?"

Dunlop paused.

"No," he said.

"We have evidence you indeed had a relationship with Ms. Hilliard and it was intimate in nature," said Charlotte.

Dunlop turned red and pushed himself out of his chair. "Who the fuck told you that?"

"Sit down, Doctor," said James, leaping up and confronting the doctor, nose to nose. "And calm down while you're at it."

Dunlop sat, his bloodshot eyes darting between the two officers. He drew his hand across his forehead, beaded with moisture.

"Please answer the question again, Dr. Dunlop. Did you have an intimate relationship with Sherry Hilliard?"

Dunlop looked down at his shaking hands and nodded his head, once.

"I'm sorry, Doctor. We need you to say it out loud for the recording."

"Yes. Yes. I did."

"When did you have this relationship? Were you engaged in it when Ms. Hilliard died?"

"No. It was several months ago."

"Can you be more exact?"

"About three and a half months ago, I think."

The timeline coincided more or less with Sherry giving up drinking.

"Did you break it off, or did she?"

"She did," said Dunlop.

"Why? What reason did she give?"

"She said she didn't want to be involved with a married man any more, and she regretted the whole thing."

"Was she drinking when you were involved with her?"

"Yes."

"Were you angry she broke it off, Dr. Dunlop?" asked Adam.

"I don't know. I guess I was. More of a blow to the ego than anything."

"Do you drive a black Porsche Cayenne, sir?"

"Yes," said Dunlop, drawing out the word. "What does that have to do with anything?"

"May we see the vehicle? Where is it now?"

"It's in the shop for servicing."

Charlotte and James exchanged looks. They could hear a slight indrawn breath from Adam over the conference line.

"Your wife told us you had taken it with you yesterday, when you went golfing," said Charlotte.

"It's a loaner."

"Did your wife know?"

"I don't know. Maybe I mentioned it to her. I don't recall."

"You weren't golfing yesterday evening, Dr. Dunlop," Adam cut in, icily. It wasn't a question.

"Of course I was."

"Which course?"

"The Willows."

"Unless you used an alias and wore a mask, sir, you were not."

"I was booked under a friend's name."

"No, you weren't. The pro shop staff knows you well. You were not at The Willows. Nor at any other course in the city. Did you think we wouldn't check?"

Dunlop did not reply. He sat rigidly, blood rising under his collar and suffusing his face. Finally, he said, "I had an appointment. A private appointment."

"With the successor to Sherry Hilliard?" asked Adam.

Another long pause. Then a nod.

"Sir, I must remind you to please answer the questions out loud," said Charlotte.

"Yes."

"Who is she?"

"I'm not answering that question."

"Where is your Cayenne, Dr. Dunlop?" Adam asked.

"I told you, in the shop."

"Which shop?"

"Why is this important?" asked Dunlop.

"Answer the question, sir."

"No. I'm done here. I'm calling my lawyer."

Adam figured that was coming. Dunlop was, if nothing else, engaged in successive extra-marital affairs, and was undoubtedly freaking out about them coming to light. It was even more interesting that Dunlop decided to call his lawyer after questions about his SUV.

"All right. Dr. Dunlop, please call your lawyer and ask him to set up a convenient time to continue this interview."

They couldn't arrest the man, but he was suspect number one right now.

The only one, right now.

*****

Suzanne's cellphone rang while she was sitting at her parents' kitchen table, sweating and drinking coffee with her mother. Her father was out on the land, checking the canola for pests.

"It's Suzanne," she answered.

"Ms. Genereux? It's Dustin here from Luxury Motors."

"Hello, Dustin. Do you have a verdict on my poor car?"

"I'm afraid so. It looks like there was some diesel fuel in your gas tank. It happens. Some people get distracted and don't notice they're putting in diesel instead of gasoline. Or I guess it could've been a gas jockey. Anyway, I'm afraid you'll need some work done."

Suzanne sighed. How could she have done such a stupid thing? When was the last time she filled up? She couldn't recall, off hand. Suzanne didn't drive very much. She worked from home and often walked to Broadway Avenue to do her shopping, so she used the car maybe a few times a week.

"How much work?"

"New fuel pump, lines, injectors, spark plugs and filters."

"*Ayoye.* How much will it all cost me?"

"Couple of grand, easy. Sorry, Miss."

Suzanne mouthed the amount to her mother, whose eyes flew open.

"*Merde*," Marie Genereux mouthed back.

"And how long will it take?" Suzanne asked Dustin.

"Day or two. Pretty busy here. Would Thursday be okay to pick it up?"

"Yes, okay. Thursday or maybe Friday morning. I'm visiting my parents right now."

"Sure. We'll have it ready Thursday afternoon, then."

"*Bien*. Ah, fine. Thank you, Dustin."

Suzanne hung up and released a stream of French and English curse words that would have horrified a less-relaxed mother.

"What happened?" her mother asked, in French.

"Apparently, I inadvertently put diesel in my car. I can't believe I did that," Suzanne said.

"*Désolée*, Suzanne, *ma jolie fille*."

"*Ça va*. So it goes. I will survive. I hope never to do something quite so idiotic again."

*****

"What I don't get," said Charlotte to Adam and James when they met by conference call in the afternoon, "is why the killer left Sherry Hilliard in the basement, or killed her at home at all. It must have been a bitch getting her through the trap door, and then down those rickety ladder rungs."

"He must have stunned her upstairs, and then finished the job downstairs," said Adam. "Even so, if he knocked her out, she would have been a dead weight. It also may have been risky carrying her out of the house. How much did she weigh, incidentally?"

"She was pretty small. Five foot two, if memory serves, and one-fifteen," said James.

"So it wouldn't have been too hard for a large man, or a strong one," said Adam. "Tricky, but possible. It was the wildest, noisiest night of the year; and the power was out, too, so killing her at home wouldn't have been too hard. There was no hope of her turning on or flicking lights, or using the phone, if she managed to get away from him for a minute.

"If she screamed or cried out, and Suzanne Genereux thought she did, it was unlikely someone would hear her. But he miscalculated that.

"The fact he left her there tells me he didn't expect her to be found until Monday, when she didn't show up for work. Makes me wonder how much he knew about her; was she living a quiet social life, and was there a good chance she wouldn't be expected somewhere? She had quit drinking. Do we know if she had a new boyfriend?"

"As far as we know, she didn't," said Charlotte. "Neither Suzanne nor her mother knew of one, anyway. Nor Carol Hall."

"Maybe the killer was her new boyfriend, but she hadn't told anyone about him yet," Adam suggested. "Or an old one. And there's Dunlop. What's his motive? Revenge for breaking off their affair? Like he said, a blow to his ego. And his car, for Christ's sake, is in the shop. We have to see that SUV. When are we going to get back at him? Has the lawyer called?"

"Not yet. We'll call him after our meeting."

"Where are we with the autopsy?"

"McDougall says Thursday. And that's with the chief poking him."

"We need to know if she had HIV or Hep C or any other diseases. The sooner the better, God damn it."

"They've all been checked out, but those things take a while to show up in the bloodwork," said Charlotte. "It would sure be better if we knew she was clean."

"Keep me posted. Anything else?" asked Adam.

"We're talking to the woman who was attacked a couple of years ago. We'll see what she can tell us. We'll send you a report as soon as possible."

There was a knock at the door, followed immediately by Joan Karpinski.

"Hey, team," she said. "We have the dog's autopsy results."

"Did he bite the killer?" asked Adam, unable to wait for Joan to roll out the news.

"He sure did. It will take a while to get the DNA profile and see if we can match it up with an actual person, but it'll be damning evidence once we catch this bastard, at the very least."

"Good dog, Argo," said Adam, fervently. "Good dog."

Twelve

Charlotte had gone alone to interview the sexual assault survivor, Deborah Clairmont. She and James had talked about it, and decided the woman might feel more comfortable with one, female questioner.

The woman's sister met Charlotte at the door, and brought her into the living room, where Deborah was sitting quietly. But her twisting hands belied the rest of her body language.

"Deborah, I'm Charlotte Warkentin. I'm so sorry this happened to you, and we very much appreciate you're willing to go over it again."

"It's okay, Constable," said Deborah. "I'm ready. It has to be done. I hope I can help you catch him."

Charlotte brought out her notebook and a tape recorder.

"I'm so grateful, Deborah. Take your time. Whenever you're ready."

With a deep breath, and after a gulp of water, Deborah began.

"It was dark out, and storming. I had been out with friends until fairly late, and a thunderstorm came up. Nothing like what we had last week, but it was dark and hard to see in the rain.

"I started to drive home, but my car quit. I drove through a pretty deep puddle and I thought it messed something up on my car. I don't know much about cars. But I was stuck, down on Spadina Crescent by Victoria Park. I had my cellphone and called a tow truck; but of course tow trucks are slow to show up during storms.

"I didn't have the car door locked. I don't know why I didn't. All of a sudden, it was pulled open; I thought it would be the tow truck driver, but it wasn't. It was a man wearing something over most of his face, like one of those wool caps with the eyes cut out. He grabbed me, pulled me out of the car and dragged me down the riverbank."

She paused, took another big, shuddering breath.

"I struggled and fought, but I'm not very big and he was much stronger. He forced me onto the ground, and held my face in a puddle. I couldn't breathe. Then he . . . " Deborah looked down, then back up at Charlotte, her eyes full of shame and remembered fear.

"Then he raped me, from behind. I thought I would pass out, or maybe die, from lack of oxygen. I was inhaling water and mud from the puddle.

"Someone came along — an older man and his dog. The dog started barking his head off; it was a big dog, a . . . a German Shepherd, I think," said Deborah.

"What were they doing out there in the storm?" asked Charlotte.

"He didn't say. But the attacker took off and left me there. I came up from the puddle gasping for breath. The man with the dog was so kind. He helped me knock on doors until someone let me in to use a phone — he didn't have a cellphone, and I lost mine somehow during the attack."

"You were able to call the police, then."

"Yes. They showed up pretty fast, then an ambulance."

"What were your injuries?" Charlotte asked.

"I had some bruises, and was kind of torn up from the gravel and stuff on the path. Torn up inside, too," she said softly. "Nothing was broken."

"Did the attacker say anything to you?"

"Yes, but his voice was muffled by whatever he was wearing over his mouth and nose. It was a bit noisy from the storm, and I was terrified, but I think he said . . . " Deborah paused and blushed. "He . . . he said, 'I'm going to fuck you and then I'm going to kill you.' Something like that. He said it several times."

Charlotte leaned closer to the witness.

"I'm going to give you a hug, if that's okay," said Charlotte. Deborah nodded. "We're going to catch the bastard, Deborah."

*****

Don Dunlop's lawyer, Richard Sealey, had weighed in very late on Tuesday. No, his client was not coming back down to the station. No, he was not answering any more questions. He had told them everything he knew.

Except, of course, where the car was, noted James. And who he was with the night of the murder.

James emailed this information to Adam, who was in the middle of yet another profiling workshop in sweltering Los Angeles. Adam left the conference room, stalked down the hotel hallway, went outside into the thick air and swore.

"Terrific," he responded, after he had calmed down a bit. "Call Sanj and get a warrant. Also warrant for dental clinic client list."

First thing Wednesday morning, James was on the horn to the Crown prosecutor.

"Sanj, it's James Weatherall. How are you doing?"

"Great, James. I hear you and Charlotte and Joan are running things down there. When's Adam back?"

"Tuesday, I think. He's taking a couple of days off after the conference."

"Well, Saskatoon is in good hands. What can I do for you?"

"Need a couple of warrants, Sanj." James explained the Dunlop situation. "Adam also wants to go ahead with the warrant for the client list at his clinic."

"They won't cough it up?"

"Nope. They're saying their clients would accuse them of breaching privacy. I guess I can see their point. If they're forced into revealing the names, at least they can say they had no choice."

"Okay, James. I'll get on it. Will you be able to come see the judge with me? Might help if she has questions I can't answer."

"Of course. Just say when. I'll be there."

"Cheers, James."

"Cheers, Sanj."

James hung up and headed over to Charlotte's office.

"Hey," he said, flopping into her extra chair. "What's happening? I've asked Sanj for the warrants. How did it go with the sexual assault survivor yesterday?"

"It was pretty awful for her, but she was a powerful witness. I'm finishing up the report now. I thought I'd give you and Adam the basics when he calls this morning."

Charlotte and James were waiting in the conference room when Adam called an hour later.

"Hey, Sarge," said James. "Just about done with those meetings?"

"Yes, thank God. One more session at eleven, lunch, then it's over. Still, there have been some helpful workshops. I may have learned a thing or two. So give me updates. Where are we with the warrants?"

"Sanj said he'd let me know when he had a date with the judge. He wants me to come along. He's hoping this afternoon."

"Great. See if you can conference me in on that. Charlotte, tell me about the sexual assault survivor."

"Deborah Clairmont, age 26, lives in Wildwood with her older sister. Severely traumatized by her attack; it was very violent and completely out of the blue, and she hasn't been able to do much since. She has only recently returned to work part-time."

"I don't suppose she's a dental hygienist."

"No, sorry, Adam; she's an English as a second language teacher. She had just graduated with her certificate when this happened."

"Tell me about the attack."

Charlotte relayed Deborah Clairmont's testimony of the night before.

"Can I see the photo of her again?"

"Yes. Here she is," said Charlotte, holding up a snapshot enlarged by the tech department. "Pretty woman. Poor thing."

Smiling back at Adam was a petite, attractive, slightly shy woman. The photo had been taken before her attack, at age twenty-three. Long, dark hair. Brown eyes. Café au lait skin.

"My God," said Adam. "You're kidding me."

"What?" asked Charlotte. "What, Adam? What do you see?"

She turned the photo around, so she and James could look at it again. It hadn't occurred to Charlotte, since

Deborah Clairmont now had short, bobbed hair. But she and James saw it the minute Adam spoke again.

"She could have been Sherry Hilliard's sister."

*****

The resemblance was striking. Could the man who raped Deborah Clairmont two years ago have killed Sherry Hilliard? Did he have a type — small women with long, dark hair?

And why was he out in thunderstorms? Was there some specific significance to storms, or was it simply because the noise and confusion of bad weather helped cover his tracks?

"Let me see those photos of the missing women again," said Adam.

Over the video link, he peered again at the pictures of eight missing women. One was blonde; one a redhead, possibly dyed; two had short, dark hair. Two were heavyset. And two had long, black or dark brown hair, were slender and appeared to be small-boned.

"The two second and third from the right. Who are they, and how tall were they?"

James opened the first file.

"Third from the right. Alexis Ironstand, age twenty-four, five feet three inches, one hundred and seventeen pounds, went missing eighteen months ago. Originally from North Battleford. First Nations. University student in education, first year.

"Second from the right," James continued, then stopped. He choked up a bit, cleared his throat. "Only nineteen. Emily Martin. Tiny girl, only five-one, about one hundred and ten pounds. Missing ten months. From a farm south of Rosetown. English by descent. She was at a business school party before she disappeared."

James looked up from the files, trying to hide his emotions, only to see he wasn't alone in being moved. Charlotte had tears in her eyes. Adam was staring into the screen, etched jaw set, full lips compressed; his colleagues could see his chest rising and falling as he took deep breaths.

He dropped his eyes, and dragged a hand through his hair.

"That makes four," he said, looking up. "Suzanne Genereux would be five."

Adam asked James and Charlotte to start putting together developed cross-referenced files on the four women — one sexually assaulted, two missing and probably murdered, one in the morgue. What did they do in their spare time? Was there any occupational connection? Did they go to the same bars or restaurants?

Where did Clairmont, Ironstand and Martin have their teeth cleaned? What was the weather like on the nights Ironstand and Martin went missing? Why were two of the victims Indigenous, but not the other two?

"We have to look at the possibility of a serial killer," said Adam. "Get Joan to help you. If you encounter any problems with staffing, let me know. I'll deal with Pearson. Hell. We really need a missing persons co-ordinator."

"You're right, Adam," said James. "I have a bad feeling about this."

"I do too," said Charlotte.

"That makes all of us," said Adam.

He swallowed. Hard.

"I'll be on the first flight I can get," said Adam, to the surprise of his colleagues. He hung up abruptly.

Then he called Grace, his heart thumping.

"Grace," he said when she answered. "I . . . don't know how to say this."

"I know, Adam. It's okay. I know you have to come home. Some other time. We'll get away some other time."

"Grace, I'm so sorry."

"Come home, Adam."

Thirteen

Mary Sutherland, Justice of the Court of Queen's Bench of Saskatchewan, was reading the hastily-compiled request for warrant to arrest Dr. Donald Dunlop, dentist and black Porsche Cayenne owner.

She glared over her glasses at Crown Prosecutor Sanjeev Kumar and Detective Constable James Weatherall. It was five o'clock on this steaming Wednesday afternoon in July. Detective Sergeant Adam Davis was on the other end of the phone, on the speaker function.

"Why, gentlemen, is it so often necessary to present a request for warrant when I should be having a cold glass of white wine on my deck?" she asked.

"With the greatest respect, Your Honour," said Sanj, "you have been in court all day."

"Ah, yes. Pesky criminals. And we feel this warrant should be executed with haste, of course? Do we fear the doctor will leave town in the dark of night?"

"We hope to remove his passport from his possession," said Sanj, "if he comes before the court and makes bail."

"Right. Possible flight risk, then. Well, he is very rich. Let us look at the facts of the case so far. The dentist decides to have an extra-marital affair with one of his employees. She chucks him for an unknown reason; his ego is damaged. Then he kills her three or four months later? And her dog? It seems unlikely timing. And a thin motive, although that's beside the point."

"Agreed," said Sanj. "Still, perhaps he was experiencing a slow burn. Or, perhaps she threatened to expose their relationship? Maybe blackmail? And he does drive a vehicle much like, if not exactly like, the SUV seen speeding down the alley, which hit a Smart Car and killed its driver. We hope it will be both crimes solved for the price of one warrant. If we can find his vehicle. We have little hope without bringing him in."

The judge chewed on her lip for a moment.

"Mm hmm," she muttered. "Constable Weatherall? Sergeant Davis? Anything to add?"

"No, Your Honour," said Adam. "Just that the police force is extremely anxious to move quickly on solving this murder."

"More anxious than usual?"

"Yes, Your Honour."

"Why is that? Are all lives not created equal?"

"Yes, Your Honour. However, this was a particularly grisly and violent murder, and we have some early indications suggesting Ms. Hilliard's attacker may have killed before. This leads us to worry he may do so again."

The judge's eyebrows rose.

"Early indications? Such as?"

"There are three young women, one having been sexually assaulted and two who are missing, who are remarkably similar to Ms. Hilliard in age, appearance and size, as well as hair colour and style."

"I see. Well done, but that's not enough to legally sway my decision on the warrant. It could be coincidence.

It says here Ms. Hilliard was stabbed. When you say particularly grisly?"

"She was stabbed at least a dozen times, and almost exsanguinated, Your Honour," said James. "We're awaiting the autopsy for an accurate count on the knife wounds. We also believe she was raped."

"Good heavens," said Judge Sutherland, stunned out of her slightly sarcastic style of communicating with law enforcement.

"You have your warrant, gentlemen," she said, after a moment, signing the papers. "Go get him."

*****

Charlotte, James and Joan arrived at Don Dunlop's home at six o'clock. This time, he was home.

"Donald Dunlop," said Charlotte, when he opened the door. "We have a warrant for your arrest. You will have to come with us."

"Let me call my lawyer," said Dunlop, turning around to find a phone. Charlotte took the excellent opportunity to cuff him.

"You can call him from the police station," she said.

Just then, Dunlop's wife came flying down the hallway. "What the hell is going on? Don?"

"Call Sealey," said Dunlop. "Now. Get him down to the cop shop."

"What have you done, Don?"

"Nothing. Ashley, shut up and fucking call Richard Sealey." Charlotte and James half-dragged him down the steps. "Go. Call him now."

James ducked Dunlop's head into the back of the waiting cruiser, and followed him in. Charlotte got into the passenger seat, and Joan put her foot on the gas pedal.

But Ashley Dunlop waited an hour before calling Richard Sealey. He didn't answer his cellphone, and by then, he had long since left the office.

*****

The next morning, Adam was standing in a security lineup at the Los Angeles airport, chewing his lip. He had managed to get a flight to Vancouver on an American airline, but a connection to Saskatoon was still, well, up in the air.

Damn, hell, damn, hell, swore his brain. Having to cancel the romantic getaway was just about killing him; now, he would be delayed getting back to Saskatoon as well.

He texted Grace and vented some of his frustration.

"Can't wait to see u. Still working on flight home, damn it."

"Hold on, Adam," came Grace's response, from Calgary airport. But he didn't know that.

Grace had had more luck with the airlines; she had managed to get a flight to Vancouver. There was the Calgary layover, but she had pulled it off. And she had landed a suite in the Pan Pacific Hotel, overlooking the bay. Luck was not with Adam, nor their trip to California; but with some help from a travel agent, Grace had moved a mountain or two.

She had carefully chosen a mid-length, light summer dress, white with slender green sprigs and tiny, hazy purple flowers. It was one of the coolest things in her closet, and she was getting sick of melting. If it was chilly on the airplane, she would throw a lavender pashmina around her shoulders.

In her luggage lurked a bathing suit and a fancy dress, also white but with a soft, powder-blue design. And carefully, on top, folded into tissue paper, her new champagne-coloured silk nightgown, edged in lace around the plunging bodice. Her fingers had trembled a bit as she tucked it into the suitcase, wondering what Adam's reaction might be when he saw her wearing it. She sat down suddenly on a bench in the Calgary airport connections area, overcome by the thought, and checked her watch. In two hours, she would see Adam again.

*****

Adam's phone buzzed, just before boarding.

"James. What's up?" Adam asked.

"I'm slapping myself upside the head," he said. "I bet Dunlop's SUV was serviced at Luxury Motors. Porsche store."

Of course, thought Adam.

"Good idea. Are you calling Luxury this morning?"

"Yeah. I know the owner."

"Great. When are you talking to Dunlop?"

"Not sure. As soon as he reaches his lawyer."

"Okay. Keep me in loop."

"When do you hit the ground in Vancouver?"

"At one. No word on a Saskatoon flight yet. I hope to know when I land."

"Sounds good. Later."

That morning in the shower, Adam had tried to let the water sluice away his misery over having to cancel the trip he had planned to Mendocino, hoping it would also calm his nerve endings. He was already a little alarmed at the way his body was reacting in anticipation of seeing Grace again. God, how long would it be before they were together again?

He felt tightness in his chest and groin. He turned the water to cold, and braced himself against the blast. Grace, you have turned me into an animal with the sexual control of a teenager. What is it about you?

He knew he was crazy in love with her. When could he tell her? He had to tell her. He was finished with hiding his feelings, bricking up his life in an effort to protect himself. He wanted her in his life, completely. Every inch of her. All of her, all the time. He had to know if she wanted him, too.

The word love had come up many times in their brief relationship, but there had not been personal declarations. Adam felt it would have been disrespectful and flippant to say such a thing only three weeks after starting their relationship. He wanted Grace to know how he felt, but he needed her to believe it, to take him seriously. How could she, after just a few weeks?

Did she feel remotely the same way?

Let her love me, too, God, or whoever is in charge up there, thought Adam, looking skyward.

Then his body reminded him it also loved her, icy shower notwithstanding. Get me home, he thought, in a thickening haze of desire.

*****

Grace climbed onto the plane to Vancouver with her heart pounding. I made it, she thought. I made it. I have actually pulled this off. I am going to see Adam in two hours.

By the time she was close to landing, it wasn't just her heart giving her discomfort. Grace's mouth was dry, and she was so sexually wet, she wondered how she was going to manage getting through the airport and to the hotel. Good Lord, she thought, what is happening to me? You'd think this was the very first time.

She asked the flight attendant for a glass of water, downed it in three gulps and requested more. She wanted to be able to speak to Adam, and preferably kiss him, when she saw him.

The jet went into its final approach, and landed reasonably gently on the tarmac. Once the doors opened, she was swept along with the other passengers, down the plane's aisle, up through the ramp and into the airport. Once she had her luggage, she ducked into a bathroom, took a peek at her hair and face, mopped herself up a bit, and squared her shoulders.

Grace tried to take a deep breath. Pull it together, she scolded herself. Right now. Do not embarrass yourself or this beautiful man in the middle of an airport surrounded by thousands of people.

She slung her purse onto her shoulder, grabbed the handle of her suitcase, lifted her chin and strode through the doors to the greeting area.

Grace stood in the waiting area, legs trembling, wondering if Adam's flight would be on time. What he would think when he saw her. What would happen next . . .

And there he was, right there. Walking through the glass doors.

She couldn't believe it. Couldn't believe how beautiful he was. In his light blue denim shirt and dark blue jeans, hair longer than it had been when he left, curling back slightly on the sides . . . he was breathtaking. And he might, just might, be hers.

He strode out the door and a few steps toward her, then stopped. He had clearly seen her, but he froze in mid-step.

Grace walked up to him smiling a little, still shaking a little. He didn't move, not at all; he simply stood there, staring at her . . . was he all right?

And then Grace saw the naked hunger in his eyes, the irises black with emotion and desire.

"Adam," she said, and pressed her body into his, her lips against his, not giving a damn about embarrassing herself or Adam or anyone else in the bloody airport.

*****

Adam thought he might be dreaming, or perhaps hallucinating. After a few seconds, though, he was pretty sure that the woman in front of him was actually Grace. The apparition smiled at him. Yes. Most definitely Grace.

His body was paralyzed, but his eyes couldn't look at her hard enough. With her tumbled, wild dark-auburn hair, her magnolia skin, and in her flowing dress, she reminded him of a crazy, beautiful, windblown wildflower. Delicate but strong, exotically-coloured, infused with nectars and scents he wanted to drink and inhale. He couldn't move. He couldn't even register he was overcome.

I am a grown man, he told himself. I am a large, fairly intelligent and fierce law enforcement officer. I can handle this.

Still he didn't move.

Another step and she was right in front of him, chocolate-coloured eyes gazing into his own, and he knew what she saw there. He heard her say his name over the blood thudding in his ears; felt her body pressing into him, her lips on his. Galvanized, finally, he opened his mouth with a low moan, slipped his arms around her waist and shoulders, and they melted together, kissing madly before hundreds of amazed and smiling witnesses.

They finally broke apart, and Adam buried his face in Grace's neck, still holding her tightly.

"Grace," he said quietly in her ear. "You . . . my God. You beautiful thing. I can't believe I'm holding you right now. What are you doing here?"

"I thought I could salvage at least one night of our . . . vacation. I can't believe it either."

"Let's get out of here, before I do something crazy."

Adam grabbed Grace's hand and led her to the luggage carousel, where his suitcase was already going around and around in a lonely circle.

As he reached over to grab it, his phone buzzed. He hauled the bag to the ground, and checked his phone, apologizing to Grace as he did. It was a text from James.

"Full autopsy report tomorrow," it read. "But McDougall says S. Hilliard pregnant."

Fourteen

Hell. Was he ever going to find time to forget about work? About violence and misery and death? About the missing and the murdered people he had not been able to protect? Could there be even one day of peace?

Adam immediately started the process of compartmentalizing. It had taken a long time, but after being shot six years ago he had slowly learned to put his thoughts into the appropriate mental boxes — with help from his psychologist. At least, that worked when he was awake; his subconscious was not as easily managed, as his nightmares demonstrated.

There is no way, thought Adam, I am letting this case beat me up right now. Not today. Not tonight. It can play havoc with me when I get back. Not. Now. Now is Grace.

He texted James back. "Let me know when report is in. Will chat then."

The other issue facing him, more immediately than he expected, was what he could tell Grace about the case and what he could not. He had a slightly sick feeling the conversation would be, if not tense, certainly intense.

Adam turned back to Grace, to see her looking at him with a soft, sympathetic expression.

"Adam, it's all right," she said, reading his mind on his face. "I know you'll be interrupted by work. This is a horrific case, and it will move along whether we want it to or not. And we'll have to talk about what we can share. But I'm here, and you're here, and we'll find time together tonight."

He was starting to see into Grace's soul — a complex and sympathetic soul, he thought, with wisdom and comfort and acceptance tucked inside. How she melded it all with her determined personality and her sexual passion, he had no idea; but he couldn't wait to figure it out.

Adam relaxed a bit — mentally, at least — although still he worried. Right now, physically and emotionally, he wanted to crawl inside her.

"Thanks for that. God, you don't know how much I appreciate it. Let's try to forget about this case at least for a few hours."

Adam was suddenly stumped. Grace smiled, interpreting the question in his eyes.

"I booked a room at the Pan Pacific."

His mouth curved into a smile as his eyes softened, registering relief.

"You did? How did you pull this off?"

"Luck, mostly. But we'll have to find lunch before check-in. It's too early for that."

Damn, thought Adam. "Let's go find some food."

They chose a seafood restaurant near the hotel, a place Grace had dined at in the past and enjoyed. Climbing into a cab, they travelled into the heart of Vancouver, dropped their luggage with the hotel's concierge, and went on to the restaurant.

"How did you get here, if I couldn't get a flight to Saskatoon?" Adam asked Grace as they walked.

"There's some huge agricultural biotech conference going on at home. So, all flights coming in are booked, but I got one out. It starts today, so we should be okay tomorrow. Good luck getting a hotel room back home, too. It's a madhouse downtown."

Adam nodded. Thank you, conference, he thought. At least I get one day with Grace.

He hadn't eaten since five in the morning, but even so, he had trouble finding his appetite once at the restaurant. His hunger for Grace had long since outraced his hunger for food. Stay patient, he told himself. Be calm.

He watched her pink lips delicately envelop salmon and tuna sashimi, declare them delicious, sip a glass of white wine. She smoothed back her hair, unsuccessfully as always, and laughed at something Adam said.

Get me out of here, thought Adam, wolfing down the rest of his lunch.

*****

"We should go and check in," Grace suggested when they had finished their meal. "Would you rather wander around first, though?"

No damn way, thought Adam.

"No, let's go and check in. I should really see if I have a flight yet."

They checked in as Adam also checked his email, and found a porter, who was apparently unwilling to give up his grip on their bags. Up the elevator, down the hall, into the expansive — and expensive — suite, and they still weren't alone. Adam finally tipped the man, showed him firmly to the door and closed it behind him.

He turned, looked at Grace, and realized he felt unsure about what to do next. He didn't know if Grace wanted to unpack first, or explore their surroundings, or make love. And somehow, what he said or did next seemed crucial to setting the tone not just for today, but perhaps for a long time into the future. Besides, they had only been together, whenever possible, for three weeks before the enforced twelve days apart; he couldn't presume, despite the electrical current snapping between them.

He walked slowly back to Grace and stood a foot away, looking into her face but not touching her. Honesty, maybe, would work.

"I've been craving you, Grace. Now you're here and . . . I need to ask you, do you want me? Now? I want you so badly I can't think. God, Grace, tell me what you want."

He could see Grace swallow hard, her face flush pink. She took the small step between them, lifted the skirt of her dress, took Adam's hand in hers and slipped it between her legs. She was wet, silky and warm; Adam closed his eyes and tried to breathe. She was always doing some erotic thing that surprised him, made him come apart.

"Don't you know yet, Adam? I wake up wanting you. I fall asleep wanting you. I . . ."

The sentence would never be spoken. Adam was undone. Her words swirled in his brain as he stopped them with his mouth. As one hand caressed her, the other held her. He felt her quiver and released her mouth; his lips travelled down her slender neck, seeking her breast. Pulling down the sleeve of her dress, he found the taut end and tugged gently.

Grace's head went back and he felt her arch against his arm.

"Adam, stop. Adam . . ." she said, trying to step backward.

"No," said Adam, holding her tightly. "No. Stay with me, Grace."

"I'm . . . oh, God, Adam . . ."

Adam pressed gently but firmly, buried his face in her breasts, and Grace had no choice but to let go. He had to grip her as she started to spasm, her legs no longer supporting her . . . she clutched Adam's head, held it against her, and screamed.

*****

Grace was wild to release Adam. After all that had happened, after the long days apart, how had she allowed him to bring her to orgasm before even touching him?

She had never in her life had an orgasm standing up; nor had she reached one in under two minutes from first arousal. Then again, it wasn't truly first arousal, she thought, somewhere in the back of her mind. She had been aroused for twelve days, and intensely so for the last twenty-four hours.

Adam had gently lowered her onto a soft area rug, and Grace didn't know whether to be embarrassed or ashamed or in her glory. Adam clearly took the third view.

"You are so beautiful when you come, Grace," he said, quietly.

He had kissed her softly as, on their knees, they faced each other afterward. Recovering, Grace urgently started to undress him. She pushed his shirt off his shoulders, pushed him back onto the floor, tugged off his clothes. Kneeling over him, she peeled off her dress, kissed his chest and stomach, and slipped him inside her.

Feeling him again was overwhelming. Grace caught her breath at the sensation, slowly took him deeply, then clenched her muscles around him and rose his entire length. She was rewarded by his body responding, his hands coming up to her hips, holding her, stroking her. Madness, she thought, how this feels.

She watched his face, saw him lose composure, felt his hips buck, felt him expand inside her.

"Grace, this is happening too fast. Stop, Grace," he gasped, as she had asked him to stop moments before.

"No," she said, softly, as he had. She wanted to make him explode, to not be able to hold back. "No, Adam. I want to make you come to me. Right now. No more holding on."

But Grace's body was ready again, and it wasn't just Adam who lost control. She felt it happening again, as she felt him try to back off; but she held him inside. Lowering her head to his chest, she love-bit him lightly above the nipple, drawing an "Oh, God" from Adam; and he was gone.

Fifteen

The room was a mess, covered in discarded clothing, cushions dragged down from the loveseat, a blanket draped haphazardly over the lovers lying tangled in each other.

Grace was curled into Adam, her hand caressing his chest. Adam's long arms embraced her, one hand gently sliding up and down her side to her buttocks. Adam finally spoke.

"Grace."

"Yes, Adam."

"That's all I've got. Grace."

She laughed. "Just keeping in touch?"

"Something like that." Another moment. "How are you doing?"

"I'm trying to decide between indescribable, which isn't terribly helpful since it's not describable, and incredible. I'd prefer to come up with something more original. You?"

"Unbelievable," said Adam into her hair, uttering the same word he had used to describe their first time together. He turned toward her.

"As much as I'd prefer to stay in bed, or rather on the living room floor — really, we couldn't make it another ten feet to the bed?" he asked.

"Apparently not. But as much as you'd prefer to stay on the floor, what were you going to say?"

"Well, do you want to go out? And do we need a dinner reservation? If so, we should slowly start thinking about getting up. I'm pretty sure I should have a shower, too. Otherwise, everyone will know."

"Do you care about that?" asked Grace, interested, propping her head on her hand to evaluate his tousled hair.

"Not much. Actually, not at all. But I do care I don't look like I'm trying to advertise my passion for you, if you know what I mean."

Grace did.

"I could use a shower too. After the travel dust and sweat, I'm amazed you wanted to kiss me."

"Always," said Adam, proving it.

Despite their brave comments about getting up and getting dressed, Grace curled back up onto Adam's chest.

"Adam?"

"Mmmm?"

"What's your middle name?"

He laughed at the sudden turn of conversation.

"We haven't asked those questions yet, have we?"

Grace shook her head, to the extent possible with her head against Adam.

"No. We're usually talking about murder and mayhem or sex. Pretty much."

"True. Adam James MacAlister Davis. And you, Grace Rampling? Have you a middle name? Is it Magnolia? Glory? Autumn?"

Grace sighed. "Now I wish I hadn't brought it up. I don't have a middle name; I have a first name."

"Ah. Something Grace Rampling. And it is . . ."

"Honor."

"Honor Grace. It's beautiful. I mean it," said Adam, as Grace made a face. "Although it's quite obvious what was expected from you by your parents. It's a lovely old-fashioned name."

"It is — old-fashioned, anyway. It was also my grandmother's name. Father's side. I feel it might be hard to live up to the moniker. What about James and MacAlister?"

"James is the family's longest-running Christian name. It was my grandfather's name, also my father's name. MacAlister is my mother's maiden name."

"Are ye a Scot, then?"

"Aye, lass. Half Scot, half Welshman, although there are a few drops of other bloodlines mixed in."

"Davis. Son of David, meaning 'beloved,'" recited Grace.

"Are you up on name origins?"

"Hell, no. I looked it up."

Adam's deep laugh resonated within his chest. "The constant reporter."

"Sadly, yes."

"Grace. How old are you?"

"Another thing we don't know about each other. I am, sad to say, twenty-nine in September. And you?"

"Thirty-two. Am I getting old?"

"Old? For what?"

"I don't know. Sometimes I feel . . . like life has gone by, a bit."

"You're certainly not too old for sex," said Grace, nipping him again, lightly. "Or anything else I can think of."

The nip shocked Adam back into an awareness of his body, and that he was cradling the naked and beautiful Grace in his arms. Oh, man, here I go again, he thought. A bit soon? He didn't want to hurt Grace.

Grace noticed, and gave a little gasp as she lowered her hand to touch him. For a moment. Then she stood up and said, "I'm going to have a shower."

He watched her walk away from him, her shapely, smooth, well-muscled backside swinging slightly. He pulled himself up on his elbows and regarded his aroused body, then Grace, again. Look at her ass, he thought, wishing his brain had come up with a more elegant word. He wanted to touch it.

Adam got up off the floor and started to put the furniture back in place, picking up cushions and his scattered clothing, as well as Grace's. Trying to ignore his arousal, he bent over to retrieve Grace's bra, feeling the satin slip across his fingertips.

"Adam?" he heard Grace call. "Are you coming?"

Almost, he thought, as he saw Grace, slippery and naked in the shower, in his mind's eye.

"Yes," he called back, through a constricted throat. At the bathroom door, he stopped. "I wasn't aware I was invited."

"You are. If you wash my back."

"I can do that," said Adam, entering the already-steamy room.

She was rinsing shampoo from her hair, back arched toward the spray, hands sluicing the water from her auburn curls. Her breasts stood up and out, her stomach was taut and hard, her legs muscled and lean, her backside round.

Oh, my God, said Adam to himself. Look at her. This was a new thing, seeing Grace behind a misted door, privately washing herself. It was an intimate moment, Grace doing something personal and every-day. His stomach clenched.

"You're a goddess," he said, climbing into the shower and putting his hands on her waist. "Is your hair rinsed? Turn around."

"What will you do if I turn around?" asked Grace, trying to sound like she was teasing. But the words caught in her throat.

"Wash your back. Price of admission, as I recall."

Adam took soap and a washcloth, and began to gently scrub her back, then her backside, and then crouched to reach her long legs. He took his time coming all the way back up. He turned her around to get the soap off under the water, and saw her eyes flutter open.

"More, Adam," she said. "Don't say no."

"Never," he said, pulling her toward him.

*****

Grace and Adam collapsed onto the bed and fell asleep. It had been a long day, with a very early start for both of them.

Grace awakened first sometime later; it was certainly darker in the room. She glanced at the bedside clock and saw it was six-thirty. Enough time to scramble into clothing and dash out for dinner. At least they were already clean.

Regarding Adam as he slept, his big chest rising and falling in a slow rhythm, she thought about the lovemaking, as if she could help herself. She had had three cataclysmic orgasms in less than an hour, and she wondered what the hell Adam thought of that. She wondered what the hell, too. It was almost embarrassing, particularly the first one. It felt like Adam had just touched her, and she was screaming in his arms. Standing, no less.

Grace was highly sexually responsive and accustomed to the ability of having multiple orgasms if the lover allowed. But this was, even for her, ridiculous — the intensity and urgency of them, all three of them.

I have it bad, thought Grace. The memory made her want again.

Adam opened his eyes to see Grace watching him, and smiled.

"How long have you been awake, goddess?" he asked.

"A few minutes. If indeed you are referring to me. It's twenty-five to seven, Adam. Are you hungry?"

"Ravenous," he answered, rolling on top of her and nibbling her neck. "I wonder what culinary adventure awaits?"

"I have no idea. Did you look at the menu at all, when you made the reservation?"

"I don't believe I had time for that. I was trying to consume you," said Adam, still nuzzling.

Grace burned. But it really was time for sustenance.

"You irresistible thing, get off me. We have to go and eat. Do I have to point out we have to get dressed first, too?"

Adam groaned. "Fine," he said, with mock disgruntlement. "Let's put clothes on."

He pulled Grace out of the bed, kissed her again, and looked at her lips. Eyebrows lowering, he touched them lightly with his fingertips.

"Grace, your lips . . . they look quite swollen. Did we . . . did I go too far?"

"No, of course not, Adam. They don't hurt; and besides, I have acquired a bee-stung, collagen-injected look."

Adam, though, looked upset. Grace took his face between her hands.

"Adam, you lovely man, it's perfectly fine. Your lips look a little ravaged too. Please don't worry."

"I am not," said Adam, then stopped to clear his throat. "I'm not used to this, Grace, to be honest. I've never, you know . . . . made love in the daytime three times in a row and I . . . " he trailed off.

Grace felt her heart thump.

"Adam, it's fine. More than fine. It's wonderful. Please trust me on this. Honestly."

The cloud passed from his face, and Grace smiled at him.

"If we do want to eat, we better move," Grace said, looking around. "Okay. Where is my stuff?"

Ten minutes later, Grace had thrown on clean underwear, a dress and heels, and skimmed traces of makeup over her face, including lipstick, hoping it would distract Adam from his concerns.

Adam had pulled on black slacks and a white shirt trimmed in black around the collar and cuffs. If they hadn't just made love and were starving, Grace would have pulled them off him. He looked incredible, dark hair in contrast with the white shirt, his clear navy-blue eyes shining.

Adam had gone into the living area to retrieve his watch, and when he turned around to witness Grace advancing on him from the bedroom, his mouth fell open. She looked bright, fresh, sexy. Her breasts pushed into the décolletage of her dress, exactly as he had imagined during lonely nights in an L.A. hotel room.

"You look amazing. Delicious. Elegant. Something I can't even describe. My God, Grace. And you're much taller than usual."

"Well, heels help. Thank you, Adam. You look . . . " she swallowed. "Very handsome. Shall we go?"

Adam crooked his arm, but then changed his mind and put his arm around Grace. "Let's go."

The bayside restaurant was full when they arrived, except for the table reserved for them. The host led them to a spot by the window, so they could appreciate the view and the sounds of the waterfront.

Adam and Grace, completely absorbed in each other, didn't notice every head turn as they walked by. But the host did. She smiled. They were beautiful together — dark and light, black and auburn, tall and young and fit. That young man, she thought, being a woman; he really is a looker.

She handed them menus.

"Your waiter will be right with you," she said, slipping away.

Indeed, the waiter was right behind her.

"Welcome," he said. "Just to let you know, the catch of the day is Summer Steelhead. We have a delicious clam chowder, and excellent steaks. First, can I get you some wine?"

Adam and Grace nodded in unison.

"Red or white, Grace?" asked Adam.

"Oh, red. We should try a B.C. wine? When in Rome, and all that?"

Adam nodded, and ordered one of the wines.

"Coming right up," said the waiter, bustling away.

Perusing the menu, Grace began to salivate at the thought of the seafood pasta. Adam decided on a surf and turf — Dungeness crab, beef tenderloin.

They ordered when the wine came, and sipped the rich red liquid. Grace's eyes widened.

"Good Lord, this is incredible," she said. "By miles the best B.C. wine I've ever tasted."

"Me, too," said Adam, "but I'm no oenophile. Do you know your wines, Grace?"

"I wouldn't say that, no. Well, maybe a little bit. Wine is a big deal for my parents and their friends, and I've tasted a few — okay, maybe more than a few — while listening to them telling me all about it. Too much about it," she added, laughing.

"I don't think you can buy this at home," said Adam, taking another sip. "Man, this is delicious."

"Saskatoon has a pretty sad selection. My parents would order wines sometimes through the Opimian Society. That sounds stuffy, sorry."

"Are they? Stuffy?"

"No. Well, they have their moments . . . discussing wine, the opera, various cultural things. But much of the dinner conversation is about healing society and defending people who can't afford legal representation. They make enough money, for sure, but they do a lot of pro bono and Legal Aid work. They're an interesting pair, no question."

"Can you give me an example?"

"Well, Mom has worked for Legal Aid and defended a lot of women who have committed crimes for reasons stemming from poverty or abuse. She was part of a group of female lawyers who lobbied hard to start a low-security prison for women. Their view is incarcerating them in the usual way is not going to help them, or society, for that matter. They need to be healed, and preferably helped — not thrown into the system."

"And now we have that facility."

"Yes, we do."

"Your mother sounds amazing."

"So does yours."

Grace remembered a story Adam had told her about his mother. She had been attacked in her farm kitchen one afternoon, and fought the man like a hellcat. Adam, just thirteen, intervened by taking his father's gun and shooting a hole in the ceiling to scare the perpetrator, then held the gun on him until the RCMP arrived.

But Elizabeth MacAlister Davis had reacted afterward with calm, soothing her children and assuring them they would take precautions in the future. She never raised the subject again. Adam viewed her as very brave; Grace thought he, too, was incredibly brave, having stopped the attack at such a young age. It was clear to Grace that the event had a profound formative effect on Adam, affecting his choice of career and his views on violence against women. Or anyone, for that matter.

Dinner arrived, steaming and fresh, beautifully arranged on white plates. Grace and Adam leaned in to devour the sensuous food, both of them having burned every calorie of their light lunches from eight hours ago.

Adam leaned across the table with a buttery bite of crab on his fork.

"Grace, taste this," he suggested. He watched her lips accept the morsel, then her eyes close in appreciation. It was how she reacted to him, he realized, when he kissed her.

"That," said Grace, once she had tasted and swallowed, "is the best and freshest crab I've ever eaten. Possibly because I live in the middle of the Prairies. But I have been to Australia. This is better."

She swirled some pasta onto her fork, speared a shrimp and a scallop, and held it out for Adam to taste.

"Fabulous," he said. "May I feed you all the time? You're very sexy when you eat."

"Wait until you see me inhaling toast on a morning when I'm late for work," she said.

Adam's brow furrowed, for a second.

"I look forward to it," was all he said.

*****

As they wandered along the water after dinner, it hit Adam how much they had in common. He hadn't concretely thought about shared interests; he just wanted Grace. But there was more, much more, than the sex. Food. Wine. Fitness. Crime. What else? He couldn't wait to find out.

His phone buzzed in his pocket. Frowning and apologizing to Grace, he pulled it out and saw who it was; then quickly rejected the call.

Grace looked at him quizzically, but Adam smoothed the expression on his face.

"No one important," he said, pulling Grace in to his body. "This is all that matters right now. Right now, I want to kiss your breasts."

He pulled her into the shadows between two enormous trees; only a sliver of light illuminated them. Adam kissed Grace's mouth, then lowered his head and gently touched the tops of her breasts with his lips. She caught her breath.

"Take me back to the hotel, Adam."

Sixteen

Adam awakened first the next morning. Desire somewhat slaked for the time being, and soothed by the lovemaking, there had been no nightmares; just sweet, surrendered sleep.

Grace was facing him, which was unusual because they often slept curled together, Adam behind Grace. He regarded her face, pink with warm sleep, her lips slightly parted, her hair in curly disarray around her face and shoulders.

He managed not to touch her, not wanting to awaken her. Not yet. He had a growing sensation Grace was one of those rare people who was constantly, immediately, ready for anything.

In the early spring, after the bishop had been murdered and she had been attacked, she was willing to help at a moment's notice — even from her hospital bed. Last week, harrowing as it was, she accompanied Suzanne to the police station at a moment's notice, in the middle of the night of the murder. Yesterday, when they had little time to get ready for dinner, she went from naked to elegantly, simply dressed and made up in ten minutes flat.

It all fit with her sexuality. Passion flowed through her like some tumbling, erotic river, he thought, as Grace moved, stretched and opened her eyes.

"Hey, handsome," she said, when she saw Adam looking at her. "Good morning."

"Hey, beautiful. How did you sleep?"

"Gloriously. And you?"

"Really well."

"Glad to hear it, Adam." Then she sighed. "We'd better get our skates on. The flight's in three hours."

"I am so sorry, Grace. About all of it. I swear we will go to California, as soon as we possibly can. I'll make it up to you. I promise."

Grace had to swallow hard, to hide her disappointment and forestall the tears from springing into her eyes. But at least they had had an interlude in Vancouver before having to face the mess back home.

Then she climbed on top of Adam.

"We have a few minutes before we have to go." Grace dipped her head and ran her tongue lightly over Adam's lips before slipping it between them.

*****

The trip back was uneventful, and quiet. Adam and Grace, sensing their shared disappointment, spoke little. They were back in their respective offices, luggage in tow, by early afternoon. Pushing down his lingering desire, Adam strode into the office.

The entire police service greeted him with "Hey, welcome back, stranger!" or "We were starting to think you were going to stay in California." Dumb shit like that, and worse. But he was privately pleased, and even moved, by the comments and welcomes.

Adam unlocked his office door to find a balloon with "Welcome Home" tattooed on it. Really? he thought, grinning; you'd think I'd been away for a year. He leaned over to start his computer and then went to find James.

"Welcome back," said the constable. "Ready to meet?"

"You bet. Come to my office."

Once settled, they started with the autopsy results.

"What killed Sherry Hilliard, and how far along was she?" Adam asked.

"Ms. Hilliard was about four months pregnant," James said. "She was definitely killed by stabbing. McDougall found fourteen wounds; the worst were in her heart and stomach and liver, which is why she bled out so badly. More like deep slashes. But she also had a significant head injury."

"How significant?"

"Pretty bad bash above and behind the temple," said James, showing Adam the photo. "It's not as bad as Grace's was on the outside, but apparently caused quite a lot of damage inside."

"Did McDougall say whether it could have killed her, if she hadn't been stabbed as well?"

"It's possible. The hit on the head came before the stabbings."

"James. Tell me. Did she have Hep C or HIV? Or any other awful blood-borne shit?"

"No, Sarge. She did not," said James with vigour.

"Thank God. Have you told Joan and the coroner?"

"Yes, Adam. First thing I did."

At least his people were safe, after wading in a bloody basement for an hour. "Anything else I should know about the autopsy?" Adam asked.

"There were bruises and the usual other injuries after an attack, all minor — obviously — compared to the head injury and the stab wounds. She had a big bruise on one hip; I'm wondering if the killer dropped her down into the basement and she landed on it."

"Okay. Any progress on the SUV?"

"Yeah, a little bit. The vehicle was on the lot at Luxury Motors for servicing, but it was stolen overnight. The dealership reported it the following morning. Of course we weren't looking for stolen cars at the time in our department, but we have the sheet now. The SUV has not been found."

"It's not going to be found unless we get extremely lucky," said Adam. "Is that it?"

"No, there's one more thing. I'll remind you of the three women we discussed a couple of days ago, as well as Sherry Hilliard: Deborah Clairmont, raped and threatened but survived; Alexis Ironstand and Emily Martin, both missing. The four sisters, as they appear."

James paused. He knew this was going to upset Adam.

"Alexis Ironstand was a dental patient at Sherry's clinic. We found her name on the client list."

Adam closed his eyes. What he already knew in his heart and gut was now confirmed in his mind.

"Who was her dentist?"

"All of them, apparently. They have a care model where whichever dentists are working on a given day handle the patients. She may well have encountered Dunlop, but also the others."

Adam took a breath. "We're officially considering this a multiple. We almost certainly have a serial killer out there. Keep me posted on any other connections between these women."

"You bet, Adam. I'm sorry, Adam," said James.

"Yeah. Me too."

*****

As soon as he left Adam's office, James dialled Nick Delacroix. The receptionist put him through.

"Hey, Nick, James Weatherall here. How are you doing?"

"Great. And you?"

"Working hard on this case, and have to ask you about the stolen SUV."

"Absolutely, James. What do you need to know? Bloody awful thing, having a vehicle stolen from the lot, damn it."

"Yes. Has it happened before?"

"A couple of times. It does happen, once in a while."

"I am assuming, since it's a Porsche, the keys were taken. Pretty hard to hotwire a high-end car."

"Yeah. Someone took the keys."

"Any sign of a break-in?"

"None I could detect. We lock up well around here. And it would be pretty hard for someone to lift the keys from behind the service desk, but it could be done. No one on staff is aware of being distracted, but you never know."

"I hate to ask this, but could it have been a staff member?"

"I hate to even think about it, James. I don't know of anyone on staff who would do such a thing. Plus, it would be pretty stupid, right? Why not steal a car elsewhere? I really don't think it was one of my people."

"No one took the day off, for sickness or anything, the day after?"

"Nope. All hands on deck."

"Okay, Nick. Much appreciated. Let me know if the vehicle turns up."

"Of course, James. Thanks for calling."
"Thanks for the information, Nick. Later."

*****

Now she was back in the newsroom, Grace's brain was on fire, wondering what the new developments were in the case. What could Adam tell her? They had to sort this out — especially for this particular murder case, since Suzanne was still, according to Adam and Lorne, not in the clear.

Her phone rang. It was Adam. They had only been back for a couple of hours; why was he calling?

"Grace. It's me. I have to tell you something," he said immediately.

"Of course. What is it, Adam?" asked Grace, worried. His tone was dark and low.

"I shouldn't, but I have to," he said. "Can you meet me right now? Maybe in the park?"

"Yes. I'll meet you by the gazebo? Ten minutes?"

"See you there."

Grace was two minutes ahead of Adam. She stood in the public gazebo, staring out over the rapidly-flowing river, wondering what he would say. Her stomach lurched.

Adam arrived, took her by the shoulders, kissed her and looked at her intently. Grace knew this was important; this was where their work and personal relationships would intersect.

"Adam," said Grace, holding his gaze. "Anything you say to me now is completely confidential, including from a reporting standpoint. You are obviously concerned about something, and I'm worried about what it is. We'll talk about the general rules of engagement later. Please, Adam. Tell me."

He looked down and ran a hand through his hair; Grace already recognized the action as something he did when upset or worried. She waited, as patiently as possible.

He looked up again, breathed in, and said, "I am positive whoever killed Sherry Hilliard has killed before. And he will kill again."

"Can you tell me why you think so?"

"There is a woman who was attacked about two years ago. She was raped, and he intended to kill her — or so he told her. There are two other women who are missing. All three of them are, or were, in their early twenties or late teens. And they look so similar, they could all be Sherry Hilliard's sisters.

"James told me one of them was a patient at the dental clinic where Sherry worked. We have a definite link between them. My gut, and now my brain, are sure we have a multiple killer."

"What," asked Grace around a lump in her throat, "do these women look like?"

"Petite. Five-foot-three or under, and slim. Medium skin, brown eyes, very long, dark hair."

Grace stared at Adam. She instantly knew what that meant. Suzanne, her beautiful brown-eyed, dark-maned, tiny friend could be in more danger than they thought, and not just because the killer might consider her a witness in Sherry's murder. Anger burned in her stomach; Grace fought back the tears forming in her eyes.

"Is there anything else?"

"Yes. Sherry was pregnant. Four months or so."

"Were any of the others pregnant?"

"Not that we know of. The woman who survived her attack was not. James and Charlotte are reaching out to the families of the other missing women."

"I know you weren't sure of this until now, Adam. But could you have told me earlier?"

"I'm not sure. What are you saying?"

"I'm wondering how long you've suspected a serial killer."

"About a day and a half." He drew a breath. "It's why I had to come back immediately."

"I have to call Suzé. Right now."

"Wait. Please, Grace. What are you thinking?"

"Suzanne is in danger. Isn't that why you're telling me this?"

"Yes. Is she not at her parents' farm, though? Safe with her family?"

"No. She's picking up her car today. Her father is bringing her in and dropping her off, then returning to the farm. She's planning to stay in the city, at least for a couple of days."

"Didn't she agree to stay out there until we got back?"

"She did, until the car thing happened. Now she has to go and pick it up. Plans change, Adam."

"You're angry with me, Grace."

Grace realized, as her stomach flipped, she was, and it was obvious in her rising voice.

"I am. I don't know how reasonable I'm being. I'm upset; I'm worried about Suzanne. I have to call her now."

"I need to be part of this conversation if there's something we need to do officially. Please, Grace."

Grace nodded. She dug her phone out of her purse and called Suzanne. Pick up the phone, her brain yelled at her friend. Pick it up.

Suzanne didn't answer. Grace tried the Genereux family home. Suzanne's mother answered.

"*Bonjour*, Grace," said Marie. "*Comment ça va*? How are you?"

"*Bien, merci, Marie*," said Grace, thinking there was little time for pleasantries. "Is Suzanne there?"

"*Non*. Henri has taken her into the city to pick up her car. Is everything all right?"

"Yes, Marie. I just need to speak with her, and she didn't answer her cellphone. How long ago did they leave?"

"Only about ten minutes ago. You just missed them."

"I will try her again. Thank you, Marie. Hope to talk to you soon, for longer."

"*Et tu,* Grace. *Au revoir.*"

Grace hung up. "She's on her way into Saskatoon, about ten minutes out of St. Denis. What can I do, Adam?"

"Where is she going?"

"Luxury Motors. A young man in a tow truck drove by her car a few minutes after it broke down, and took it there."

Grace glared at her phone, willing Suzanne to call her back, but the damn thing was silent. She tried her again. Nothing. Grace looked down, trying to keep her nerves from splitting.

"Now what?" she asked Adam.

"Here's what," said Adam. "I'll get someone out to Luxury Motors in an unmarked car. We have to persuade her to go back to the farm, with one of us as escort, or she has to find a hotel room. Also with escort. She can't go home."

"I doubt a hotel will take Bruno," said Grace. "She can stay at my place, can't she?"

"Yes. She can." Adam's heart sank; he wanted more time with Grace, and he wasn't expecting this change in plans. He grabbed his own cellphone and called James.

"Sarge," said James. "What's up?"

"James, I need you to get a detective over to Luxury Motors right now. Plain clothes. Unmarked car. Do it now, and then I'll explain. I'll hold on."

What the hell? James looked at the staff board, and decided to give Lorne Fisher the assignment. Lorne was free, apart from paperwork, and in plain clothes.

"Lorne," he called. "Got a minute?"

"What's up?"

"Can you grab a ghost car and head over to Luxury Motors right away? I'll get on the radio with you as soon as I figure out what's going on. Adam's on the phone."

"Right," said Lorne, plucking keys off the board and heading out. Man of few words, but a man of action, thought James.

"Lorne is on his way. What's going on?" James asked Adam, returning to the phone.

"Suzanne Genereux is, right now, coming back into Saskatoon. Her father is driving her to Luxury Motors to pick up her car, which broke down on the highway a few days ago. It got towed to Luxury to be fixed. Particularly in light of our conclusions of this morning, I don't want her going home. Tell Lorne if she won't go back to the farm to take her to Grace's. Obviously, she knows the address."

"And you're also worried because the SUV was stolen from the Luxury lot."

"Yes."

"Got it. I'll tell Lorne. And I'll tell him to keep a low profile." James laughed hard at his little joke. Lorne Fisher couldn't keep a low profile in a crowd of Sumo wrestlers.

Even Adam laughed, a little.

"Call me when Lorne gets her."

"Of course, Sarge. Don't worry. We've got this."

Adam profoundly hoped James was right, as he watched Grace sprint back to the StarPhoenix, and her car.

Seventeen

Lorne was already halfway to the car dealership when James got him on the radio.

"Lorne."

"Yeah, James."

"Suzanne Genereux is on her way to the dealership to pick up her vehicle. We weren't expecting her to come back into town, but Adam learned from Grace she's on her way, and Grace can't reach her on her cell. Adam doesn't want her to go home, so if she can't be persuaded to go back to the farm with her dad, she has to go to Grace's."

"So how do I handle this? I can't just walk in there and kidnap her."

"I know. And we don't want everyone to know you're there in an official capacity, especially because the SUV was stolen off the lot."

"I'll check out the cars in the outdoor lot," said Lorne. "With any luck I can intercept her before she gets to the service area. I'm almost there, by the way."

"Make sure you're not followed when you leave. Last thing we need is for someone to know where Suzanne is staying. Not to mention where Grace lives."

"You think?" said Lorne, snark dripping from the words.

"Sorry, Lorne. I guess I'm a little jazzed about this case, and Adam sure as hell is."

"No problem. I'm there. Will get back to you."

Lorne parked the unmarked police vehicle on the street, did a quick visual check and climbed out as nonchalantly as possible. It was hard for Lorne to go anywhere unnoticed, so he affected a shambling sort of innocence whenever he had to go undercover. It usually worked.

He wandered onto the car lot and began checking out the used vehicles, which were closer to the service department door than the new inventory. Besides, used cars matched up with his persona better than shiny new Porsches.

No one bothered him, and five minutes later, he saw a very big truck turn the corner and come down the street. Inside were a man, a woman and a huge dog.

Suzanne's father manoeuvred his enormous Ford through the used vehicles and stopped near the service door. Lorne walked quickly over to meet them, trying a hail-fellow-well-met expression on his face. As Suzanne opened the door, she saw Lorne; but before she could react, he plunged into a greeting.

"Well, hello! Fancy meeting you here," he said, words he had never uttered in his life. His back was to the dealership, and the warning look on his face belied his greeting. He held out his hand.

"Nice to see you again."

"Nice to see you, too, Mr. Fisher," said Suzanne, with a question in her voice.

"Follow me to the other side of the truck," said Lorne in an undertone. "Introduce me to your father. Say I'm a friend."

Suzanne did as she was told. "Papa," she said, "this is Lorne. He is a friend of Grace's and now mine. Lorne, this is my father, Henri Genereux."

"Sir. Pleased to meet you," said Lorne, formally, shaking the older man's hand.

"And you, Mr. Fisher."

"Lorne, please."

"Lorne. Are you here to buy a car?"

"Yes, I am," said Lorne a bit too loudly. "Always wanted a sporty car. But I think I'll have to stick to a used one."

He dropped his voice, and said, "Suzanne. Pretend you are talking to us. Okay?"

"Yes, Lorne. What's this all about? What are you doing here?"

"It's a long story and we don't have time," said Lorne, as Suzanne feigned talking. "Sarge says you are not safe to go home. You must go back with your father or to Grace's."

"I have clients to meet this afternoon," said Suzanne.

"Can you cancel?"

"I'd rather not. Is it really a bad idea to go home?"

"We'd rather not take the chance. Please, Suzanne. Pick up your car and either follow your dad home or I'll follow you to Grace's."

Suzanne looked at her father, who by this time had figured out Lorne Fisher was a cop. "Come back with me, *ma chère fille*," said Henri Genereux.

She considered. "*Non*, Papa. Perhaps I will come back tomorrow or Sunday. I must meet with these clients. I've been away all week, besides."

By now, Bruno was getting agitated in the back seat of the truck.

"I must go pick up my car before Bruno eats Papa's truck," she told Lorne.

"I'll be watching," he said, quietly.

Lorne shook Henri's hand again in an elaborate display of bonhomie, and returned to the used car selection. From there, he could watch Suzanne through a window. He drank in every movement, every moment of seeing her again.

Several minutes later, she walked back out, following the service man — Dustin, although Lorne didn't know his name — who led her to the car and seemed to explain something. He handed her the keys, nodded, and went back inside.

Lorne's eyes widened. Had she given the dealership her entire keychain, with her house keys on it? From his vantage point, it looked that way.

How well had those keys been protected, especially since the SUV had been stolen from this very lot?

Suzanne and Henri began unloading the truck. Suzanne's clothing, computer equipment, the dog food and sundry other items were transferred back into her car. Lorne hesitated, then decided it would be okay if he helped, having established they were acquaintances.

He shambled over, grabbed a huge box and put it into the Honda's trunk. Bruno was led out of the truck by his leash and stuffed into the car.

"Drive straight to Grace's," muttered Lorne. "I'll be one minute behind you in a light blue sedan. Unmarked car. Don't get out of your car until you see me."

"Yes. Okay. *Au revoir*, Papa. I will see you soon."

"Goodbye, Suzanne. Please, please be safe. Your mother is going to kill me. Are you sure you won't come back to the farm?"

"*Oui*, Papa. And I will be safe. *Maman* will kill you, but the police are handling this. Don't worry. I love you," said Suzanne, hugging her father and kissing him on both cheeks.

"*Je t'aime*," said Henri, a catch in his voice.

Suzanne got into her car and drove away with a cheery wave to her father. As Henri watched her disappear around the corner, Lorne said, "Sir, I will not let anything happen to your daughter."

Henri Genereux looked at Lorne with a forlorn expression on his face.

"Promise me."

"I promise."

There was no way in hell anything was going to happen to Suzanne on his watch, if he had to stay up all night. Every night, until the case was solved.

"Thank you. I will hold you to that. Goodbye, Mr. Fisher."

"Lorne. Goodbye, sir."

Lorne walked quickly to his car, got in, and drove like a maniac to catch up to Suzanne. What were they going to do, give him a ticket?

Grace's little home in Buena Vista was not terribly far from the dealership, and Suzanne made it there in twelve minutes. By the time she pulled up, Lorne was right behind her. He looked around, checking for cars, as he had every second during the short trip. He saw no one.

Lorne got out of his car and went over to Suzanne's door, indicating for her to roll down the window.

"Is this necessary, Lorne?" she asked, through the open window.

"Yes," he said. "It is. I can't explain, but it is. Please, Suzanne. Trust us. Trust me."

Lorne bent from his great height to speak to Suzanne face to face, expressing himself as powerfully as he ever had. His frame filled the window, and then some. Suzanne felt a strange emotion verging on awe as she regarded the massive man with the wide brown eyes, passionately pleading with her to trust him.

Suzanne nodded speechlessly, staring at Lorne. He held her gaze for a moment, then abruptly stepped back.

"Sorry, Suzanne. I'm holding things up here. Let's go inside. I see a light on; Grace must be there."

"*Non, non*, do not apologize. Thank you. Again. Are you my blue knight in shining armour? This is the second time you have intervened to save me, *oui*?"

Lorne swallowed, hard. Knight? Now he was speechless, momentarily.

"I . . . yes, I guess it's the second time. I hope I can live up to the knight thing."

"You already are," said Suzanne. "Let's get Bruno inside. I can deal with all the stuff later."

"I can grab a suitcase and a box or two," said Lorne, opening the car's back door to be met by a big, slobbery lick from Bruno.

"He remembers you from the night of the murder," said Suzanne. "I think he likes you."

Lorne drew his sleeve across his wet face, and laughed. "I like him, too."

The procession of little Suzanne leading her huge dog, followed by a huge man carrying huge boxes, was noted as adorable by the woman waiting inside. Grace thought she looked like a little queen leading her subjects.

She went to the door and threw it open.

"Suzanne," said Grace, advancing to give her a hug, and the dog a pat. "Hello, Bruno. Hello, Lorne."

Lorne gave her a big nod. "Where should I put all of this?"

Grace took a suitcase from him and led the way to her second bedroom.

"We'll see what we can fit in here. Suzanne, do you want your computer on the kitchen table, maybe?"

Once all Suzanne's things, and dog, were moved in, Grace handed her a key. "I have to get back to work. I'll see you later, and we'll catch up. But Suzé. Keep your phone on. And turned up. Okay?"

Suzanne nodded. "I'm so sorry about this."

"Don't worry about it at all. Just glad you're safe. Bye, Lorne."

Suzanne and Lorne were left in Grace's kitchen, in a suddenly awkward silence. Suzanne felt the weight of something serious going on; Lorne felt the responsibility of protecting this witness. This beautiful, tiny witness.

"I'd better call James," Lorne said. "He needs to know I got you. Back in a minute."

He fled out the door and jumped into the car, picked up the radio and identified himself.

"Weatherall, you there?"

"Here, Lorne. What's happening?"

"She's at Grace's. She has to meet clients this afternoon; she refused to go back to the farm, but said she might on the weekend.

"Here's the thing, James. I think she gave the car dealership her entire key ring. When the service guy gave her back the keys, from where I was standing, it looked like a big bunch. Not good considering the stolen SUV."

"Shit. You better ask her and find out for sure."

"Will do. What happens next?"

"I'll ask Adam what he wants to do. It's his call. He was hoping she'd go back to the farm. I'll keep you posted."

"Okay. I'll go back in and find out about the keys. Let me know if I'm hanging out here or what the hell."

Lorne went back to the house and knocked. Suzanne opened up right away.

"May I come in for a few minutes?" he asked.

"Of course. Would you like some coffee? I don't think there's much for food since Grace had planned to be away for a few days, but I can do coffee."

"Sure, coffee would be great."

Suzanne bustled around Grace's kitchen, which she knew almost as well as her own. She found the coffee, filters, brewing machine, milk and sugar.

"I have to ask you something," Lorne blurted, while Suzanne measured rather a lot of coffee grounds into the filter. "Were your house keys on the same chain with your car keys? The ones you gave the car shop?"

Suzanne looked around at him, and went white. "Yes," she said. "That was stupid? Lorne, what is going on?"

Lorne decided she had to know, at least some of it.

"Please, come and sit down," he asked her. Suzanne turned on the coffee maker and complied.

"The SUV you heard behind your house the day before the murder — the one that also hit the Smart Car," he said. "We think it was in for servicing at Luxury Motors, and was stolen from the lot. We haven't found the car, we don't know who stole it, but there's a chance the key was taken from the dealership. They tell us it's missing, along with the car."

"I see," said Suzanne, in a very small voice. "But no one would want my Honda."

"No," said Lorne, smiling, "probably not, on a car lot with Porsches and Audis. But if the vehicle was stolen to assist in a crime . . . by the same person who killed your neighbour . . ."

He couldn't finish the thought. Then you're in potential danger too, especially if that person has copied your keys. But Suzanne got it.

She knew Grace had reached out and touched Adam for the first time right here, while seated on these chairs, in this kitchen. Why did she want to touch Lorne? She had the oddest feeling Lorne needed more comfort than she did, right now; but why? She barely knew the man, but he had saved her from crashing to the pavement, and now had intercepted her at the dealership.

Instinctively, she held out her hand and when Lorne didn't take it, she placed it on his muscular forearm.

"I understand, Lorne," she said. "I was stupid. Several times. I will try to do better."

"Not stupid," Lorne managed to growl, looking down with incredulity at Suzanne's hand. "Most people don't go around worrying about leaving their keys at the dealership. But you have to be careful. Don't go anywhere alone, okay?"

"What about my clients?"

"Are they in an office somewhere? Downtown?"

"Yes."

"That's fine. Public place, middle of the day, is okay. If you want to go out at night or somewhere private, though, don't go alone."

"I won't," promised Suzanne. "I won't. Thank you, Lorne."

"I better go," he said. "I'm not sure what happens next, but we'll keep you informed."

He didn't tell her he'd be outside, all night if necessary.

Eighteen

"I'm going back to the farm," Suzanne told Grace after work. "I'm just too much in the way."

"No, you're not."

"Well, if I'm not, Bruno is."

"What about your clients?"

"I saw them this afternoon, and it's all good. I . . . I need some time to think, away from all this, Grace. You need time with Adam. I'm going back."

Grace hugged her friend, and had to admit to herself that hashing out some issues with Adam while not worrying about Suzanne would be a good thing.

As Suzanne drove away, Grace noticed the big blue sedan crawling down the street behind her, with a very large police officer in the driver's seat. She smiled. Safe.

She called Adam, and told him Suzanne was heading back to the farm.

"I'm very relieved. Can I see you tonight, Grace?"

"Come over for dinner?" she asked.

"That'd be great. Thank you. See you at seven or so?"

Grace had dinner ready when Adam arrived. Conversation across the table was stilted; they had not resolved the issue that had arisen earlier that day. But once they took their wineglasses out to the patio, Adam plunged in.

"Grace. Talk to me."

She heard his deep voice in her heart, saw his worried face with sympathetic eyes, and felt her resolve melt. She couldn't bear it. But they had to hash this out, or any possible future would ever after hold conflict.

Grace put her face in her hands, and tried not to cry. The awful events of the spring, when she had been attacked twice, came back to her in a wave even as she worried about her friend, safe for now, but possibly in a similar situation. She couldn't hold back the tears.

"Oh, Grace, don't," said Adam, reaching for her.

"No, Adam," said Grace, looking up with wet eyes. She had trouble speaking through her constricted throat.

"We have to finish this," she said. "You have to understand when you tell me things, I am not going to call the newsroom and tell them what you've said. Nor will I write it. We have a personal relationship and I will go through normal channels to verify stories.

"I understand there will be things you'll feel you shouldn't tell me, or can't tell me, or don't want to tell me. But I'm not going to betray your confidences, and I needed you to tell me what was going on. Like it or not, I'm involved here."

"I know. I'm sorry I didn't tell you earlier, when I started to suspect a multiple killer. I honestly didn't think of it, knowing Suzanne had gone home. And I'm not used to having someone I need to tell, either.

"But you're right; we can't manage other people's actions, and I should have told you sooner. Still . . . " Adam paused, not wanting to make this a tit-for-tat conversation.

"What, Adam?"

"Someone should have told us Suzanne's car broke down on the highway."

Grace's eyes widened. "Oh, hell," she said. "You didn't know."

"No."

"I didn't tell you, did I? And who else would have?"

"It might have been important, Grace."

Grace tried to absorb his comment. Adam was often way ahead of her.

"What do you mean?"

"What was wrong with the car?"

"Apparently, she inadvertently put diesel in it."

Adam nodded. "It's all good. She got to the farm, she picked up her car, it was just a mistake at the gas pump. But what if someone had cut her brake line or something? We would need to know."

"Wouldn't she have had an accident, then, or something? Been unable to stop the car?"

Adam shook his head. "Not necessarily. When the brake fluid seeps out, most cars will simply stop, depending on how old they are and what technology they have. The computer picks up the information and the car quits."

Grace, horrified, stared at Adam.

"The possibility of sabotage. Oh, my God. Adam, I'm so sorry. I've been an idiot."

"As have I," he said. "We have to talk to each other, Grace. I promise I will tell you everything I can, and will think hard before I hold back. I promise to trust you. Can you trust me?"

"I can. I will," said Grace. And realized, at least for his intent if not his actions, she did. She trusted this intelligent, intense man. When had it started? And how far did it go?

"Tell me about Paul," said Adam, abruptly. Grace had mentioned her older brother a few times, but always changed the subject before Adam could learn anything about him.

It was a strange segue, but Grace knew that question was coming; she had deflected it several times previously, in the spring. Grace was the mistress of deflection, if she found it too hard to talk about something; or if she felt someone getting too close. But this was Adam, and they had just agreed they would really *talk* to each other. Seconds ago. She was obliged to answer.

"Paul," said Grace, baldly, "was my older brother, by a few years. He died in a single vehicle accident when I was fifteen."

"Oh no, Grace," said Adam, leaning over the little wicker table that held their glasses to take her hand. "I'm so sorry. What happened?"

Grace took her hand back. "I can't talk about this while you're offering sympathy," she said, giving Adam a shaky smile. "I will cry. I'll give you the short version.

"Paul was a sweet, sensitive, handsome boy and man. He built doll houses for Hope and me, fixed our toys, played games with us and with David. You met David, when I was in the hospital, right?" Adam nodded, remembering Grace's big, blond younger brother. "And of course you remember my sister.

"Paul wanted to be an engineer. He had an incredible brain, profoundly understood how things worked; a spatial genius. But somewhere along the line, he decided to become a minister. Lutheran. Some love thing he wanted to share with a flock somewhere," said Grace, a bit bitterly.

Then she sighed.

"I shouldn't have put it that way. I'm not angry with him. I'm angry with Melissa. Melissa was his girlfriend. Well, fiancée; they were engaged until he told her he was going to attend the seminary. But she didn't want to be a minister's wife, even if the minister was sweet and kind and handsome. She wanted him to be a rich engineer.

"She broke it off. He called Mom to tell her. He said he was okay, needed to be alone for a while. He got in his car and hit the highway, going north to Prince Albert, to burn off some of his pain. He hit an icy patch, which spun the car around southbound. It flew over the ditch and hit a power pole. He died in minutes.

"I never forgave Melissa. She came to the funeral, and I screamed at her in front of everyone. Then I ran out of the church."

Grace tried to collect herself, but failed.

"How could she do that to him? How could she not love Paul?"

Adam tried to hug Grace, but she pushed him away.

"While I was walking around the city," she went on, "a man approached me. Asked for a cigarette. Of course, I didn't have one; I told him so. I didn't understand what was going on. I was fifteen, and pretty innocent even for that age.

"He followed me to the park near our house, then pushed me up against a tree and started to kiss me. If you could call it that. I tried to push him away, but he just closed in and tried to take off my dress. Put his hand over my mouth."

Adam was white, his hands clutching the arms of his patio chair.

"I bit him. His hand. Just like I did the guy in the spring. He hit me, and I fell; but he couldn't . . . you know, he couldn't . . . couldn't get it up. While he was dealing with that, I scrambled up and got away. It was a near thing. I blamed Melissa for that, too. But it wasn't her fault. It was mine. And his."

Adam had had enough of not touching Grace. He got out of his chair, took the step between them and pulled her up out of her chair and into his arms.

"I'm so sorry, Grace," he said, holding and rocking her. "I'm so sorry."

Even as he held her, and knowing the attack was bad enough, he thought: Thank God. At least she wasn't raped. And she got away. Could the bastard have killed her?

Grace was naturally protective of her friends, and until now, Adam thought excessively so. But he began to understand how her experiences at the hands of men informed her feelings and her actions. There was more to learn about her previous boyfriend, too, he was sure; but that conversation was for another time.

And as Grace wept in Adam's arms, she let Melissa go.

*****

Adam felt her shudder and quieten. She put her arms around him, and stood there, not moving, not speaking, for several minutes.

"I am in desperate need of a tissue," she said, with a little hiccup of a laugh.

Adam let her go and regarded her face, smoothing the tears from her cheeks. "Come back, Grace."

She nodded, went inside, blew her nose, washed her face and returned to the patio bearing the bottle of wine.

"How do you feel, Grace?"

"Better. Much better, actually," said Grace. "Can I ask a question?" she asked.

Adam blanched. He was pretty sure he knew what was coming, too. He nodded.

"You said, once, after you had been shot, you behaved badly. I don't want to open those wounds, Adam, if it's not important. Is there anything I need to know?"

Adam did not want to tell Grace about the few months after he had recovered from being shot; how he lived in the bars when off shift, and sought solace in the arms of women who threw themselves at him. It was a drunken, manic, miserable period of his life. But Adam also knew he had to tell her. He wanted no secrets, and if Grace couldn't love him because of his past, better to know now than later.

He held her gaze, and started in.

"I went a little insane, after I got out of the hospital and was healthy enough to get back to work. They had me on the desk for several months — just like James, after he was shot in the spring. It takes a while to come back, and they don't need a cop out there on the streets limping around or blowing an artery.

"Being sidelined drove me nuts. I felt useless. Broken. So I started drinking, first at home and then out in the bars and clubs downtown. Going downtown allowed me to walk home, at least, and not drink and drive, which I might have done in the frame of mind I was in. I was picking fights and . . . hell." He stopped.

"And picking up women, Adam?" asked Grace.

Adam looked down and ran his hand through his hair, his signal he was feeling something hard to bear.

"I still can't believe that was me. It makes me sick to think about it. It was a few months of this drunken blur, meaningless sex, stupidity. I treated people badly, and I treated myself badly. I never spent more than one night with anyone. I was probably too drunk and definitely too angry to connect.

"One night, I woke up screaming, after one of my nightmares. Scared the hell out of a young woman, and she didn't handle it very well. Neither did I. I yelled at her to get out of my condo.

"The next morning, I was seriously hungover. I went into the station anyway — no way I was missing work — and threw up the minute I got there. I looked like shit. Charlotte could see something was wrong, and she let me have it; wanted to know why I was ruining my life and career. I almost told her to get the fuck away from me, but I didn't. What she said pierced the fog.

"I . . . collapsed. Literally. I was on the floor, on my knees. She comforted me, and helped me find counselling, and I quit the drinking and, well, womanizing. That's what I was doing, if I'm honest with myself. I was looking for something. Not sure what — comfort? Some kind of reassurance I wasn't completely busted?

"Charlotte helped me find a way out. I swear to you I had no conscious intention to hurt anyone. But it's no excuse for what I did. And when we talked about sex and protection, Grace, I told you the complete truth," Adam said, taking her hands and looking at her with the most intense expression Grace had ever seen on his face, which was saying something.

"It ended, the bad time, about five years ago. I had myself tested every which way I could. And I . . . I hadn't been with anyone for a long time before I met you. I was still trying to be the superhero, staying away from anyone I might get close to or might hurt, either with my behaviour or because of my job. It got too hard to try relationships at all.

"And then you stood up in the middle of the cathedral next to the bishop's body, and stopped my heart. So when I tell you this is all new to me, it's true. I've never made love like this before. I've never felt like this before. And I hope you can forgive my past."

Adam stopped talking, and waited for Grace to respond. He was determined not to say any more, to give her time to think and decide. The five seconds it took felt like forever.

Grace, processing this information, could see it all in her mind's eye: the women watching Adam, a murmur and a tension in the air. And a dash for the most beautiful man in the room.

Adam never noticed it, but she was right. When he walked into a bar, the room went from deafening din to quiet hum as every female head turned in his direction. Then the lineup formed. And hell, yeah, she was jealous. Of all of them. Why did he choose her? Would he want to go back to that life in the future? Was she enough for him?

But it was one of the alluring, appealing things about Adam, that he really didn't see, or understand, his own beauty. It drove Grace crazy; she was sure it drove other women mad, too.

"You have no idea, do you, Adam?"

"Of what?"

"Adam, you are heart-stopping. Do you not notice every eye following you?"

Adam swallowed, digested the compliment, felt it in his groin. His face, though, registered confusion. He just didn't get it.

Grace slipped off her chair and knelt in front of Adam, her hands on his.

"There's nothing to forgive. You were trying to deal with the post-trauma stress. You do know no other man in history would feel so badly about a few months' madness, don't you?"

"I don't know," said Adam. "I do know, though, that I want you."

"Stay, Adam," Grace whispered. "Stay with me tonight."

Nineteen

Adam had blood on his hands. He was on his knees. A streetlight spread its thin beam over a dark-haired woman lying before him, whom he didn't recognize; but he knew it was Suzanne.

Grace was behind him, screaming her friend's name, then his. She turned in a blur of auburn hair and ran down the dark, wet street — Adam realized it was raining — calling out for Mick to save her, to comfort her. Adam couldn't move. He tried to rise to his feet, but he was glued to the pavement. He wanted to shout, don't go, Grace. Don't go, Babe . . . but no sound would come.

At the end of the street, Grace climbed into a black SUV, and Adam tried to call to her: *No.*

Then Suzanne sat up, and shape-shifted into Sherry Hilliard. She began to scream at Adam. *I'm dead. I'm dead because of you.*

The bed was shaking, Adam was crying out, and Grace awakened in shock. Oh, my God, Adam, my poor love, this is a bad one. On top of him in a second, she tried to rouse him from the nightmare, crooning and soothing.

"Wake up, Adam, wake up now," she said, her body half covering his, her hand over his pounding heart. "Oh, Honey, wake up. It's okay, it's okay . . ." Grace couldn't say it was just a dream. It was never just a dream.

Adam's eyes opened as his body gave a massive start, and Grace moved up to kiss his face, feeling his pain in the moment her lips met his tears.

Suddenly, he sat up, pushing her away, and Grace flew over the bed, landing hard on the floor below. Stunned and wide-eyed, she looked up at Adam. He was crouched on the bed like an animal ready to spring, staring at her. Finally, awake.

"Grace," he gasped, as he realized what had happened. "Grace. Oh my God. What have I done?"

He leapt off the bed and put his arms around her, so tightly she had trouble drawing a breath.

"Are you all right? Did I hurt you? Grace, talk to me."

"I'm . . . I think I'm all right, Adam," she said, touching a sore spot on her hip. Just a bruise, she thought.

"Grace, don't leave me," he said, arms still around her. "I finally found you. Don't leave me."

Oh God, thought Grace. This is awful. What happened in this dream?

"I am here, Adam. I am not leaving. I am here, with you." Grace said every word firmly, slowly, deliberately, hoping he was hearing her. *Wild horses, Adam.*

His eyes changed expression. Narrowed.

"Hell," he said, abruptly disentangling himself from Grace's embrace and heading for the bathroom.

This is not supposed to go this way, thought Grace. She gave him a few minutes, but was damned if she was going to leave him to suffer alone. What the hell was that dream about?

She stood up somewhat gingerly, put on a robe and then stood uncertain in the dark room. She had been very concerned that this might happen one night. How worried should she be about Adam right now?

Very worried, Grace decided. She had heard water running, but now, as she crept to the bathroom door, she heard nothing.

"Adam," she said through the door. "Adam, please, can you tell me you're all right? Can you come out and be with me? Talk to me. Adam?"

Another moment passed, Grace aware of nothing but her heart thumping and aching in her chest. Then Adam opened the door.

Thank God.

She backed up a couple of paces, looked into his beautiful, sad face with her frightened eyes.

"Adam?"

He stood there for a moment, seemingly uncertain about what to do after powerfully ejecting Grace from her own bed. Grace opened her robe, opened her arms, and he came to her. No words yet, but at least she was holding him.

Adam's arms tightened around Grace. She could feel him shaking, breathing heavily, trying to regain control, and she swallowed her own emotion. He lost the fight.

"I have to go, Grace," he said hoarsely. "This can't happen. I have to go."

"No, Adam. Don't. Please. We can figure this out. I don't want you to be alone, especially right now."

"No. I have to go."

Adam threw on his jeans, grabbed his shirt and wallet, jammed his feet into his shoes and flung himself out the door.

Grace slumped to the floor, and wept in huge, gulping sobs.

*****

Sunbeams scattered weak morning light as Adam stared out his window. The beautiful dawn was utterly incongruous with the darkness enveloping him.

All he could see in his mind's eye, all his body memory would register, was Grace asleep in his arms, her backside cuddled into his groin, in their usual sleeping position. The sun setting the reddest threads of her hair alight, painting her creamy skin with shadows. Her breasts, so soft and full, rising and falling with each breath. Just a few hours later, he already missed her with every atom of his being.

Oh, God. How could he expect her to put up with his darkness, his deep plunges into this hell of nightmares? He couldn't bear it. He was dangerous to her, this woman he loved. He had to let her go.

The intercom buzzed, but he couldn't answer it. He didn't know what to say, or what to do. Five minutes later, there was a knock at the door.

"Adam. Let me in please."

Someone had let her through the main door.

"I'm not leaving," she said. "I will stand here until you let me in. If I have to wait all day."

"Grace. I can't."

"You can. You must, Adam. I have to see you."

Adam stood at the door, hands spread widely across it, as if bracing himself.

"I'm begging you, Adam. Please."

He couldn't resist her. He opened the door; Grace slipped in and took him in her arms.

He stood against her woodenly, then buried his face in her neck, preparing to ask her to go ... but Grace began to move her hips against him. Her body stretched in arousal; she kissed him deeply, moaning from her throat. Like a wave, the full length of her body flowed along his. He felt her hands slip down his back and over his buttocks, pulling him closer.

Adam almost couldn't stop, a pulsing desire for this fiery ribbon of woman blocking all other thought. Every nerve in his body registered her soft skin, touching his.

He mustered all of his self-control, and drew away.

"Please go, Grace. Please. I can't . . . I don't know what to do. I'm sorry."

Grace stared at him for a moment, desperately; but she saw the determination in his eyes. Left with little option, she nodded, turned and walked out the door.

*****

Saturday or no Saturday, dreams or no dreams, Adam dragged himself into work and met James at the station.

"Where the hell is Dunlop, right now?" Adam asked James, his temper simmering.

"In jail. There was a snafu with his lawyer, and he got stuck in remand. I'm not sure why yet. We'll find out on Monday. Oh, and the baby's DNA has been sent for testing," added James, "and we've asked for a sample from Don Dunlop, but I highly doubt he's going to provide one willingly. But, Adam, I think I've found another connection."

"Tell me," said Adam. "What?"

"Emily Martin. She's the youngest and tiniest of the women on our list. She was attending business school, you'll recall, and went missing after an end-of-term party. We determined she had no connection to the dental clinic, and so far, we haven't found any other connections to the other women.

"The school she attended was Hartz School of Business, owned by that Shawn Hartz guy. I'm sure you've seen him on TV, and he's perpetually in newspaper ads announcing donations to things.

"Adam, Emily Martin was not a patient at the clinic. But Shawn Hartz is."

"Holy hell, James. How did you make the connection?"

"Well, I'm working my way through the patient list. It's taking longer than I thought, because you can't just look at a name and hope it rings a bell, right? In this case, I recognized his name, and remembered Emily Martin was a business school student."

"Wow, James. Good work. When can we get him in? We have to find out if he knew Sherry Hilliard. But even if he didn't have her as a hygienist, he had likely seen her there."

"He's apparently at the lake. I'm working on getting him in as soon as possible."

"Thanks, James. Can you please take the rest of the day off?"

"Yeah, I'll try, as soon as I reach this dude and persuade him to show up at our shop. You too? Take the rest of the day off?"

"Yes. Me too."

Adam had no idea what he was going to do with himself at home, so he stayed at the station and tried to focus on paperwork. All he could think about was Grace. What the hell was he going to do?

Twenty

The old man pushed his shopping cart, filled to the top with cans and bottles, over the bumpy dirt trail along the riverbank. His long, thinning grey hair spun about his head in a freshening breeze, obscuring his dimming vision.

If, as a bottle collector, you weren't out early in the morning, you'd miss the bounty within the blue bins dragged out by bleary, hungover homeowners. Someone else would beat you to it. The old man was also bleary, but bottles and cans were critical to staying fed, so he was up and out of his filthy one-room apartment with the dawn.

He was getting tired already. He'd done the burrowing and collecting, and now was taking the shortcut to the recycling depot. He stopped to brush the hair from his eyes, and sat heavily on a boulder by the active river. The whole damn city of Winnipeg sat on a flood plain, and there had been plenty of rain, as there had been upstream in Saskatchewan. The Assiniboine was rolling.

His stomach growled. It was already three hours since his insubstantial breakfast. He had to get to the depot, deliver his goods, and get something in his gut; he already felt faint, and the depot was still blocks away.

Heaving himself off the rock, he immediately lost his balance and stumbled toward the water. Bad idea to get caught in the current, he thought with a small thrill that brought on a slick of sweat. *Shit,* he swore, as he shifted his weight violently backwards, and landed on his ass in wet sand and rocks. His hand came down hard between two of the smaller boulders.

He scraped and twisted his wrist on the unyielding rock, but his hand landed on something odd, both soft and hard at the same time. Swinging his head around, he saw a woman, her own arm caught by the rocks and soggy waterweeds.

"Shit! Lady! Are you okay?" he yelled, as he scrambled to his knees and scurried on all fours around the larger of the two boulders, to see the rest of her.

She was definitely not okay. She was white and blue, black hair twisted around her neck and face. Dead, if the old man knew anything about life and death. Which he did.

*****

In the north part of Saskatoon, on a sandy bank of the South Saskatchewan River, a woman was walking her dog. She normally didn't go down so close to the water, but it was a beautiful day and her dog loved to splash along the shore.

The dog began to behave strangely. He sniffed, and pulled at the leash, very much like Bruno had two weeks before. He dragged his person along the shoreline, where she almost tripped over an extremely decomposed body. A tiny body, for a woman, who still had some of her long, black hair.

The desk constable put the call through. Adam was silent, listening to the woman describe the scene. She was dead, then. He had been clinging to a faint hope she was only missing.

"It could, of course, be someone else," Adam said to James. "But this woman fits Emily Martin's basic description."

"Could it be Alexis Ironstand?" asked James.

"I don't think so. She had a couple of inches on Emily, right? Meet you at the car. I'll call McDougall. I'll be there in two minutes."

Adam called McDougall on his cell. Despite it being Saturday, he answered, and Adam quickly explained the situation.

"Can you meet us down at the sandbar, Jack? We need to find out how she was killed as fast as possible. If she was drowned, this is a different killer. The rest can wait. Even her identity."

McDougall drew a heavy sigh, but it was an act, Adam was sure.

"Fine. I'll be there," said the pathologist. "Speed limits being what they are, of course."

Ten minutes later, Adam crouched over the little body, or what was left of it, in the gathering darkness.

"What do you think, Jack?" he asked McDougall.

"It appears she was strangled, Adam. Of course, I won't know for sure until I do the full autopsy, but see here? Obvious. Windpipe crushed. And it will probably be impossible to say whether she was drowned."

"Right. Okay, let's get her out of here. Thanks, Jack."

Walking away, his phone buzzed. He wondered if it would be Grace, and almost picked up the call; but it wasn't. It was *her*, again. The second time in the past week. Hell. He let it go to voicemail, then listened to the message in the car.

"Hey, gorgeous," she said. "Jilly again. Give me a call. I miss you. I need to talk to you."

Jilly. That was all he needed right now. The nightmares, this case, missing Grace. Oh, God, what the hell was he going to do about Grace?

*****

Grace wandered alone, desperate and miserable around her tiny home, all weekend. What the hell had happened? Before the planned trip to California, and the abbreviated time in Vancouver, there had been a few difficult nights, but the last one was different. She had to admit it had frightened her a bit; but it had terrified Adam.

Reality was now facing her, and biting her hard enough to draw blood. How did she, how could she fit into Adam's world? A terrible world, punctuated by his post-traumatic stress, and his nightmares. And now, he had driven her away; asked her to leave. She couldn't stand it.

Grace stretched in pain, tears blurring her vision and dripping down her cheeks; her lover had left her, holding her life in his hands.

She poured a glass of white wine she really needed, returned to her bedroom, and looked at the champagne negligée she didn't have the chance to wear in Vancouver. She had hung it on the closet door to let the wrinkles fall out. Remembering the day she had packed the silky thing, she doubled over with a sudden, sharp physical craving, spilling some of the wine.

I'm not going to make it, she thought. I want him, want him now. Now. Oh, God, now.

Grace sank to the floor, gulped some of the remaining wine in her glass, and tried to figure out what to do. Try to sleep? Read a book?

No. I can't.

Unable to help herself, despite his rejection of her, Grace reached over to the bedside table, plucked the phone off its stand, and dialled Adam's number. She wondered if he'd be home, or at least on his line.

What was she going to say? She nearly hung up.

A big voice answered.

"Grace. Are you all right?" it asked, anxiously.

"No. Adam, can you come to me? Adam, I'm . . . I miss you."

I'm dying for you to touch me. To be with me. Grace barely managed to hold the thought back. She couldn't say it, knew she couldn't go that far, couldn't stand a further rejection at his hands.

Grace couldn't see Adam close his eyes, open them and look heavenward.

"Don't move. I'm coming now." That was all he said, and hung up.

Ten minutes later, Adam was hammering on the door. Grace opened it, clad only in champagne silk and lace, and backed up into the kitchen, eyes wide.

"I'm sorry if . . . I know, you asked me to leave, but I . . ."

"Sh," said Adam, advancing, his eyes roving over Grace quivering in a slippery wisp of a garment.

Her nipples were red, erect, poking through the lace of the bodice. Adam, stunned, was instantly beside himself. He cupped her breasts with his hands, rasped the lace against her nipples with his thumbs and opened her lips with his, plunging his tongue into her mouth.

He finally released her, tried to catch his breath.

"Desire is getting the better of me, Grace," he said, staring into her eyes. "Do you hear me?"

Grace heard. Holding his gaze, she nodded.

"Do you want me to back off? Go home? I don't know if I can . . . but Grace, I'm not safe for you to be with. I'm not safe."

"No, Adam," she gasped, squirming in his powerful arms. "Stay with me. I want you."

A flicker of fear pierced Grace's fog of desire: she had never seen Adam like this, maddened, his blue irises gone completely black. Was it not just the PTSD? Was there a wilder animal inside him? Would he strip her of all composure?

No. She couldn't believe he would ever intentionally hurt her. It just wasn't possible. Adam was ferocious, passionate, broken; but he was also a good, decent and beautiful man. She was as certain of that as she had ever been of anything.

"I will never take your dignity, Grace," said Adam, more softly, as if he read her mind. He had certainly read her eyes. "I will not ever knowingly hurt you. I do want to take you all night. If you say yes."

He slipped his hand under the silk to the silkier place between her legs. "I need to hear it, Grace. Only if you agree. Say it. *Say it.*"

"Yes, Adam," whispered Grace.

He swept her up against him by the buttocks and curved her legs around his hips, kissing her hard and striding purposefully down the hallway to her bedroom, erection pushing against her.

"Grace," he said, stopping abruptly. "God, I'm so sorry about last night, this morning. I . . . can't believe I pushed you away. You have to decide if you can bear my passion for you. I've never wanted anything so much. But the price may be too high to pay. The job. The nightmares. I need to know what you're really thinking. About me. Us.

"Tell me, Grace, what you were going to say on the phone. You said, I miss you. But what were you going to say? I'm . . . what?"

He was still holding her against him, staring into her eyes. It was impossible for Grace to move or look away without struggling, without breaking the powerful embrace. I have to tell him, she thought. He wanted to, had to know.

"I was going to say I'm . . . I'm dying for you to touch me," admitted Grace, hoarsely, staring back.

Adam's body trembled as if a wind gust had blown through him.

"Oh, my God," he said, as if to himself. "And now? Now, Grace?"

"I'm going to come apart if you don't make love to me."

"I've already come apart."

Adam lowered Grace onto the bed and removed the silk gown. Leaving her naked and shivering a little, he watched her intensely as he stripped himself quickly, throwing his shirt and jeans to the floor.

He bent over and took Grace in his arms, sliding her up the bed until her head was on the pillow, hair wildly flowing around her, and entered her deeply. Grace screamed at the first thrust, so aroused was she by his passion; so open to him she could hardly bear the sensation.

He held her down at the hips, keeping her from stroking up against him, and went in again and again, in long, shuddering, slow motions that filled her body and stopped her thoughts. As Grace started to reach climax, he paused for a moment, breathing hard, before beginning again.

Grace writhed under him, so close she almost begged him not to stop. Then remembered her vow to stop the deflections, the silly efforts at humour. *Say it. Tell him.*

"Adam, please, I'm . . . please keep going . . ." she still couldn't quite get it out.

"You're what, Grace?" he muttered.

"I . . . I want to . . . with you . . ."

"Tell me, Grace. Tell me."

"Come with me, Adam . . ." I'm almost incoherent, she thought.

"We are coming together, Grace, now, tonight," Adam said, in a mixture of need and command.

He stopped thrusting and buried himself in her, brought his hand under the small of her back and lifted her pelvis. At the contact, she began to climax immediately. Released, she began to move her hips, grinding against Adam, panting and digging her nails into his back. His orgasm joined hers then, his hips pressing into her.

"Grace! You make me crazy with wanting you. God help me, I couldn't stay away."

Adam collapsed onto Grace, then lifted his face and kissed her softly, as if to make up for the ferocity. He spoke again, big voice adamant but gentle.

"I want you to be mine, Grace. In bed and out of bed. Here, at home. Not just in California or Vancouver or wherever the hell. But I don't know how. How will you be safe in my arms?"

So, that insane lovemaking wasn't the end of it, then. He was still expressing himself forcefully, still inside her.

"Do you have any doubt? Tell me, Grace. What do you want? I want this. You. Help me."

"Yes, Adam," she said. "I want this. You. I wept when you left me yesterday. Taking bits of me with you. I will risk it, Adam. If I will, so must you."

Adam held Grace tightly against himself.

"I can't promise the dreams will end."

"I know, Adam."

"How can we sleep together, Grace?"

"Adam. That's enough; please stop this, this beating yourself up. You pushed me, once — while you were asleep. You haven't tried to cut me, shoot me, throw things at me, strangle me or even yell at me. We'll get help. We can do this, Adam. Do you remember asking me not to leave, after the nightmare?"

"Yes."

"I'm not leaving. What happened, Adam? Can you tell me? Can we exorcise the dream?"

Haltingly, he told her, and Grace began to cry.

"Oh no, Adam," she said, turning her head to kiss his face again and again. "It was a hard day. So many things we talked about. I see how your brain knitted those together into a nightmare. For my part in it, I'm sorry, Adam."

"No, Grace. Not your fault. We have to be able to talk to each other. I feel like a piece of glass, sometimes; the tiniest chip makes me shatter. But I will not shatter you."

Grace paused.

"We come to each other, Adam," said Grace, slowly, "with our bits of baggage clenched in our hands, and we pry them open to say look, here I am. These are the things which have made us who we are; we're not perfect, but we are strong. You won't shatter, and I won't run from a nightmare."

Adam wondered if he was hearing her, interpreting her, correctly. He propped his head on his hand, and looked into Grace's eyes, the reflective, dark pools that intrigued him so.

Adam drew her into himself again, and hoped she was right. That he was safe for Grace. He couldn't leave. He couldn't.

And Grace was damned if she was going to let him go without a fight, fucking dreams or no fucking dreams.

Twenty-one

The morning came much too soon for Adam, who wrenched his body out of Grace's bed at six, threw on his clothes and kissed her desperately.

"I can hardly stand to leave," he said, softly. "See you tonight?"

"Oh, Adam," said Grace, stretching as she came fully awake. "I'm going to miss you today. Yes, see you tonight. Come for dinner."

"Babe. I'd love to. Are you sure?"

"Yes. Please, Adam," added Grace, remembering she had flung herself off the cliff of restraint, begged him to come to her. "I can pick up groceries on the way home."

Adam's upper lip curled. How domestic.

"I can't wait. Is seven okay?"

"Perfect. Adam . . . "

"Grace?"

"I want you."

"Even after last night?" Adam coloured a little. "Grace, oh, God . . . I was out of control. I was desperate to hear you, feel you . . . . and your lips. Your lips. Oh no. They're succulent, but swollen again."

"I wear my badge of carnality with pride."

That sounded more like her. But he had heard what he had wanted to hear, needed to hear. *I'm dying for you*

to touch me. I'm going to come apart. I will risk it, Adam.
And so would he, because he could not help himself.

Adam, in an agony stirred by passion, got in his car and drove home for a shower and to dress for work. He wrenched his mind away from Grace, and tried to focus on the case.

We're going to find this bastard, he told himself. We're going to find him.

*****

"Hey, partner," said Adam, leaning over the partition of James's carrel.

"Hey, Adam, "said James. "You look different," he added, cocking his head judiciously, one eyebrow raised.

"Do I?" asked Adam. "How?"

"Fucking happy," said James, who knew what that looked like. Adam had the grace to colour, a little. "And you need a haircut. Where do you want to start?"

Adam silently thanked James for not going too far with his observations, but also appreciated the comment. Somehow, it was validating.

"Let's move. Set up a meeting for nine with Charlotte, Joan and Lorne, in the case room."

"I have just the thing. Wait'll you see, Sarge," said James, obviously pleased with himself about something.

"Look forward to it. See you in a couple of hours."

Adam spent the next hour answering emails and, at eight, looked up the new number for Inspector Jeannette Villeneuve, now of the Winnipeg Police Service. He had been meaning to call her for a week, but there had either been no time, or there had been Grace.

"Winnipeg Police. Inspector Villeneuve's office, Constable Sophie Harwood speaking. How can I help you?"

"Constable Harwood. Good morning. Detective Sergeant Adam Davis, Saskatoon Police. I was hoping to speak to the Inspector. Is she in?"

"Yes, sir, Sergeant," said the constable. "Let me see if she's free. Can you hold for a moment?"

"Absolutely."

Villeneuve had been in London when Adam and his team were chasing the bishop's killer around the country a few months ago. A priest had been murdered at St. Peter's Seminary, and Adam had been convinced the murderer was the same person. Villeneuve had been a big help on the case.

"Hello, Sergeant," said a beautiful, Québécoise voice a moment later. "*Bonjour.* So lovely to hear from you. How are you? Are you calling to solve another case for me?"

Adam laughed.

"No, Inspector. This is a social call. I wanted to congratulate you on your new position, and promotion. Are you enjoying Winnipeg?"

"I am, so far. This coming winter, however, I may not feel the same way."

"Stay away from Portage and Main, and you may survive," said Adam. "What made you decide to take the job?"

"Well, largely the promotion, of course. It has been quite a learning curve, becoming inspector. But Winnipeg has its lovely aspects: excellent music scene, museums and galleries, and proximity to the lakes. It was not too hard to move here."

"Glad to hear it. I've been away for nearly two weeks at those police conferences in L.A., or I would have called sooner. Anything interesting going on?"

"The usual, unfortunately. Too much gang activity, too many drugs, too many missing or murdered women." She sighed. "We've just had another one. Probably murdered."

"So did we," said Adam. "That case is my primary focus right now. What happened in your case?"

"This poor girl was found down on the bank of the Assiniboine by a . . . well, not a homeless man, but a gentleman down on his luck. She was a pretty little thing. Heartbreaking."

Pretty little thing. Poor girl. On the bank. Water. Adam's body froze. *It couldn't be. God, no.*

"Jeannette," said Adam, in a low, warning tone.

"Adam. What?"

"What does she look like? Exactly, if you don't mind. Height, weight, eye colour, hair, the works."

"Adam, what are you saying? Wait. I'll send you the file."

A moment. Adam's eyes were riveted on his email. It pinged.

Adam opened the file and clicked on the photo. His stomach tightened.

"Do you have it, Adam?" asked Jeannette.

"Yes." He swallowed. "Give me a minute, Jeannette."

He pulled up the woman's file. Sinclair, Della: age twenty-one, one hundred fifteen pounds, five foot two, black hair, brown eyes . . . Adam stopped reading.

"Did she have long hair?" asked Adam. "As she does in the picture?"

"She did. She looked very much like she does in the photo."

"How did she die?"

"She was likely strangled and then dropped into the river. We're not sure where. She came ashore near The Forks," said Jeannette, referring to the shopping area at the confluence of Winnipeg's two rivers. "Adam, what is going on?"

"We have, I believe, at least four women here who have been attacked, killed or spirited away by the same man. At least two of those women were also raped. They all look so much alike, they could be sisters. As could this young woman. Ms. Sinclair."

Adam couldn't see Jeannette Villeneuve, but he could almost hear the blood drain from her face. She made a small, awful noise.

"*Mon dieu*, Adam. Could it be coincidence?"

It could be, but it wasn't. Adam knew it with terrible certainty. He felt himself shake his head, with an out-of-body sense of watching his own actions from far away.

"No, Jeannette," he said. "The woman we know was raped and murdered was originally from Winnipeg. Her name is Sherry Hilliard." His fingers were flying over his keyboard. "I'm sending you the file now. Tell me what you think when you see her."

Another moment. Adam could hear Jeannette clicking the keys on her computer, and gasp.

"Goddamn it to hell. Just a minute, Adam." He heard her calling to Sophie Harwood. "They look so much alike, it is quite incredible, Adam. And they are identical in size. I'll ask Sophie to cross-reference the two. Can I call you back?"

"Of course. I have a meeting at nine — ten your time. I expect it to take an hour. Call me on my cell — do you still have the number, Jeannette?"

"*Oui*, I do."

"I'll pick up if I'm in the meeting when you call. Do you have a new cell number?"

She gave it to him.

"I feel . . . ill, Adam," said Jeannette.

"I do too, Jeannette."

*****

Adam walked into the case room with his mind and stomach churning. But he stopped short when he saw the huge bulletin board, covered in photos, notes, newspaper clippings and arrows pointing in all directions.

Despite his swirling thoughts, he smiled broadly.

"Look at this," he said approvingly, legs planted wide apart, arms crossed, muscles straining against his sleeves. "I see you've made progress. I thought I told you to take Sunday off, James."

He looked first for the photo of Shawn Hartz, the business school owner, whom he wasn't sure he had seen before. James had unearthed a newspaper ad with a photo of Hartz, grinning and shaking hands with someone from a hospital foundation. Adam did recognize him. The man gave his share to charity, but never shied from the publicity it offered, either.

"Well done, team," he said, looking at all of them individually. "Okay, let's see where we're at."

They looked at all the victims' photos and bios again, now that they were organized on the board in some kind of order.

Deborah Clairmont, raped in the park two years ago but alive; no obvious connections to anyone else.

Alexis Ironstand, missing 18 months, dental clinic patient.

Emily Martin, missing 10 months, business school student. Likely found dead along the river.

Shawn Hartz, business school owner, dental clinic patient.

Don Dunlop, owner of dental clinic, lover to Sherry Hilliard.

Sherry Hilliard. Raped. Dead. Dental clinic employee. Found in her flooding basement during a historic rain storm.

There was also a picture of a black SUV, a Porsche Cayenne. It was not the specific SUV in question, since it had not been found. And a photo of Suzanne Genereux: witness, neighbour, potential victim. Grace's friend. Thinking of that made Adam's stomach muscles clench.

"Shawn Hartz has been at the lake, as I mentioned, Adam," said James. "He's back in town today. I've invited him down for a chat."

"What time?"

"Two. And Don Dunlop is finally coming in with his lawyer again. At eleven."

"Has he been in remand this whole time?"

"Yes. Apparently some problem getting in touch with Sealey."

"That's bizarre. Big important guy like Dunlop? Can't reach his lawyer? You'd think Sealey would have a separate cellphone just for him."

Adam's phone started vibrating in the middle of his comment. Adam nodded in apology to the assembled officers, looked at his phone and saw it was indeed Jeannette.

"Inspector," he said, sticking to protocol in front of the others.

"Adam," said Jeannette, her voice very low. "Della Sinclair and Sherry Hilliard were cousins."

"Fuck," said Adam, viciously. Then collected himself. "Sorry, Inspector. You know what this means."

"Fuck, indeed," said Jeannette. "Do not apologize for language matching the crime."

"I'll be on the first flight tomorrow morning," said Adam.

*****

Don Dunlop looked quite awful, particularly in contrast with his sharply-dressed, thoroughly-rested, well-groomed lawyer.

"Thank you for coming back in, Dr. Dunlop," said Adam. "And you, Mr. Sealey."

Adam did the formalities for the recording, identifying Dunlop, Sealey, James and himself.

"We have a number of questions for you, Doctor. Are you comfortable?"

"Yes," said Dunlop. "Thank you," he added, a bit weakly.

"It took a while for you reach Mr. Sealey, as I understand it."

"Yes . . . Ashley said she had trouble reaching him."

Adam's eyebrows lifted.

Sealey cleared his throat. "Miscommunication, I think."

"I see," said Adam, but he didn't. What was that about? "Can you please start by telling us where you were the night Sherry Hilliard was murdered, the night of the rainstorm."

Dunlop looked a little wildly at Sealey, but the lawyer nodded. "Get on with it, Don."

"I was with someone. Else," he added, as if to clarify.

"Another mistress?"

"Yes."

"Her name?"

"Is that necessary?" Dunlop asked, but the tone of his voice showed he knew the answer.

"Obviously, sir. We will have to check your alibi." *Duh*, Adam added mentally.

"Monique. Um. Monique Delacroix."

That name, thought Adam. Do I know that name? But James placed it right away.

"Related to Nick?" asked James.

"Yes. Sister."

"How did you meet her?"

"At one of those charity dinners."

"A hospital foundation dinner, maybe?" asked James.

"Yes. How did you know?"

"Was Shawn Hartz there?"

"Probably. He always is."

"How well do you know Shawn Hartz?"

Dunlop paused, and glanced at his lawyer, who raised his eyebrows.

"Not very. He is a patient. I see him at these endless events. Sometimes we get young women, occasionally a young man, in the office from his school. They do their practicums with us. That kind of thing."

"Do you know a young woman called Emily Martin?"

Dunlop's brow furrowed. "I don't think so. It doesn't ring a bell."

"Do you know where your Cayenne is, Dr. Dunlop?" asked Adam.

"No. I don't. It was stolen from the car lot, I was told. They gave me a loaner until it could be found, or we could get the insurance people on it."

"Were you the only driver of the vehicle?"

Dunlop gave a barking laugh. "No. My wife would take it at every opportunity. Not that I gave her too many of those."

"Why didn't you tell us about the vehicle the first time you were in?"

"It was obvious from your questions that my car was important. Maybe you wouldn't believe me, that it was stolen."

"Do you ever visit Winnipeg, Dr. Dunlop?"

"Occasionally."

"Have you been there recently?"

"Not very, no."

"Did you know Sherry Hilliard was pregnant, Dr. Dunlop?"

The effect of the question on Dunlop was visceral. He stared at Adam for a moment, then doubled over, holding his gut, making a small gasping noise.

Adam's eyes would have flown open in surprise if he was not expert at exerting control over his facial features during interviews. What the hell? Dunlop obviously could not hide his emotion. But what was he feeling?

"Are you all right, Doctor?" asked Adam, worrying Dunlop might vomit or something.

"Yes," said Dunlop, but sweat poured down his face. "And yes. I knew Sherry was pregnant."

"Was it your baby?"

"She said it was. I don't know for sure. But I believed her when she told me."

Light blue eyes, filled with misery, met Adam's navy gaze.

"The baby died too," he said. "Not just Sherry. The baby too. Oh, God."

"You broke up, though."

"She broke up with me. I told you."

"Is that why she quit drinking? The baby?"

"Yes, I think so. She intended to keep the baby. But not me. Not me."

Adam looked at Dunlop sharply, as Dunlop ducked to peer down at his hands, clasped together. His voice was filled with — what was it? Sorrow. It was sorrow, thought Adam. And something else.

"How did you feel about her breaking up with you, Dr. Dunlop? The truth, now. Let's have it, man."

"I was . . . oh God. Devastated. I was crazy about her, Sergeant. You've seen my wife." Adam hadn't, but the description from James and Charlotte was telling. Icy, angry, beautiful Ashley.

"Sherry was . . . quiet. Unassuming. Sweet. Warm. Fucking unbelievable in bed. She made you feel like a . . . a god. But how could I leave my wife for a little hygienist? My employee? I would have done anything for her, and the baby."

"But you didn't."

"No. She wouldn't have me. She wanted to start over, she said. I didn't know what the hell to do. And now she's dead."

Dunlop slumped on the table, head on his arms, and wept in wracking sobs. It was all Adam could do not to comfort him. He knew despair when he saw it.

But Dunlop was still, despite or perhaps because of his testimony, suspect number one.

Twenty-two

Don Dunlop, post-interrogation, had gone to court. He was in the process of making bail, and having his passport removed from his possession. He had agreed to a DNA sample.

Adam printed out the photo of Della Sinclair after the meeting with Dunlop, and tacked it up beside Sherry Hilliard's picture on the case room's bulletin board. He considered the two women, side by side. Cousins. No. Not a coincidence.

James followed Adam into the room.

"Jesus Christ," said James, a Catholic who seldom took his saviour's name in vain when he chose to swear. "Cousins. Or twins. Did you get the morning flight to Winnipeg?"

"Yes, at great expense to the Saskatoon Police, considering the short notice. I'm on the six a.m. Why is it necessary for hour-long flights to cost well over a thousand bucks in this country?"

"That's ridiculous. Adam, I came to say Shawn Hartz should be here any minute."

"Right. Feel ready?"

"Yes. Ready."

Hartz appeared, lawyer-free, and swaggered into the interview room with outstretched hand. Cocky bastard, thought Adam.

"Thank you for coming down, Mr. Hartz," said Adam.

"Hey, no prob," said Hartz. "What's happening? How can I help?"

"We're investigating the murder of Sherry Hilliard," Adam began.

"Heard about it," Hartz broke in. "Terrible."

"And we were wondering if you knew anything about that, or about her."

"Why the hell would I?"

"You're a patient at Dunlop Dentistry, I believe. Was Ms. Hilliard ever your hygienist?"

"Well, yeah . . . but it doesn't mean I know shit about her death."

"I assume you also know Dr. Donald Dunlop."

"For sure. My dentist, eh? Well, one of them."

"You also have a business relationship, I understand. You have provided business school students to the clinic, for office-work practicums."

"Yeah, a few times."

"Was one of them Emily Martin?"

That got a reaction. Shawn Hartz's face began to turn an unbecoming, blotchy red, starting at his starched collar and moving inexorably upward.

"No," was all he said.

Less cocky now, thought Adam.

"You're sure?"

"Yeah. I'm sure." Hartz visibly zipped his lips, pressing them together so hard they turned white.

"Emily Martin is missing, as I'm sure you know, Mr. Hartz." Adam wasn't going to share that her body may have been found.

"Yeah. I had nothing to do with that, either."

"Did you have a relationship with Ms. Martin, Mr. Hartz?"

"No." But the word fell unconvincingly from his mouth.

"Are you telling the whole truth, Mr. Hartz?"

"Well . . . I . . . yes. I mean, I didn't have an actual relationship with her. I did . . . um . . . see her a couple of times outside the school."

"Under what circumstances?"

"A couple of parties. No big deal."

"What kind of parties?"

"Just parties. Women, men, parties. You know."

"No, I don't think I do. Maybe you could explain."

Hartz sighed.

"I asked some of the girls if they would . . . you know, come to parties, be nice to people, look pretty, serve drinks. No sex, I promise. Just, ah, window dressing. Emily agreed a couple of times. I paid them very well; most of them needed the money."

"So, this . . . window dressing," said Adam, choking a little on the term. "It was an act of charity. They needed the money; you came up with a way to give it to them. Is that right?"

"Yeah, exactly," said Hartz, brightening.

"You're big on charity, as I understand it."

"Yeah. Always giving back, that's me."

"Very good of you. And how did you guarantee the safety of these young women after the parties, Mr. Hartz? May I remind you, we're talking about a missing woman. Nineteen years old," said Adam, mentally adding, *asshole*.

"Hey! I only invited friends, guys I knew were okay. They'd never do something bad. Okay, okay, maybe one or two of them got lucky. But they'd never hurt a girl."

"Something, Mr. Hartz, has happened to Emily Martin. Did you have a party the night she went missing? After the business school event?"

"I — I don't remember," said Hartz.

"Okay. I'm going to need a full guest list from your parties. As soon as possible."

"I don't keep guest lists. I just invite people."

"Then think hard, Mr. Hartz. Very hard. You have until tomorrow to compile a guest list, as well as the dates of your parties over the last two years, and get the information to Detective Constable Weatherall," said Adam. "Don't even think about leaving anyone off the list."

"What if I do? What if I can't remember?"

"If I find out, I will have you charged with obstruction of justice. I guarantee it."

Hartz paled. "Can you really do that?"

"I can, and I will. Tomorrow, Mr. Hartz. Without fail."

*****

At day's end, Adam was in Chief Dan McIvor's office, giving him updates and telling him how much of the police budget he was spending on a trip to Winnipeg.

"Well, it's still cheaper than taking our plane," said McIvor. "How in hell did you connect the woman in Winnipeg with our victim?"

"I asked Jeannette Villeneuve what was going on in Winnipeg. She said, the usual: gangs, drugs, missing and murdered women. She volunteered they just had another death — top of mind for her — and it went from there. I've been thinking, Chief, we need to connect with other police services about this kind of case more often. This is a huge break, finding out so quickly. That's five women at least who we think are connected, not to mention Suzanne Genereux."

"Any theories on the killer?"

"I'm working on one," said Adam. "You're not going to like it."

"Let me have it."

"I'm starting to think this guy is pretty high profile, possibly a businessman or professional. Smart. Rich. The stolen Porsche Cayenne could, of course, have been taken by anyone, but that doesn't feel right. I think it was a customer of the dealership. Your average car thief, even if he's also a killer, is more likely to peel something off the street. Of course, it could also have been Dunlop."

"Point taken. Anything else?"

"It could also be someone who works for that rich business owner or professional. Someone close to them. And we can't discount family members, now we know Ms. Hilliard and Ms. Sinclair were cousins."

"Right. Any more ideas?"

"He has a thing about water."

"Water?" McIvor's eyes widened.

"Water. I'm sure it comes into this somehow. Sherry Hilliard was found in her flooding basement. Why didn't he remove her body? Maybe he's increasingly cocksure, since he's getting away with attacking and murdering women. He may simply have killed her during the lightning storm because of the noise, but again, why did he leave her there? It has something to do with the fact her basement was going under water.

"Ms. Sinclair was found by the river in Winnipeg. She'd been dead about two days and washed up on the bank of the Assiniboine. The first victim, if we're right about this being the same guy, was Deborah Clairmont; like Sherry Hilliard, she was also attacked during a rainstorm. The attacker pushed her face into a puddle while he was raping her from behind. And now we've found another body by the river.

"We're almost certainly going to find the other missing woman somewhere near water. But she won't have been drowned. Ms. Sinclair was strangled. As you know, Ms. Hilliard was stabbed, and possibly hit on the head.

"He's killing a particular type, too, but they are all especially vulnerable somehow. Three of them were not from Saskatoon. And two are part-Indigenous; one is First Nations."

"God Almighty, Adam," said McIvor. "Well done. And Adam, thanks for coming back early. I'll find a way to pay you back."

"Yes, sir," said Adam, vaguely. "Thank you, sir."

Dan McIvor, who was not chosen to serve as chief of police because he was an idiot, saw the tiny glint in Adam's eyes and understood his sacrifice. He smiled sympathetically.

Adam walked out of the chief's office and down the hall to his own, where he almost ran into Terry Pearson. The inspector was waiting for him.

"Terry," said Adam, holding back a sigh. "Have a seat."

"Adam. Got a question for you. Where the hell has Fisher been?"

"What do you mean?"

"I tried to reach him the other day. Weatherall said he was out of town, following some woman. Did you sanction that?"

"Yes," Adam said.

"In a police vehicle?"

"As far as I know."

Pearson was turning red in the face, and Adam knew something was coming. Something he didn't want to hear. He recognized the signs. The man regularly went apoplectic when things weren't going his way.

"What is she, his fucking squaw?"

Adam was on his feet and around his desk in a second; Pearson rose to face him, defiance in his expression. Adam was immediately nose to nose with his superior, his eyes flashing, nostrils flaring.

"What did you say? Are you fucking kidding me, Pearson?"

Pearson made a guttural sound.

"What's your problem, Davis?"

"Don't ever use that language in front of me again," said Adam. "Or in front of anyone. On second thought, try it on Fisher. Please. Maybe he'd have the guts to kick your ass. Get the hell out of my office, Pearson."

"Fuck you, Davis. You're gone. I'm writing you up for insubordination."

He stormed out.

*****

Grace had stumbled into the newsroom with work most definitely not on her mind. Her lips were, indeed, quite swollen, as were certain other parts of her body. She had applied a darker lipstick than she usually wore, trying to minimize the puffiness. Peering at herself in the mirror, she sighed. Well, that didn't work, she thought.

She didn't want to advertise her passion for Adam, as he did not for her; but the evidence was there. I can't do much more about it, thought Grace.

Nor did she have the focus to care much. She was floating in a new space which both frightened her and made her deeply happy. They had blown apart the last — well, almost the last vestige — of restraint between them. The passionate intercourse, the building of their connection, the acknowledgement that they would work together on Adam's PTSD. And she had managed to be open with him, tell him the truth. No deflections. That wasn't so hard, Grace, now was it? she asked herself. Well, yeah, it was, but she had to do it. She wanted Adam, and he wanted the truth.

How can it be, that this beautiful, ridiculously beautiful, man wants me? She still found it hard to believe.

She dropped her gear and headed for the city editor's desk. After greeting Grace, and casting a knowing look at her lips, Claire Davidson sent her to court. A violent domestic dispute had resulted in assault charges, and the man was being sentenced today. Children were involved. Grace hated these cases, but then, which cases made her day? Still, the domestics were among the worst.

"Have the police offered any more on the Hilliard murder?" asked Grace, on her way out the door.

"Just got a new release, but not a hell of a lot new," said Claire. "Makes me nervous. Makes me wonder what's going on, you know?"

"Yes. I know. What have they said?"

"Well, let's see. They've admitted Sherry had been stabbed several times, and hooked up the dog's death with hers. They're looking for a vehicle, a newer black Porsche SUV. That's been fun this morning. People have been calling every time they see a black SUV, regardless of age or make. It's driving the cops crazy, according to communications, not to mention us."

Grace nodded.

"I can't be any more help, Claire," she said. "But I'll see if I can move any mountains."

"He is rather large, isn't he?" said Claire with a twinkle.

"Rather. And not just physically."

*****

Adam left work fifteen minutes early, and ran the few blocks to his condo. Since Adam lived so close to the station, he rarely drove his personal vehicle, a semi-ancient BMW, to work.

He had to pack before going to Grace's for dinner. The plan was to throw his carry-on bag into the car, in the hope she would invite him to stay for the night. He knew he shouldn't stay, but maybe it would be okay? He could leave for the airport straight from her place, very early in the morning.

Adam expected he would have to spend two days in Winnipeg, if he was going to get any face-to-face interviewing done. Another hotel room, he thought, with a mental sigh. Damn. At least it was two days, not nearly two weeks, away from Grace.

Packing delayed him, so he called Grace to warn her.

"Grace," said Adam, when she picked up. "I'm going to be a few minutes late. I'll explain when I get there. Would you like me to pick up some wine or something? Anything?"

"No, I'm fine, Adam. There's lots of wine. Come over as soon as you can."

"See you in about fifteen."

He was there in twelve, knocking rather more gently than he did the night before. Grace opened the door, and Adam swung her into his arms, kissing her.

"Goddess," he said. "Sorry to be late."

"You're only twelve minutes late. Come in. Let's eat. And talk."

Adam helped her serve the pork tenderloin, mushroom rice pilaf and salad; he poured wine, and they settled in.

"Yum, Grace. This is delicious. Thank you."

"You're so welcome," said Grace, thinking, *he's adorable when he says yum*. "So tell me all. What happened today?"

"I have to go to Winnipeg in the morning," said Adam. "I can't believe I have to get on a plane again; and worse, stay in a hotel, alone. Just one night, I hope," he added, seeing Grace's face. "Oh, Babe, two days, one night. Don't . . ."

"It's fine, Adam. I'll be fine." Okay, so she wasn't telling the whole truth. And oh, she loved it when he called her 'Babe.' A new thing. She missed him already.

"Suzanne is coming back to town, possibly Wednesday, otherwise Thursday. That might . . . complicate matters, too."

"Another excellent reason to solve this blasted case," said Adam. "For Suzanne's freedom and, frankly, mine. To make love with you whenever possible."

Grace leaned over and kissed him, between bites of pork and rice.

They ate for another moment.

"Why Winnipeg, Adam?" Grace asked.

"There's been a murder in Winnipeg similar to Sherry Hilliard's," said Adam. "This has to stay between us, but she was Sherry's cousin. I'm going to see what the hell is going on."

"Holy shit, Adam. What? Obviously you're thinking it's the same killer, even if it's a different city?" Adam nodded. "When do you think you can release more information about the situation here?"

"Soon. The trip should shed more light on the case. In fact, I'm counting on it. But Grace, we have to be careful. We don't have any hard evidence pointing to a serial killer. What if I'm wrong? So we're a bit stuck."

"I see," said Grace, slowly. "You know, I was wondering today . . . I was in court covering the sentencing of a man who brutally beat his wife. She barely survived the attack. His tiny children witnessed it, and are, according to the testimony of a social worker, traumatized in the extreme."

"How old are the little ones?"

"Four and five, at the time. Much too small to intervene, but old enough to sort of know what they saw."

"What did he get?"

"Seven years. He ended up being sentenced for aggravated assault, not attempted murder, which in my view, it certainly was. You know plea bargains. But he endured terrible abuse himself, which was a mitigating factor at the sentencing."

"You're not just telling me about your day, are you, Grace?"

"No. I'm wondering if there's a family member involved, and if a traumatic childhood event comes into this, either for the killer or the victims."

"Yes. The family member had occurred to me earlier today, when I was briefing the chief. I take your point about the children as witnesses to abuse, or even victims . . . worth considering."

Before she could respond, Adam leaned forward, changed the subject.

"Grace, I'd like to talk to someone at the women's prison. Can you suggest someone?"

"Don't you police people connect with Elders and prison staff on a regular basis?"

"Yes, but most of them are men. I'd like to speak with a woman, especially one who understands what the women have gone through."

"Well, Justice Deborah Lafond was very involved in getting the prison built, when she was still a lawyer," started Grace. "She'd be worth talking to. So would Elder Eileen Bear. She runs the place; I've interviewed her a few times. She's amazing. A pragmatic mystic."

"What I'm looking for is some kind of an epiphany. I'm sure we have a serial killer, but I also think Sherry Hilliard's murder was not random. He knew her. There's a domestic element there. And some of these women are Indigenous. Why not all of them? It would help me with the profile."

"Absolutely. Are you going to talk to Sherry's family, while you're in Winnipeg?"

"That's the plan. Inspector Villeneuve — I've told you about her, yes?" he asked, to a nod from Grace. "She's setting up interviews."

"It'll be interesting to see if there is a cycle of abuse in Sherry's family. What time do you have to get up in the morning?"

Adam groaned. "Stupid early. Four-thirty."

"Will you stay with me? Seems ridiculous to go home . . . unless you have packing to do?"

"No. I'm ready to go. I hoped you'd ask. I will stay with you. If you're sure, Grace."

"I'm sure, Adam. The more often you stay, the more you'll get used to it. We'll be fine."

And they were.

Twenty-three

Adam awakened at the unholy hour of four-thirty in the blasted morning to find Grace tucked tightly against him. Oh, Babe, he thought, I could get used to this. Waking up next to you, wildflower, every morning.

I am going to be with you every day and every night, and I will never hurt you. I will fix this, with your help.

He tried to slide silently backward out of the bed, but the contact was too close. She awakened immediately, turned, and demanded a kiss.

"I'm sorry to wake you, beautiful," said Adam, complying with the request. "God, I don't want to go."

"Go you must, Adam. I'll be waiting for you. Here, with any luck," she added, patting the bed.

Adam groaned dramatically, kissed Grace again, and hit the shower. By the time he was dressed, Grace had made coffee and poured some into a travel mug.

"Best of luck in Winnipeg. Call me tonight?"

"Absolutely. See you in two days, if all goes well."

Adam forced himself out the door, into his car, and to the airport.

*****

Inspector Jeannette Villeneuve herself met Adam at the airport.

"Detective Sergeant," she said. "So nice to meet you in person."

"Inspector. And you," said Adam. "Thank you so much for picking me up."

"My pleasure," she said. "Do you have any checked luggage?"

"No. I'm ready to go."

Jeannette told Adam what they had learned so far about Della Sinclair. She had worked in a restaurant, was single, and had no criminal record. She had been admitted to hospital a couple of times for what appeared to be the results of beatings, but her chart showed she had denied physical assault. Apart from a few old bruises and scars, the autopsy indicated she had been healthy at the time of her death.

"Do we have time to drive by the site where she was found? Or do you have immediate plans for me?" asked Adam.

"No; good idea. I've arranged a couple of interviews for this afternoon; I hoped we could discuss the case first, this morning, but we'll have plenty of time."

Half an hour later, Adam was standing on the bank of the Assiniboine. Jeannette showed him the exact spot where Della Sinclair had been found by the bottle-collector, George Anderson. She indicated how Della had been lying, tucked behind two large rocks with her hand caught between them.

"She'd been missing for two days?" asked Adam.

"Yes. Well, not quite two days. We aren't sure how far down river she came."

"Do we know where she was the day she went missing?"

"She was at work; she showed up for the lunch shift, so it happened in the afternoon."

Adam crouched down and looked around the rocks, trying to envision the young woman washing up on the riverbank. He stood, then, and gazed upstream, absorbing the environment and wondering where the hell she was murdered.

"Damn," he said, under his breath. "Okay. Let's go. Forgive me, but I have to make a call on the way."

Adam dialled James's number.

"James. Listen, could you look up the Hilliard autopsy? Or maybe you remember . . . did McDougall find any evidence of old bruises, cuts, anything like that? Injuries indicating a history of beatings?"

"Let me take a look. I don't recall it being high up in the report but there was something . . . here, I've got it. Okay." James was speed reading. "Yes. There were some old injuries, a few scars on her back and buttocks. A healed broken bone in her cheek. Why are you asking, Adam?"

"The autopsy on Della Sinclair indicated she had been beaten, and her hospital records did too — although she denied it. I'm wondering, considering they're cousins, if there's a family member we should be looking at. If he was beating them, did he kill them? And, what he was doing in Saskatoon, if we're right about the other women? Remind me, James. How long had Sherry been living in Saskatoon?"

"Not very long. About a year."

"Hasn't Alexis Ironstand been missing for eighteen months? And Deborah Clairmont was assaulted two years ago. Maybe we have two killers?" asked Adam. But he didn't think so. He shook his head to clear his brain, dragged a hand through his hair.

"I hope something starts to make sense," said Adam. "Call you later. Thanks, James."

*****

Inspector Villeneuve was hands down the most elegant cop Adam had ever seen. Her appearance meshed perfectly with her lovely voice. Dark and slim with perfect posture, beautifully groomed and dressed, she was the quintessential, stereotypical, gorgeous Frenchwoman.

In her mid-forties, Jeannette Villeneuve also had a commanding presence very similar to Adam's own. He recognized a sister in crime solving, and had resisted the urge to kiss her hand in respect when they met at the airport.

In her office, over excellent cafés au lait since the inspector had her own expensive espresso machine, she told Adam about the people they had interviewed. The man who found Della Sinclair, George Anderson. Della's siblings. Her parents. Her co-workers. Everyone they could think of. And now, at Adam's request, she had set up an interview with Corey Hilliard, Sherry's older brother and Della's cousin.

"He's coming in at one," said Jeannette. "Della's sister Angela will be in at three."

"What do you know about the Sinclair family?"

"There are two sisters, Della and Angela, and one brother, Richard Jr., who is younger — seventeen, if memory serves — as well as the parents. Their mother is Helen, sister to Sherry's mother, Hannah."

"Got it. Would you excuse me again for a moment, Jeannette? I have to call a colleague."

"And then, I will treat you to lunch, Adam."

"Perfect, thank you." He was very, very hungry. His five a.m. airport bagel seemed a distant memory.

Jeannette turned to her computer, and Adam went into the hallway to call Charlotte.

"Char," said Adam, when she answered. "How are you doing?"

"Fine, Sarge. And you? How's it going in Winnipeg, so far?"

"Very well. Inspector Villeneuve is all over it. Char, can you contact Carol Hall? First of all, find out how she's doing and whether she's resigned yet. Also ask her what the office buzz is about Dunlop. But mainly, ask her about Sherry's brother, Corey. See if Sherry ever mentioned him, or any family member."

"Will do, Adam. What are you thinking?"

"I'm wondering if Corey has anything to do with her death, or their cousin's. We're interviewing him this afternoon, but it would be great to get some direction from Carol."

"Do you suspect Corey Hilliard, Adam?"

"Theoretically, sure. His sister and his cousin died within days of each other. Who else is connected to both of them? Della Sinclair's brother would be the other obvious option, although I gather he's younger than Della — quite young, and he's less likely for that reason. I'm starting with Corey, and Carol Hall might be able to help."

"Right. I'm on it. Will get back to you as soon as I reach her."

Adam knocked quietly at Jeannette's door, and entered at her greeting.

"Thanks for waiting, Jeannette. I should drop my gear off and check in at some point."

"Where are you staying?"

"The Fort Garry."

"Excellent food there. You can check in, we'll have lunch a bit early and be back in plenty of time for one o'clock."

*****

Adam wasn't sure what he was expecting from Corey Hilliard, but this wasn't it.

Cool, self-assured, much taller than his sister and fashionably dressed, he seemed a very different personality from Sherry, apart from a shared composure. Adam detected something else . . . a contained sort of power, under the surface.

Jeannette initially took the lead, as Corey came in — stalked in — and settled into a chair, crossing his legs casually.

"Mr. Hilliard, *bonjour* and thank you for coming in," said Jeannette. "This is Detective Sergeant Adam Davis from Saskatoon. My condolences, sir, on your sister's death."

"Thank you," said Hilliard. "What have you learned about her murder, Sergeant Davis? I trust you have made some progress on finding her killer. And my cousin's, while I'm at it, Inspector Villeneuve."

Ah. He was going on the offensive, then, thought Adam.

"Indeed, we have," said Adam, with a confidence he didn't entirely feel. "That's why we've asked you to come in."

"Whatever I can do to help, Sergeant, Inspector."

He didn't seem particularly cut up about the deaths of his sister and cousin, thought Adam. Why not?

"How close were you to your sister, Mr. Hilliard?" Adam asked.

"Fairly, especially when we were younger."

"Did you discuss personal matters with her, such as her romantic life?"

"Not much. She was quiet, kept to herself."

"Did she tell you about Dr. Don Dunlop?"

"Who? Oh, her boss. Or one of them. Tell me what?"

"They were having a sexual relationship, and she was pregnant, likely with his child."

The cool brown eyes flashed, and the lips parted slightly. Adam was quite sure Corey Hilliard was surprised.

"No. I did not know. Pregnant? What do you mean, 'likely' with his child?"

"According to Dr. Dunlop, Sherry said the child was his. You didn't know any of this?"

"No. I said that."

"What did you know about her life?"

"She worked hard at the clinic. She had few friends in Saskatoon; she'd only been there a year and a bit. She used to have a drinking problem, but she stopped a few months ago."

"Did you visit her?"

"A couple of times."

"Did you get along?"

"Yes, of course."

"Why did she move to Saskatoon, Mr. Hilliard?"

"For the job, I guess."

"She couldn't get a job at a clinic in Winnipeg? As I understand it, hygienists are in considerable demand, here and in Saskatoon."

"I don't know," said Corey Hilliard. "She applied, got the job, packed up and left. Soon after she arrived, she bought that crappy little house."

"Was she being threatened here, in any way, Mr. Hilliard? Perhaps running from a bad relationship? Could there be another reason why she moved, if it was so sudden?"

"Not that I know of."

"Tell us a bit about yourself, Mr. Hilliard. Married? Kids? Job?"

"Not married. Girlfriend. I work at Garden City Motors. Sales."

Interesting, thought Adam. But he decided against going any further. He had no ammunition from Charlotte yet.

"Thank you for coming in, Mr. Hilliard. If you think of anything else, please call me," said Adam with some force, standing up and handing Hilliard his card.

Adam used his height and size to make an impression on this witness. Let's be clear, said his posture: I'm in charge here. Corey Hilliard stood and stayed impassive; but his face twitched, ever so slightly.

"Sure, Sergeant," he said, casually. "Be in touch if I think of anything."

Hilliard turned on his heel and left the room.

Jeannette waited a moment to ensure he was out of earshot, then asked, "What was your impression of him?"

"Self-assured, on the surface. Contained, like his sister. Too contained, perhaps. There's something I can't quite put my finger on. I'm certain he was surprised at learning Sherry was pregnant. I'm also positive he's not telling us everything. I just have to find the right questions. What did you think?"

"He definitely flinched at the end, when you stood to claim control. There is absolutely something he doesn't want us to know."

Adam's phone buzzed. He snatched it off the table.

"Charlotte," Adam answered. "What's happening? Any luck with Carol Hall?"

"Yes, I just talked to her."

"Has she quit?"

"Not yet. Dunlop, as you know, hasn't been around much. She thought she had a bit of time before she had to resign."

"What did she say about Sherry's brother?"

"This is weird, Sarge. You know how people go for lunch with a new colleague, ask about family and pets and stuff. So Carol asked, to the best of her recollection, do you have any brothers and sisters? And do you know what Sherry said?"

"No idea."

"She said no. No siblings. So when I asked Carol whether Sherry had ever mentioned Corey, she was, to say the least, shocked."

"As am I," said Adam. "That's bizarre. Why the hell would she deny having a brother?

Twenty-four

Adam strode down the Winnipeg police station hall, his brain on fire and his body vibrating. Who is this killer? Is it indeed Corey Hilliard? How often does he get to Saskatoon?

He knocked on Jeannette's door and told her the news from Saskatoon, including that Sherry told a colleague she had no siblings. Jeannette blinked at him, her face registering bafflement.

"Now why would she do that?" she mused. "Did she hate Corey for some reason, and essentially disown him? Had he done something she didn't want to be associated with, and she denied him out of fear? Or, perhaps, disgust?"

"Those are my thoughts. What does his sheet look like?"

"There are a few minor incidents from his youth. He was a brat, but not an extremely bad kid, according to his record. A bar fight, a stolen car, that kind of thing. Nothing recent."

A head poked in. "Inspector, Detective Sergeant, Angela Sinclair is here."

"Thank you, Sophie. Please direct her into the interview room and wait for us."

"Yes, ma'am."

When Adam entered the interview room and saw Angela Sinclair for the first time, he couldn't have been more surprised if the queen had been sitting there. Or, perhaps, an angel.

Clad in a white dress, Angela had hair the colour of ripe wheat, skin almost as fair as Grace's, and bright green eyes. When she stood to greet the police officers, it was clear she was at least five foot six. Apart from the length of her tresses, she could hardly have looked less like her sister, or her cousin.

"Thank you very much, Ms. Sinclair, for coming in," said Jeannette. "This is Detective Sergeant Adam Davis of the Saskatoon Police."

"Pleased to meet you, Ms. Sinclair," said Adam, frankly peering into her face, seeking resemblance to her relatives. He immediately knew Angela Sinclair would not be the next victim.

"As you know," Jeannette began, "we are investigating the deaths of Della and Sherry. It is hardly a coincidence for both of them to be killed within days of each other, yet they did live in different cities. We are hoping you can help us."

"Yes, of course."

"May I ask, Ms. Sinclair," said Jeannette, in a very gentle voice, "why you did not seem surprised when your sister was found deceased? My officer said you were devastated, but did not appear shocked. Is that a reasonable evaluation?"

"Yes," said Angela. Her lip quivered. "After I heard about Sherry, I guess I wasn't particularly surprised. It seems to me whatever happened to Sherry, happened to Della. So why not this?"

"Can you give us an example?"

"They were so much alike in many ways, Sherry and Della. You've seen, I'm sure, how much they looked alike. They both were a little tormented. Both drank a bit too much. They had bad luck with men. They were quiet, reserved, sweet. As you can see, I'm blonde, tall and outgoing."

"Do you mind me asking if you have the same biological parents as Della? I apologize," added Adam, "but you do look very different, and it's important."

Angela dug in her purse, pulled out a photograph and presented it to Jeannette and Adam. It was an image of Della, Angela and their brother, Richard. Della was quite dark; Angela very fair; and Richard somewhere in between, with brown hair.

"I know. It does amaze a lot of people. But I apparently got the European genes; Della looks much more like our First Nations side. Looked, I mean," said Angela, choking on the words.

"And your mother?"

"She looks like Della and Sherry. And like Sherry's mother. Inspector, when can we have Della's and Sherry's bodies? Tradition on my mother's side calls for wakes and other rituals. We must honour those customs."

"Ms. Sinclair, I'm so sorry about the delay," said Jeannette. "Autopsies take some time. I will see to it that your sister and cousin will be released as soon as possible."

"Thank you," said Angela, quietly.

"I'm sorry to ask you this, Ms. Sinclair," Adam said after a moment. "Are you aware Della had, at some point in the past, been beaten? At least twice?"

The woman's face registered only acceptance. She nodded.

"And Sherry also had been beaten."

"Yes."

"Were they the victims of the same person?"

"Yes."

"Was it a family member, or perhaps a boyfriend they shared consecutively?"

"A family member. Yes."

"Can you tell us who it was?" asked Adam, although he was now sure he knew.

She sat, rigidly, her face working.

"Yes. It's time. They're both dead, for God's sake. Both dead! Damn," she said, and lowering her face, began to cry. "Corey. Of course."

"Can you tell us about it?"

"The whole family knew. No one would do anything about it. Corey was the golden child, the handsome one, the one with the big future. But he's a violent bastard when he's drinking; sometimes even when he's not. He's also a coward. He rarely got into fights with other boys or, when he grew up, other men. He preferred to take it out on his sister and his cousin."

"Did he beat you, as well?"

"Just once. I think I wasn't as much fun to beat on. I fought back, refused to cry. I stayed the hell out of his way. But Della and Sherry would go out drinking with him once in a while, meet his friends. It was a bad scene. They were more vulnerable, and maybe they shouldn't have gone out with him; but they didn't deserve what he dished out. Afterward, like an abusive husband, he'd apologize. Say it would never happen again, give them presents. All that bullshit."

"Is that why Sherry moved to Saskatoon, do you think, Ms. Sinclair?"

"It's absolutely why she moved away. Saskatoon is not too far from Winnipeg, but she thought she'd be safer there, from Corey."

That explains why she denied him, thought Adam.

"Why didn't they come forward? Why didn't someone come forward, to make it stop?"

"Like I said, he was the golden boy and was forever saying it would never happen again. We were protecting him, I suppose, from a bad reputation and from jail, or a criminal record. And now they're dead. Oh, God. Please tell me Corey didn't kill them, Detective."

"I can't tell you that, Ms. Sinclair. I don't know yet. Do you know if he visited Saskatoon in the last year?"

"Once, as far as I know. Some work thing, he said. It was some time ago . . . months ago, anyway. He may have gone since then, but I don't know for sure."

"You've decided to break the silence, Ms. Sinclair."

"Yes. This has gone on far too long."

"Thank you. It's very brave of you."

"No. It's time. Corey has a girlfriend — small, pretty, dark. We have other cousins. There are other women out there. For the love of God, Detective. Stop him."

*****

It was almost four o'clock. If they got moving, they would make it to Garden City, not far away, by four-fifteen. They might well catch him there.

"Sophie!" called Jeannette, speed-walking down the hallway from the interview room. "Get us an officer and a car. Make that two officers. Right now. Tell them to meet us at the south door. Adam, are you ready? What do you need?"

"I'm ready," said Adam, buckling his duty belt.

By the time they made the south door, the police car was waiting with one officer behind the wheel and one in the back seat. Jeannette jumped into the front, and Adam into the back.

"Sirens, Inspector?" asked the officer behind the wheel.

"No. Just lights. Go as fast as possible, though, Constable."

Constable Bruyère made it in under fifteen minutes, turned off the spinning red lights and slipped into the parking lot of the car dealership. All four police officers leapt out, and despite being on someone else's turf, Adam charged forward, his long legs taking the distance to the front doors in seconds.

He flashed his warrant card at the receptionist. "Detective Sergeant Adam Davis, Saskatoon Police and Inspector Jeannette Villeneuve, Winnipeg Police. Where is Corey Hilliard?"

Her expression blended awe at the sight of Adam with shock at the peremptory demand for Mr. Hilliard. She pointed mutely in the direction of his office.

Adam gave one curt nod in thanks, and abruptly turned left with Jeannette and the two constables right behind him.

Hilliard wasn't there. Through the window, Adam could see him on the lot, talking to another salesperson. To his right, Adam could see the exit sign, and made for the back door.

"Corey Hilliard," he said, as loudly and authoritatively as only Adam could. "Do not move."

But Corey did. One look at Adam's intense face powered his legs, and he took off across the lot, weaving between the shiny new cars. He was no match for Adam, who caught up to him within twenty metres, slammed him against the side of a car and cuffed him.

"You are under arrest, Corey Hilliard, for assault against Sherry Hilliard, Della Sinclair and Angela Sinclair," Adam said. "And God only knows who else. You are also under arrest on suspicion of murder in the cases of Sherry Hilliard and Della Sinclair. You are coming with us."

"I didn't do it! I didn't do it!" Corey shouted, loud enough to reach the ears of his shocked colleague, who appeared frozen in place.

"You definitely assaulted your sister and cousins. There is no doubt. Let's go."

As they dragged Corey Hilliard back to the police cruiser, Adam noticed something. Several somethings. Silver Audis, money-green Jaguars and midnight-black Porsche Cayennes.

*****

"Jeannette, I am so sorry. My anger got the better of me. I can't believe I've arrested someone on your turf." Adam looked stricken. "I don't know what the hell I was thinking."

"Adam. Forget it. I'd describe that as passion more than anger. And, you were the first to catch up to him. It's fine."

Corey Hilliard was being processed; Adam and Jeannette were waiting for him in an interview room. Adam's hand went up to his head and through his hair.

"I do apologize."

"*Merci*, Adam. Do not worry."

Adam was quiet for a moment, and Jeannette let him be.

Corey Hilliard appeared after being booked and was directed into a chair, with some force. Constable Bruyère kept his hand heavy on Hilliard's shoulder; the suspect was struggling and twitching.

"Welcome back, Mr. Hilliard," said Adam, as coolly as he could manage. "Coffee?"

"Whisky?"

"Very funny, Mr. Hilliard. Let me start by asking, did you kill your sister, Sherry Hilliard, and rape her? And did you kill your cousin, Della Sinclair?"

"No," hissed Hilliard. "Fuck no."

"You did beat them. Badly enough to break Sherry's cheekbone. Did you not?"

"No," he denied, but with less force.

"I have a very important question for you. Concentrate. We know you travelled to Saskatoon some time ago, perhaps ten or eleven months ago. Why? And have you been to Saskatoon since then? You know we can prove you were there the first time. Please don't deny it."

"Went for work, didn't I," Hilliard said sullenly. "Almost a year ago."

"Did you go subsequently? You told us you visited your sister once or twice in Saskatoon."

"One other time."

"When?"

"A few months ago."

"When you went for work, what was the exact reason? What did you do in Saskatoon on business?"

"Helped out at Luxury Motors. Was there about a week, training some new sales staff. The owner didn't trust anyone else."

"You know the owner?"

"Yeah. He used to work at Garden City until he bought Luxury, couple of years ago."

"Did you happen to borrow a car from the lot?"

"No. Didn't need to. I had my own."

"Maybe you needed another car for some reason, the second time you were in Saskatoon."

Corey Hilliard's eyes flew open.

"What the fuck are you talking about?" He seemed to realize he was floundering in very deep water and couldn't feel the bottom. "I'm not saying another word until I get a lawyer. Fuck you, Davis."

But Adam was okay with ending the interview. He had enough, for now.

Twenty-five

"Grace," said Adam over the phone. "I miss you."

"I miss you, too. How are things going in Winnipeg?"

"Very well. Horribly. Depends how you look at it. Grace, I'll be home tomorrow morning. I managed to get a seat on the morning flight."

"Something has happened, then."

"Yes. Tell me about Suzanne. Where is she?"

"She's coming back from the farm tomorrow. Would you like to come and meet her? Over dinner?"

"I'd love to. I will try. Tomorrow might be a wild day. Will I be allowed to kiss you passionately?"

"God, I hope so. I will dream of it."

"I will dream of more than that."

Adam went to say goodbye to Jeannette. It was getting late.

"Thank you, Jeannette, for everything. Especially your patience with me. This case has a piece of me. I suppose they all do, but this one . . ."

"I know, Adam. We will stay in touch."

"Do you think you might get back to Corey Hilliard tomorrow, as well?"

"It's possible. I've heard from his lawyer. I'll let you know."

"Thanks again. I guess I'm off. I have to admit I'm looking forward to seven or eight hours' sleep before getting up at four."

"I don't blame you. Those early morning flights are the worst. Take care, Adam. You're welcome any time."

"Thanks, Jeannette." Adam took Jeanette's hand in his, and, this time, he did kiss it.

"*Merci*, Adam," said Jeannette, smiling and accepting the salute. "Safe travels."

Sophie drove Adam to his hotel, where he headed straight for the rotunda-style bar at the far end of the lobby. He ordered a pint of beer and a large rare steak. Absorbed in the music of a trio playing cool jazz, he did not notice the hot stares of all the women in the room, and felt himself relax.

Vibration alerted him to a phone call. He pulled his cellphone out of his pocket and put it to his ear, simultaneously walking out of the noisy bar.

"Grace," he said, making an assumption.

"Who the fuck is Grace?" asked a female voice.

Hell.

"Jilly. What's up?"

"I'll be in Saskatoon this weekend. I was hoping we could get together and talk. See what's new with you, handsome."

"I'm sorry, Jilly, I'm very busy with a big case. I'm afraid I won't have time."

"Come on, Adam. You still have to eat."

"I just can't. Jilly, I have to go. Sorry. Goodbye."

Adam hung up. He didn't want to argue. And he was not going to tell Jilly about Grace, nor Grace about Jilly. He wondered if that decision would prove to be a mistake.

*****

James opened his email one last time before end of shift to see the missive from his sergeant.

"James, I'll be on the six-ten flight, so I should be on the ground about six-forty with the time difference. Can you meet me for breakfast about seven, at the Bessborough? We'll make plans for the day."

James and Charlotte were waiting for Adam as he came into the hotel restaurant shortly after seven.

"Hi, Sarge. Welcome back. Did you bash your head again?" asked James.

"No. Did on the way out, though," said Adam, touching his temple ruefully. The tiny, low-ceilinged planes serving the Saskatoon to Winnipeg route were a point of misery with Adam and every other tall Saskatonian or Winnipegger.

Adam briefed James and Charlotte on the interviews with Corey Hilliard and Angela Sinclair over coffee at the beautiful, stately downtown hotel. The city's residents referred to it as the castle on the river, and it indeed was majestic. Adam privately loved going to the hotel whenever he could find a reason.

"He's the link, or he's the killer," said Adam of Hilliard. "First, we have to visit Luxury Motors. I want to see the place and talk to the owner. James, you know him. Can you set it up as soon as we get back to the station? We need to find out what he knows about Corey Hilliard. Do we know any more about the body? Theoretically, Emily Martin?"

"No. McDougall promised me cause of death, if it's possible to tell, this morning."

"What I want to know is why she emerged after ten months, when Della Sinclair washed up on the riverbank after two days," said Adam. "The usual thing is for people to pop up within a couple, three days — if they've drowned, anyway. But even if they've been killed another way and dumped, it doesn't take ten months. But I'll take a definite cause of death for now. How far out are we on Sherry's baby's DNA?"

"Couple more days, probably," said Charlotte.

"Okay. Suzanne Genereux is coming back into town today sometime, and will be staying at Grace's. I'm not terribly concerned, but I'd like to have a car sliding by Grace's every so often again. Char, can you arrange that?"

"You bet, Sarge."

"Here's another thing," Adam said. "We have to remember our killer is armed. Not just strong hands, but knives and at least one handgun. It seems pretty obvious there's some escalation here.

"The first woman," Adam continued, "Deborah Clairmont, was raped, but she survived. She may not have lived if a man with a dog hadn't shown up. We don't know how he intended to kill her.

"Then Alexis Ironstand went missing. God, we have to fucking *find* her. Then Emily Martin, then Sherry Hilliard, then Della Sinclair. Della was strangled. I'm betting Emily was too. But Sherry was absolutely cut to ribbons. Why? What was special about Sherry, or did he switch weapons for some other reason? And he shot the damn dog. So, he's packing, too."

Breakfast was delivered. All three officers dove in, the constables mulling over what Adam had said. After a couple of bites, Adam continued.

"We have to think about where Alexis Ironstand could be. My bet is somewhere along the river, maybe in a shallow grave, or at one of the nearby lakes. Pike Lake? Blackstrap?

"But I don't think she's *in* the river, or a lake. It's been eighteen months, and no sign of her. It took ten months for Emily Martin to appear. That's a long time. He has a thing for water, uses it as a terror technique. But he doesn't drown his victims. Why?"

Adam shook his head, and closed his eyes, in an effort to force his mind to see Alexis Ironstand's grave. Damn it. Where could they start?

He had another thought.

"Have we determined if Shawn Hartz ever hired Ms. Ironstand for one of his disgusting parties?" asked Adam.

"No, we haven't," said James. "She wasn't a student at his school — she was attending university — and he said he hired the young female students. But hey: she was a patient at the dental clinic. What if he met her there? Two patients making small talk in the waiting room? She's young and pretty. He gives her a card; she's hard up, and agrees to be . . . what do you call it, window dressing? What do you think?"

"Yes. Brilliant. James, call Hartz again and ask him. Also, has he coughed up the guest list yet?"

"No. He was supposed to send it by end yesterday, right? I can harass him for the list while I'm at it."

"Okay. Tomorrow, I'm heading out to the women's prison. And, I'm planning to meet Suzanne tonight, if I can get away. I hope she'll say something that will ping in my brain."

"By the way," James said, as they prepared to leave, "we're having an impromptu pool party Friday. You two are invited, with your special others, if you can make it. Short notice, I know; but what the hell. It's still hot."

* * * * *

"Davis," Adam answered, somewhat absently, when his cellphone rang. He was buried in the women's case files.

"It's Jack McDougall, Adam. Are you back from Winnipeg?"

"I am. Got back early. Don't tease me, Doc. What's the story on the body?"

"Strangled. No question. Crushed windpipe. No evidence of bullets, knives, or blunt instruments. For what it's worth, anyway. There's not much of her left."

"Help me with this, Doc. Why did we find her now? She's been missing ten months. Has she been in the river all this time?"

"I don't think so, although she's certainly been saturated for a very long time. There's a lot of sand stuck to her, along with some unpleasant plastic and rope fibres."

"Does that mean she was bound?"

"Aye," said the old Scot, whose brogue became more pronounced when he was moved. "If I had to guess . . . and Adam, I am guessing right now. But I'd say the poor wee thing was placed in a shroud, weighted and tied, and buried in sand. It would have been in, what, November?"

"Yes, sometime in November. So did he bury her in sand specifically, for some reason? Sand wouldn't freeze that early, in some years, like ordinary dirt would," Adam mused.

"Maybe he buried her too close to the river? The river doesn't normally rise in the winter, but it does in the late spring. So after the spring flow rushes in, it comes over the bank, and over time, washes her out of her grave? What do you think? Would the water eventually have removed most of the shroud? And maybe the shroud was caught on something, keeping her under in the river for longer."

"You're onto something, Davis."

"I can start with that?"

"I think you've nailed it. I'll get on this today, Adam. Let's get this bastard. With any luck I'll have your identity by noon."

"What about my other missing woman, Jack? How am I going to find her?"

"Let me talk to a forensic anthropologist I know. I'll keep you posted."

"I can't thank you enough, Jack. I mean it. Scotch coming your way."

"Don't mention it. Although perhaps, once you catch him, we can share a dram of Glendronach or two."

"I look forward to it. And I'm paying."

"Yes, Sergeant. You are."

*****

There was a knock at Adam's door, a few minutes after he hung up with the forensic pathologist.

"Come," said Adam.

The door opened to reveal Lorne Fisher.

"Got a minute, Sarge?" he asked.

"Of course. Come in, Lorne. How are you doing?"

"Uh, fine, thanks. I was kind of wondering . . . is Suzanne Genereux still out at her parents' farm?"

"Yes. She's coming back into town sometime today, and staying at Grace's again. I still don't feel comfortable with her staying alone, big dog or no big dog. Big dog did not work for Sherry Hilliard."

"Right."

There was a long pause.

"Lorne, would you like to sit down for a minute? Something on your mind?"

God, the look on his face, thought Adam.

He knew in a flash of understanding he too had worn that expression, in the long months he waited for Grace between the death of the bishop and the trial of the man who assaulted her. A great certainty hit him in the gut, along with a little jolt of joy.

"Lorne," said Adam, sympathy in his voice. "Let me help. I've been there."

Lorne Fisher sank into the chair opposite Adam, and dropped his massive head into his huge, powerful hands. Oh, oh, thought Adam; those feelings are a little more advanced than I knew.

"Do you want to tell me about it? Or should I start?" asked Adam.

Lorne nodded, presumably to the second question. Adam cleared his throat.

"As I'm sure you know, along with the rest of the police force, I fell for Grace right at the beginning of the bishop's case. I couldn't go near her personally, but I had to see her professionally. I thought I'd go crazy. So I have to warn you that Suzanne is a witness and a potential victim, as Grace was in the other case. You are working this case, and you cannot go near her. Am I clear, Lorne?"

He nodded again, miserably.

"I know," he said. "How did you deal with it?"

"I didn't deal with it very well. I did talk to someone about it, though, like you are talking to me now, and it helped. You have to gut it out, Lorne. Wait until we catch this son of a bitch. Take pride and solace in your professionalism, and know we are all doing our best to protect her, and to catch this killer. You can do it. I know you can. You are one tough bastard, Lorne Fisher."

"Not when I'm near her," he mumbled.

"What happened, Lorne?"

"I met her the night we found Sherry Hilliard, first here at the station, and then later when she fainted in the street. I caught her, and by the time I laid her on the couch I was ... God, I don't know. But why the hell would she even look at a galoot like me? Christ, I'm three times her size. Oh, shit," he ended, choking.

"Then," he continued after a moment, "at Grace's, after I followed her home from the dealership, she asked if I was her blue knight in shining armour. Later, inside, she touched my arm. I couldn't move."

Adam had to swallow hard. If someone had told him Lorne would ever, in six lifetimes, reveal his feelings like this — or even have them — Adam would have laughed the person out of the room. He was impressed.

"I know," Adam said. "I know, it's brutal, falling for a woman when you don't know what she's thinking. And for us, in some cases, the law keeps us apart from them, and you can't even ask. Look, it's pretty obvious she likes you, right? She wouldn't have touched your arm or said those things otherwise."

"Sure, she could have. You know, in thanks. She's very nice."

"No," said Adam, suppressing a laugh. Very nice, indeed. "I don't think so. I have no idea what she's feeling or thinking, Lorne, but for Christ's sake cut out the 'I'm a galoot' thing. Maybe you should see yourself through the eyes of someone else."

"Like my ex-wife?" he asked, bitterly.

"No. Of course not. But you're strong and big and a hell of a cop. Not a bad start, right? And I know I'm talking to a man who also knows how to feel, and can admit it. I couldn't do that a few years ago. I couldn't do that until a few months ago."

"Really?"

"No. I was messed up. You are not. Well, maybe about Suzanne, but not generally. Can you try to be patient, and help me solve this case? Then see what happens? Keep being a pro, Fisher," added Adam, remembering Sanjeev Kumar's advice when he was pining for Grace. "You can do it. You'll feel good about doing the right thing. Besides, if there is a possibility of a relationship, you don't want it screwed up by any disciplinary action."

Lorne sat up a little straighter, and squared his incredibly wide, muscular shoulders. Even Adam, who saw Lorne almost every day, was amazed all over again at his size; and Adam was not a small man. He smiled at his constable.

"You are one impressive guy, Fisher. I know you can wait. I know you can do this. And I know how you're feeling. I can help, if you ever need to talk again."

"Thanks, Sarge. Thanks. Thanks so much."

"Do you feel any better?"

"No. Not about Suzanne. But maybe a little better about myself."

"That's what it takes, man. Hang in there."

Adam stood up and held out his hand. It disappeared into Lorne's.

"Lorne, another thing," Adam said, a thought occurring to him. *This is the right person.* "Would you consider, if I can get this past the chief, becoming our new missing persons co-ordinator? You have what it takes. You have the smarts and the sensitivity and the cultural knowledge we need on this force, and for that job. Would you?"

"I'd sure think about it, Sarge. Thank you."

"Thank you, Lorne. And about Suzanne. It's going to be okay," Adam said. And hoped like hell he was right.

Twenty-six

At ten minutes to eleven, Adam and James rolled into customer parking at Luxury Motors in an unmarked car.

The place was impressive. All the cars were parked in tidy rows; there were no garish sales signs in the windows of the expensive, spotlessly clean vehicles. The dealership building itself was modern, with huge glass windows and an elegant logo flowing in script above the large main doors.

Adam walked around the lot for a couple of minutes and headed over to customer service. He glanced up and around, looking for evidence of the security system. Its cameras had shown no evidence of anyone absconding with Don Dunlop's Cayenne keys.

"James," he said. "We need to have a chat with Monique Delacroix. Verify Dunlop's relationship with her. Can we get it done today or tomorrow?"

"Sure. I'll see if she's in."

"Does she work here?" asked Adam, surprised.

"Yes, she does. She's the general manager and co-owner. It's a family show."

"Let's see if we can make a date with her, before we leave. There's someone else we have to talk to. The service guy."

"Right, Adam."

They approached the receptionist, identified themselves in low tones, and waited as she called her boss.

"They're here, sir," she said.

"Send them in," they heard him say over the line.

They took the stairs two at a time, and once at the top, immediately saw which office would belong to the president of the company. He rose to meet them, hand outstretched, a big smile in greeting.

"James. Great to see you again. And you, of course, are Sergeant Davis."

"Nice to meet you, Mr. Delacroix."

"Sit down, sit down. I have coffee here, or soft drinks?"

"No, thank you, I'm fine," said Adam. James accepted coffee.

"If you don't mind, I'll get right to it," said Adam, who was feeling very pressed for time. "We're here to ask you about Corey Hilliard. He has been arrested, in Winnipeg, for assault against at least three female family members. I hope you can tell us a bit more about him. I understand you worked with him in Winnipeg, at Garden City Motors."

"Arrested, for assault? Wow. Well, yes, we worked together for a few years. I decided to buy a dealership a couple of years ago and ended up here. There was less competition at the high end of the market in Saskatoon than in Winnipeg."

"I understand you hired him to do some staff training, about a year ago?"

"Yes, I did. We purged some of the sales staff. They had become, shall we say, complacent under the former owner. I hired some fresh faces, and got Corey to come down and give them some sharp lessons in selling. He's one of the best salesmen I know. You should see his numbers at Garden City."

"You didn't want to do the training yourself?"

"No. Don't have time. And frankly, Corey's better. Assault, you say?"

"Yes, against his sister and cousins. Since you know Corey, I'm sure you know it was his sister who was murdered here a couple of weeks ago."

"Yes. Terrible thing. But I never would have suspected Corey would have anything to do with it."

"His cousin was also murdered. In Winnipeg, a few days after Sherry."

Delacroix's eyes widened. "I did not know that. Terrible."

"So you see why we have to ask some questions. It's hard to imagine the deaths of these two related women would be a coincidence."

"Of course. I see. Well, what can I tell you about Corey? Like I said, one of the best salesmen I've ever had the pleasure to work with. Handsome guy, very cool; doesn't lose his head on the sales floor. What else can I tell you?"

"Did you ever go drinking with Corey?"

"Sure, a few times."

"Did you ever meet his sister or his cousin? Apparently, he would sometimes go drinking with them."

"I'm not sure. They may have come along a time or two, but there were, forgive me, often lovely ladies around."

Adam's stomach turned a bit. Nick's language reminded him of someone else.

"Do you know Shawn Hartz, sir?"

"Not well. I know who he is, and we're friendly at charity events."

"Have you ever attended one of his parties?"

"No. We're not that friendly."

"So, you've never heard a word about Corey Hilliard beating his sister or his cousin."

"Well . . . I wouldn't say that. I had no direct knowledge, but there were rumours. But they were only rumours. We weren't close friends, more like colleagues; it's not something I'd ask him about."

"Did he come back to Saskatoon in the months after the training session?"

"He did come back, briefly. A few months ago. I don't recall when."

"Did he have the run of the dealership while he was here, either time?"

"I suppose he did," said Delacroix, heaving a sigh. "I trusted him. He had security codes, keys, that sort of thing."

Adam nodded. It would indeed have been easy for Corey to snag Dunlop's car, or any car, if the timing lined up. There was no evidence that he had been in Saskatoon recently, but that didn't mean anything; he could easily have driven in, and knowing the dealership, stolen a black SUV.

But where was the connection between Corey Hilliard and the other victims?

"Was Corey Hilliard here when you first bought the dealership, Mr. Delacroix?"

"He did come by at the beginning, to check it out."

"Okay. Thank you. Appreciate your time. We'll see ourselves out."

Adam and James rose, shook Delacroix's hand, and were back in the hallway, looking surreptitiously for Monique Delacroix's office. It wasn't on the second floor, so they headed back downstairs. There, in the middle of the big showroom, was a stunning, well-groomed woman who looked like she could be her handsome brother's twin. The two officers bee-lined for her.

"Monique Delacroix?" asked Adam.

"Yes," she said. "And you are?"

"Detective Sergeant Adam Davis, and my colleague, Detective Constable James Weatherall." They showed their warrant cards, careful not to make it obvious. "Do you think we could have a private conversation?"

"About what?"

"Don Dunlop," said Adam, keeping his voice low. "And Corey Hilliard."

Monique's heavy lids closed for a moment, then fluttered back open.

"Not here," she said, very quietly. "The walls have ears."

"At the station?"

"All right."

"Later today?"

"All right. Say four?"

"That'll be fine," said Adam, handing her his card. "See you then. Come to the front and ask for me."

*****

Adam and James walked out the sales door and in the service door, where they asked the young man behind the counter for Dustin.

"That's me," he said. "What can I do for you?"

Adam showed him his warrant card.

"Is there somewhere we can talk for a few minutes?" he asked.

"Sure," said Dustin. "Come through."

Dustin led the way into a small and relatively filthy office, and shut the door.

"What's up?" he asked. "Is this about the stolen Cayenne?"

"Partly," said Adam. "First, could you please give us your full name? And what is your position here?"

"Dustin Wheeler. Assistant service manager."

"What do you know about the SUV?"

"Not much. I came in that morning, and realized it was gone. I told the bosses."

"Did you lock up as usual? Or is that your job?"

"It is my job, but one of the higher-ups checks after me."

"How often do you handle the tow trucks?"

"Never."

"But you picked up Suzanne Genereux's car two weeks ago on the highway, correct?"

"That was different. I was delivering the truck out to our dealership in Humboldt. I couldn't very well drive by the poor lady."

"How long have you worked here?"

"A year and a half," said Dustin. "I was one of the new guys hired after they bought it."

"Where were you on the night of the storm, a week ago Thursday?" Adam asked, changing up the questioning. He hoped to take the service man off guard.

Dustin thought for a moment.

"At a party. Until about two, I'd say. Then I went home. I was pretty drunk, so I slept through most of the thunder."

"Do you live alone?"

"Yes. Why are you asking me these questions?"

"We have to verify where everyone was that night. Can you give me the name of the person who held the party? Or was it a public one?"

"Yeah, it was at Prairieland Park. Big rock show. But I can give you a couple of friends' names."

"Please."

Dustin scribbled names and phone numbers on a card.

"Where did you work before Luxury Motors?" asked Adam, accepting the card.

"Dan's Service."

"Did Dan's Service have a tow truck?"

"Yeah, sure."

Tow truck. Deborah Clairmont called one. Another picked up Suzanne's car.

"Okay, Dustin. Don't leave town, okay? We'll get back to you."

"You bet, Sergeant. I'm not going anywhere. But I didn't do anything wrong."

*****

Adam had been summoned into the police chief's office to talk about the event with Terry Pearson.

Pearson and his attitude dated back to the dark days of the police service, when some officers would drive Indigenous men outside the city limits with a directive to "sober up" as they tried to find their way back to town. They were called Starlight Tours.

It often happened in the cold Prairie winter, when freezing to death was a real threat. And then it did happen, more than once. Rodney Naistus and Lawrence Wegner died of hypothermia, although no police involvement was found at their inquests.

A young Indigenous man, Neil Stonechild, had also perished in the cold, and two police officers were implicated in his death. An inquiry ensued in 2003, just a few years ago, and the city, largely, no longer trusted its police force — nor its chief, who was widely excoriated for creating the culture that allowed for the tours to take place.

The inquiry was, in part, forced by the StarPhoenix's coverage. The paper dove deeply into the crimes, and one day, after months of investigation, the news exploded, sickening an unsuspecting public. The entire front section of the paper was devoted to the roots of the problems in the police force. It all came to light thanks to the paper's city editor and a very tough, committed reporter.

The city managers were forced to respond. The chief was fired.

The Board of Police Commissioners ever afterward would choose their chiefs carefully. Those chiefs worked hard to clean up the racist elements of the force.

But neither McIvor nor Adam, who joined the force after that time, were under any delusions the situation was perfect. McIvor had organized training sessions with Elders, workshops with university professors and everything else he could think of. Adam attended them all, as had his staff. Pearson had not.

Pearson was a nauseating hangover from the 1990s and early 2000s. Adam clashed with him on every case that involved people of colour, women, and every other possible minority: he was positive that Pearson had largely ignored the Ironstand and Martin missing persons' files.

Over the last two years, the relationship had become so toxic that Adam went around him whenever possible; and although it was hardly protocol, McIvor let him.

This time, though, McIvor had to talk to Adam. He looked up when Adam knocked, and invited him to sit down.

"Pearson's complained about you," said McIvor.

"I was sure he would," said Adam.

"What happened, Adam? Come on. That's not like you."

"Did he tell you what he said?"

"He complained he couldn't reach Fisher for something, and apparently Fisher was out following your witness back to her parents' place. He said you sanctioned it, and when he questioned you, you swore at him."

"That's pretty close," said Adam, evenly. "Except he also asked if Suzanne was Fisher's 'fucking squaw.'"

"You're fucking kidding me."

"That's what I said. I admit I lost my temper. I came around the desk and let him have it. I'm not sure if it was the slur against Fisher's heritage, or against Suzanne, that set me on fire. I'm sorry, Chief. Do what you have to do."

The chief leaned back in his chair and regarded Adam, twisting a pen in his fingers.

"What the hell," he said. "Consider yourself severely reprimanded. I'll try to get it past the union, and I'll talk to Pearson again. One more time."

"Thank you, sir," said Adam. "Very much."

Adam knew he had gone too far with Pearson, regardless of his inspector's racist views. He allowed himself a deep breath of relief, and a personal promise that he would not let Pearson get under his skin again.

*****

Adam's phone rang an hour later, and he saw the Winnipeg area code. He snatched up his office phone.

"Davis."

"Adam, it's Jeannette."

"I hoped it was you. How are you, Jeannette?"

"Very well, and you, Adam?"

"Well, thanks. What's new?"

"We had another chat with Corey Hilliard. I believe we scared the ever-living hell out of him on the murder charges. He admitted physical abuse on his sister, cousins and another woman."

"Progress," said Adam.

"But, Adam, he adamantly denied ever having broken someone's bone, or hitting anyone in the face," said Jeannette. "He said he wouldn't have been so stupid, number one, since everyone can see facial bruises; and two, he admitted he's 'angry and fucked up and drinks too much,' but said he would never go that far."

"Did you believe him?"

"Adam, I did. Obviously I could be wrong, but I don't think he's a psychopath, despite his cool and cocky exterior. I think it's an act. He cracked like a little boy when we went after him in the interview. He said he had been an asshole but he had never killed anyone, and begged us to believe him."

"I trust your gut, Jeannette. Will he remain in custody?"

"Yes. We are still charging him with assault. We'll see what happens at his bail hearing. We also caught up to Angela Sinclair and put this information in front of her. She agreed she had never seen facial evidence of a beating, nor had he hit her above the torso."

"Where does his anger come from?"

"Angela described his mother as distant, depressed, self-medicating — mostly alcohol but some drugs as well. As a teen, she got into some trouble and ended up in foster homes." Jeannette sighed. "It's that terrible cycle, you know, Adam. She shouldn't have been fostered; she should have been helped.

"It all trickled down to her kids; her emotional unavailability had an effect on Sherry and Corey. They both became quite withdrawn, reserved.

"Angela described herself and her brother, Richard, as fairly well-adjusted, calmer types. Della was a little wilder; she and Sherry were thick as thieves, Angela said. Very close."

Adam was madly processing what Jeannette was saying. And he knew, suddenly, what he was looking for.

"Inspector Jeannette Villeneuve. Can I persuade you to move to Saskatoon? You're genius."

She laughed.

"Is it coming together for you, Adam?"

"It's starting to. We'll talk soon, I hope. Goodbye, Jeannette."

"Goodbye, Adam. Best of luck."

Adam turned to his computer, to see a message from James.

"Let me know when free," it said. "News."

"Free now," Adam wrote.

James was at the door in less than a minute.

"Shawn Hartz claims he never hired Alexis Ironstand to, ah, help out at one of his parties," he said. "He claims he had never seen her, at the clinic or elsewhere."

"Shit. Okay. Well, the connection is at the clinic, but not via Hartz. If he's telling the truth, of course. Has he coughed up his guest list?"

"Yeah, he finally emailed it; I sent it to you a few minutes ago while you were on the phone. Adam, you won't believe some of the names on there. I have to admit I started looking for the ones I didn't want to see — you know, the chief, the mayor — and I didn't find them. Thank God. There is one city councillor, though, and a few very prominent guys . . . "

"Is Dunlop on there?" Adam interrupted.

"No."

"Delacroix?"

"No. But Adam . . . Pearson's on there."

Twenty-seven

Jesus, thought Adam. Pearson, an inspector in the police force, attended Hartz's parties. Did the man have no respect, no scruples?

A knock at the door was immediately followed by Joan Karpinski's head.

"Hey Sarge, James, Monique Delacroix is here. You wanted to see her?"

"Yes. Could you take her into the interview room, and please stay? It might make her a bit more comfortable to have a woman officer in the room. We're going to be asking her some intimate questions."

Adam greeted Monique Delacroix, and felt the hairs on the back of his neck standing up. He was sure she held a crucial piece of evidence.

"Welcome, Ms. Delacroix," said Adam. "Thank you for coming down. Can we offer you something? Water, coffee, soft drink?"

"No, thank you. I'm fine."

"As you know, we are investigating the murder of Sherry Hilliard at her home about two weeks ago."

"Yes."

"Do you know Don Dunlop had a relationship with Ms. Hilliard?"

"I do. He told me after you interviewed him. For obvious reasons."

"How long have you been seeing Dr. Dunlop, Ms. Delacroix?"

"A couple of months."

"Where did you meet?"

"We had met several times, usually at business or charity events. I think the first time was at a hospital charity dinner. I've also seen him on the lot, although I've never dealt with him directly."

"How were you introduced?"

"Nick introduced us. Obviously, they know each other. Nick tends to get to know his most valued customers."

"Were you with Dr. Dunlop the night of Ms. Hilliard's murder?"

"We were together most of the night, but not all of it. He felt he had to go home. Ashley, you know; bad idea to make her too suspicious, Don thinks, although I personally feel it's far too late for that."

"Did you see or speak to him after he left?"

"No."

"How close are you and Dr. Dunlop?"

"If you're asking whether we're having sex, Detective, yes, we are."

"And you feel his wife is aware of it."

"I do. She obviously knows about Sherry, too, since her husband is the prime suspect."

Yes, she does, thought Adam. But when did she find out?

"Ms. Delacroix, do you know Ashley Dunlop at all?"

"I've met her at these functions. Just to say hello to, a little small talk. I try to avoid her now."

"Did you know Sherry Hilliard was pregnant when she was killed?"

"Yes. Don told me. He was very upset."

"Did he tell his wife?"

"Yes. I think he had to. She caught him talking to Sherry on the phone. I don't know when. He had no choice, I gather, but to tell her."

If Monique was accurate, Sherry was not blackmailing Dunlop, eliminating that motive.

"You seem to have a very open relationship."

"Let's just say Don has needed some support, Detective Sergeant. I've been willing to give it to him."

Adam raised an eyebrow. Monique Delacroix sighed.

"I also told him there would be no relationship if he lied to me."

"Why are you with him, Ms. Delacroix? What's the attraction? If you'll forgive me, he is a married man, with a propensity for serial affairs."

"There's more to Don than you might think. Sure, I wish he wasn't married, but it's also not really a marriage anymore, not for him."

"You are being very forthcoming, Ms. Delacroix, and we greatly appreciate it. Can you tell me why?"

"Don Dunlop, Sergeant, may not be a prince among men in some ways," she replied. "But I'll put the dealership up against him being a killer. He didn't do it. I won't lie for him, but I believe truth finds a way. Maybe my testimony will help clear him.

"And, Sergeant, I am in love with him."

*****

Adam was at Grace's door by six forty-five, holding an enormous bouquet of red roses and white chrysanthemums, and a bottle of Napa Valley wine.

He knocked, feeling a little like a suitor meeting a family member. Suzanne's opinion of him was going to matter, certainly to him and likely to Grace, too. A butterfly teased his stomach.

Grace swung the door open, looking like the slightly-windblown and delicious flower he always saw in his mind's eye. Her lips parted when she saw the bouquet.

"Adam, they're beautiful, thank you . . . but come in. Quickly."

"Quickly, Grace?"

"Suzanne is walking Bruno. And you, lovely man, are early."

"What? Oh!" said Adam, getting it, and immediately rising to the challenge.

Grace relieved Adam of the flowers and wine, placed them on the table, took his hand and led him firmly down the hallway. She closed the door to the bedroom, turned, and they fell on each other, lips and tongues meeting hungrily.

"Adam, do you think we could . . . ?"

"Yes. Quickly?"

"Yes." Grace rapidly undid his shirt buttons and yanked the fabric back.

"I missed you, Grace," Adam said, a little out of breath, watching her undress him. "Two days were two too long."

"I missed you, beautiful man," said Grace, mumbling a bit since her tongue was tracing his pectoral muscle. She licked his nipple.

Adam groaned. "You're getting ahead of me."

He peeled off her sundress; she pushed his jeans down, and they were suddenly on the bed, raging and pushing and trying to consume each other. Five minutes of madness, but it was enough. After a moment of panting and staring into each other's eyes, they both started laughing.

"Hopefully, this will keep us going for . . . how long, Adam?"

"I don't know. I hope not long. When Suzanne can go home, we can . . . figure things out. I feel like something is going to break, Babe. I feel like I've eliminated some suspects. If the, uh, longing gets too much, you could pop over one evening?"

"Beware. I'll take you up on that."

"Please, Grace. Please do."

*****

"How well do you know Lorne Fisher?" Grace asked Adam as they prepared the meal and waited for Suzanne.

Adam inclined his head. "Fisher? Why?"

Grace told him about the day Sherry Hilliard had been murdered, and how sweetly he had treated Suzanne, and the expression she saw on his face. Longing. Wondering.

"I know that expression," she told Adam. "I felt it on my face all the time, in the three months we waited for my attacker to go to trial."

"Oh, Grace," said Adam, who had thought the very same thing. He cleared his throat, and said quietly, "Thank you for telling me."

There was a quiet moment as Adam collected himself, forced his heart to stop pounding.

"Fisher. Well, he's an interesting character. Man of few words, most of the time. Hell of a cop. We tease him a bit about his size, you know? He's the biggest guy on the force, by a wide margin. Works out like a madman.

"He comes in pretty handy. I gather from Joan Karpinski he broke down Sherry Hilliard's door like it was made of toothpicks; and you'll remember he took most of James's weight when we carried him out of that basement in Westmoreland, after he was shot. I was feeling pretty shaky, too, from the head wound.

"I wish they had used the ram, of course, on Ms. Hilliard's door; I don't want my people hurting themselves. But it saved a few minutes and Lorne, of course, was fine. He's a little younger than I am; he's been a cop seven years, I think. Great work ethic. A bit of a rough exterior, at times, but a softie inside. Especially with women.

"He's from the Prince Albert area, originally. I heard about him through the police grapevine, and went up to P.A. to meet him. I persuaded him to come to Saskatoon. We don't have enough Indigenous cops, as you know — which might be the understatement of the decade — and Fisher is fantastic. We badly wanted him."

"Fisher? Is he Métis?" Grace wondered, because of the name.

"That's something I wonder about. When is it appropriate to describe someone's heritage as Métis? As I understand it, it's only correct if you're from Red River ancestry. Fisher's father is German, a farmer — a massive man, just like Lorne — and I gather the family took the 'c' out of Fischer when they came to Canada. His mother is First Nations. Cree. He is part-Indigenous, I guess."

"We struggle with it at the paper, too," said Grace. "It's important to be culturally sensitive and to use the right language. Sherry Hilliard, too. She was Scottish and First Nations.

"Is Lorne married? Divorced? Girlfriend?" asked Grace, feeling it was a horribly nosy question. But she had to know.

"Divorced. She didn't treat him very well, if I remember correctly. He's been on his own for about three years now."

By the time Suzanne and Bruno appeared, ten minutes later, Grace and Adam were ready to put the meat on the grill.

"Suzé!" Grace greeted her friend. "And Bruno. Meet Adam Davis. Adam, this is Suzanne and, of course, the great Bruno," she added, patting the big dog.

The lover and the friend shook hands, murmuring the usual pleasantries, as Bruno snuffled and evaluated this new person in his life . . . until Suzanne reached up and gave Adam a very big hug.

"Thank you, Adam," she said.

"For what?" he asked, startled.

"For Grace. And for me. You know what I mean."

His eyes searched Suzanne's.

"Thank you," he said, a little unsteadily. "You're a wonderful friend to Grace. I'm honoured by your hug."

Grace's eyes were blurring. I am so stupid lucky, she thought, to have this wonderful friend and incredible lover. They both heard her sniff behind them.

"Oh, Grace," they said, more or less in unison, and turned to her.

"Hugfest," she said, drying her eyes and laughing, after four arms enveloped her. "Okay, you two. Let's get dinner down us."

They cooked and ate, leaving the case aside, and chatted and laughed, and fluffed Bruno's head from time to time. After dinner, Grace stood, and said, "I'll clear this up. You two talk."

They both protested, but Grace was firm.

"Talk. Suzanne has something to tell you, Adam."

"Suzanne. What is it?"

"I am sometimes an idiot. Your Lorne Fisher told me, for example, never to leave my house keys with anyone, such as at the dealership when my car was being repaired. I actually did that.

"However," she continued, "I am, in other ways, very together. I keep track of all my expenses, *comprends*? I have a business to run, and while I am happy to remit my taxes — to pay for excellent policing, *oui*? — I do not want to contribute more than my share. Therefore, I have all of my receipts, organized in files, and I also keep track of them on my computer."

Adam knew what she was going to say. *Oh, my God.* But he waited for her to continue.

"It occurred to me, and perhaps should have sooner, to check those receipts. I have never put diesel fuel into my Honda." Suzanne's face was white. "I cannot find any evidence I have ever done so."

"Someone did it for you."

"I believe so. Yes."

"At a gas station, do you think? Or by jerry can?"

"I fill up regularly at two stations, one on Eighth Street and one on Broadway. I don't even know if they have diesel; I've never noticed. But it would have to have been the last time I did so, right? For it to have effect, at that time, on my car?"

"Yes."

"Here is the receipt," she said, handing it over. "I don't know if there could be an error of some kind, but it shows gasoline, *oui*?"

"We will be there tomorrow," said Adam, looking at the address on the receipt. "Was there a time you can recall when someone might have used a jerry can?"

Suzanne thought back to the morning she packed up before going to the farm.

"I stopped at home to pick up some work equipment on the Monday after Sherry's death," she said. "I was only home for about fifteen minutes, so I didn't put the car in the garage."

That would do it, thought Adam.

"Very helpful, Suzanne, thank you. I also have a couple of questions about Sherry," he continued. "How well did you know each other? I know you've said you knew very little about her personal life."

"We were neighbours, and very friendly, but not what I would call friends," said Suzanne. "I think she had a lover when she first came to Saskatoon, but she mentioned no one by name. Then there was no one for a little while; then she had another relationship. Then no one again for, oh, about three months. And she did tell me that."

So there was someone else, earlier. Adam made a mental note.

"I'm going to show you some photos, Suzanne. None of them will show anything upsetting, but two of them are of deceased people. Are you all right with taking a look?"

"Yes. Yes, of course. Anything I can do to help."

He went to his black leather bag, and pulled out a fat file. He laid photos and newspaper clippings all over the kitchen table, but said nothing. The names of the people in the newspaper photographs had been clipped off, and removed from the bottoms of the photos.

There were images of the missing women, Don Dunlop, Corey Hilliard, Della and Angela Sinclair, and the StarPhoenix clipping of Shawn Hartz. They had no photo of him, since he had not provided one; nor had they arrested him for anything. Yet.

Suzanne pulled her heavy hair back, bent at the waist and pored over the photos, slowly shaking her head.

"This one," she said after a moment, pointing at Della. "Is this Sherry's sister?"

"No," Adam said. "Her cousin."

"Oh," said Suzanne. "They could almost be twins. Is she . . . all right?"

"No."

"Oh. *Désolée*." She didn't ask any more questions.

She kept looking. A few seconds later she stopped, hovering over the newspaper clipping. She picked it up and peered at it.

"Adam," she said. "Who is this?"

"Why? Do you recognize her?"

"I do. I think so. It's a bit small, but I think so."

"Where do you recognize her from, Suzanne?"

"She came to Sherry's one day. Sherry wasn't home, and I was walking out the door to see a client when I heard her knocking. The noise made me look around. I told her I thought Sherry was out; she nodded, said okay, and dropped something in the mailbox. Just delivering something, she said, then turned and walked away, rather quickly. I only saw her face for a few seconds, but she was beautiful. And so, I noticed."

The woman Suzanne recognized was standing behind Shawn Hartz in the photo taken at a charity event and published in the local newspaper.

It was Ashley Dunlop.

Twenty-eight

If Adam had his way, he was going to pick up Ashley Dunlop now. Right now. What had she done?

He called James.

"Hey, partner. Are you available?"

"I might be," said James, who had had one whole sip of beer and was ready for dinner. "What's up?"

"We have to try to pick up Ashley Dunlop. Can you attend?"

"What? What's happened?"

"I'll tell you on the way. Can I pick you up in ten? You're between Grace's and the Dunlops' place."

"I'll be ready."

Adam apologized to Grace and Suzanne, kissed Grace swiftly and was out the door less than a minute after Suzanne identified Ashley in the newspaper clipping. Since he was driving his own car, he called the station and asked for a cruiser to meet him at the Dunlop home.

James was waiting outside and jumped into Adam's car ten minutes later.

"What the hell is going on?" he demanded.

"Suzanne recognized Ashley Dunlop in the newspaper photo with Shawn Hartz," Adam said. "She recognized her, because Ashley Dunlop has been to Sherry Hilliard's home. Suzanne saw her banging on the door."

"What? Holy shit, Adam. Have we been wrong all along? Can the killer be a woman? It can't be, can it? Of course, we haven't found any semen, but we assumed it was because the killer sensibly wore a condom. Could she have raped her with something? Could she be strong enough to carry Sherry into the basement, or strangle Emily Martin? Fuck, this is wild."

"It's hard to imagine our killer being Ashley, and Deborah Clairmont was definitely raped by a man. But Ashley knew Dunlop was having an affair with Sherry," said Adam. "She knew, according to Monique Delacroix, that Sherry was pregnant; and she was at her house. There's motive. It's enough to bring her in."

Adam drove as fast as he could, south from James and Bruce's home to the Dunlop residence, arriving at the same time as the cruiser, populated by Lorne Fisher.

"Heard the call, Lorne?" asked Adam.

"Yeah," said the man who wanted this case to be solved yesterday.

"Okay. Let's go get her."

Adam rang the doorbell, and heard steps coming down the hallway. Ashley Dunlop opened the door, and started the sentence, "What the hell are you doing here?" when Adam interrupted.

"Mrs. Dunlop. We are here to talk to you about the murder of Sherry Hilliard. May we come in?"

"No. Fuck you. You've caused enough problems."

"It may be wise for you to talk to us, Mrs. Dunlop. We know you have visited Sherry Hilliard at her home." That wasn't precisely true, but it would do, Adam thought.

"Bullshit. You know shit. I'm not talking to you! I'm not coming with you!" she screamed, backing up into the hallway, bent over with fury, rage contorting her face. She looked around wildly, and spying a bronze statue on a nearby table, picked it up and held it in front of her.

"That's not necessary, Mrs. Dunlop. Please, calm down," said Adam, advancing on her slowly.

But Ashley Dunlop was beside herself. She hurled the heavy artwork at Adam, who was forced to deke to his left to avoid being smacked in the head. It banged into his shoulder and clattered to the floor as Ashley Dunlop took off down the hallway.

But Adam caught her, cuffed her and dragged her screaming and squirming into the cruiser.

"It didn't have to be this way," he said. "Ashley Dunlop, you are under arrest for assaulting a police officer."

Lorne Fisher sat in the back with the crazed woman, as James took the wheel of the cruiser and drove back downtown to the station, with Adam following in his own car.

His shoulder hurt.

*****

Ashley Dunlop wouldn't say a word until her lawyer appeared, so James gave her a phone, let her make the call and put her in a cell.

Adam went into his office, removed his shirt and inspected his shoulder, which was indeed developing a large bruise above the blue scar marking the place where he'd been shot. He shivered.

He put his shirt back on and went in search of ice.

Then he called Grace to tell her he would not be able to return. He could hardly get the words out.

*****

Richard Sealey came, and had an extremely difficult time calming Ashley Dunlop down enough to get her to make sense. He explained he could not represent both her and her husband in this case, which sent her into a second meltdown, screaming her head off in the interview room. Sealey told her he would find her a lawyer as soon as possible, and got the hell out of there.

An hour later, a lawyer from a different firm appeared. Fifteen minutes later, she summoned Adam.

"I think I have her calmed down enough to talk," said Diana Elliott, known in legal circles for her success in family law. She was a great negotiator.

"Thanks, Di," said Adam. They knew each other fairly well, having crossed paths several times on domestics. "Meet you in interview room two."

Ashley Dunlop was quieter, but sullen. Once the obligatory recording device was set up and Adam had identified everyone in the room, he started in.

"Mrs. Dunlop. We have information you have been to the home of Sherry Hilliard. What can you tell us about that?"

"Nothing. Maybe you should ask my husband," she spat.

"We have indeed spoken to your husband, as you are well aware." Adam felt a spear of inspiration. "You didn't call the lawyer the day we arrested him, did you?"

"Of course I did."

"But not for a long time. Mr. Sealey didn't appear for quite a while. Why?"

The woman chewed on her lip for a moment, but then her anger broke through.

"Bastard. He was cheating on me. Fucker. Fucker! I didn't give a shit how long it took for his stupid lawyer to show up. Served him right to spend some time in jail."

"You knew he was having a relationship with Sherry Hilliard. You knew she was pregnant. You went to visit her. Is that correct?"

"Yes, I knew. I also know he has some new bitch he's fucking."

Adam suppressed a sigh.

"You went to visit her shortly before she was killed."

"So?"

"She wasn't home. What did you put in her mailbox?"

"A little letter. Telling her to fuck off."

"Did you visit her at a later time?"

"Nnn . . . no."

"You don't sound very sure. I put it to you that you did visit Sherry Hilliard. Why?"

"I didn't."

Diana Elliott put up a hand to temporarily stop Adam's next question, leaned over and whispered in her client's ear. Ashley Dunlop went white, with an unbecoming blotch of red patching her face.

"No. I won't," said Ashley to her lawyer, voice rising.

"I can't force you," said Diana Elliott, "but I'm advising you. Tell him. This could get a lot worse, Ashley."

"Fuck. Fine. I did visit her that night."

"Why?" asked Adam.

"I wanted to tell her never to see my husband again. Never to bring her bastard brat anywhere near him, or me."

"She had already broken off the relationship with Dr. Dunlop. Why was it necessary to have this conversation?"

"Sure, she broke it off, but how long was that going to last? Stupid little bitch could easily have asked for child support, and told everybody about how it was Don's kid. I wanted to warn her."

"You wanted to scare her. Did you?"

"Yes, I fucking wanted to scare her. Badly enough so we'd never hear from her again."

"And did you? Scare her?

Another long pause. Diana Elliott touched Ashley Dunlop on the arm, and gave her a warning look. "Talk, Ashley."

"Yes. I scared her. I told her never to come near us or she would regret it. Then I . . . I pushed her."

"How hard did you push her?"

"She fell. Banged her head on the coffee table."

"Was she unconscious?"

"For a while."

"Did you rape Sherry Hilliard, Mrs. Dunlop?"

"What the fuck do you mean?"

"Did you rape her? With a . . ." Adam was having trouble finding a word for it. "A device."

"No! I didn't! What the fuck do you think I am? I only pushed her! She was breathing when I left. I swear to God, Detective."

"But you didn't call an ambulance."

"No. She was breathing."

"Because you did not call an ambulance, Sherry Hilliard was home, and even more vulnerable when someone came to finish the job, instead of in the hospital. And now, she is dead. You are under arrest, Ashley Dunlop, for aggravated assault."

*****

Adam turned the woman over to the staff sergeant for processing, thinking he had seldom met anyone he disliked as much as Ashley Dunlop.

He walked home, occasionally feeling his shoulder, and knew what awaited him in the night.

Once in his condo, he pulled out a bottle and poured two ounces of Scotch into a glass, then downed it and poured another. He sat alone in the dark, on his gleaming black leather couch, head in his hands, wondering how people could be so fucking stupid and vindictive. Ashley Dunlop had hurt Sherry Hilliard, but then had the chance to save her life, and didn't. Jesus Christ.

And what was he doing here, in this plate-glass and chrome condo, which had never felt like home, even after six years? It held no comfort for him. It belonged to someone else, a former self Adam no longer recognized.

He was a farm boy. A kid brought up by loving parents who supported him, dragged him through the hard times and gave him hell when he needed it. How did he turn into a fucked-up, womanizing jerk in a glass house?

Now, he wanted to be a better man. For himself, and for Grace. But his past kept screwing things up. How could he control his temper, when the smallest reminder of the bad time set him off? And the condo was a continual reminder, his own strange prison. How could he move beyond his nightmares, and be with Grace whenever he wanted?

He drained his glass and suddenly threw it at full power into the open kitchen, where it hit a cupboard door, fell and shattered on the granite countertop. It wasn't enough. He picked up a tall island chair and flung it across the room, where it smashed into pieces against the concrete wall.

He was looking for the next victim when his intercom buzzed. What the hell? It was midnight, Adam noticed, when the noise surprised him out of his fury.

"Yes."

"Adam, it's me."

"Go home, Grace. It's late."

"No. Let me in."

"No."

"Let me in. I want to see you."

"I don't want you to see me right now. Like this."

"Like what? Adam, what is going on? Let me in this minute, goddamn it. If you don't I will call the police."

"I am the police."

"No. You're not the only goddamn detective sergeant on the Saskatoon police force. Not to mention all the other officers. You said so yourself. Let me in now. I mean it."

"You would really do that."

"Yes. Don't try me. I heard your voice when you called earlier. Something is wrong. Now. Let. Me. In."

Adam looked around the condo, at the destruction he had begun to wreak, and wondered what Grace would make of it. *Hell.* This tantrum was happening while he was awake. That made him fully responsible.

Grace buzzed again. And Adam, feeling his anger drain out of his muscles, pushed the entry button.

She was at his door in less than a minute, banging on it with her fist.

"Adam. Let me in."

He did. Grace stepped in, kicked the door shut behind her and took him into her arms.

"I'm not leaving this time," she said. "Don't even try me."

Twenty-nine

Early the next morning, Grace awakened and turned to Adam. His eyes were already open.

"How are you feeling, Adam?" she asked, as softly and tenderly as a mother.

"Better. Thanks to you. She got to me, Grace," Adam said, turning toward her and flinching as he leaned on his shoulder. "Sherry Hilliard didn't have to die. She could have been in the hospital when her killer arrived."

"I know, Adam. It's heartbreaking. Your shoulder hurts, doesn't it?"

"More than it should. Because it reminds me." Of being shot.

"Ice it again, before you go to work."

It had been a crazy night. Grace had grabbed Adam and held him as he shook in her arms, the fury seeping out, shame over his tantrum creeping in, the disgust over Ashley Dunlop's actions rippling through his body.

"I lost my temper. Grace, I'm so sorry," said Adam, when he had calmed down enough.

"I've thrown things," she said. "I threw a stainless steel pepper mill weighing three pounds against the back door once. Which made a poor substitute for Mick. And it made quite the hole."

Adam didn't laugh, though. A woman throwing a pepper mill was not equivalent to a man in an uncontrollable fury. Grace read his face.

"You would never have touched me, Adam. I know it as sure as I'm alive."

"Oh, Babe."

"It's okay, Adam. We're okay now. I'm staying with you. It's going to be fine."

Adam wasn't so sure about that.

*****

"James," said Adam, leaning over his desk later that morning. "What have we learned about Dustin Wheeler?"

"I've reached two of his friends. I sure as hell wish we had witnesses other than friends. Both said he was extremely drunk. One said he drove Dustin home, got him inside, and left. It was about two in the morning."

"And Sherry's murder was between two-thirty and four a.m., and likely close to three, based on Suzanne's evidence. He could still have done it. I don't like the tow truck connection."

"I know. If his friend is telling the truth, he would have been too drunk to kill someone, drag her into the basement, and cover his tracks. If he was faking, it's perfect timing."

"Have you pulled his sheet?"

"Yeah. One charge," said James, with a strange grin. "Impaired driving, a few years ago."

"That fits, then. Maybe he's smartened up and doesn't drive to parties anymore."

"Kind of looks like it. Unless his friend is covering for him."

*****

Adam went alone to the women's low-security prison. At reception, he was greeted by Elder Eileen Bear, a spectacularly beautiful woman with dramatic, long, thick greying hair peppered with black. Regal, was Adam's first thought. Her bearing was regal.

"*Tanisi*, Adam Davis," said the elder. "Welcome. I am very glad you are here."

"I am honoured to meet you, and to be here," said Adam, taking in her wise and smiling eyes as he shook her hand. "Thank you very much for seeing me."

"Justice Lafond," said Eileen Bear, "is on her way. She was held up by a bail hearing."

Adam knew all about that. Ashley Dunlop.

"Shall we take a tour, first?" suggested the Elder. "We can walk and talk together."

"Yes, thank you."

She walked him through the commons, including a cafeteria, a crafting area, a gym, and then out into the garden. There was also a large therapy room fully populated with women participating in a group session.

"I can take you through because all of our women are in the session," explained Bear. "That's why I asked you to come at ten."

"How many women do you have, presently?"

"Thirty. We work with them very closely. Therapy comes in many forms, Detective. Talking. Exploring one's creativity. Participating in life — they are all given tasks, such as laundry, cooking, making beds. But they never do the real grunt work, like cleaning bathrooms or mopping the long hallways. We take care of those jobs with janitorial services. They don't need it."

"Tell me about one of them. Tell me what brings her here."

"I will tell you about 'Susan.'"

Bear described the woman's hideous marriage, the beatings, the drinking, and the murder.

"She couldn't take any more. One night, her husband came home in a drunken fury, as he had so many times before. On this night, he had a weapon. But he was intoxicated, and Susan was not. She stabbed him, and he died. And now, she is here.

"This is the cycle of abuse, Detective. Susan's husband came from a dysfunctional family, where his father beat him. And his father was beaten and otherwise abused at a residential school. So, Detective. Where does the fault lie? It lies in our past. It lies in our present. It lies in our system. Susan's husband had deep scars, but did they give him permission to hurt her? In the last moment, when he tried but failed to hurt Susan again, and she ended his life, where did her fault lie?"

"Why is she even here?" asked Adam. "Was it not self-defence?"

"Not in the eyes of the justice system, Detective. She wielded a knife. He held a statue."

Adam immediately relived Ashley Dunlop hurling her own bronze artwork at him, just last night. But he could cuff her and drag her away. Susan couldn't have done that.

"The two weapons were not considered equal," Elder Bear continued. "She was convicted of manslaughter. I'm not convinced it was a fair finding."

"Why do they stay with these men?"

"Love. Kids. Money. Nowhere to go. Is it better to be homeless, take your children onto the streets, or be beaten every week? How do you make those decisions?"

A young woman was approaching them. "Elder Bear, Justice Lafond has arrived. She's in your office."

"Thank you, Andrea. We're on our way."

Adam had testified before Justice Deborah Lafond many times, and they greeted each other with familiarity.

"What can we do for you, Detective?" asked Lafond, who was used to getting down to business.

"I came for a clearer understanding of what women, particularly Indigenous women, are facing, in terms of violence, domestically and otherwise," said Adam. "Elder Bear has been very helpful. But I have an immediate and difficult problem. I believe we are seeking a serial killer of women, many of them Métis and First Nations. The women are young, petite, dark, and either employed or taking education. We haven't found any victims of this killer who are living on the street.

"I don't think the killer is Indigenous, for several reasons; among them, that most serial killers are white men. But why is he doing this? Who am I looking for? Can you help me?"

Adam felt he had stripped the women's faces bare with his words, so horrified were their expressions. He could hear them thinking, *oh, my God.*

"I'm sorry," he said quickly. "I don't pretend to know how upsetting this is for you; it must be terrible. But I need your help. I have to catch this man."

Adam laid it out for them, as gently as he could.

"Obviously, he's a psychopath, or a very, very disturbed human being in some other way. But why is he choosing to kill Indigenous and other women, all of whom look much the same, on a serial basis?"

"You know, Detective, about the Highway of Tears in British Columbia," started Eileen Bear. Adam nodded. *Right.* Most of the women who had disappeared along the infamous highway were Indigenous, but not all. The other women were marginalized, poor, isolated, addicted, abused.

"You know Indigenous women are more vulnerable, in countless ways, than most people in society. I'm sure you also realize when an Indigenous woman goes missing, it sometimes takes longer for it to be noticed; and much more often, to be taken seriously. Many police forces — including your own, sir — will think she simply ran away. Or she will eventually show up on her reserve. Or she's a street worker, or a drug addict; she will be hard to find, so why bother?

"This may be at work with your case. How long did it take for the disappearance of Alexis Ironstand to become a serious case file?" she asked.

Adam didn't know the answer, since neither Ironstand nor Martin had been his cases; but he was damned well going to find out from Terry Pearson. That fucker.

"And then your killer leaves Sherry Hilliard in her basement, thinking no one would care to find her for a few days, and he would be long gone, along with much of the evidence. So let's say it's easier to kill Indigenous women, and not be caught."

"I don't have to tell you, Detective," added the judge, "the colder the case gets, the less likely it will ever be solved. Killers know that too. They also get cockier; if you didn't catch them the first time, the second time, the third time, why would you catch them the fourth or fifth? Then we have more dead women. As to his motive, Detective, I can't imagine."

"How many serial killers have there been in or around Saskatoon, Your Honour?" Adam asked. "Have any appeared before you?"

"There was one a few years ago," she said. "He was always on the move; he had killed women in three provinces, but we ultimately caught him here. And there was your very own bishop murderer, although he was not a serial killer, by definition, even though he killed three people. He kept killing to cover his secrets. There was also David Threinen, in the mid-1970s, who killed four children.

"Serial killers like to change locations, usually, Adam," she added. "Although not necessarily by large distances, as the Threinen case showed."

Adam knew that, but hearing it from Justice Lafond turned a light on in his brain. Alexis Ironstand was not in, or near, the South Saskatchewan River. She was somewhere else. He was sure.

"What about Emily Martin and Deborah Clairmont? They look very similar to the Indigenous women, but one is English and the other French by descent."

"Men often kill to type, Adam," said Lafond. "You have to look for why the other women are marginalized, or isolated somehow, or perhaps living in poverty. It has to be fairly easy for him to find them, and get to them; maybe he culls them from their groups. Is he a misogynist? A racist? An opportunist? Or all three?"

"Any thoughts on why there's a connection to water, or storms?" Adam asked.

"He could connect water with something terrible in his past," said Justice Lafond. "Perhaps he almost drowned? Or someone he loved drowned? Or, could it be some warped cleansing ritual? For example, if he is washed by water during the crimes, or if the victim is, has he been somehow absolved? Or, has she?"

The first motivation had occurred to Adam, too, especially after talking to Grace about the children in the domestic case she had covered. But not the second.

It was his turn to look like he had been blanched by disgust and horror. He could not imagine this man being absolved, nor his warped arrogance over absolving others.

Eileen Bear reached out to Adam, her eyes deep wells of sadness, and took his hand.

"This is our River of Tears, Detective."

*****

Before Adam left the women's prison, Eileen Bear took sweetgrass down from a high shelf in her office, lit it, and brought it over to him. She showed Adam how to cup the smoke in his hands, and waft it over his face and shoulders.

She murmured in Cree as the small smudging ceremony took place, and told Adam afterward what she had said.

"You have a sadness within, that you carry everywhere. But you also have found a great passion, at great emotional risk. You must carry those together. They will help you understand.

"I have blessed you. I have asked the Creator to make you strong for us, and for our sisters. We do not have enough of our own warriors in your world. Not yet."

The Elder paused.

"Detective Davis. I know your police force has made some strides in the last few years. But there is much more to do. You need Indigenous cops, and you need Indigenous women cops. There must be greater sympathy and understanding. Your society exists on our lands, but we are ignored upon them.

"Your presence here tells me you are doing your best, and I appreciate it. But more must be done. I'm counting on you."

Aside from his experiences with Grace, Adam had never been so moved in his life. Nor had he felt the weight of responsibility so heavily. He felt his spirit shudder within him as he looked into the Elder's eyes, heard her words. What had Grace called Eileen Bear? A pragmatic mystic. A perfect description.

He bowed his head to the Elder. "I will move heaven and earth and water to stop this man."

*****

Immediately, he moved on his vow.

"Chief, it's Adam. Do you have a moment?"

"Sergeant. How are you doing? I heard about your shoulder. That woman sounds like a piece of work."

"I'm doing okay, thanks. Chief, I'm wondering how hard it would be to get a boat out to Pike Lake and Blackstrap."

"What are you searching for?"

"Anything that looks like a grave. It will be near the shore."

"You've got to be kidding. Do you know how long those shorelines are?"

Both Pike Lake and Blackstrap Lake were very long, narrow bodies of water, which posed some problems; but Adam still thought it was worth a shot.

"I know it sounds crazy, but hear me out. I talked to McDougall about this, and he talked to a forensic anthropologist. I know what we're looking for. I have a strong feeling our other victim, the one still missing, is at either of those lakes."

"Or at any slough or pond in southern Saskatchewan."

"It's possible, but I don't think so. I think this guy takes the women out somewhere. Makes nice, does dinner or drinks or something. He's not going to end up on a farm or in a ditch. He acts the Lothario. He pretends to himself he's looking for someone special, but of course she never measures up. No one could. He becomes furious. He intentionally creates anger within himself."

"What about the first victim? He didn't take her out somewhere."

"Practice. As he goes along, things change. He tried the first attack in a park, but screwed up because he was in too public a place. Someone came along and he didn't get it done. Now he meets these women first, controls the situation. He thinks about the murder scene, and how to get rid of the bodies. He doesn't pick them up on the street."

Chief McIvor heaved a sigh.

"I can't believe I'm agreeing to this," he said. "Okay. Prep the guys and get them out to whichever lakes you want. You have four hours of boat time. I'll clear it with Pearson so he doesn't freak on you if he finds out you asked me first."

"Thanks, Chief. I know it sounds ridiculous. But they can avoid all the heavy traffic areas; she won't be near a cabin, or a store, or a boat launch. We have to try. We might get lucky."

"I guess that narrows it down." He sounded unconvinced. "A bit. Good luck with this, Adam."

*****

Joan Karpinski popped into his office with updates later in the afternoon.

Ashley Dunlop had not made bail. She freaked out in court, and Justice Deborah Lafond was forced to shout, "Remanded into custody. Get a grip on yourself, Mrs. Dunlop."

Probing the tender spot on his shoulder, Adam had to admit the ruling made his day, to the extent possible.

"And Sherry Hilliard's baby was Dunlop's," Joan said. "They've confirmed it."

"Okay, thanks," said Adam, somewhat absently. Somehow, it didn't seem to matter anymore. Both Don and Ashley Dunlop believed Sherry's child was his, and that was the point.

Adam roamed through files, stewing, trying to force his brain to concentrate, to put the pieces together. He tried not to will the phone to ring, with news from the officers in the boat.

Another rap, and James was at the door.

"I hope you haven't forgotten about our pool party," he said, sticking his head in.

"Shit. I haven't. But I did forget to tell Grace."

"Ah. Will you bring her?"

"Yes. It's time."

"Coming out, then?"

"You could put it that way," said Adam, a thrill sliding up his spine. "I'll call her right now. Thanks for the reminder. I'm a little distracted."

"I don't blame you. See you at seven-thirty or so?"

"Yes. Later, James."

Adam dialled Grace's work number.

"Babe," he greeted her. "How's work?"

"Fine. How are you feeling, Adam?"

"Sore. Okay. But listen, I forgot to tell you yesterday James and Bruce have invited us to their pool party tonight. The weather's holding, so they're going impromptu."

"Us?" asked Grace.

"Yes," Adam said, firmly. "Us. Would you like to go?"

"Yes. Sounds divine. A party with water."

"I'll pick you up at seven, if that's okay?"

"Perfect. Will we eat there, then, Adam?"

"It's a barbecue, too. See you later, beautiful."

A party with water. Grace's words chimed with Adam. With *water*.

And then the phone did ring, but it wasn't a constable of the police service on the line. It was Jack McDougall.

"Jack. What's up?" asked Adam, after the pathologist identified himself.

"Adam. We've found your victim."

"What the hell? What are you doing out there? Where are you?"

"I have a cabin at Pike Lake. After I talked to you about where your victim might be, I decided to knock off early today, take a little canoe ride. There's an area up the shore where an unused dock sits. The area was cleared to make way for it, but the owners never did build the cabin that was supposed to go with it. It's quite secluded.

"There's a very strange bit of growth there, Adam. Cattails and grasses. About five, six feet of them, in the middle of nothing —just sand and dirt. At first, I thought a poacher had maybe buried some remains. Now I'm sure your victim is there. Well, a victim, anyway. Your boys are digging now."

"Are you shitting me, Jack?"

"No. I'd noticed it before, a few times, and thought it was odd. After our chat, it clicked. I thought, what the hell? There's something going on there. Can't hurt to check. Oh, just a minute, Adam. Jones is yelling at me."

Adam could hear the pathologist yell, "What?" Then silence. Then, "A what? Okay."

McDougall came back on the line.

"She's pretty much gone, Adam. But there are fibres, like the ones we found on Emily Martin. And, there's a ring in the grave. I'm surprised the murderer left it on her. Maybe it wasn't on her finger, and she had it tucked away in a pocket or something. Anyway, it's a signet ring. Initial A."

Adam scrambled to grab Alexis Ironstand's file. Flipped it open.

"Is it silver, with a tiny diamond set into the initial?"

McDougall hollered. Jones responded.

"Yes, Adam," said Jack.

"It's her."

*****

The email came to reporters Grace Rampling and Lacey McPhail, city editor Claire Davidson and news editor John Powers of The StarPhoenix, at five o'clock.

The press release it contained had the names of Detective Sergeant Adam Davis and Chief of Police Dan McIvor at the bottom.

It said the Saskatoon Police had found a third body in the vicinity of Saskatoon, and they were now potentially seeking a serial killer. Circumstances led them to believe the same person was responsible for at least three and possibly four deaths. They asked women to take extra care in their daily activities, and also urged the public to continue to watch for a Porsche Cayenne, black, about two years old, likely with significant damage to the front of the car.

Here we go, thought Grace. She could feel Adam vibrating from two blocks away. Felt his sadness, his fury, his certainty; and started to worry about his hell.

"Holy shit. Lacey!" yelled Claire. "Did you see the release? Let's go. Put a call in to McIvor. Grace, can you start pulling together the background? John, see you in Steve's office in five, okay?"

Editor Steve Delaney, who had just presided over the four o'clock daily news meeting, looked up with surprise when Claire, John, Lacey and Grace churned into his office less than half an hour after it ended.

"Steve," said Claire without preamble, "the cops have finally admitted they're looking for a serial killer. They found a third body this afternoon."

"Where?"

"They don't say exactly; just in the vicinity of Saskatoon."

"Bloody hell. Well, you know what to do. Do I need to call the press room?"

"No, I don't think we'll be late. A couple of interviews should do the trick; we have everything else. Lacey has already interviewed the family of Emily Martin, and unless we get lucky, like a call from the third woman's family, we won't get her identity until there's an autopsy. We'll get what we have online right away."

"Okay. Get at it, team."

Grace returned to her desk and texted Adam.

"Are you okay?"

"Yes," came the response, a minute later. "At least we found her."

"Incredible. Sending hugs."

He had to go. His phone was already ringing off the hook, and he still had to call Alexis Ironstand's family in North Battleford.

Thirty

The StarPhoenix, August 4, 20__
Online edition

Serial killer sought
By Lacey McPhail and Grace Rampling
of The StarPhoenix

Saskatoon Police are seeking a serial killer in the deaths of Sherry Hilliard, Emily Martin and at least one other local woman, the service said Friday.

Sherry Hannah Hilliard, 25, was killed in her home two weeks ago. Emily Elizabeth Martin, 19, had been missing for several months when her body was found by a woman walking her dog on the riverbank a few days ago.

During a planned search, police found the body of a third woman near Saskatoon on Friday afternoon. She has not yet been identified.

The killer may also have murdered a woman in Winnipeg, where police are looking for someone with the same modus operandi in the death of Della Delores Sinclair, 24.

All four women were very similar in appearance, including their height, weight and general colouring. They were between the ages of 19 and 25.

"We extend our deepest sympathies to the families of these women," said Police Chief Dan McIvor. "We are throwing all our resources behind finding this killer.

"However, until we find him or her, we must advise all women in Saskatoon and area to take the greatest care while participating in all activities."

Detective Sergeant Adam Davis, lead on the case, said he could not give any new details because they might jeopardize the investigation.

"I would like to ask everyone in Saskatoon to continue to keep their eyes open for a vehicle we believe is involved in one of these murders," he said. "This is a newer Porsche Cayenne SUV, black in colour, likely significantly damaged. It may, of course, have been repaired by now. But it's a crucial piece of this investigation."

While the police had not yet positively identified the third woman found Friday, Davis added, they had spoken to the family of a woman who disappeared more than eighteen months ago.

*****

Adam's eyes were ringed with lines of fatigue when he came to gather Grace at eight. Grace didn't feel fantastic, either. It had been a wild three hours for both of them, although much worse for Adam.

"Do you still want to go to the party?" Adam asked Grace, after they embraced at her door.

"Not particularly," she admitted, "but we should go. First, we have to eat. Second, it's James and Bruce. Third, maybe it will relax us a bit."

"Okay. Let's go for a while."

"Have you spoken to the family of the third woman?" Grace asked.

"Yes," said Adam, and his head went down.

"Adam, I'm so sorry. That must have been hard."

"Not a fraction as awful as it was for them."

Adam had called the Ironstand home, and reached Alexis' mother. As gently as he could, he told Martha Ironstand they thought her daughter had been found. She dropped the phone, and Adam could hear her weeping, could see her on the floor in his mind's eye. God, he wished he didn't have to tell her. He took a breath.

"Let's go, Grace, if you're ready."

He wasn't sure if he was. But Grace was right; they had to carry on.

They climbed into Adam's old BMW and headed out to James and Bruce's spread. James answered when they rang the doorbell, also looking haggard. He hadn't had time to change yet.

"Come in, come in," he said, sounding very tired. "What a rotten day. How are you holding up?"

"Beat," admitted Adam.

"Beat," echoed Grace, "but not like you two. And you have to play host," she said to James, with sympathy.

"I'll be fine. Do you feel like a dip first? We just started the barbecue."

"Perfect," said Grace, nudging Adam, who nodded vaguely.

Once in the back yard, where perhaps twenty people milled around or splashed in the pool, Adam stripped off his shirt and headed for the diving board. Every eye —

heterosexual and gay — followed his six-foot-two sculpted form. He was, thought Grace, as beautiful as a man could possibly be.

She watched him, mesmerized, as he dove cleanly into the pool, swam a few strokes, then came up shaking the water from his hair. He called to her, and held out his hand.

"Grace, come in. Come in with me."

A bit shyly, since she was in a new crowd, Grace removed her cover-up to reveal an aqua and black one-piece, and saw Adam's eyes darken.

She dove in, and met Adam in the middle of the pool, somewhere on the edge between shallow and deep. He kissed her quickly, and slipped his hands around her waist.

"You look incredible," he said in her ear. "I could eat you alive. Let's get out of here as soon as possible."

"You do too. Look incredible," she said. "Like Michelangelo's David."

"Hardly," said Adam. "But thanks, Babe."

"Idiot," said Grace. "If anything, you're more beautiful. You still have no idea, do you?" She looked around. "Every single person here watched you walk to the pool and dive in. Every single one was salivating. They wanted to lick you."

Adam stared at Grace.

"Believe it, lovely man," said Grace.

"Not as beautiful as you."

"Wrong. But let's swim a bit, before burgers, and before I can't help but make love to you right here."

Adam's eyebrow went up; Grace smiled and swam away from him.

Afterward, they pulled shirt and cover-up on and joined James at the barbecue, where he was madly turning burgers and steaks.

"Can I help?" asked Adam. "You need a drink."

"How good a cook are you?" asked James, warily.

"He's very good," Grace testified. "Wonderful steaks."

"Okay. I'll be back in five. Thanks, Adam."

But Adam did rather absently flip the chunks of meat, prompting Grace to give him a poke.

"Pay attention," she said, gently, grabbing some tongs to help.

As they tended the barbecue, Bruce wandered over with a glass of wine in his hand, and gave Grace a hug. Bruce had found Grace bleeding in an alley near the city's gay club that March, and possibly saved her life. Now, they were the best of friends.

"So great to see you, Grace," he said, as she awkwardly hugged him back with one arm, the other engaged in helping Adam with the meat.

"So great to see you, Bruce," she said. "Lovely party. Oh, there's Charlotte," she added, spying Adam's colleague and waving. Charlotte came over, also with a quick hug in greeting.

Soon, there was a growing, hungry group around the barbecue, chatting, laughing and drinking wine and beer. People grabbed plates and piled them with green salads, artisan breads and baby potatoes, then came over to be served off the barbecue by Adam and James.

Bruce had gone off to talk to Nick Delacroix about his Audi, until James yelled at him to get back to work.

"Coming," Bruce said, laughing, and shrugging at Nick.

"I'll come with you," said Nick. "Getting hungry."

Relieving Adam so he could get some food, Bruce introduced him to Nick.

"We've met," said Adam. "Good to see you again."

"And you, Detective. Or would Adam be all right in this environment?"

"Of course. How's business?"

"Well, I'm not selling a lot of Cayennes," said Nick. "Thanks to you guys."

"That's interesting. Why, do you think?"

"Buyers think they might be mistaken for your killer."

Adam took a bite of his steak, and mulled that over. "Have you sold any in the last couple of weeks?"

"Sure. Two. It's not like the whole city would be out buying Cayennes, anyway. They're not cheap, as you know, but that's still a bit light."

Adam's face became suddenly serious. He steered Nick slightly away from the crowd.

"I need those buyers' names, Nick," he said. It dawned on Adam the SUV used in the crime might not be Don Dunlop's. He doubted it, but it had to be checked out.

The car dealer appeared to understand immediately.

"Okay. Call me tomorrow. I'll be in until three."

"Thanks. Oh . . . watch out," said Adam, grabbing Nick's arm. Nick had taken a step backward, toward the pool; he was wearing dapper slacks and a perfectly-pressed shirt, hardly dressed for a dip. "Don't fall in."

"Shit," said Nick, breaking into a sweat. He shook off Adam's grip, but a moment later smiled ruefully. "Sorry. Embarrassing."

"Didn't come for a swim, obviously," said Adam, in reference to his attire.

"No. Not big on the changing and being wet all night in a crowd. Came straight from work, too. Still, these are great parties. Can't resist. Do you want another beer? I'm buying," he quipped.

"No, thanks. Driving. I think Grace has had a couple."

Adam put his plate down on the nearest table and went to find Grace, who was deep in conversation with James, Bruce and Charlotte. Adam smiled and spirited her away toward the bar, making noises about a fresh drink.

"Are you almost ready to go, Grace?" he asked. "I'm beat. And I want you to myself."

"Whenever you're ready, Adam, I am," said Grace, looking into his eyes.

His low voice dropped another half an octave. "Let's get out of here."

*****

Grace called Suzanne as they left the party, and confirmed she was doing fine.

"I think I will go to Adam's for a while," said Grace. "I'll see you later?"

"Depends how late you get back," said Suzanne. "But I'll be here."

"How was your meeting with the new client?"

"Fine, *merci*. As first meetings go."

"We'll have to chat about it tomorrow. Thanks for understanding."

"Of course, *chère amie*. See you soon."

Adam was unusually quiet on the way back to his condo, and Grace let him be, wondering if his mind was going over the case or if he was simply blasted from the long day.

The condo had returned to its tidy, plate-glassy state; Adam had pitched the broken chair and made sure no evidence of his fury remained.

"Would you like a glass of wine, Grace?" he asked, once within.

"No, thanks, Adam. A shower, maybe?" she asked, feeling the film of chlorine on her skin. She wanted Adam to kiss it, but only if it was clean.

He nodded, took her hand, led the way, and turned on the shower. Once under the water, Adam soaped Grace from neck to feet, slowly, saying nothing. He was in an enigmatic mood; so she returned the favour quietly, trying to match his stillness, his state of mind.

Towelled and fresh, they slipped into bed. Grace lay softly against him, waiting for a clue, and he began to stroke her gently, running his hands slowly down her arms, her sides, her stomach. He reached her breasts, and continued his slow, ruminative caresses.

After a while, though, Grace was thoroughly aroused and had to break the quiet.

"Adam," she said, panting a bit, "are you all right? You seem distracted, a little. Whereas, I am not."

"Grace, I'm so sorry. I am a bit distracted. I was thinking . . . it's not the same, here. I much prefer making love with you at your home. I can't explain it."

"Perhaps we could dive into that conversation later? For now, let me see if I can temporarily change your mind."

Grace curled herself on top of him and began to kiss him everywhere. She slipped his erection inside her; but Adam soon turned her on her back, entered her slowly, and gently moved his hips, ensuring his pelvis met hers. It was slow and dreamlike and very different from any other encounter they had had, and Grace was finding it not just erotic but emotionally moving. Rising and falling, then straining and crying out; the orgasm shook her to the core. Adam came to her a moment later, burrowing and holding her hard.

Later, Grace snuggled into him and stroked his chest.

"Anything you want to talk about, Adam? Is everything all right? How did things go at the women's prison?"

"It was intense. Incredible," said Adam, briefly describing what had happened, but leaving out what the Elder had said to him about sadness and passion and risk. He wanted to be in a better frame of mind when he explained it to Grace.

"What an honour, Adam. And a responsibility."

"I think I'm close to solving this case, Grace," he said. "And then, things are going to change. I'll be in the office tomorrow morning, but can we get together later?"

"Of course, Adam. Can I do anything, say anything to ease your mind?"

"I don't know. I enter this zone when the pieces start to come together. Once I have the puzzle almost finished, I get a little, well, excited. Focused. I guess this is our first time together during a big case, where you are neither victim nor prime witness."

"Yes, it is," said Grace, privately thrilled by the 'first time together' comment. "I don't know how to help, if I can, but I'm here."

"Yes. You're here. God, I love that you're here," said Adam. And that was as far as he could go, for now. He wanted and needed time and space to declare himself. It was going to happen soon.

Thirty-one

Grace forced herself to leave Adam and go home in the middle of the night, unable to stop worrying about Suzanne. She was sleeping soundly, though, and Bruno did the equivalent of putting a finger to his lips. He raised his massive head, shook it slowly from side to side, and promptly went back to sleep.

Adam was in the office by eight Saturday morning. He had not had time, as he had planned, to examine some of the outstanding bits of evidence; but he needed to now.

He was so close he could taste the ending, thick and metallic, like blood in his mouth.

He had asked James to connect the dates Alexis Ironstand and Emily Martin went missing with Environment Canada information. Was it raining, storming, snowing, anything?

It was snowing on the day Alexis Ironstand went missing, but the weather, for November, was fine on the day Emily Martin was reported gone. So storms were not necessarily part of the killer's MO.

Emily was found along the South Saskatchewan, which did not freeze in the winter and supported Adam's theory that the killer terrorized his victims by threatening to drown them. Explaining the death of Alexis was more difficult, since she was discovered at Pike Lake and went missing in the winter. She may have been killed somewhere else.

Then he looked at the time between the attacks. Deborah Clairmont, as far as they knew, was the first victim, two years ago. Alexis Ironstand went missing six months later, but then Emily Martin came eight months later; Sherry Hilliard and Della Sinclair were killed ten months after that.

They were missing someone. There was at least one, and probably two, other women. It was very unlikely their killer had been inactive between Alexis and Emily, and Emily and Sherry.

He also heard Justice Lafond's words ringing in his brain. How were the women marginalized, or isolated? Alexis and Emily were from out of town, new to the city, possibly with few friends or relatives nearby. Was that all it required? Did the killer ask them or know about their lives, and then choose them based on their isolation? Was he racist, misogynist or opportunist?

Who were the other missing women? Where were they, and what were their stories? Was it possible one was in Regina, Calgary, or another in Winnipeg?

Adam sighed heavily, and started looking for missing women's stories from across Western Canada. As he turned to his computer, he noticed a new file folder on his desk, which must have landed late yesterday in the midst of the madness after finding Alexis Ironstand.

It was a report comparing Don Dunlop's DNA to the blood and tissue found in Argo's mouth.

*****

Monique Delacroix read the print edition of the StarPhoenix Saturday morning on her acreage north of

Blackstrap Lake, south of Saskatoon. "Serial killer sought" in eighty-point letters shrieked across the page.

Unsettling, to say the least; especially since Don had been involved with one of the dead women. It was time to climb onto her horse, ride around the property, let the exercise and fresh air blow through her mind.

She pulled on her jeans and boots, ate a quick breakfast and went out to saddle Bête Noir — a name that did not suit her gelding's personality, so she privately and affectionately called him Big Boy. Monique was quite a horsewoman, having competed in equestrian events in her teens and twenties. She was more at home on a horse than in one of the expensive cars she sold every day.

Kicking Big Boy into a canter, she let the wind mess her hair as she rode around her eighty acres. Then she slowed the horse to a trot and began to check the property fences, the out-buildings, the corral, the garden. She hadn't done it in quite a while.

A door had blown open on the big shed at the bottom of a hill at the south end of the property. That was strange. She hadn't been near the shed for ages; it simply housed, well, crap. And a lawn mower. But she didn't want vagrants or even large vermin on her land, so she kept it locked.

She pulled the reins to stop Big Boy, swung out of the saddle, and went to shut the door. The lock had not been properly clamped; it must have pulled away, maybe in the storm.

A second later, she stopped in horror. Inside her shed was a black Porsche SUV.

It had to be.

It couldn't be.

She had to know.

She walked around to the front of the vehicle.

Shaking so hard she couldn't stand, she slumped to the ground, mouth stretched open in a silent scream.

*****

Adam's office phone rang at about eleven. He looked at the phone, but the number and name didn't come up. The display said "private."

"Davis," he answered.

"Detective, it's Monique Delacroix."

Her voice was low and quavering. It was impossible to miss the emotion in her voice.

"Monique," he said, abandoning protocol and titles. "What's wrong?"

"I was . . . I have something . . . I have to show you something . . ."

"Monique. Please, take a deep breath. What's going on?"

"I'm frightened, Detective. I found something. Can you come to my acreage? Now?"

"Yes. Tell me where you are."

Monique gave the acreage address and quick directions.

"I'll be there right away. Are you safe?"

"I — I think so. I don't know."

"Can you lock yourself in, somewhere? No. Forget that. Get in your vehicle and meet me on the road. Is there a grid road along the highway there?"

"Yes. I'll be in a half ton. Navy blue. Ford, believe it or not," she said, with a shaky laugh.

"Go now. Take your phone. I'll be no more than fifteen minutes. If anything comes up, drive away, toward me. Flash your lights when you see me, three times, so I know it's you." There were thousands of Ford pickups in Saskatchewan.

"How will I know it's you?" she asked.

"Oh, you will know, Monique. Now go."

"Yes. Thank you, Detective."

"No. Thank you. I'll be there right away."

Adam leapt to his feet, grabbed his duty belt, and called James all at the same time.

"James. I'm coming to get you. Can you do it?"

"Yes," said James, hearing the urgency in Adam's voice and asking no questions. "I'll be on the road waiting. Bring my belt."

"On my way."

Adam sped into the locker area, snagged James's belt — Adam had emergency access to his constables' lockers — went to the garage and hopped into a cruiser. He had the lights and sirens on within half a block, and tore toward James's home.

James was ready, and leaped into the police car. "What the hell is going on?"

"We're going to see Monique Delacroix. She called and sounded completely freaked. And scared. There was no time to ask her what was going on. She said she had to show us something, but she was frightened. She'll meet us on the grid road near her place in a blue Ford truck."

"Ford?" asked James, eyebrows up. "Well, I guess they're useful on acreages and farms, even if you usually drive a Jag. Do we need backup?"

"Yeah. Call it in. Tell them to drive an SUV."

James hit the radio, and Adam hit one-fifty by the time they reached the Grasswood gas station on the highway to Regina, pushing the vehicle to two hundred a moment later. It wasn't ten minutes before he saw Monique's truck, stopped on the grid road. He slowed down, relief washing over him. It hadn't escaped Adam's notice that Monique was petite, pretty and dark.

Monique waved at them to follow her, and so they did, down the grid road to her property and into the driveway.

She leaned over, opened the passenger door and said, "Hop in. Your cruiser will never make it where we're going."

Her hands gripped the wheel tightly, forearms shaking, her foot unsteady on the gas pedal. She didn't say anything.

In moments, she pulled up next to a large shed at the end of her property and jumped down from the driver's seat.

"Monique," said Adam, as he got out of the truck. "Slow down for a moment. Is there danger inside? Anyone in there?"

She shook her head.

"Is there . . . a body?"

"No."

"Are you okay?"

Again, she shook her head. She drew open the door, which she had closed earlier, and nodded for them to go in.

There it was. Don Dunlop's Cayenne.

Adam blinked for a moment; he couldn't believe it. He seriously thought they would never find it, that it was hidden somewhere, far away, or possibly burned. It would have been next to impossible to have the vehicle crushed, because every facility had been warned to watch for it. Even torching it might have been tricky, because the vehicle identification numbers usually survived burning; but the killer may have tried it. He hadn't. Here it was.

Adam turned to Monique.

"What does this mean to you? Who has access to your shed?"

"Well, in theory, the world does. I mean, you can't see it from anywhere, so if you break the lock, you're in, and no one will find you for weeks. I come down here maybe once a month; never, in the winter. But the lock. It wasn't broken. It was not closed properly. It must have worked its way out; maybe in the storm? I don't know."

"Who, besides yourself, has key access to this shed, Monique?"

She began to shake again.

"Don," she wailed. "Oh, God. Don! My property keys are in a drawer in the kitchen. And Nick, of course; he has all my keys. I — I can't think of anyone else."

The car dealership owner put her face in her hands and wept.

Adam put his arm around her shoulders.

"You are very brave, Monique. Can we go up to the house and talk? You need some tea. Or a drink."

He led her back to the truck, took her keys, and drove her back to the house. James stayed behind with the Cayenne, and started taking photos. They heard the siren from the second police vehicle; backup had arrived.

Adam told Lorne Fisher and Derek Jones to go down to the shed and to bring James back to him, then to go back and collect the evidence. He called James.

"James. Lorne and Jonesy are coming down to you; they're going to bring you back to the house. I need you to get back to town. Take the cruiser. Find Dunlop now. And Shawn Hartz. Get them to the station."

*****

Adam poured whisky into two glasses at one o'clock in the afternoon. One for Monique Delacroix, and one for himself. It had been a long time since he'd done that so early in the day.

He brought the glasses into the living room, where Monique was on the couch, still shaking. After she downed the fiery alcohol, she sat quietly for a moment, turning the crystal glass around and around in her hands.

"I knew," she said, "it was too good to be true."

"What was, Monique?"

"Don. Our relationship. God damn him. I finally found someone I cared about, and I didn't fuck it up. But he did."

"Maybe you shouldn't jump to conclusions, Monique."

"What do you mean?"

Adam didn't answer her question. Instead, he asked one.

"Why did you call me, Monique?"

"The — the story in the paper. All those women. I would never have guessed Don could do such things. Then I saw the Cayenne. I thought my heart would stop. Then I got so angry. It was the only thing I could do. I didn't know, Detective; I didn't. But this . . . this has to stop."

Adam nodded, but abruptly stood up and walked over to a cabinet where a photograph had caught his attention.

He knew it all, with certainty. His brain clicked; his body thrilled; he felt sick.

He took a breath, picked up the photograph, and brought it to Monique.

"Who is in this photo?" he asked her, sitting beside her on the sofa.

"Well, that's me," she said, pointing, "and that's Nick. That's our Mom — she died a couple of years ago. A little more now, I guess. And that's our sister, Véronique. She, too, has passed."

Monique touched the photo gently with her forefinger.

"I miss them," she said.

Adam drew out his phone, and scrolled through a series of photographs until he found the one he wanted. He handed the phone to Monique.

"Who is this?" she asked.

"Sherry Hilliard."

"She's so pretty. I've never seen a picture of her. Oh, no. Oh, so sad."

"And this is Della Sinclair," said Adam, showing her the next photo.

"She's pretty too. They both are. They look a bit like Véro. And like Mom, I guess. And me."

Adam waited. It didn't take long.

Monique's huge brown eyes widened; her lips parted, and she looked up into Adam's sympathetic face.

"Oh, my God," she whispered, and slipped to the floor.

Thirty-two

Adam lifted his shaking witness to her feet.

"I need you to be brave," he said. "I need you to come into Saskatoon with me. I need to talk to you. There isn't much time. Can you do that?"

Monique shook her head. She was in shock; Adam could see the signs. Somehow he had to bring her back, get her to function.

Adam took her glass, refilled it, and asked her to drink the Scotch. She did, tossing it back as if it were a lifeline. Adam waited.

Finally, she nodded.

"We'll have to take your truck," Adam said. "I have to leave my men here with the Cayenne until it's ready to tow; we can't risk tampering at this point. Please, Monique."

"Yes," was all she got out.

"Can you get whatever you need? A jacket or your purse? I'll have to talk to my officers. Then we'll go."

"Yes. Okay."

That was a little better, Adam thought, watching her walk unsteadily toward her bedroom.

Adam called Lorne Fisher.

"Sarge."

"Lorne. As soon as you've done what you can with the SUV, get it towed to the station, and come back in."

"Okay, Sarge. See you in maybe half an hour. We're almost done."

"Great. Thanks, Lorne."

"Sarge. Do you know?"

"Yes. I'll explain at the station," he said, as Monique returned, carrying her purse.

"Let's go," she said, tipping up her chin.

They climbed into the Ford and headed back to the city. Adam gave Monique a moment, and said, "There's no father in the photograph."

"No."

"What happened to him, Monique?"

"He died on the job. He worked for the power utility in Manitoba and was electrocuted."

"How old were you?"

"Eight. Véro was twelve. Nick was . . . Nick was ten."

"Was he a good dad?"

"Oh, yes. I loved him very much. We all did. He was funny, warm, loving. We were devastated when he died."

"Did your mother remarry?"

"Yes, a few months later. Mom didn't do well on her own; and it was like she froze the day Dad died. She needed a partner. She didn't choose as well the second time."

"Tell me, Monique."

"He was a fucking asshole. Violent. Didn't want us kids around." Her voice caught; Adam was silent, waiting for her to regain composure.

"He liked to smack us around, all of us. But he was the hardest on Nick. Nick had attitude; still does. He — his name was Harold — hated it. Hal would take Nick out back and beat the shit out of him whenever Nick gave him lip."

"Was that the worst of it?"

"No. One night I got home from something — maybe a birthday party, I don't recall — and Hal had Nick out back as usual. We had a fish pond out there, and Hal was holding Nick's face in it. He pulled him up, and Nick was gasping for air. Then he did it again. Nick wasn't very big yet; he was eleven at the time. I walked out and screamed at Hal; he let Nick go. I guess it was the first time, but it wasn't the last."

"And your mother? Did she know?"

"Yes, I think so. But she couldn't do anything. Hal hit her, too, and like I said, she was frozen inside after . . . after Dad."

"How long did this go on?"

"Nick ran away when he was fifteen. Two years later, Hal died. Cancer. Served him right," Monique said. "Bastard."

"The photograph. How long ago was it taken?"

"A few years before Mom died."

They had reached Saskatoon. Adam stopped asking questions, and let Monique take an emotional break as he drove through the city to the station.

They went inside, and he took her into his office.

"Rest, Monique, for a few minutes. I'm going to ask Sergeant Joan Karpinski to come and be with you for a little while."

He closed the door gently, and then stormed down the hall.

"Joan! Can you please sit with Monique Delacroix? She's in my office. And where the hell is James?"

"Interview one."

"Who's he got?"

"Dunlop."

"Okay. Thanks, Joan," Adam said, forcing himself to calm down. "Sorry. I'm being rude. Thanks."

Adam strode to the interview room and slammed through the door.

"Dunlop," he launched in. No pleasantries this time. James's head snapped around in surprise; this wasn't like Adam.

"Why the hell is Nick Delacroix not on your patient list?"

"He's not a patient anymore," said Dunlop, looking with alarm into Adam's face, his darkening eyes, his set jaw. "He stopped coming about a year ago. What the hell is going on?"

Adam watched Dunlop's face. He saw realization, anger and misery, in quick succession.

"Holy fuck," said Dunlop. "You've got to be kidding."

"Did you know Nick Delacroix had a relationship with Sherry Hilliard?"

"No. I did not."

"You better be telling me the truth, Dunlop."

"I swear to you, I did not know. I swear, Detective."

"Did he know you were involved with Sherry?"

"I don't know. I never told him. Why would I? I didn't advertise our relationship for obvious reasons. I don't know if she did."

"Okay. There's a woman in my office who needs you right now. I'll get someone to take you there," said Adam.

Dunlop's eyebrows rose like a question mark.

"Monique," Adam explained. He didn't have time to talk to Dunlop about his wife. "Go comfort her. James," Adam added, nodding his head at the door.

Outside the room, Adam asked, "Where's Hartz?"

"Charlotte's got him in interview two."

"Let's go. And call the staff sergeant. Ask him to gather Lorne, Joan and anyone else available in the case room in fifteen minutes."

Shawn Hartz was a rather terrifying shade of purple when Adam and James entered interview two. Charlotte stood against the wall, arms crossed and glaring at her charge.

"Hartz. Don't fuck with me. I mean it," said Adam. "Did you, or did you not, invite Nick Delacroix to your disgusting parties?"

"Yes," spluttered Hartz.

"Then why is he not on your guest list?"

"He never came."

"You left him off because he never attended one of your parties."

"I thought I was supposed to tell you who came to the parties."

"No. I specifically asked you for your guest list. He would have known when and where your parties were held, right?"

"I guess so. Yeah."

"I am so close to charging you with obstruction of justice my fingers are itching to sign that paper," said Adam, pointing to a document sitting ready on the desk.

But he relented. He was starting to worry the man might have a heart attack, right there and then.

"Instead, here's what we're going to do," Adam continued. "One of two things is going to happen. Either you stop with the 'window dressing,' or I will be attending every single one of your parties. Standing outside, taking names and photos. Don't think I won't. And don't think I won't find out. Your actions have contributed to the death of at least one young woman in this city. It will not happen again. Am I clear, Hartz?"

Hartz turned from purple to white.

"I never meant for that to happen," he whispered.

"But it did. Because you did not take care. Get the hell out of here."

Charlotte dragged Hartz to his feet, out the door, and into the lobby. A moment later, she joined the officers coming into the case room, where Adam was standing in front of the photo board, thrumming with certainty.

Charlotte walked up to Adam, as the officers streamed in.

"Breathe with me, Adam," said Charlotte, very softly, almost under her own breath. "Breathe, now. Take one moment. You're going to get him. Breathe."

Adam looked fondly at the police service's mother superior, and breathed. "Thank you, Char."

"Okay. Let's go," she said.

Adam cleared his throat and started in.

"Everyone. Our killer is Dominique Delacroix, co-owner of Luxury Motors with his sister, Monique Delacroix. He is usually called Nick.

"I'm going to make this as short as possible, because we're going to go and pick him up now. We just found Don Dunlop's Porsche Cayenne on Monique's property. Two people besides Monique have key access; Dunlop, with whom she is having an affair, and her brother. The killer is not Don Dunlop. His DNA does not match the blood found in the mouth of Sherry Hilliard's dog.

"Okay. Let's go find him. James and I will take the dealership. Lorne, Jonesy, go to his home. Char and Mac, you'll back us up. Let's remember, people, he's packing. He shot Sherry Hilliard's dog. Vests, the works. Let's go."

The officers pulled on their gear and streamed out of the station, into cruisers, and headed for Nick Delacroix's home and workplace. Once in the car, James started asking questions.

"So, Adam? What's his story?"

"As far as I have pieced this together, Delacroix lost his father at age ten. By eleven, his new stepfather was beating him and shoving his face into the fish pond, threatening to drown him. He used it as discipline, if you can call it that. When I talked to Delacroix last night at your place, he almost stepped backward into the pool and had a very intense reaction. He swore, started sweating. I was pretty sure then it was him."

"Shit. I wonder how Bruce is going to feel about it being Nick."

"Badly, I would think. Anyway, Nick had easy access to the Cayenne's keys. It could have come in handy to use Dunlop's car, in case Delacroix wanted to cast suspicion on him. He also, by the way, tried to implicate Corey Hilliard. Remember when he said there were rumours about Corey beating his sister and cousins? Delacroix was spreading the net of suspicion as widely as possible.

"He didn't count on ramming the Smart Car. That was the big mistake; that, and leaving the dead dog as a terror tactic. He couldn't help himself.

"He knew about Dunlop's affair with Sherry Hilliard. He had a relationship with her first. It was violent; he broke her cheekbone. I originally thought Corey did that, but it was Delacroix.

"Sherry broke up with him. Then his mother died. She was emotionally 'frozen,' as Monique calls it, after their dad died. She became unavailable. Delacroix started his rampage after her death.

"That's also when he moved to Saskatoon; and later, so did Sherry, to get away from her violent brother. I'm guessing Delacroix tried the abusive husband tactics and apologies, got her back for a while, and she dumped him again. Maybe she was scared of him; maybe he hit her.

"Later, I think, he tried again. She told him she was seeing someone else — Dunlop — and that she was pregnant. He lost his mind. To him, it was betrayal; it gave him the licence to kill her. Unlike the other victims, though, they had a relationship. He did feel something for Sherry, at least at first, in his way. He felt betrayed, like he felt betrayed when his mother married again.

"He stabbed her over and over again in a vicious rage, instead of strangling her. And he killed her dog first, to hurt her, as a calling card, and so he wouldn't get in the way."

"Why the water, though, but no drownings?" asked James.

"He used the water as a threat, as his stepfather did, then left the women buried nearby or threw them into the lake or river. Justice Lafond wonders if there's a cleansing aspect to this; either he feels absolved, or he feels his mother has been absolved of her dual crimes: being unavailable and leaving him in the clutches of his stepfather.

"I'm sure he held Sherry's face in the water in her basement before she died. The water was right there, so he didn't have to move her. And it would have destroyed evidence if Suzanne and Grace hadn't been brave enough to come downtown that night, and we didn't find her for a few days."

They had arrived at the dealership. Adam and James jumped out and ran inside. They asked the receptionist if Nick was in, but she shook her head.

"I'm sorry, officers, but he has left for the day."

Adam nodded, and raced upstairs anyway; but Nick Delacroix was not there.

He radioed Lorne Fisher.

Neither was Delacroix at home.

*****

Late that morning, having slept in, Grace and Suzanne curled up on the couch with coffee and caught up on the news in their lives.

"So, your new client."

"Yes, Dom," said Suzanne. "He's opening a new ad agency, and wanted to see if I was interested in working for him. I'm not sure. At the end of the interview, he started making personal noises. He suggested we should go for dinner sometime."

"Would you be interested?"

"I might be. He's very handsome, smart and charming. But that would knock out working for him."

"Yeah, you'd have to decide," said Grace. "You didn't make further plans with him, though?"

"No. Nothing concrete. I guess I'll wait and see."

Phew, thought Grace. She was still rooting for Lorne Fisher in the race for Suzanne's heart. Besides, who was this Dom guy?

"And Adam?" asked Suzanne. "How are things going? You were worried about him the other night."

"Yes. He is . . . very passionate about his work. Sometimes too much so. This case has been very hard on him." She didn't say she was concerned about whether it would trigger more post-traumatic stress episodes. Adam still worried about them, constantly.

"Have they solved the crime yet?" Suzanne asked hopefully.

"Not as far as I know. But Adam says he feels they're very close."

By one o'clock, the two friends felt they should get something done. Suzanne offered to clean the house while Grace did the grocery and wine shopping, and Grace gratefully accepted.

"What would you like for dinner?" Grace asked.

"Mmm. Don't care. Everything you make is delicious."

"Aww," said Grace, embracing Suzanne. "That's so sweet of you."

Grace hopped in the shower, tied up her mane, threw on jeans and a T-shirt and was out the door by two-thirty.

An hour and a half later, she pulled into her garage and started lugging grocery bags toward the house. She unlocked and opened the door to be confronted by Bruno barking his head off and twisting his huge black body in a strange frenzy.

What on Earth . . . ?

"It's okay, Bruno," said Grace, trying to pat his head, but Bruno turned away and flung himself toward the front door.

Blood surged into Grace's brain. Something had gone very wrong.

"Suzé!" she yelled, hoping her friend was somewhere else in the house. Knowing she wasn't.

Grace dropped what she was carrying onto the floor and frantically looked around. The house was tidy; Suzanne had done the cleaning. She hadn't been gone long.

Bruno had licked Lorne Fisher, Grace remembered Suzanne saying. Now, Bruno was freaking out.

There was a note on the kitchen table, obviously written in a hell of a hurry. A scrawl.

"Out with Dom . . . sorry . . . later. S."

Oh, my God. Oh, no, Suzanne.

Grace lunged for her purse, grabbed her cellphone and dialled Adam. It rang four times, the longest four rings of Grace's life. But he answered.

"Grace, I can't talk. We're trying to find the killer. I'm driving around out here with James."

"Adam, wait! Suzanne is missing. Bruno is freaking out. She's with him, whoever he is. I know it. I think it's the guy she had coffee with yesterday. He was supposed to be a client, but he came on to Suzanne. She said she had no plans with him. She said he didn't know where I lived. I thought she was safe, and now she's gone."

"Who is it?" Adam asked. "Do you have a name?"

"She called him Dom. Dom Damien."

Dominique, Dom, Nick. *Fuck.* No wonder it hadn't registered with Grace. Besides, she had only met Nick last night.

"There's a note on the table," Grace said, "saying she went out with him at the last minute."

Adam's brain glued the final pieces of the case together. Delacroix hid his identity from Suzanne, posing as someone else — a client. He must have followed her to Grace's, somehow.

As soon as Grace went out, he struck. He convinced Suzanne to go out with him on the spur of the moment, spouting flattery and adoration.

But he wouldn't kill her until he found out what she knew; and he didn't know they were hunting for him. Suzanne was the witness Delacroix feared. She hadn't identified him, obviously; but had she described him to the police? Did she have evidence he didn't know about?

So he put diesel in her tank. Sent his tow truck to try to catch her on the highway, when the car broke down; but her father came to pick her up. He was forced to wait until she came to the dealership, which took much longer than he'd hoped; but Lorne Fisher was on the job. And then she had gone back to the farm, and later, to Grace's. The whole protection scheme almost worked. Almost. It had likely driven Delacroix crazy. He switched tactics, and called Suzanne posing as a client. The dealership had her cell number.

Now, he had her.

"Grace. Any idea where they could be?"

"None. You're telling me I'm right, aren't you?"

"Yes." He didn't want to add it would be impossible to put out an all-points bulletin for Delacroix's car. No way he took his own. So which car? One of two hundred from the dealership? A customer's car he had taken the keys for, as he had Dunlop's Cayenne? How the hell were they going to find him?

"Give me her cell number," said Adam, and Grace did. "Stay on the line, Grace, while I try her on James's phone."

No answer. She had been polite and turned her phone down, or off. She was bad for that, even when she wasn't simply being socially correct. Adam passionately wished he could enact a law forcing all women to have their phones on, volume up, at all times. Courtesy be damned.

"Hell," he said under his breath. "We'll keep calling her. If you think of anywhere they might be, call me, Grace."

"Oh, God, Adam. Find her. Please find her."

"I will. I will find her, Grace. I'll call you back soon, okay? I'll find her."

But he had no idea how.

Thirty-three

Adam got on the radio and told the other officers Nick Delacroix had Suzanne Genereux. He knew what kind of a reaction that would bring from Lorne Fisher, and wondered what he could say, in the other officers' hearing, to keep him focused.

"Think, everyone. Stay calm and think. Where would he take her?"

"Monique's, maybe?" asked Jones.

"Possible. You and Fisher get over there."

"We're on our way, Sarge."

"Anyone else?"

"You were thinking he wined and dined his victims first, right, Adam?" James asked. "Does that mean they could be at a restaurant in town?"

"Could be. He wants to know what Suzanne knows, what she has told us. James, call the sergeant on duty. Get him to start calling the more expensive restaurants in town. Make it sound like it's a family emergency or something."

And Adam knew, suddenly, where they were.

Water. Restaurant. Not the South Saskatchewan, not Pike Lake, not a slough or a pond.

"Never mind. We're going to Blackstrap. Hole in the Wall restaurant. Let's go."

His cell rang again. Grace.

"Babe," he answered quickly. "I think I know where they are. Heading there now."

"Where, Adam? Where?"

"Blackstrap. I'll keep you posted."

To hell with that, thought Grace. She and Bruno were going for a ride. If anyone could find Suzanne, it was Bruno.

*****

Suzanne sat across from the man most people knew as Nick Delacroix with a glass of wine in her hand, thinking it was time she relaxed, went out, had some fun. Maybe he wasn't the one, but he had good taste, made decent conversation. *Bien.* For now.

He had knocked on Grace's door, and Suzanne opened it, surprised to see him there.

"I met Grace last night," he said. "At James and Bruce's. She mentioned a friend was staying with her, and it turned out to be you! Can I buy you dinner? I know it's impromptu, and a bit early, but I've been thinking about you ever since yesterday morning. We won't get into the restaurant I'm thinking of if we don't go now."

"I'm not really dressed for dinner."

"I can wait."

Bruno was unimpressed. He obviously didn't want her to leave, but Suzanne managed to shut the door on her dog's writhing, frenzied body.

And here she was, in one of the area's finest restaurants, after a lovely drive through the countryside.

Somewhere into the salad, he said, "Terrible about those killings, isn't it."

"*Oui*," said Suzanne, carefully. She was trying not to think about Sherry, and knew she had to keep her mouth shut about the bits and pieces of the crime involving her.

"Terrible for you, too, I guess," said Delacroix.

"Why?"

"One of them was your neighbour, wasn't she?"

Suzanne took a bite of her salad even as her brain suddenly began to scream. Cells on fire. Synapses snapping. What was wrong with that question?

No one knew Sherry Hilliard was her neighbour — unless, of course, he had purposely looked up her address, and Sherry's. No. That didn't work. Sherry's was unlisted.

Unless he had been there.

She patted her lips with a napkin.

"If you'll excuse me for a moment, I need to use the washroom. Be right back," she said, as lightly as she could manage.

Suzanne took her purse, and slowly walked away toward the bathroom and out the front door.

She frantically searched for her phone, which she had indeed turned off, and fumbled to turn it back on. She had to call the police.

Come on, come on, she yelled mentally at her phone. And then Dom was at the door, and right behind her. A few feet away.

Suzanne took off, running down the road leading to the lake, where she hoped trees and brush would hide her until she could reach someone on the phone. Too late to turn back to the restaurant. *How could I be so stupid?* she asked herself. *Quelle idiote*. She thought she was being so clever with the washroom excuse. He had clearly realized his mistake the moment he said it.

She heard his heavy breathing, his running footsteps, and knew Dom was right behind her. In her heels, she couldn't outrun him, so she kicked them off; but the gravel ripped her feet. They were bloody and torn in seconds.

Terror fuelled Suzanne's legs and lungs. Then she saw a way out: not a cabin, but a house on her right, and she headed for it. Knocking madly at the door, she realized with a sinking heart no one was home, and she was making a lot of noise which Dom would certainly hear.

She dashed off the porch, turned right toward a clump of bushes, and hit what felt like a wall. Delacroix had come around the corner. He caught her around the middle, knocking the wind out of her, and tore the phone out of her hand, throwing it far from reach.

"What did you tell them?" he hissed in her ear. "What?" he insisted, grabbing her mane of hair and pulling her head back.

"Nothing," said Suzanne. "I didn't know. Until right now."

"You didn't see anything?"

"No."

"You did. You saw me in the back yard. I know you did. You must have. You're lying. I heard you banging on the door. You called the police. They were there that night. Don't fucking lie to me."

Suzanne stopped talking. She had to think. Fast.

*****

Two cruisers screamed up to the restaurant and the officers surged inside. There was no sign of Suzanne or of Delacroix.

"Was there a couple here, a little while ago?" asked Adam. "Dark, petite woman and dark man, slender, tall?"

"Yes, sir," said the wide-eyed maitre'd. "They ordered, had some wine and salad, and suddenly left."

"Did you see which way they went?"

"No, I'm sorry. I wasn't watching them. Their car is still here, though. I thought perhaps they might come back."

"Thanks."

Adam raced back to the cruiser and got on the radio. "They're here. Somewhere lakeside of the Hole in the Wall restaurant. Get out here."

Before Adam could put the radio back in its slot, he saw a very familiar car drive by, with a beautiful redhead and an enormous black dog inside. It was headed for the lake.

*****

Delacroix dragged Suzanne down toward the water, spewing fury.

"Fucking bitch. You should never have called the cops. You wouldn't be here now. You should never have married that fucking bastard. I'm going to show you. You're going to see what that was like. I'm going to fucking kill you. Fuck you. Kill you."

Suzanne realized he was insane with anger; he wasn't making any sense. Which fucking bastard should she not have married? All she could do was fight back, as well as she could.

He dragged her, a hand twisted in her hair, an arm around her neck, backward to the water's edge. Suzanne couldn't kick him, and could barely breathe, but she managed to reach up and over her head to claw his cheek. He screamed, let go of her hair and hit her, hard.

It was enough, a second of furious inattention. Suzanne spun away, and started running again — until he caught up with her, tripped her, and sent her sprawling. He yanked her toward the water again and forced her face into the lake.

This is it, thought Suzanne, even as she struggled. I'm going to drown.

But he pulled her face out of the water, dragged her back to the shore and began to tear at her clothing. He ripped her blouse, pushed up her skirt. With what was left of her breath, she screamed — until Delacroix's hands closed around her throat.

The scream reached Adam's ears. He had sent James and Lorne in other directions, and was jogging down the road, looking everywhere; now he started to run. A moment later, he came through the trees to see Delacroix straddling Suzanne's pelvis.

"Delacroix!" he boomed. "Hold it right there or I swear to God I will shoot you."

In a flash, Delacroix stood up, dragging Suzanne with him and pulling a handgun out of the back of his belt. He trained the weapon on Suzanne's temple.

"Welcome to our party, Detective. What do you want to do now?"

"You're going to drop the gun, Nick. Now."

"No. I don't think so."

"None of this is Suzanne's fault. We have you on evidence. We have eight cops surrounding you. Give it up. No one has to die here."

A car skittered on the gravel, slid across the grass. Grace had found them.

"Who the fuck cares if we die? If she dies, if I die? Or maybe your girlfriend?" Delacroix gave Grace an obscene stare as she got out of the car. "Not my type. Happy to shoot her, though. Or, say, you?"

Hell, thought Adam. Suicide by cop? God help me. In the same instant, he realized Grace was heading for Suzanne and the killer.

"Grace! Stop! Get back. He's armed, for God's sake. Grace!" Adam shouted.

Grace turned to him, eyes black with fear. She turned and opened the passenger door; Bruno bounded out and headed straight for Delacroix, murder in his eyes.

When he reached the man who held his person captive, he lunged and sunk his teeth into his leg. Delacroix didn't react. For a moment, it was as if he felt nothing. He lowered the gun from Suzanne's head and shot Bruno. The huge dog fell to ground with a thump, whimpering. Then he was silent.

Suzanne did not scream. A new jolt of adrenalin crackled through her veins, carrying fury instead of fear to her brain. In a split second, she elbowed Delacroix in the stomach and wrestled the gun from his still-lowered hand. Spinning around and away from him, she held the firearm with both hands and trained it on Delacroix's forehead.

"You fucking bastard," she said, in a low, menacing tone. "You killed Sherry. You killed her, you killed her dog, and God knows how many other women. You were going to kill me, and you killed Bruno. I want to know why. Talk. Or I will shoot you."

Adam wondered if, in Delacroix's mind, being shot by a woman was different from being shot by a cop. Would her threat carry some weight? But he didn't say anything. He just stood there, snarling.

"Suzanne," Adam said, in as even a voice as he could muster. "Don't do it. We've got him. Don't do it. You don't want to go to jail over this sick fucker. Please, Suzanne."

"No. I'm going to shoot him if he doesn't confess right now. Maybe I'll shoot him anyway. For revenge."

Adam spied Lorne Fisher creeping along the shore behind Delacroix and Suzanne. He had found them, had managed to come around from behind. Thank God. Did she see him?

Keep her talking.

"We have enough evidence, Suzanne. We've got him. I swear to you. Please put down the ..."

He didn't get the last word out. Lorne pounced out of the brush and in a second was all over Delacroix, pushing him down, grabbing his arms and pulling them behind him. Adam closed in on Suzanne, and held out his hand for the gun.

"I swear, Suzanne," he said. "We will avenge you, and the other women. Please."

Suzanne stared at Lorne holding Delacroix for several seconds, then dropped her arms and handed Adam the firearm before crashing to her knees.

A second later, Lorne pushed Delacroix's face into the sand as Adam cuffed him. Grace dove toward her friend, touching her bruised face and hugging her. Suzanne, her body turned to stone by shock, was weeping and calling Bruno's name in a one-word litany.

Grace, by now shaking so hard she couldn't walk either, crawled over to Bruno and saw he was breathing. The bullet had gone into his hindquarters, and he was bleeding; but he was, so far, all right.

"He's breathing, Suzanne," Grace called to her. "He's alive."

Suzanne collapsed, and Lorne Fisher, having given custody of the killer over to Adam, caught her for the second time. But this time, he sank to his knees in the wet earth, pulled her into his arms, cradled her against his heart and did not let go.

*****

Three officers dragged Dominique Delacroix, of the many names, into a cruiser, as he swore and spat and squirmed. James called an ambulance.

Adam plunged toward Grace, who was sprawled in the sand hugging Bruno and sobbing.

"Grace. Grace. Are you all right?" asked Adam. "What were you thinking? God, Grace. Don't do shit like this, Babe."

"I knew Bruno would help me find Suzanne. He would pick up her scent, and find her." She shuddered. "We found you instead, but he did help save her. He did, Adam."

It was not the worst idea Adam had ever heard. A K-9 would have come in handy, and as it was, Bruno's attack on Delacroix let Suzanne get away. He saw Grace's logic, as upset as he was. All of this was his fault, for telling Grace where they were going to look for Suzanne.

"How did she know how to get the gun away from him?" Adam asked. "That was incredible. Would she have shot him? Could she?"

"Her fiancé. Leo. Special Forces, killed in Afghanistan. He taught Suzé how to shoot. Looks like he taught her more than I know, about how to defend herself. Delacroix's face looks pretty bad."

"Still, Grace. For God's sake, he could have shot you."

He wrapped his arms around her, and they knelt, Grace shivering and Adam shaking, in the wet sand.

Sirens and lights announced the ambulance, and Suzanne and Bruno were both carefully loaded inside.

"Which hospital?" Lorne asked the paramedics, after allowing them to take Suzanne out of his arms.

"RUH," one of them said, referring to the Royal University.

"Okay," said Lorne. "Suzanne. I'll see you there. Suzanne. Hang in there."

Suzanne made an incomprehensible noise. The paramedics slammed the back doors shut, and screamed away toward Saskatoon.

*****

"The one time I couldn't follow you," Lorne said to Suzanne, much later that night. She had been thoroughly checked over; her wounds were dressed, and although she was bruised and beaten and torn up, she was more or less all right, the nurse assured Lorne.

"The one time. Did you trust him? Why did you trust him? What were you doing there?"

"What do you mean?"

"I — we — were out looking for Delacroix this afternoon. We thought you were safe. Grace told Adam you were at home, you were going to have dinner together. She told him, always, where you were. If you were on the move, I was right behind you. This wasn't supposed to fucking *happen*. Why did you trust him?"

"I don't know. We had coffee; he was supposed to be a client. He seemed nice."

Damn. He should have gone into the coffee shop, to see who she was with. At the time, though, it seemed unnecessary; Suzanne was in public, with a theoretical client. And somehow, he had followed her home. Must have.

"He surprised me at Grace's. He said Grace told him I was staying with her," Suzanne continued. "They had been to the same party. He was part of the social scene. So, he seemed to be some kind of friend by association. Obviously, he lied."

Lorne was quiet for a moment, looking at Suzanne's scraped and bruised face. He realized that yeah, Delacroix was part of the social scene. How fucked up was that?

"Does it hurt?" Lorne asked a moment later, hand hovering over one of Suzanne's bloody scratches.

"Yes," Suzanne admitted.

"Where else are you hurt?"

"Several other locations."

"I've never seen anyone as brave as you."

Suzanne held out her hand. Lorne got up from his chair, sat on the side of the bed, and took it.

"My blue knight," she said, softly. She reached up a hand and touched Lorne's cheek. "I'm alive because of Adam, and Grace, and Bruno. And you."

"No. You were your own hero."

She lifted her head and kissed the cheek she was touching, simultaneously smoothing the troubled lines in his face. Lorne flinched, his body involuntarily and powerfully reacting to her touch. Suddenly he had his arms around her. A moment of confusion. Then he turned his face to look at her, and her lips touched his.

"*Merci*," said Suzanne, against his mouth.

Thirty-four

Dominique Delacroix, shackled, stared at Adam. Adam was hoping for a full confession, but Delacroix was completely crazed. Even so, he was not legally insane. The man knew what he was doing, Adam was certain. It was impossible to apply sane moral logic to a serial killer.

"You know," said Delacroix, "it was easy. So easy. You won't find the rest of them."

Adam's heart skipped. That was Delacroix's final card.

"We'll find them," he said to the killer.

A slow smile spread over Delacroix's face. "No. You won't."

Swallowing his anger, Adam let it go. He wasn't going to make it if he started arguing with this wild-eyed bastard. He changed his tactics.

"Maybe it wasn't so easy. Maybe you were good at it. Look how you found Deborah Clairmont."

"Who?"

"The woman in Victoria Park, two years ago."

"I didn't 'find' her, detective. I fucked with her car. Saw her, followed her, cut her brake line. Easy."

"How did you know it was Suzanne who contacted the police?"

"I heard her banging on the door. It had to be a next-door neighbour, or they wouldn't have heard Sherry scream. And it was a woman's voice calling Sherry's name. Two guys live on the other side. Besides, I'd seen her before, when I went to visit."

"Genius. But you didn't do anything about her at the time?"

"I was a little busy."

"Great idea to put diesel in Suzanne's car. Everyone would think she did it, a mistake at the pump. When did you manage that?"

"Again, easy. I watched her house. She came home on Monday, and left her car out back for a few minutes."

"But you didn't kill her."

"Cops everywhere. Besides, I wanted to talk to her. Maybe fuck her first."

"How did you know where she was going?"

"I didn't. Not for sure. She was either going to stay home, or head to her folks' place, or stay at a friend's. Sending out the tow truck that morning was a gamble, but it worked, eventually. I got her keys, and her cell number. Of course, she was staying at your girlfriend's place. But I was going to catch up to her no matter what. I found her alone, didn't I?"

He had done his leg work, Adam privately agreed.

"Women are so stupid," Delacroix suddenly continued. "About cars. About not looking behind them. Women are so stupid about men. Always picking the wrong ones."

"Like your mother."

Delacroix's eyes narrowed.

"Stupid fucking bitch. Why didn't she get rid of him? It was all her fault. See? Women are stupid. So easy to suck them in. 'Oh, you're so pretty. I'd love to take you out for dinner.' They fall for that shit every time. Even your little friend."

"What I don't get," said Adam, although he did, "is why you didn't kill the fucker. Your stepfather. He deserved it. It could have been self-defence."

"No. She deserved it. It was her fault."

"But you didn't kill her."

"She died."

So Adam was right. Her death triggered Delacroix's killing spree. His fury spilled out, and he murdered her over and over again.

"She deserved it, then. But did these other women deserve it?" asked Adam.

"Sure. They're all the same. If they're not yet, they will be someday."

*****

"Why was Sherry different?" Crown prosecutor Sanjeev Kumar asked Adam, when they met a few days later. "She was stabbed, not strangled, and it took him a long time to get around to killing her."

"Two things, I think," said Adam. "He knew her in Winnipeg. They met through Sherry's brother, Corey. Delacroix hadn't been triggered yet, and they had an earlier relationship. His mother died two years ago, of natural causes, and he knew then he'd never get an apology from her, for marrying the violent man who became his stepfather. He would never feel her love. That was the trigger."

"That's the other thing I was wondering. Why was he killing women, and not fifty-year-old men? As I understand it, then, the answer is he blamed his mother."

"Yes. She was emotionally unavailable to him, after his real father died."

"Why did he kill Della, so soon after he killed Sherry?"

"Sherry and Della were 'thick as thieves' according to Della's sister. She was likely the only one who knew about his relationship with Sherry, and the one who would have suspected him. He had to kill her, too. Plus, she fit his type, so she scratched the itch."

"So he came to Saskatoon after his mother died to take on this dealership with his sister. And when Sherry came too, he started up the relationship again?"

"Yeah. She took him back; he hit her again. They broke up. He tried again, but by then she was seeing Don Dunlop. She got pregnant. She decided she'd had enough of both violent and married men, and tried to make a new start. Sherry Hilliard was a smart and brave woman, Sanj. She worked hard to get a good job, moved away from her toxic brother, tried to get away from bad relationships with men. She was trying to break the cycle.

"For Delacroix, Dunlop and the pregnancy sent him over the edge. He killed the dog, left his body as a message. When he got to Sherry's later, someone had already attacked her: Ashley Dunlop. Sherry was woozy, maybe semi-conscious; it may have been partly why he stabbed her again and again. He had to get her attention, so she knew this was him, killing her.

"That, and this betrayal was personal. It wasn't just any woman who didn't come up to his exacting standards. No woman could, of course."

"He met Alexis Ironstand at the dental clinic?"

"Yes, he was still a patient at Dunlop Dentistry at the time. It was a terrible coincidence; she was there only on an emergency basis; she would normally have gone to the university clinic. Delacroix stopped going to Dunlop when he discovered Sherry had been hired there. He probably knew, somewhere in his twisted mind, he was going to kill her, and didn't need the connection with the clinic."

"And Emily?"

"Stalked her at one those parties planned by Shawn Hartz. He stalked the first victim, too. Damn, I wish I could charge that Hartz asshole with something. If you come up with an idea, I'm listening."

"I'll think about it."

*****

Adam and Chief McIvor held a news conference that went on for an hour and a half, providing details on the case. They asked the families of Alexis Ironstand and Emily Martin if they would like to make statements, to honour their memories. They invited Suzanne Genereux and Eileen Bear.

Alexis's aunt, Carrie Ironstand, described her niece as a beautiful, intelligent, outgoing woman who was studying education at the University of Saskatchewan. Tears poured down her face as she told the media how dearly Alexis was loved.

"Alex came down from North Battleford to study at the U of S. She was smart, determined, wonderful with little children," said Carrie. "Now she will never be a teacher, will never have her own little children, will never have this life she worked so hard for."

Emily Martin's mother, Doreen, clutched a stuffed animal that had belonged to her daughter — so young was Emily, she still had her childhood toys. Doreen could barely speak, but choked out how proud she was Emily was going to business school, how beautiful she was, how much she was missed.

Suzanne stood up and hugged both women, tears raining down her cheeks.

She cleared her throat, but didn't wipe away the tears. And spoke.

"I survived," she began. "I am very fortunate. I am part of this community, and have been for many years. I have wonderful friends who looked after me, who saved my life. I have a small business and make enough money. I have a wonderful dog, who also helped save me," she added, pointing to Bruno, who was there because Suzanne was going nowhere without him, not even a news conference.

"I once had a fiancé who loved me enough to teach me how to protect myself. I am lucky, and privileged. I would not have survived if all of these things did not come together.

"Three of the women who were killed came from other backgrounds, they came from other communities. They were trying to live their lives here, to improve their lives here, but they were more vulnerable than I. They didn't have the connections, the friends, the network. This man took advantage of them, in anger and fear and, I think, misery. He took their lives.

"I don't know if he could have been helped. I don't care, I hate him so much. But we all have to support each other. I should have helped my neighbour more. I tried, but it wasn't enough. I have to live with that for the rest of my life."

Completely devastated, Suzanne grabbed Bruno's leash and stumbled away from the news conference table. Lorne, standing at the side, did not give a damn what people thought, including the chief. He grabbed Suzanne as she stepped away and held her hard, as she wept in his arms.

Elder Eileen Bear walked over to Suzanne, gently touched her shoulder for a long moment, and went to the microphone.

"It is a terrible day," said Bear. "We mourn all our sisters. The broken bodies, the broken families, the broken lives. We ask the Creator to take care of them in the other world. We ask for peace and healing to come to their loved ones.

"In this world, however, we ask the government, the police services, and the educational agencies to change their policies. To follow the missing women, and the men. To create safe places and institutions of cultural understanding. It is time.

"I leave you with an ancient blessing: Let us walk safely on the Earth with all living beings, great and small."

Adam feared he wouldn't be able to speak. He thought of his mother, fighting an intruder in her kitchen so many years ago. He thought of Grace, battling an attacker in her home that spring, and in a park as a budding woman. He thought of the young, beautiful women whose lives were cut short.

When he did speak, his voice was raw and low.

"This killer is now in prison and he will never leave," said Adam, knowing the public needed reassurance. "Our evidence is beyond question.

"We may have done our jobs, but it wasn't good enough. We lost these women. I don't know how we can stop the violence, but in my department, we are going to change things.

"We are going to look closely at every single missing person's case the moment it comes in, and compare those cases to other crimes in the Saskatoon area. We will have a missing persons co-ordinator, who will cross-reference their files with other police services.

"We are going to find and train and hire more Indigenous police officers as detectives, who will bring cultural understanding to our investigations. We will meet with Elders, particularly women Elders, on a regular basis."

Chief McIvor found himself nodding as Adam spoke. But Inspector Terry Pearson, standing nearby with his arms crossed, made an unpleasant snorting noise. Every head in the room turned. McIvor shot him a look that would wilt an iron bar; Adam ignored him.

"This was the worst case I have ever worked on," continued Adam. "Elder Bear called it our River of Tears. And it was."

Grace was at the back of the room, taking in the words and weeping for the families, for her dear friend, and for her ferocious lover.

*****

"Pearson," said Chief McIvor after the news conference. "In my office."

Pearson gave the chief a "who, me?" look and followed him down the hall with an annoyingly nonchalant swagger.

"Sit down," said McIvor, shutting the door behind the inspector.

"What's up, Chief?" asked Pearson.

"What was that about, at the newser?" asked McIvor.

"What?"

"The snort."

"Fucking Davis. He's such a cry baby. 'We're going to change things and everything is going to be okay.' Right. Nothing's going to change, and you know it, McIvor."

"Actually, Pearson, everything is changing. We have a long way to go, but we're making some progress. And you have to get with the program. I also found your name on a certain list, Pearson. Some parties you've been invited to. So cut the shit, do your sensitivity training, and get your act together."

"Or what?"

"You're gone. I have to give you this one last warning, Pearson. Figure it out, or you're outta here."

Pearson nodded, smirked, got up and left.

"Fucking Davis," he muttered later to a colleague. "I'll get him for this."

*****

"Grace."

"Yes, Adam."

"I want to go home to the farm for a few days over the long weekend."

It was the end of August. The hot summer had ripened the canola early, and James Davis was ready to take it off on the Labour Day weekend. Adam, God knew, needed a break, or at least a change of scene.

"Harvest time, Adam?"

"Yes. Will you come with me?"

Grace was stunned. That would mean meeting his family. She swallowed.

"If I can get the Friday off, I would love to come with you."

Mark gave Grace the day off. Thursday night, she was packing and talking to Suzanne on speaker phone at the same time.

"How are you feeling?" Grace asked her.

"I feel fine, *chère amie*. Physically, at least."

"How is Bruno?" Grace felt the grip of her contracting heart. If Bruno had died, it would have been her fault. Still, Bruno, as part of Suzanne's circle, had saved her life. Grace knew she would do the same thing again. And again.

"A little limpy. He's fine, Grace. And, *ma belle*, I understand. You were trying to find me, and you saved my life," said Suzanne, a catch in her voice. "I love you."

"Oh, Suzé. I don't know what I would have done without you, my dear friend."

Grace had to stop talking for a moment. Her voice wouldn't work, as she contemplated the worst. She cleared her throat.

"And with Lorne?" she croaked. "All is well?"

"All is more than well. And you? And Adam?"

Grace paused. He had been angry, torn to shreds over the murdered women's case; distracted, dreaming, distant. He wouldn't spend the night, worried that he would hurt Grace again in his agitated state. Adam was constantly wondering where to go, what to do next, to find the other women Delacroix had killed.

Grace missed him horribly. She had to find some way to break through those damned dreams, once and for all. She had made an appointment to confer with a psychologist, but it was still a week away.

"I'm fine," she said eventually, then decided not to deflect anymore. "No, I'm not. Adam is having some trouble accepting what happened in this case, and is working hard on trying to get the new co-ordinator's position established. I'm worried about him, Suzanne. I hope I can help him. But it might take some time."

"You're leaving tomorrow?"

"Yes, in the morning."

"Perhaps being home will help him. I send you good luck for Adam, and for meeting the family, *mon amie*. But I feel it will be *très bien*."

Please, God, let her be right, Grace begged.

Thirty-five

Adam and Grace pulled up to his parents' home in his truck, a vehicle Grace did not know he owned. She was used to the old BMW, but here he was in a massive half ton. It was a small indication that there were still so many things to learn about Adam Davis.

Grace took a deep breath, and hopped down from the running board. Nervous didn't begin to describe how she was feeling.

"Grace," said Adam. "They will love you. Especially Mom."

Even so, he was showing evidence of a few nerves himself. Several times during the trip, he had dragged a hand through his hair.

He tugged their bags out of the back seat, and they walked up to the house. Elizabeth Davis was standing on the porch, arms outstretched.

"My bonny boy," she said, with a hint of rich Scottish accent, and took her big son into her arms. Grace was surprised again; she hadn't realized Elizabeth was an immigrant.

Then she turned to Grace, standing quietly beside Adam, and gathered her in her arms.

"Grace," Elizabeth said. Grace could hear the emotion in her voice, and hugged her back. "Ye're the most welcome sight of my life, after my own two babes and grandbabes. Come in."

Grace couldn't see Adam, who stood behind her; but his mother could, and in her son's face she read that this woman, the first he had brought to meet her, was without question the one. The only one.

They went together into the farmhouse kitchen, and a second later Adam's sister flew at him with her arms wide. Behind her, two little boys hopped with excitement, waiting for their uncle to notice them.

"Jen," he said to his sister. "God, it's been too long."

Then he turned to the boys, crouched down and opened his arms. "Matt. Alex. Come here."

"Uncle Adam! Uncle Adam!" they squealed and threw themselves at him, in an effort to knock him onto the floor — which he allowed them to do. It was clearly a ritual.

The squirming mass of boys and man bonding was beautiful to Grace, who saw yet another side of Adam in the melee of mutual adoration.

Jen turned to Grace. "Hug?" she asked, opening her arms again.

"Yes. Hello, Jen," said Grace, embracing Adam's sister.

Elizabeth broke in to say Adam's father and brother-in-law would be back in from combining soon, and lunch would be in half an hour.

"Can I help?" asked Grace.

"No. Jen and I will manage. You two get settled in. Off you go, now," said Elizabeth.

Adam disentangled himself from his nephews on the promise of future roughhousing. He picked up the bags again, and inclined his head toward the staircase.

"This way, Grace."

Up they went to Adam's childhood room, now furnished with a queen-size bed and decorated for guests rather than a boy. Grace didn't know what to say to Adam, overwhelmed as she was by meeting his family.

"Grace. Are you all right? It's a lot, I know."

"I'm fine. I think. They're all so . . . warm. I'm a little blown away."

Adam hugged her. "I'm sorry, Babe. I've been far away. But the case is now in Sanj's hands, and I hope I can move on, for now. I'm so glad you're here."

"I'm glad to be here."

Grace put her arms around him. She craved him; they hadn't slept together for too long. She hoped they could move on, too.

By the time they returned to the kitchen for lunch, Adam's father, James, and Jen's husband, Richard Ashton, had come in. There were more hugs, and much catching up over the big, protein-heavy farm meal. Grace watched and listened, answering the questions that came her way.

Yes, she was a reporter. Yes, she was from Saskatoon. Yes, she, too, was very glad Adam had found that serial killer.

But after lunch, Grace had to let Adam go, and her heart hurt. She felt they had started to pull back together, and now he was off to harvest.

"Later, Babe. Here we go," he said, kissing her.

"Later, Adam."

Grace insisted on helping with the dishes, and stood in front of the kitchen window watching the men walk across the yard, toward the farm machinery. Fascinated by seeing Adam in his first milieu, she continued to watch as he swung himself up with one arm into the cab of the combine, so easily. He was so strong. He was so sexy. Was he hers? He'd been so distracted. Was there room in his mind and heart for her? Could they find help with the nightmares, now that this case was over?

Jen was watching her own man. "They're beautiful, aren't they?" she said, noting the expression on Grace's face.

Grace turned to Jen, recognizing a sister who understood, if ever there was one.

"Yes. Very."

"We'll miss them today. But we'll be back together at dinner."

After the dishes were done, Elizabeth suggested they go out to the porch and chat. Seconds later, Matt and Alex ("Matthew Richard James and Alexander Adam McAlister," Jen had told Grace) came tearing outside, apparently to check out this new person in their uncle's life.

Matt was seven and Alex five, and both were vibrating with curiosity. They stood before Grace, questions leaping from their lips. After a few minutes, Matthew asked, "Are you our Auntie Grace?"

Grace thought she would die, although Jen laughed.

"That will do, Matthew," she admonished him. "Let poor Grace catch her breath, now. Off you go. Both of you. Go and play."

After they scooted away into the yard, Jen turned to Grace.

"I'm sorry, Grace. They're just wee boys. It means they like you, for what it's worth."

"I like them, too."

"Do you have an answer for them?" Jen asked, hopefully.

"Not . . . really, no."

Elizabeth leaned over and patted Grace's hand. What could she say? If Adam hadn't declared his intentions, she certainly couldn't. She changed the subject, and the afternoon rolled along as the women talked and learned about each other.

*****

Finally, it was six o'clock. Normally, the men wouldn't be coming in yet, but it was a special occasion: they were all together.

Dinner was in the oven, and Grace was doing a few more dishes, getting them out of the way before the meal. She saw Adam striding across the yard, and her heart lurched.

Before he could reach the porch, a white SUV sped into the yard. It stopped a few metres from Adam, and a curvy woman threw open the door and launched herself out of it. She was heavily made up, with big blonde hair, and she wore expensive city clothes.

She marched up to Adam, threw her arms around him and kissed him as if she wanted to devour him. Grace saw his hands go down to her waist, and her head instantly spun in a whirl of disbelief. With a little cry, she turned away from the sink, flung herself out of the kitchen and flew out the back door.

"What the . . . Grace? What's wrong? Are you all right?" Jen called, then looked out the window herself.

"Hell. Jilly," she said to her mother.

"Oh, no," said Elizabeth. "Go after Grace. Hurry."

Jen turned and ran. But Grace, fleet as a cheetah, had a minute on her; and by the time Jen hit the back porch, there was no sign of her.

"Grace!" she called. "Grace! Come back! It's not what you think!"

No answer. Jen swore again, and went back into the house.

Adam was still in the yard, by now talking with Jilly. Jen leaned out and yelled at her brother, "Adam! I need you. Can you come inside? It's important. Hi, Jilly," she added.

"On my way. One minute," said Adam.

"Adam. Now, please, if you can."

Adam was nonplussed. He wondered what the hell was so important; or maybe his sister was trying to save him from this woman? Jen knew the trouble Adam had had with her over the years.

"Jilly. I have to go. This can never happen again, okay? I'm with someone. I'm . . ." he wanted to say, I'm in love with someone. But he hadn't told that someone yet. It was only right she should hear it first.

"It's this Grace person, isn't it?" she asked, spitting out the name. "Adam, oh Adam, you know I love you. I want you. We can make it work," she wailed, slipping her arms around his neck again.

But Adam grabbed her arms, forced them down to her sides and said, "No. Jilly, you must go. This will never happen. Do you understand? Never. Please. Go."

He turned on his heel and walked toward the house, where his sister was waiting impatiently on the porch.

"Adam. Grace saw," she said.

Adam's nostrils flared. "Where is she?"

"I don't know. She gave a cry and ran out of the house. But Adam," said Jen, sniffing, "you reek like Jilly. Do something about that first."

"What if she left?"

"How? Unless your truck is gone."

"No, it's here. I saw it in the yard."

"Okay. So she's around, somewhere. Take the fastest shower of your life and go find her. Besides, you're filthy."

"No. I have to go now."

"I will go. I'll take my phone. Get." Adam started to protest again, but Jen stopped him by reaching up and taking his face in her hands. "Adam. Mark me. Grace will never forget that smell as long as she lives. Now go."

Jen grabbed her phone and headed out the back door, in time to hear spitting gravel from Jilly's car as she tore out of the yard. "Good riddance," Jen muttered.

Where would Grace go? Jen did a quick check around the yard, then hurried down the trail to the barn. Not there. Jen ran toward the grid road and looked right, to see Jilly's vehicle disappearing in a cloud of dust. She looked left, and spied a tiny Grace at some distance, easily half a kilometre out.

Jen texted Adam. "G on road, headed west. U need car."

Adam was already pulling on jeans. Clean ones. "Coming now."

He grabbed his keys and phone, yanked on his sneakers, dashed out of the house and jumped into the truck. Speeding out of the yard, he drove past Jen and turned left.

He saw Grace, walking down the middle of the road, her arms wrapped around herself, and if it's possible to feel one's heart melt, Adam did.

"Oh, no, Grace," he whispered to himself. "Hold on, Babe."

Adam pulled over behind her, and leaped from the vehicle. She started to run.

"Grace!" he called, his huge baritone in full cry. "Wait! Grace!"

"Get away from me, Adam. Leave me alone."

Adam started after her, then heard something behind him. A vehicle. He moved over toward the ditch, out of the car's way, and bellowed, "Grace! Get over. There's a car coming."

But instead of slowing down, the car sped up, and Adam understood in a flash of fear it was Jilly. She had turned around for some reason — to try another plea? — and must have seen Adam chasing Grace down the road.

She was aiming for Grace. Adam couldn't believe his eyes. Was she crazy?

"Grace! Dive for the ditch!" he yelled.

Grace turned to see the big white vehicle bearing down on her, and froze for a second, unable to register that someone was trying to hit her. Then she spun, took two steps and threw herself off the gravel and onto the side of the road, rolling into the wet ditch.

Jilly sped by, missing Grace by a breath. And kept going.

Adam, terror firing his leg muscles, ran full speed the few metres toward Grace. He skittered over the gravel and slid down the incline to the ditch, to find Grace lying limply at the bottom, face scratched and bruised, shirt torn, jeans ripped, a bloody gash in her arm.

Adam barely held himself back from lifting Grace into his arms. He first had to make sure she had no serious injuries.

"Grace, Grace," he said, touching her scraped cheek. "Talk to me. Grace."

Eyelids fluttered, then opened, and the deep brown pools were staring up at him. Thank God.

"Where are you hurt? Does your neck or back hurt? Grace, can you talk? Tell me, Babe. Tell me."

"I . . . I think I'm okay," said Grace, tentatively touching her head. Possible concussion, Adam thought. Then, "Ow," as her hand found the torn arm.

Adam, well-trained in checking for injuries, said, "Hold still," and looked at her pupils, gently felt her neck, and asked her to wiggle parts of her body, one at a time, in succession.

And then he grabbed her, emotion breaking through.

"Grace. I'm going to call Jen. Hold on."

Bracing Grace against his chest with one arm, he dialled his sister.

"Jen. We need a doctor. Can you call Doug Smith, get him over here?"

"What the hell, Adam? Are you okay? Is Grace?"

"Jilly tried to run her down. Grace needs checking and some stitches. I'll be back at the house in five minutes."

"Holy fuck." Jen knew better than to waste time asking questions. She hung up and called Doug Smith, family friend, neighbour, farmer and doctor.

Adam gently picked Grace up in both arms, carried her back to the truck, placed her carefully in the back seat and drove her to the farmhouse.

*****

"She should probably go to the hospital," said Doug Smith, who arrived fifteen minutes after Adam had put Grace on the couch in the living room.

"No," said Grace, in a voice so low they could barely hear her. "I'm not going to the fucking hospital. Ever again, if I can help it."

Doug turned to Adam with an eyebrow up.

"Long story," Adam answered his eyebrow. "Grace was in the hospital for a week this spring."

The doctor sighed. "Okay, well, I have anaesthetic and antibiotics. Grace, I'm going to have to stitch up that gash."

"Do what you need to, doc," said Grace, already feeling weird from the pain medication he had administered.

"Maybe we should get her upstairs. She's going to be pretty much out after all these drugs."

"Right," said Adam, who lifted her as if she were weightless and started up the stairs.

"Put me down," said Grace, wriggling. "You liar."

"Grace, let me explain, please."

"Sure. You go right ahead and explain why you brought me out here and then decided to kiss some other woman in front of me. Who also decided to run me over. Put me down."

Adam held on to her, hard, and kept going up the stairs. "No."

Grace looked into his face and began to cry, huge fat tears rolling down her face.

They reached the bedroom, and he put her down on the bed, but held her gently by the shoulders to keep her there. Doug Smith was right behind.

"Would you like some privacy for this, Grace?" he asked, holding up a needle destined for her backside.

"I'm not leaving," said Adam.

"It's not up to you, Adam," said Doug.

"You should leave, Adam," said Grace. "What are you doing here anyway? I assume that's the person who's been calling you lately. Or maybe she always calls you. How would I know?"

He kneeled by the bed, took Grace's face in his hands.

"Grace. I've been trying to get away from Jilly all my life. She was my friend Bobby's girlfriend. Three days after he died in a farm accident, she was over here trying to . . . hook up. I thought she was desperate and lonely and grieving. It's been ugly ever since.

"I don't know how she knew I was home, but news gets around out here. It never occurred to me she would show up — she lives in Regina — much less try to run you down.

"I have never been near her, Grace, much less with her, apart from the occasional scene similar to what you saw. I swear to you, Grace. Please believe me. I want you. Only you."

Doug Smith was turning red at witnessing the intimate scene, and nodding at the same time. That Jilly. She had it bad for Adam to this day, fourteen years after she'd first tried, and failed, to latch onto him. Everyone knew it. But no one would have expected her to try to kill his girlfriend.

Grace started to cry again, but this time she reached up and wound her fingers in Adam's hair. Doug left the room.

"I'm sorry, Adam," she whispered.

"For what, Babe? I'm sorry."

"For not trusting you. But you've been so far away, and I thought . . . I don't know . . ."

"Oh, God, Grace. I know. I'm so sorry, so sorry."

The embrace was clumsy and passionate, and only lasted a minute. The doctor was back.

"Adam. Grace," said Doug. "I have to get on with this, or you might end up in the hospital whether you like it or not, with an infection. Do you want Adam to leave?"

"No," she said. "Adam, hold me."

"I'm right here, Grace."

Doug injected the antibiotic, and the anaesthetic, which hurt like hell and made Grace cry out. After a moment, he started to sew up her arm. When he was finished, he started to pick gravel out of her face and knee.

*****

An hour later, Grace was asleep, knocked out by all the medications. Adam sat beside her, touched her face, her lips, her shoulders, and wondered how it all came so close to going very wrong. It was bad enough as it was.

After a while, he went downstairs to update his family.

"How's she doing?" asked Jen, anxiety stretching her voice up a few tones.

"She seems okay. Doug said she'd be fine, but she'll be in some pain for a few days, and tired from all the meds."

"Here, Adam," said his mother, putting a plate in front of him. "Eat something, dear. You need some strength after the day you've had."

"Thanks, Mom," he said. But he didn't eat. He sat at the table, head down, fingers combing through his hair.

"My poor bairn," said Elizabeth, kneeling before her son. "It will be all right. But you must tell Grace, Adam. Soon. You almost lost your chance."

"I know, Mom," he said, his voice low, breaking. Even in his state, Adam was amazed at his mother's intuition. "I know. We'll stay tomorrow — she'll need to rest, anyway. But I'll take her home Sunday. And I will tell her, Mom."

Thirty-Six

Grace was in more pain than she had expected, and much groggier. She limped around the farmhouse or slept most of Saturday. Adam suggested they go home Sunday, but Grace said no way. Finish your part in the harvest.

But it was time to go on Monday afternoon. There were a few tears, many hugs, and they were on their way back to Saskatoon. Grace kept falling asleep in the truck, off and on.

"I'm bringing you home with me," said Adam at one point, piercing her fog. Grace nodded and passed out again.

They struggled into Adam's condo, and Grace went straight up to the loft and to bed. Adam awakened her later for a light dinner of omelettes and toast, and let her go back to sleep.

Adam roamed around the condo. He had a Scotch, tried to calm down. Finally, he went to bed, too, and slept for a while.

The inevitable nightmare came to him, forcing him to relive the sight of Jilly trying to kill Grace. And in his dream, succeeding. He awakened, sweating, with a start, and quickly turned to see if he had roused Grace, but she was still asleep. He crawled silently out of bed and down the stairs to the main floor.

Naked, he walked to the soaring window overlooking the street. Trying to cool himself, he put both arms over his head and leaned his entire body against the wet window. It was raining, but a streetlight managed to cut the darkness and the streaming glass.

But Grace had awakened. She came up through layers of dreams and deep sleep, and knew Adam would not be there beside her. Pulling a blanket around her shoulders, she crept to the top of the stairs and saw Adam stretched long and hard in the dim light. She stopped, awestruck at his perfect, powerful body, aware of how the light gleamed on the muscles in his shoulders, his side, his buttocks.

This incredible man. Passionate and ethical. To a fault, sometimes. She thought of how different her circumstances were from the women who were murdered. How privileged she was. How unbelievably lucky to have found her fierce and tender lover.

"Adam," she said.

He turned. "Grace. Should you be up? How do you feel?"

"Much better. I think I've had enough sleep."

She came down the stairs and stood before him.

"Adam, what's wrong? Did you dream?"

"Yes. I saw Jilly driving like a madwoman toward you. Hitting you."

"Oh, Babe," said Grace, putting a hand on his cheek. "What has happened to her?"

"The RCMP picked her up. She's in remand, as far as I know."

"I understand that she's in love with you. Trying to kill me, though, might have been a little extreme. Is she . . . all right, do you think?"

"She's crazy," said Adam, flatly. "Obviously. I hope she gets some time, and some help. Under other circumstances, I may not have been able to protect you."

"But you did, Adam. I'm here, and more or less fine, because of you."

"It was close, though. And the women who were killed by Delacroix. I couldn't protect them, either, or Suzanne. You did a better job at it than I did. What the hell good am I, then?"

"Adam, you found the killer. I know it's not enough for you. But you did what you could. Everything you could."

"No. We're not doing enough to stop this."

"You have started to change things, at least to the extent you can, in your department. Opening a position for missing persons co-ordinator will help. If you can get Lorne to take it, you have a really good start."

"Do you think so? Be honest, Grace."

"I do. Every time a good policy is made, we take a tiny step forward, toward equality. You've seen some differences already, since they fired the previous chief. You can't stop murder, Adam. You can only help break the cycle and change the system."

Adam shivered. Grace opened the blanket and wrapped it around him, and herself.

"I don't want to live here anymore," he said simply. "It's not me, it's not home. I feel so far away from myself. I'm going to sell the condo."

"And then?"

"I don't know yet. But I have to get out of here."

Grace's body was starting to awaken. It had been too long since they had made love, and she wanted him badly, particularly after having been so frightened by Jilly — not the attempt to run her over, but by the horrible scene in the farmyard.

"Adam. I need you to make love with me. Please. I've missed you so much."

He bent his head and kissed her, so gently, as she had kissed him the first time their lips had ever met. Her arms went around him, and she held him tightly against her breasts and belly and thighs. She felt him respond, and he kissed her deeply, swung her up against his chest and took her back to bed.

Adam laid Grace on her back and gently kissed her neck and breasts; and as she moaned, he entered her and held her tightly.

His body shuddered, the sensations luring him, but he had to stop. The time had come. He had waited too long as it was.

"Grace, look at me," he asked, softly. "Into my eyes. Sh, now. Stop for a moment."

Grace writhed under him, and stopped moving with an effort.

"Adam? What's wrong?"

"Listen to me, Grace. Hear me. I love you. I am in love with you. I have loved you from the very start. I should have told you before now. I should have, but I thought it was too soon, that you wouldn't believe me."

He moved inside her involuntarily, the physical connection and intense declaration rocking his emotions and body.

"Do you love me, Grace? Tell me." Adam was still looking into her eyes. He had to hear the truth, and see it.

Grace moved her arms from his shoulders and took his face in her hands, holding his gaze firmly. She moved her hips, smoothly caressing him inside her.

"I wanted you from the start. I feel like I've loved you forever; I was just waiting to find you."

She paused.

"Adam. Come live with me."

"Live with you? Come live with you? Grace, are you sure? I can't . . . what if I hurt you again?"

"I'm as sure as I've ever been of anything. We will find the way to cope, if we are together. Say yes, Adam. Say it," breathed Grace, rocking him. "Come live with me, love."

Adam shuddered again, a tremor pulsing through him, bringing Grace with him. The spasms rose and fell and left them helpless to each other.

"Grace," he said, finally, holding her tightly. "Yes. Oh, God, yes. I will come and live with you."

Notes and Acknowledgements

The second crime in Broken Through, after the death of the dog in the first chapter, is not entirely fictional.

Indeed, a woman lost her life, was found in a basement, and may have been murdered by a man she knew well. He was never charged or tried for the crime. We will never know if he was indeed the killer; there was most certainly domestic abuse.

How often does that happen? How many people are actually guilty of many more crimes than they are ever charged with? How can the police better piece together the motives, the factors and locations of missing and murdered people, particularly women? And particularly Indigenous women?

In the late-2000s, Canada did not yet have a country-wide missing persons database or protocol among law enforcement services. Some dedicated and horrified police officers in this country have made that happen, many of them good white men. They are, in part, represented in this book by Adam Davis.

The remainder of the book deals with other men and some women who are not good. Some are blind; some are evil. None of them exist in real life, although some of their crimes certainly do. There was never an intention to vilify any particular profession or person. The plot found its villains for their capabilities and circumstances.

I have had an enormous amount of support in the writing of Broken Through. To my husband, Ken, and primary beta reader: Love and thanks.

Bev, Kathy, Ann, Bruce and Caroline (thank you for the beautiful cover), I appreciated every excruciating criticism and word of support. Jennifer, you are the beta reader of beta readers. Jan, I couldn't have published without your note: Yay, Book! I do love you both, so much.

Bev Katz Rosenbaum, thank you for your professional editorial advice.

Lori Coolican, you Graceful editor, thank you for everything.

Joanne, you genius counsellor: not only do you help me navigate life, but also sleep at night over the profiles of my villains. I can't thank you enough.

Avalon Auto in Saskatoon, you awesome guys, thanks for all your help on the car front. Free book coming your way!

CeCe Baptiste. It is hard to describe how meaningful your support was, how helpful your advice, how deft your touch in handling me and massaging into the book the correct elements of Indigenous culture.

Whether you read Broken Through as a murder mystery, a love story, a morality tale or a fury, I suppose it was intended to be all of those. Many thanks, gentle reader.

Also by this author

Adam's Witness
(Adam and Grace Book 1)

Reporter Grace Rampling is expecting a routine interview. What she finds is the bloodied body of a Catholic bishop.

Suddenly, she finds herself central to a murder case, not just as a key witness but a suspect and potential victim.

Enter handsome but troubled Detective Sergeant Adam Davis, who is thrown by the fierce attraction he feels toward his witness. Legally and ethically, he cannot act on his feelings without throwing the entire case into jeopardy.

With Grace at risk and off limits, Adam races to unravel an increasingly disturbing mystery while he struggles to both protect and resist the woman of his dreams.

Adam's Witness "simmers with intrigue, suspense and sexual tension. Five stars."
— Amazon reviewer

About the author

J.C. (Joanne) Paulson was born in Saskatoon, the beautiful prairie city she loves so much, she has never managed to leave for longer than a few months.

A long-time journalist with the local daily newspaper, The StarPhoenix, as well as other news outlets, Paulson awakened one night with the plot of Adam's Witness swirling in her brain. There was nothing for it but to write the thing.

The transition from fact to fiction was a strange relocation into a very different world of words, characterization and plot creation, but Adam and Grace quickly became part of the household. Book two, Broken Through, came a year later.

She lives in a rambling older bungalow with her husband, goldsmith Ken Paulson.

www.jcpaulsonauthor.com

Made in the USA
San Bernardino, CA
01 November 2018